The Memory of Lost Senses

Judith Kinghorn

W F HOWES LTD

This large print edition published in 2013 by
W F Howes Ltd
Unit 4, Rearsby Business Park, Gaddesby Lane,
Rearsby, Leicester LE7 4YH

1 3 5 7 9 10 8 6 4 2

First published in the United Kingdom in 2013
by HEADLINE REVIEW

A CIP catalogue record for this book is available
from the British Library

ISBN 978 1 47123 976 2

Typeset by Palimpsest Book Production Limited,
Falkirk, Stirlingshire
Printed and bound by
CPI Group (UK) Ltd, Croydon, CR0 4YY

MIX
Paper from
responsible sources
FSC
www.fsc.org   FSC® C013604

For Max and Bella.

In Memoriam

JME Shepherd 1895–1917

'Italy was mostly an emotion and the emotion naturally centred in Rome. Rome, before 1870, was seductive beyond resistance . . . shadows breathed and glowed, full of soft forms felt by lost senses.'

Henry James

'If any one faculty of our nature may be called more wonderful than the rest, I do think it is memory. There seems something more speakingly incomprehensible in the powers, the failures, the inequalities of memory, than in any other of our intelligences. The memory is sometimes so retentive, so serviceable, so obedient; at others, so bewildered and so weak; and at others again, so tyrannic, so beyond control! We are, to be sure, a miracle every way; but our powers of recollecting and of forgetting do seem peculiarly past finding out.'

Jane Austen, *Mansfield Park*

*S*ometimes it's easy to be blind, to run into the blackness and know you are heading in the right direction. Know that beyond the dark is light, and that behind you all is dark. Know that your destination – wherever it may be – will be infinitely better than your point of departure. This is how it was that night.

And though the girl already knew about the need to take flight, she had not anticipated her own escape, had never been out in the dead of night, the witching hour, grazing dripping brick and corrugated iron, the backsides of tenements and factories and warehouses; clamouring over ramshackle fences, sidestepping rat-infested ditches and sewers.

But fear of the night – its other-worldliness – was nothing compared to what had just taken place at home.

At the end of the alleyway the woman finally stopped, released the girl's hand and dropped the bag to the ground. The girl was still whimpering, and shaking; shaking so violently she thought her legs might give way, thought she might fall to the sodden ground and be swallowed up by Hell and Damnation. Her feet were numb, her shoes and the hem of her dress caked in wet mud from cutting through the market gardens. She could smell the river, its stench permeating the fog, and knew they were close. But she must not make a sound. No, no sound. She had been told that, and slapped.

And so she tried to hold in her sobs, her breath, and kept her hand – its congealing stickiness – clasped over her mouth, her eyes fixed on the blurred shape of the woman beside her, now pulling a shawl back over her head. Ahead of them, a solitary hansom cab creaked westwards, wheels spraying, lamp swaying.

'Was he . . . is he . . . dead?' the girl whispered.

The woman made no reply. She watched the yellow light fade, picked up the bag, and led the girl on across the highway, into the blackness, into the night.

PROLOGUE

England 1923

The photograph had been torn in two and later repaired. Now, a crinkled line of severance ran through the background pine trees, the top of the tented gazebo and the statue by the gate to the sunken garden, decapitating the marble lady. But the image continued to exude the effulgence of that day, and Sylvia squinted as she brought it closer, glancing along the line-up and then at herself: eyes closed, hand raised, as though about to sneeze, or laugh, or speak; the only one to have moved. I was nervous, she thought, remembering, not used to having my photograph taken . . . not used to posing.

She lifted the magnifying glass, levelling it over the figure seated at the centre: a broad hat shading the eyes, the memory of a smile about the mouth, the dated costume, out of time – even then. Accustomed to scrutiny, impervious to the occasion, she thought. But she could hardly bear to think the name. She was still in shock.

She sat back in her chair, closing her eyes, already

moving through shadows towards brightness and warmth, and the sound of a band and the hulla-baloo of children drifting up from a village green, and that day, that day, that day.

But something else tugged at the edge of her senses. Another memory, faded almost to white and worn thin as gossamer with time. And emerging from it, into it, a familiar dark-haired young man, standing by a fountain in the sun-drenched piazza of a foreign city. As he moves towards her she feels the incandescence of the stone surrounding her, the weight of it upon her, and one name, on their lips, about to be spoken, about to be broken.

'My dear,' he says, reaching out to take her hand, 'your note has me quite bamboozled . . .'

He holds her gloved hand in his. His dark eyes are serious, searching; his brow is furrowed. He is indeed perplexed. But there is no turning back, she must tell him, she must tell him everything. And so she releases the appalling words in whispers, and as he leans towards her she can smell turpentine and stale sweat. When he steps away from her he raises a paint-smudged hand to his forehead, and she can feel his pain. But it had to be done. She had no choice.

'I had no choice,' she said, opening her eyes, coming back to now. 'He needed to know . . . needed to know the . . .'

She had been going to say *truth*. But it would have been a lie.

BOOK I

ENGLAND 1911

CHAPTER 1

Within weeks letters would be burned, pages torn, photographs ripped in two. Names would be banished, memories abandoned and history rewritten, again. Within weeks promises would be broken and hearts made fit to bleed.

But for now there was little movement or sound.

The countryside languished, golden and fading and imbued with the lassitude of weeks of unwavering heat. High above, the cerulean sky remained unmoved. It had been there early. Stretching itself from treetop to treetop, resolute, unbroken, never touching parched earth. Only the ratter-tat-tat of a woodpecker interrupted the wood pigeon's lullaby coo.

It was shortly before noon.

Sylvia would remember this – the time of her arrival – ever after, because she would later write it down, along with the words and events of that day, and the rest. She would for years to come ponder upon whether she could have, should have, done things differently. But when she stepped down from the vehicle her heart knew only love.

As the wagonette disappeared back down the curving driveway she gazed up at the house, smiling. It was typical of Cora to have played it down. Now, I shall be able to imagine her *here*, she thought, lingering beyond the shadow of the building. Ahead of her, the front door and glazed inner door stood open. It was fine weather and they were expecting her. But still, it seemed a tad foolhardy, reckless even, to her. Anyone at all could walk in.

The hallway was dark and cool, the place silent, and as she put down her bag she called out, 'Hello-o! It is I, Sylvia . . . anyone home?' She immediately recognised the long ornately carved table next to her and, placing her fingertips upon it, reassured by familiarity, she moved along its length. A red leather frame – next to a large earthenware bowl containing an assortment of calling cards – read, 'OUT'. A folded newspaper and yet to be opened letters lay on a silver tray beneath an oversized and, to her mind, rather haphazard arrangement of flora. She glanced through the letters – brown envelopes, all bills – then lifted her hand and tugged at a large open bloom, pulling it free from the tangle of waterlogged bark and stems, plunging it back into the centre of the vase. Raising her eyes to the wall, she gasped. It was not a painting she recollected having seen before, and was surely inappropriate to have hanging in an entrance hall, or anywhere else, she thought, turning away.

Opposite her, a settee of gilt and pink velvet she remembered from Rome made her smile. And above it, the zebra's head, mounted high upon the wall. But hadn't Cora said she loathed the thing? Would never have it in any of her homes?

She walked on, glancing through open doorways into tall sunlit rooms, revealing more familiar polished mahogany – magnificent antiques, glinting crystal and objets d'art. She smiled at Gio and Louis – Cora's two beloved pugs, stuffed by a renowned Parisian taxidermist and now sitting either side of an ottoman, staring glassy-eyed at the empty hearth – half expecting the little things to scramble to their feet and clip-clap across the ebonised floorboards to greet her once more. Oh, but it was marvellous to be in a place where one could immediately connect with so much of it. Almost like coming home, she thought. And yet it was queer to see it all again, together, here, in this place. Cora's world could never have fitted into any cottage. 'A cottage indeed!' she said, shaking her head. Cora was a collector, a traveller, and her new home was testament to this. Each of her homes – her apartments in Paris and Rome, her chateau in the Loire – had surely been testament to this. And though Cora had never planned to return, had vowed she would die in Rome, circumstances – tragic as they were – had dictated otherwise, and Sylvia had secretly been pleased. For Cora was finally back in England, and back for good.

A young male voice broke through the silence and she turned.

'You must be Sylvia,' he said. 'I'm Jack.'

Jack. So this was he. Ah yes, she could see the resemblance.

He smiled, stretched out his hand to her, and as she took hold of it she said, 'What a pleasure to meet you at last.'

He told her that they had been expecting her a little earlier. And she explained that she had taken the later train in order to avoid the day trippers. She did not tell him that this plan had failed, that the train had been chock-a-block with families bound for the coast.

Unused to children, their eyes and their noise, she had sat in a tight huddle on board the train, her notebook and pencil in her lap. She had pretended to be busy, keeping her mouth shut, restricting her breathing to her nose. In her notebook she wrote the word *miasma*, then doodled around it in small squares and boxes, interlinking and overlapping. Until the word itself was covered. When the child dropped the ice cream at her feet, splattering her shoes and the hem of her skirt, she simply smiled. And when a nursing mother unbuttoned her blouse and exposed her breast to feed a screaming infant, she smiled again, and then looked away.

'All tickety-boo? Cotton was still there, I presume.'

'Yes, Mr Cotton was there, waiting on the platform as arranged.'

10

When she stepped off the train, with her small leather satchel and portmanteau, she had stood for a while with her eyes closed. She had seen the man at the end of the platform, knew from Cora's description that it was Cotton, but she needed a moment – just a moment – to herself. She had allowed him to take her bag but not the satchel. She had hung on to that.

'And the train? Not too busy, I hope.'

'No, not too busy at all,' she replied.

'I imagine Linford was quite deathly . . . by comparison to London,' he added.

The market town had been quiet, very quiet. Sylvia had noticed this. Sun-bleached awnings sagged over the darkened shop windows and empty teashops, and the wilting flags and bunting and banners proclaiming 'God Save the King' still draping buildings and criss-crossing the street looked sad and incongruous; like Christmas in summer, she thought. But the coronation and its celebrations had been quickly forgotten in the stifling heat, the effort of remembrance too much.

Sylvia shook her head. 'It's the same up in town. *Everything's* shut down, ground to a halt . . . the streets are quite deserted.'

This was something of an exaggeration. Though many city businesses had been closing early, the main thoroughfares quieter, the pulse of the capital continued to throb. People had adapted, altering their habits. The city's parks were busier than ever and any pond, stream or canal, not yet dried up, filled with bathers. And though Mrs Pankhurst and her suffragettes had called a truce to their window smashing for the coronation, and for summer, they were still out and about with their banners and placards: 'Votes For Women'.

'Ah well, perhaps you won't find it quite so quiet here after all,' he said and smiled.

Yes, she could see the resemblance, in the line of the jaw, the nose and, most particularly, the eyes. She said, 'You remind me very much of your grandfather.'

He looked back at her, quizzical for a moment, then said, 'Of course, I forgot . . . forgot that you knew him, that you lived in Rome as well.'

'A long, long time ago,' she replied, glancing away, removing her gloves.

'My namesake,' he said, wistfully.

She kept her eyes fixed on the ivory lace in her hands. They were talking at cross-purposes. He knows nothing, she thought.

'Come,' he said suddenly, and with an assurance that surprised her. He walked on ahead of her down the passageway, saying, 'I was outside . . . it's not too hot for you, is it? We can sit in the shade . . . I'll organise some coffee, if you'd like . . . wait here.' He turned, walked back along the passageway, put his head round a door, and Sylvia heard him laugh and say, 'Yes, please, if you don't mind . . . on the lawn, please.'

She followed him out through a broad sunlit veranda, across a south-facing terrace to stone

the woods . . . a tiny replica of ancient Rome. She likes to sit there.'

'I see.'

Gestures to ancient Rome were scattered all about the place: the sculptures and bronzes within the house, the urns and more sculptures outside in the garden. Sylvia had seen some but not all of them before, and at that moment she noticed and recognised the marble figure next to the gateway in her line of vision.

'She was always a connoisseur, you know? Not just of painting and sculpture, but so very well-informed and knowledgeable about architecture as well. Far, far more than I,' she added and laughed.

At one time in her life it had seemed unfair. Cora's blessings – her beauty, aptitude and style, her ability with people – had inspired resentment, left Sylvia feeling impoverished, lesser. But fate had intervened, the way it did with the appearance of good fortune. Cora, she had come to realise, many years ago, was not to be envied. She was to be loved, cherished and, above all, protected.

He moved forward in his chair. 'I understand you're penning my grandmother's memoirs,' he said, without looking at her, lifting his cup and saucer.

'Yes, that's right, I am.'

'Well, I shall be the first, the very first to read it. But I rather think it'll be an interesting exercise for you. She seems somewhat reticent to talk about the past . . . to me, at any rate.'

Sylvia did not say anything, not immediately. She was a little irked to be classified as the memoirist. It made her feel like a hired amanuensis. After all, she and Cora *were* dear friends, close friends; they had known each other for over half a century, been through so much, confided in each other. Added to which, she was doing this as a favour. Memoirs were not her expertise. She was a novelist. Some would say *romantic* novelist. She preferred the term *literary*.

She said, 'Sometimes it's not easy to revisit the past. It involves confronting everything we've done and said, all our actions, mistakes, and regrets.'

The memoirs had always been Sylvia's idea, always. Though it had, admittedly, been many years since it was first mooted, and then later begun. At that time Cora had been angry about the innuendo and gossip surrounding her marriage to her late husband and Sylvia had suggested to her that if she were prepared to write about her life, the truth, it would at the very least silence her critics. 'After all,' Sylvia had said, 'in the absence of fact people do rather like to invent things.' Cora had agreed, then, and they had made some headway, mainly via their letters to each other. But later Cora appeared to change her mind, writing cryptically to Sylvia that she felt the enterprise to be *somewhat foolhardy* and *possibly dangerous*. Over the intervening years it had become something of an issue between the two women, with Sylvia often writing to Cora, *when we finish your memoirs* . . .

However, when Cora stayed for a few nights with Sylvia prior to coming down to the country, she had been surprisingly enthusiastic, appeared newly committed to the plan. Yes, she wanted to put the record straight, she said, not least for Jack's sake, and added, 'The truth needs to be told. Indeed, the truth *must* be told.' To that end, Sylvia had been invited to stay for an indeterminate time at Temple Hill. When Sylvia mentioned that she would have to return to London – once a week, perhaps – to check on the flat, collect post and so on, Cora had clapped her hands: 'Barely an hour by train!'

'Of course,' Sylvia began again, 'your grand-mother and I have known each other for a very long time. We have few secrets from each other . . . and writing one's memoirs is a . . . an intimate process. I don't suppose she would wish just *anyone* to record her memories.'

'Of course,' he replied, smiling. 'I understand you met when you were both quite young.'

'Yes, at Rome, when Cora first arrived there. Though my parents and I had lived there for a good few years by then . . . My father managed the English bank there.'

He nodded, and they moved on. She asked him if he had met any other young people in the village, and he mentioned some names, including two girls: a Sonia and a Cecily. She smiled. 'Nice girls?' she asked.

'Perhaps,' he replied, shrugging his shoulders, glancing away.

A few minutes later, Cora appeared. She emerged from what Sylvia already knew to be the gateway to the sunken garden. She raised a hand and then moved towards them, slowly, looking downwards and pausing to tap at the dried lawn with her cane. Sylvia and Jack rose to their feet. 'Dandelions!' she called out. 'Coming up everywhere.' She did not smile, did not ask Sylvia about her journey or how long she had been there. But later, when Sylvia finally said, 'I do like your *little cottage*, my dear, but think it rather cramped by comparison to Bayswater,' Cora had laughed. And the joy Sylvia felt at hearing her laugh was incomparable.

Weeks earlier, when Cora had arrived at Temple Hill, the yellow gorse was still in bloom and tiny pink flowers covered the branches of crab apple trees. Trees she could not recall having seen before. But it had been over twenty years since she had visited the place, it was quite different to how she remembered. The house itself was smaller, its interior – the layout and dimensions of rooms – not at all as she pictured, and the landscape surrounding the place more wild and rugged.

She had acclimatised quickly to the unseasonable warmth and to her new surroundings. After all, it was home. She had come home. And though she was privately anxious – and by this thought more than anything else – she considered the place an

18

oasis of calm in a troubled and turbulent world; a world she no longer fully understood.

Before Jack arrived, before Sylvia came, she had spent a great deal of her time in the garden, wandering the overgrown pathways with Mr Cordery, her gardener, explaining her vision, how it had looked in her mind's eye: remembering, or trying to. And as the heat grew increasingly intolerable, building up day by day, and the house, despite every sash being pulled open, so claustrophobic, she sought refuge in the temple.

The temple – a small, circular structure, comprising seven ivy-clad Doric columns and a cupola atop – had been erected some years after the house was built, the limestone shipped from Tivoli. But inclement weather, damp and spores from the trees had aged it prematurely, bestowing it with the look Cora intended: a well-preserved ruin. Open to the elements, it had once been open to the views also, north, south, east and west: across the valley to uninterrupted pastures and meadows; across the village with its clusters of smoking chimneys, picture-postcard green and church steeple; and westwards, to glorious sunsets. These vistas were now obscured by woodland but light continued to filter down through beeches and birches, bouncing off stone encrusted with tiny particles of glass and silver and sand. It was a quiet, private place, a place of meditation and remembrance.

And yet it appeared to commemorate nothing.

There were no carved initials or dates, no inscriptions in Latin or lichen-covered busts, no statues here. But for Cora it was a small piece of Italy, a reminder of a time and a man. Here, there was stillness and peace; here, she liked to ponder what had been . . . and what might have been, had her life been different.

But facts were inescapable now she had come to a halt. And reflection, the inevitable backward glance, the search for a perfect moment in which to luxuriate and wallow and take comfort, offered up other moments too. Reminding her of how and where her journey had started. Reminding her of who she had been, and what she had done. An involuntary remembrance that caught in her throat and sucked out her breath. A memory she had spent a lifetime trying to forget.

And yet, and yet, surely the only fact that mattered was her love: her love and devotion to a man, one man. And it was at this place, the temple – her temple – that she often saw him, spoke with him. That he had been dead almost two decades mattered not. When he came to her there he was young and beautiful, exactly as he had been when they first met, and exactly as he had been at Lucca . . .

She stands before him, aware only of his gaze, his concentration upon each curve, each undulation, each and every part of her being. And in the silence, in the dusty ether that lies between them, the possibilities are endless and eternal, beyond a here and now. And when

20

he finally meets her eyes, when he looks at her and says her name – as though it's the very first word he has ever spoken, the first word to ever escape his lips – there is a frisson, a frisson that will sustain her and fire the years to come.

Sylvia made it her business to find her bearings, to learn her way about the place and be at meal-times promptly. She wished to be an inconspicuous houseguest: a pleasure to have. Thus, each morning, whilst Cora – never an early riser – remained upstairs in her suite of rooms, Sylvia quietly worked on her new novel. She had been instructed on the morning room. The light was better there, Cora told her, and there was a desk in front of the window. Perfect, said Sylvia.

Jack, too, it seemed, was not a morning person, which perhaps explained why that particular room, with its lack of curtains, crates and boxes, had had so little use. When eventually he rose – an hour or so before his grandmother, who made her entrance on the day at around eleven – he appeared to Sylvia to float about the place aimlessly. She sat listening to the sound of him moving through rooms, opening and closing doors, as though unsure of what to do, where to be, or perhaps looking for something: a clue. She watched him through the window, wandering, lost in thought. Understandable, she supposed, that he'd need time to himself. Time to take in the events of the preceding months, his circumstances and new situation. Time to ponder the woman who had broken her vow and quietly slipped back into England, his only living relation. Understandable.

And it was understandable, too, that Cora had a lot on her mind. Understandable she appeared so distracted. How could she not be? Sylvia thought, trying to imagine, trying to imagine what it must be like to be Cora.

During those first few days Sylvia watched Cora closely. She tried to access that troubled mind, watching and waiting for signs. She noted and logged each nuance in manner, each and every hesitation or tremor. She smiled a great deal, asked few questions, and sometimes hummed through a silence.

It was plain to see that Jack knew nothing and it was certainly not her place to tell him. If truth were told, he made her nervous, though she would, she thought, be the first to admit that all men, young and old, remained an enigma. There were, had always been to her, things off-putting – in their countenance, shape and smell. And it was the way they breathed. It must have started, she presumed, with her father who, banker or not, had always been a heavy breather . . . and with some decidedly queer habits, too. And it was, she imagined – whenever she looked up and saw Jack at the table – in no small part due to the way they chewed and swallowed their food, as though they had not eaten for weeks, as though no one was watching, as though they were not human, but animal. But Cora seemed not to notice, and who was she to cast aspersions?

Seven days after her arrival, Sylvia did indeed find herself 'back on the train'. It was in fact her fourth train journey that week. The day-return to London had been arduous enough, the tube like a furnace, and now, less than twenty-four hours later, she was on board another, this time heading south. Of course it was an altogether different experience travelling with Cora. There were no filthy children or bare-bosomed women in first class. And the upholstered velvet seats, gilt-framed mirrors, oil paintings, polished brass, and mahogany panelling made it an altogether more enjoyable and aesthetically pleasing experience. But still, so much toing and froing had left her feeling quite lacklustre.

And she had had to tread carefully with Cora, for there seemed to be issues, new issues. Whether to do with Jack or something else Sylvia was not yet sure. But today her friend appeared more distracted than ever, and Sylvia could not help but wonder if it was related to a letter she had received in the morning post.

In anticipation of their day Cora had risen early, been at the breakfast table – in navy blue silk and smelling sweet with the fragrance of violets – by nine. She had pronounced it a 'glorious' day, telling Sylvia that she was in fact an early riser at heart, and that the lack of a siesta was the root cause of many of the problems in England.

'Tiredness! Fatigue!' she declared, raising her hands in that way she did. 'It so interferes with one's judgement . . . one's ability to enjoy life . . . its simple pleasures.'

Sylvia watched her pick up the envelope, slice the pale yellow paper with a silver knife, pull out and open a single sheet – typewritten, it appeared from the reverse. She saw her wince, heard her gasp. And as Cora put the page back inside the envelope and the envelope inside her pocket, Sylvia tentatively enquired, 'Is everything quite all right?'

At first Cora offered no reply. She stared straight ahead at the open window, and with such intensity that Sylvia, too, turned and looked in that direction. Then Cora rose up from the table and said, 'We must make haste, Sylvia. Cotton will be here in a few minutes.'

Perhaps because of these matters, matters yet to be disclosed to Sylvia, they had made no progress on the memoirs. None whatsoever. Each time Sylvia mentioned it Cora shook her head. 'Not now,' she'd say, 'now is not the right time.' But when, Sylvia wondered, would it be the right time?

On board the train, Cora sat for some time with her eyes closed. She was not sleeping, Sylvia could tell. She watched Cora's breathing, watched her lips part and move, saw the flicker of a smile. And Sylvia knew she was remembering, knew she was back there with *him*. She was always back there with him: *George Lawson . . . Lord George Lawson.*

Sylvia had been there when they very first met,

when they were introduced to each other at Mrs Hillier's palazzo apartment on the Pincio hill in Rome, so many years ago. They exchanged few words that night, Sylvia remembered, though it had been enough for Cora; enough for Cora to change who she was or had been, enough for her to forget what came before and look forward. She had been beautiful, then, young and beautiful, Sylvia thought, studying the lined face opposite her. And he? Yes, he was handsome, and exceptionally talented, that was undeniable, but he was also conceited, and selfish. He did not deserve her love. Had never deserved her love. That had been proven by his actions. He had been put to the test – and failed. And yet, when Cora finally took her revenge, and it *was* revenge, Sylvia was in no doubt about that, she had actually felt sorry for him. 'Him!' she said out loud, and then quickly raised a finger to her lips. But Cora did not look to her, did not hear her.

And to think she had allowed Cora to take him back – after everything, after everything he had done to her; to think she had allowed Cora to nurse him through his final days . . . *and to think what he knew about Cora* . . . But she tried to push that thought away. After all, he had spoken to Sylvia in Paris about *that* matter. And he had been the one to bring it up, not she. She would never have done that. Would never have mentioned it. And it was not the right occasion, a wedding: Cora's wedding. Oh yes, he had quizzed her, and just as though *she* were guilty, as though she had committed the crime! None of it was how it should have been, not in her mind; not the way she had envisioned or written it.

When Sylvia lifted her satchel, slamming it down upon the table between them, Cora opened her eyes. Sylvia smiled at her. Then, pulling out her notebook and pen, she said, 'You know, I've been thinking . . . we could change certain names if you wish . . .'

'Hmm. It's an idea. But then it's not the truth, is it?' Cora replied. She opened a small mother-of-pearl case with two intertwined silver 'Cs' upon its lid, slipped a cigarette into an ebonised holder. Sylvia looked on as a liveried guard swiftly appeared with a match. She watched Cora tilt her head, release a plume of smoke towards the lacquered ceiling of the drawing-room carriage. '*Grazie*.' She looked back at Sylvia. 'Well, we can think on it, can't we? It's not as though we're in any rush.'

'No, but I rather thought now might be a good time to make some notes.'

Cora frowned, raised her hand to her brow. 'But I'm still not altogether sure where to begin,' she said.

'At the beginning, of course. We must begin at the beginning. It's what I came down here to do . . . the beginning.'

'But I'm not sure, not sure it's relevant.'

'Not relevant?' Sylvia repeated, attempting a smile.

'Yes. I think we should simply begin at Rome.'

Sylvia tried to laugh. 'But if we are to write the truth—'

'Sylvia!' she snapped. 'If you had any real notion of how life can be . . . if you had had children, for instance, a husband, or husbands,' she went on, in a terse, hushed voice, and leaning forward now, 'homes to run, others to think of, you would understand how exhausting it can also be. *Exhausting*.' She turned her head away, and Sylvia watched her as she gazed at her reflection in the carriage window, puckering and pursing her lips.

Morning coffee was served.

The sight of starched linen and polished silver appeared to assuage Cora's nerves, and she smiled benignly to the young waiter as he bowed and disappeared off down the carriage. Earlier, the stationmaster himself had helped her to board the train, and Sylvia had seen him whispering to the guard as though he knew a secret. Oh, it was plain enough to see that Cora was someone, or had been, once. And though men had always been dazzled, as much by the enigma as by any reality, there had only ever been one who had dazzled Cora.

Sylvia knew that in Cora's mind it had been a Great Love Affair. She knew that in Cora's mind it still was, for she had not been able to let him go. But what niggled Sylvia more than anything else was, why? Why did she hold on to him? And, more importantly, why did she hold on to her secrets? After all, *the beginning*, that part of her story she would not speak of, happened long, long ago. Everyone involved would surely be gone by now. And she owed *him* nothing. Nothing. He had broken promises: promises of marriage, children and that bohemian gypsy life Cora had described to her all those years ago: '*We will move around, he says; live like gypsies. Spend winters here in Rome, spring in Paris, and summers . . . oh, I'm not sure now where he said we would spend the summer . . . but I'll be back each year, so I'll still see you.*' Then he abandoned her. Left her high and dry in Rome. And all because of *circumstances*, circumstances so appalling and shocking as to be unbelievable, circumstances Sylvia had waited over fifty years for Cora to confirm. But patience seemed to count for nothing, and now Sylvia was determined.

Before coming down to the country, in anticipation of the weeks ahead, Sylvia had gone through some of their early correspondence, archived, and filed in chronological order in various numbered shoeboxes at her flat. It had been a time-consuming process due to the sheer volume. And confusing, because of the crossings out: corrections made at earlier dates in Sylvia's own hand. She had half-wondered whether to bring the letters with her to the country. But no, there were too many of them, and Cora would have reacted badly, for she had long ago asked Sylvia to burn them. Why? Because Cora's tales from overseas (commentaries spanning half a century) had been illuminated by observations others would have had neither the courage nor inclination to put down on paper, and because of the names involved.

Sylvia wanted Cora to elucidate, she wanted to hear her final version, and from her own lips, face to face and in person. *Not* the stories around the Story. That was what Cora was good at, had always been good at, deflecting, detracting. Even now, so many of her sentences began, 'You know, I had a dear friend in Paris who once told me . . .' or, 'My friend, so and so, in Rome used to say . . .' and continued by way of a circuitous route of name-dropping and digressions to a startling revelation. From a peccadillo to a double life, her tales of scandal had always been littered with abandoned wives, illegitimate children, lunatic asylums, mistresses, lovers, murders and duels. Sylvia had heard them all before and, even when they were fresh, even when they were new(s), nothing, no matter how scintillating, had ever been able to compare to Cora's own and yet to be concluded story.

'I do hope Jack enjoys his cricket,' Sylvia said at last.

Cora said nothing. She appeared to be deep in thought, and continued to stare at the pane of glass, transfixed by her own image.

'It's so nice that he's able to join in with the other young people,' Sylvia persevered. 'Lovely that he's made a few friends . . .'

Silence.

Sylvia lifted her cup, looked down into it. 'I believe he's rather taken by a certain girl in the village.'

Cora turned to her.

Sylvia took a sip. 'I must say, this coffee's really very good.' She placed the white china carefully back upon the saucer, lifted the napkin to her mouth. 'Yes, awfully good,' she said again. She looked up at her friend, smiling. 'You haven't tasted yours.'

Cora sighed. 'Well . . .'

'Well?'

'Are you going to tell me? And don't, for heaven's sake, ask *what*. You know perfectly well *what*.'

'He mentioned two names . . . but the hesitation before the second gave him away.'

'And the name?' Cora asked.

CHAPTER 2

Cecily remained indoors. Spread out on the long, blue-cushioned window seat in the square bay of the parlour, she was immersed in her new novel, *Zuleika Dobson*, which had arrived in the post the previous day. The summer curtains were drawn halfway across the open window, shading the room, Cecily and the book from the glare of the afternoon sun. And but for the distant sound of Rosetta's singing, all was quiet.

When the doorbell rang Cecily jumped, dropping the book to the floor. It seemed unnecessarily loud and whoever it was, they were of determined character, she thought, pushing the book beneath the cushioned seat.

'I'll get it, Rosetta,' she said to the maid in the hallway.

She turned the brass handle, pulled opened the door. 'Annie—'

'There's a cricket match on the green this afternoon and *he's* in it, he's bowling, Walter just told me,' Annie said rapidly, clutching the handlebar of her bicycle. 'I thought I should come . . . come and tell you.'

'I'll get my hat.'

The girls cycled slowly down the track, through the shallow ford and up the hill on the other side, moving in and out of the shadows of overhanging hedgerow and trees. At the newly gated entrance to Mount View, where the road widened and the sky suddenly seemed bigger than ever, they passed the rector, Mr Fox, wobbling back towards the village on his bicycle, and Stephen Burrows, emerging from a field with a reap hook in his hand. They parked their bicycles under the trees by the steps down to the village hall and walked up the pathway towards the green. The match was already underway. Languorous half-hearted shouts and desultory clapping drifted through the air. Barefooted children zigzagged about with hoops and people stood in huddles. A group of young men raised their boaters, smiled and nodded to the girls as they passed. 'Too hot for cricket, eh?' one of them said, wiping his brow with his handkerchief. 'Hottest day so far, I reckon.'

In the middle of the green the yellowing grass turned to molten silver, the players blurring into the pool of liquefied metal: like a mirage, Cecily thought. Only a few wore white flannels, the majority were in their usual working clothes, with shirtsleeves rolled back and braces exposed. And beyond them, at the other side of the field, clear and solid, and dazzlingly white, stood Bramley's new pavilion.

'Oh cripes,' said Annie, 'look who's here . . .'

Sonia Brownlow stood out that day, but for none of the reasons she would perhaps have wished to. In a broad-brimmed, top-heavy hat, tight-fitting frilled blouse, and skirt, tightened further by a broad belt, she resembled a great white galleon about to set sail. Sonia lived with her parents, brothers and sister at Mount View, the biggest and newest house in the village, situated opposite the village green. Mr Brownlow had made his money in shipping, enough for his family to live in deep-piled comfort, with every modern convenience and luxury and a dazzling array of new, gilt-edged furnishings. Sonia had been born in Rangoon and, as she liked to remind people, had travelled the world. And to Cecily and Annie she had made some bold claims: she had swum with giant turtles in the Pacific, shot wild boar in Africa, and learned to ski at St Moritz. And she could, she had told them, if she wanted – though not to them – speak half a dozen languages.

When Sonia saw the girls, she flapped a hand about under her fringed parasol, beckoning them over to where she and a few others stood. Cecily glanced at the figures in the centre of the field. She could see Walter, Annie's brother, standing in front of the wickets, bat in hand, and she recognised a number of other familiar figures, but she could not see *him*. And the possibility of his absence, of his not being there, gave her a sudden pang, a quick and sharp sensation of loss.

Sonia was laughing, wobbling her head about in that affected way Cecily loathed. As the girls drew nearer she turned to them, wide-eyed, and asked, 'Here to watch the match, are we?' And then quietly added; 'Don't worry, none of us gives a monkey's about cricket, but perhaps we rather like certain *cricketers* . . . hmm?'

Cecily whispered, 'I think I'm going home.'

'Now? But we've only just arrived.'

Cecily turned, about to walk away.

'But Cecily . . . Cecily,' Annie hissed.

She glanced over her shoulder, saw Annie's nodding gesture and, beyond, a white-clad figure striding out across the pitch, rubbing a ball against his thigh. For a while all conversation stopped as the girls focused their collective attention on cricket, without any commentary. Then, with her eyes fixed ahead, Sonia said, 'I don't suppose you know Jack.'

'Jack?'

'Jack Staunton.'

'Yes, I've met him,' Cecily said. 'I met him last week, very briefly, though I didn't catch his name.'

It was true. She had crossed paths with him, literally crossed paths with him. He had been heading up the track when she stepped out through the garden gate and almost collided with him. And she had known, known immediately, who *he* was, even before he mentioned the word 'neighbour'.

But so unprepared had she been that she missed the name and then stumbled over her own, reducing it to *Silly* Chadwick. 'Cecily,' she had said again, shaking his hand and looking downwards, too embarrassed to ask him to repeat his own, too embarrassed to say anything else at all. She had swiftly turned and walked on, cringing at the clumsy introduction. But at the bottom of the track, on the bend before the ford, she had glanced back, and caught him doing the same.

Sonia moved closer. 'I was introduced to him the day he arrived. *She* invited us over . . . wanted him to meet some young people he'd have things in common with, I suppose.'

Annie said, 'Is he her grandson then?'

'Well, yes,' Sonia replied, sounding vaguely amused. 'But he's only just finished at school. Because of all of his travels he's a year or two behind – which must be rather odd,' she added, crinkling her nose. 'He's going up to *univarsity* in October. Better late than never, I suppose.'

'And is he really an orphan?' Annie whispered.

'Indeed he is,' she replied. 'His father died *yars* and *yars* ago, when he was no more than a baby, and his mother . . .' she paused, looked around her, 'committed *sewicide* . . . only earlier this year,' she whispered.

'Suicide?'

'Sshh! Yes. Awful business, one imagines.'

'But how do you know all of this?' Annie asked, moving closer, narrowing her eyes. 'Did *he* tell you?'

'No! My mother told me. She read about it in the newspaper. There was an inquest and it mentioned the name, said the old lady had returned to this country after a lifetime abroad. His father's death was in the newspapers too, apparently. He died in a hunting accident, you know. He had just returned from South America.'

'South America,' Cecily repeated.

'Mm, thrown from his horse. Tragic really. Mama says the poor woman must be cursed for everyone around her to die in such tragic circumstances.'

Cecily was about to ask the name, the full name, for no one ever seemed inclined to refer to it, but Sonia continued, 'To lose all of her children, and five husbands . . .'

'Five!' Annie repeated.

'I believe so.'

'And is she English?' Annie asked.

'Oh, I should say so. Old aristocracy . . . titled family scattered the length and breadth of Europe. You know how they all intermarry. She has a palazzo in Rome, and a chateau somewhere in France, I believe. And of course one can see from her manner and style that she's from a very old family. Temple Hill is quite something, I can tell you. Wall-to-wall antiques and art . . . Though Papa says old families like hers always like to have their heirlooms on display, no matter how chipped or tatty, just to remind them of who they once were.' She laughed.

'And Jack, Jack Staunton, he has no brothers or sisters?' Cecily broke in.

'No, he's the only one left.'

'So what happened? To the others, I mean,' Annie asked, leaning in once again, her eyes fixed on Sonia.

Sonia shrugged her shoulders. 'I have no idea but I believe they all died in quite tragic circumstances.'

'Golly, a curse . . .' said Annie, sounding excited.

'And what of the companion?' Cecily asked.

'The novelist?'

'She's a novelist?'

'Oh yes. And one imagines she could tell you the whole story.' She threw back her head, and affected another, this time silent, laugh, then continued, 'They've known each other forever, since they were girls in Rome.'

'Rome?'

'Yes, she grew up there with—'

'But I heard it was Paris,' Cecily interrupted.

'Paris and Rome.'

'Paris and Rome,' Cecily repeated quietly, trying to take it all in.

'Crikey, she gets about,' Annie said, not entirely untruthfully, Cecily conceded.

'She's a peculiar sort though, awfully timid . . . scribbles away all the time.'

'Which one?' Annie asked.

'The novelist! Miss Dorland.'

'Dorland?' Cecily repeated. The name was

vaguely familiar. Wasn't there a Dorland in the village? Hadn't she seen or heard that name somewhere recently?

'And is he Italian?' Annie went on.

'Jack? No! He's more English than you or I, dear. Oh, but yes, I see . . . he does rather look *Latino*,' she added dreamily, staring across the field.

Then Annie said, 'And so, what's he like, Sonia? Do tell.' And Cecily wished she hadn't; wished she hadn't sounded quite so eager.

'Well,' Sonia began, without looking at either one of the girls, 'he's really rather charming, and quite different to anyone here, of course. You see, he's travelled a great deal, like me . . . like us.' She glanced at Cecily and smiled. 'And I told him Bramley's really rather dull . . . perfectly suitable for a summer, perhaps, but not to spend one's *entire* life.'

Cecily looked away. She longed to know more, wanted to ask questions, but it seemed to her that both she and Annie, particularly Annie, had indulged Sonia Brownlow long enough. And she resented the remark about Bramley. Despite her desire for new horizons, a desire growing ever stronger, Cecily felt inherently loyal and protective of this small world. She gazed out across the field, watched Jack Staunton run forward, describe an arc and release the ball.

Due to Mr Cotton's wagonette having over-heated and breaking down en route from the rectory with scones, cakes, sandwiches, as well as the tea urn

38

on board, there was only a very brief interval at 3.30p.m., when the players filed into the pavilion for cold refreshments. Tea would be served after the match, Mrs Moody informed everyone, circumnavigating the field with a megaphone as Miss Combe tried to keep pace holding a parasol aloft. And every so often, forgetting to remove the mouthpiece from her lips, and entirely forgetting her public-speaking voice, Mrs Moody's offside remarks reverberated through the sultry air: 'This ruddy heat'll have me yet . . . it'll make us all go mad . . . as though I haven't enough to do . . . well, I'm not carrying anything from that blessed motor . . .'

Minutes later, Mr Fox, Mrs Fox, Miss Combe and a few others could be seen weaving their way through the long grass of the rectory field in a crocodile formation, carrying trays and platters, with Mrs Moody a few yards behind, bringing up the rear. And later still, inside the sweltering pavilion, laid out upon a long trestle table, were the plates of curling sandwiches, scones with dollops of melting cream on top and fat slices of cake that had been rescued and carried through the fields. Mrs Moody stood poised with a knife behind her lemon meringue pie; Mr Fox, his whiskers smeared with jam and cream, was already seated and tucking in.

The girls sat in a row on a bench outside the pavilion with their tea. Beyond them, on the far side of a densely wooded valley, the tall chimneys of Temple Hill rose up into the blue. And it was this vista Cecily was contemplating when Jack Staunton emerged from the pavilion holding a cup and saucer in his hand. Sonia quickly rose to her feet and invited him to join them.

He smiled. 'Miss Chadwick.'

'Oh yes, you two have already met . . . and this is Miss Annie Gamben,' said Sonia, wafting a hand, 'from the post office.'

He reached out and took hold of Annie's hand. 'Jack Staunton, a pleasure to meet you,' he said, and then sat down on the grass in front of her.

Annie said, 'You played very well. I'm not sure we'd have won without—'

'*Remarkably* well,' interrupted Sonia, seated once more. 'One rather thinks you were the man of the match, Mr Staunton.' And as she arched her back and lifted her head up to the sun, he glanced at Cecily, smiling, and said, 'It's Jack, please, and I have to say it was a team effort . . . the whole team played well.'

'My, but it's hot!' Sonia went on, tugging for a moment at the lace of her blouse, and then fanning her face with her hand. 'Makes one think of the South Seas . . .'

'Or Southsea,' said Annie, 'on a hot day. No different.'

'Southsea? Ha! Oh Annie, you do make one laugh. The South Seas are, I think, a tad different to Southsea. Wouldn't you agree, Mr . . . Jack?'

'I'm afraid I really can't say. I've never been – to either.'

Sonia laughed, as though Jack Staunton's reply was the funniest thing she had ever heard, as though there was some private joke hidden in his response to her, Cecily thought.

'But I'd like to,' he added, quietly.

'Southsea or the South Seas?' Cecily asked.

'Both,' he replied. 'But perhaps one is nearer, more accessible than the other.'

'And duller.'

'Hmm. Not necessarily, not if it's where one wishes to be, not if the sun shines.'

'*If* the sun shines . . . that's a condition.'

'A secondary condition. Happiness can't be dependent on fine weather.'

'No. But it can be defined by a sense of *place* . . . and . . .'

'People?'

'Yes, people,' Cecily agreed.

'Then we're in agreement. Nowhere is dull, only people are dull.'

Cecily smiled, and Sonia, whose head had been turning from Jack to Cecily and back again, said, 'One hasn't the foggiest notion . . . what *are* you two on about?'

'Only the weather,' Jack replied. 'So queer you should mention fog . . .'

Sonia laughed again, and for a few minutes they sat in silence before she started, 'I must say, your grandmother's a remarkable lady, Jack. It was such an honour to be invited to meet her . . . to hear about Rome and Paris and all. One could listen

41

to her for *ars* and *ars* . . . and one simply can't wait to read the book, the memoirs. But,' she paused and frowned, 'it must be unspeakably dull for her here.'

Jack looked at Cecily and smiled. And Annie, leaning forward, staring along the bench at Sonia, said, 'Oh dear, one appears to have spilled some tea on one's blouse, Sonia.'

Sonia glanced down at her frilled bosom, 'No . . . really? Where?'

'Perhaps not,' Annie replied, sitting back, turning her face away. 'It must've been a shadow.'

For what seemed to Cecily excruciating *ars* and *ars*, Sonia monopolised the conversation, determined Jack Staunton should understand the nuances of being Sonia Brownlow, determined to make the distinction between herself and the two sitting next to her. When, eventually, she rose to her feet, she said, 'Well, my dears, I'm afraid it's toodle-pip time *pour moi*. One has one's pianoforte lesson at six.' She opened her parasol. Jack Staunton stood up. She extended a gloved hand to him. He took it in his. 'So lovely to see you again,' she said, blinking. 'I believe you and your grandmother and Miss Dorland are to dine with us tomorrow.'

'I look forward to it,' he replied.

Cecily watched him as he watched Sonia stroll off across the grass. She wondered what he made of her. She was handsome, yes; and she could certainly speak of things that neither she nor Annie

– nor most in Bramley – had any experience of. Sonia wanted to impress, and she was impressive. How could she not be? How could anyone not be impressed by her knowledge, accomplishments, even her wardrobe? And Jack's grandmother was obviously impressed too. After all, she had invited Sonia up to Temple Hill to meet him, her beloved grandson. Hand-picked, Cecily thought. But then Sonia had a proper family, a mother *and* a father, and the requisite full complement of siblings. And the family had money, more money than anyone else in the parish. Mr Brownlow's seemingly endless pounds had funded the modernisation and extension of the village hall, an extra class-room at the school, and the new cricket pavilion. Oh yes, the Brownlow's weren't short of a bob or two, or ten.

When Walter, Annie's brother, appeared, he squeezed himself on to the seat and turned to Cecily. 'My, my, you're looking very fetching today, Cecily.' He placed his arm along the bench behind her, moved his head under her hat. 'And we don't usually see you here . . . do we?' he whispered, his mouth to her ear.

Cecily stared ahead, smiling, and said nothing. Walter liked to tease her. He was two years older than Annie and had recently celebrated his twenty-first birthday with a rumbustious dance at the village hall, which Cecily, her mother and sister had attended, and left long before its end. Cecily considered Walter solid and dependable, a brick:

Annie's big brother. And he was. He was easily over six foot tall, with broad shoulders and huge hands. Like Annie, he was fair-skinned, with mousy coloured hair and pale far-seeing grey eyes. His disposition, too, was like Annie's, with a natural inclination towards happiness. Walter, Cecily thought, was innately kind; comfortable with himself and his lot in life, without pretension, malice, or ambition.

Jack Staunton sat tugging at the grass, his head bent, listening to Annie. She was going on and on about a fair at Linford, saying what a ripping idea it would be for them all to go. It had been at the Whitsun fair, right there on the green, that Annie had been told she would be married before she reached twenty. She had been euphoric, over the moon, had spent all of the following week cogitating upon her future, that forthcoming marriage, and with whom it was likely to be.

'So where's Ethne today?' Walter asked.

'Oh, probably at church,' Cecily replied.

He threw his head back and laughed.

'It's not *that* funny Walter.' She turned to him: 'She may well be.'

He leaned closer. 'Really?' he replied, looking into her eyes, 'But you always make me laugh.'

Walter had been like this a lot recently: staring and intense. And it made her feel awkward, uncomfortable. Weeks before, at his twenty-first birthday, a little befuddled and bleary-eyed, he had pulled her close as he danced with her and said, 'You know I have plans, Cecily Chadwick . . . plans for the future. I'm going to make something of my life. You wait and see.' She had said, of course, she wouldn't expect otherwise. Because Walter had a brain, a very good brain, and it would be wasted at a post-office counter, she thought. 'So don't you go running off with anyone whilst I'm not looking,' he had added, smiling, half-joking. She had laughed. 'I'm not planning on running off with anyone,' she replied, turning away from him, towards her mother's watchful gaze.

Now, she could hear Annie telling Jack Staunton everything the fortune-teller had told her at the Whitson fair. '. . . she said she saw the letters R and W, and a large stone-built house and lots of animals.'

'A farmer?' Jack suggested.

'Yes! You know, that's exactly what I thought. It has to be, doesn't it? But I can't think of any farmers, not round here, with those initials . . .'

'Could be middle names.'

'Yes, or someone who's going to take up a tenancy, because I've got almost another year yet, you see. He might not have arrived yet.'

'There's that old buffer, Richard Wakeford,' Walter broke in. 'He's got a big stone-built butcher's shop, no wife, and plenty of *dead* animals.'

'Ha-ha,' Annie replied, flicking a hand in her brother's direction. 'I seem to recall that you, Walter Gamben, weren't quite so glib at the time, were you?'

'It's bunkum, Annie. All of it.'

'Oh really? And I suppose that's why you were so keen to know if your name had been mentioned in connection with a particular young lady – whose name I shan't mention . . .'

Walter's face reddened, and for a short while no one spoke.

When Cecily stood up, saying, 'I should go now,' Walter and Jack simultaneously rose to their feet.

Walter said, 'I can walk you home . . . if you want.'

'There's no need. And anyway, I have my bicycle.'

Jack Staunton stood kicking a toe at the grass, his hands in his pockets. 'I'll walk with you,' he said. And then, looking at Walter, as though he might say something, object, he added, 'After all, I'm going that way too.'

At first, without Annie and Walter there to chivvy things along, the atmosphere was awkward, and they walked in silence down the road. He had insisted on taking her bicycle, pushing it along between them.

He said, 'Annie's a jolly sort.'

Cecily smiled, nodded her head.

'And Walter,' he said, turning to look at her: 'He seems like a nice chap.'

'Yes, he is, although . . .' she paused.

'Although?'

'He's become a little . . . solemn of late. But he's a very nice person. One of my favourite people.'

'I could see,' he said, looking away.

'Sonia says you're going to university, to Cambridge.'

'Yes. I've been offered a place at Trinity.'

'How exciting.'

'I suppose it is. Yes . . . I suppose it is,' he said.

'So you're here for the summer then?'

'Mm,' he said, pushing the bike along, lost in his thoughts.

'Well, you know a few folk here now,' she went on, wanting him to feel . . . What was it she wanted him to feel? At home, welcomed, part of the village? Yes, all of those things and more. She wanted him to feel happy. She wanted him to look forward, not back.

'You know Sonia,' she said, 'And now you know Annie and Walter, and me.'

'Yes, it's good to make new friends.'

When they reached the hill that led down to the huddle of the village, he stopped, stepped over the bike, turned to her and patted the seat behind him. 'Come on, hop on.'

He stood upright on the pedals and she sat on the saddle, her hands behind her, clutching it, as they glided down the hill. As they swerved to the right, towards the ford, she felt the tilting of the bike and grabbed hold of his waist. 'Not through the water!' she shouted, but their approach was too fast, and then they were in it, and through it.

He stopped the bike on the dirt track on the other side of the stream. 'Sorry about that, I forgot about the ford,' he said, laughing.

'And I'd forgotten it's almost dried up,' she replied, climbing from the bike, glancing along the path of the stream to the pool where watercress and forget-me-nots grew. The yellow water lilies were in full bloom, the air above thick with tiny white butterflies.

They continued up the track. He said, 'I'm getting a motorcycle next week. I'll take you out on it, if you'd like.'

'A motor bicycle? I don't suppose my mother would allow me to go out on one of those.'

'Don't ask her . . . don't tell her. I shan't go too fast, you know. I promise. Just a spin through the lanes, but only if you'd like to, of course,' he added, without turning to look at her.

When they reached the privet hedge they stopped. She took the bicycle from him. The rubber grips of the handlebar were warm and wet where his hands had been. He pushed his palm up over his forehead into his hair and said, 'My God, it's hot. Hard to believe we're in England, eh?'

'Yes,' she said, though it wasn't for her, because she had never been anywhere else.

He stepped away from her, to the other side of the track, staring out over the scattered rooftops, the straggling line of the village beneath them. Across the valley a hot-air balloon rose up above the trees and he raised his hand to his brow, watching it. 'Wouldn't it be wonderful to do that? To go up into the sky, just float above the world,' he said, and she smiled. Because every summer, every time she had seen one of those huge, coloured balloons rise up over the hill, intermittently roaring, breathing fire, she had thought the very same thing.

'One day I'm going to fly,' he said, his eyes still fixed on the balloon.

'You mean go up in a flying machine?'

He turned to her. 'Yes, why not? Geoffrey de Havilland's already building himself another flying machine, as you call it, at the balloon factory at Farnborough. He'll be taking it up sometime next year, I imagine. And you know, one day, one day soon enough, people will be flying all over the place in them, across mountains, land and seas, travelling the world through the air.' He smiled. 'It's a stunning thought, isn't it?'

'I'm not sure. I think a balloon's far safer, and more sedate.' She moved the bicycle towards the open gate.

'If we only ever did what was safe we'd never learn anything, never have new experiences . . . never move forward. We have to take risks in order to progress. Science has, at the very least, taught us that much.'

'I'm afraid I'm not very scientific, and I simply can't believe science has *all* the answers.'

He stood with his hands pushed deep into his pockets, looking downwards and kicking at the ground once more. He said, 'No, well, you might be right . . . I don't know anything really. I thought I did. In fact, up until quite recently I rather thought I knew it all. But things happen, inexplicable things that one never saw coming . . . that one couldn't possibly have foreseen or anticipated, and then everything . . . everything goes back to the beginning. Right now, I'm probably as clueless as the day I was born.'

'Sometimes all of us, no matter what our circumstances, feel like that,' she offered, searching for something better. 'I lost my father when I was very young, rather like you . . . but of course I still have my mother.' No, that wasn't what she meant, not what she meant to say at all. 'What I mean is . . .' she faltered, and he smiled.

'It's all right, I know what you mean.'

Seconds later, when she turned her head, saw his white figure disappearing into a tunnel of shadows, it was all she could do to stop herself from dropping the bicycle to the ground and running after him.

CHAPTER 3

He says he thought it was her in the bed, and she simply stares at him, her breathing loud and fast – as though she has been running, running very fast, her chest rising and falling, her jaw clenched. She shakes her head and speaks quietly when she says, 'It can't happen . . . can't happen again.' He laughs, turns to walk away and she reaches out, grabs hold of the back of his shirt, pulling on it and saying, 'Do you hear me? I'm telling you now.' His fist glides through the air so smoothly, so swiftly, swivelling his body, almost lifting him off his feet, meeting the side of her face in a loud crack. Then he looks across the room at the girl sitting on the chair by the fire. And he raises his finger to her as a warning.

Cora sat alone, staring out towards the tops of pine trees. Had she needed a prompt, a visual reminder, they would have served her well, for she had stared at that very same image – a blur of darkest green against brilliant blue – many times before. But at that moment she saw no wooded hillside and no English sky; she saw only the blush of ancient stone, the sunlit ruins of a distant place.

She saw the velvet contours of seven hills, a hundred steeples and domes and, beyond them, the windswept meadows where the land met the sky in an azure haze. And with this image came the remembrance of the weightlessness of youth, when her world had been a small empire of infinite possibility.

'Such plans, such dreams,' she whispered, 'such promises.' Had it really only been a season? Yes, between autumn and spring. He had swept into her life without warning, turning winter into summer and her world upside down. But hadn't she known, even before she met him, even before she set eyes on him? Wasn't there something in the name, she thought, trying to remember that very first time she had heard it, which sounded . . . familiar, anticipated? She could hear her aunt say it, picture her standing in the hallway of their apartment in Rome. That was the beginning, she thought; that was when I came alive, truly came alive, when I heard that name for the first time.

Knowing he was in Rome for only the season made every minute of every hour of every day count. 'It's why and how I began to live . . .' She smiled as she recalled her boldness on that first solo visit to his studio, and she could see the place once more: the violets she took him, standing in the dirty jam jar; the canvases stacked up against the walls; the kettle on the open fire; the paper-strewn floor; and him, standing in his chalk-smeared, crumpled velvet jacket, holding up a teapot. 'China or Darjeeling?'

'China or Darjeeling,' she said to herself, half laughing.

But her memory, as it was wont to do now, moved on at random to a later date, and with an intake of breath she closed her eyes . . .

'We'll come back each year,' he said, lying back, folding his arms behind his head. 'Yes, we'll return here each winter.' He glanced at her. 'What do you say?'

'I say, *yes*!'

She threw herself down next to him. The remnants of their lunch – grapes and peaches, cheese and bread – lay scattered about them, the bottle of wine and two almost empty glasses on the table next to him.

'Of course, once we're married I'm going to have to sell heaps of bloody pictures to support you and our horde of badly behaved children.'

'And how do you know they'll be badly behaved?' she asked.

'Because I do . . . because they'll be just like you,' he said, turning to face her.

She lifted her hand to his brow. 'We'll be happy,' she said, tracing a dark curl with her finger, 'so happy.'

'We will, and we'll live in total squalor.'

'Squalor?'

'Chaos . . . Total and blissful chaos.'

'But where will we live, George?'

'I've already told you, everywhere. We shall live *everywhere*! All over the place and wherever we like. We'll live like gypsies . . . but we may need more than one caravan. We'll come here each winter, divide our time between Rome and Florence, head to Paris in the spring, and the south of France perhaps in autumn.'

'But not England?'

He stared at her and smiled. 'No, not England. Who needs England?' he asked, pulling her to him . . .

She opened her eyes, glanced down at her hands, her wedding band – immovable now. 'I was the gypsy,' she said out loud.

There was a muted rhythm to the evening. The air was soft and still. But it had been a long and arduous day: too long, and much too hot. And it had been a relief to get back to the solitude and peacefulness of her garden, the place that was now her home. Stiffly upholstered in navy, faded with age and wear, she felt heavy and weary. Not simply from that day's journey, but from a lifetime's journeys, and the journey of a lifetime.

A seasoned traveller, undaunted by timetables, foreign languages and customs, she had spent decades criss-crossing Europe by land, by river and by sea. But there would be no return to Rome, not even for the winter, and there could be no more trips to Paris. She would never again stroll through the gardens of what had once been the Tuileries Palace, or catch a steamer and sail from Rhône to Avignon, or from Marseilles to Civitavecchia and, later, stand on the deck of another, heading upriver to the Ripetta. Her wings had finally been clipped.

But there were other things sapping her once renowned energy. Things she could not speak of, which thrashed on the periphery of her thoughts and lay heavy on her conscience. If she could only exhale, fully exhale, she thought, she might be able to release the burden, feel lighter. *Breathe*, her aunt had told her, breathe, as though it was the easiest thing in the world to do. But it had never been easy. And now, this holding-in was almost too much.

She moved her hand, feeling for the paper in her pocket: yes, it was there, still there. She had not dreamt it. She would look at it again later, in private; decide then what to do. She must not panic, must not imagine the worst. After all, it had happened before. Been dealt with before. This time would be no different . . . though there was, of course, Jack to think of now.

She had thought of telling Sylvia, and had come close to it on the train earlier that day. Sylvia's instincts had always been so very acute. She knew when something was amiss. But it would be wrong, selfish, to burden poor Sylvia, who would undoubtedly panic and imagine the very worst scenario. And yet, when Sylvia had taken hold of her hand and said, 'Something is troubling you, Cora, I can tell,' she had longed to tell her: to tell her everything, all of it, from beginning to end.

But the train's movement, a gentle rock and forward motion, that familiar sensation of transit, and a landscape, albeit foreign to her, gliding swiftly past had soothed her. The upper windows of the drawing-room carriage had been pulled open, and she had closed her eyes, savouring the caress of warm air upon her skin, searching for that familiar bouquet of cedar, cypress and pine. And fleetingly, for a second or two, she caught it, the memory of it, heady, intoxicating, life affirming; then it had gone. Gone forever, perhaps. And the tightness about her chest – the restriction, lack of breath, the weight – returned, and with it a sense of sorrow.

When she caught her reflection in the carriage window she had been surprised once more by the aged face staring back at her; the inclination of what had once been upturned to now be down-turned; the eyes, once sparkling and wide, now small; unreadable, even to her. Oh, that she could turn back time, that she wasn't in England, surrounded by English people and their need to know; their voracious hunger for information. And for what reason? To know where and how she fitted in? People had stared, people had smiled; yes, they always did. They bowed their heads as she passed by, and then bowed them again each time she caught their eye.

Early on in life she had become aware of this dichotomy: how easily the succour of attention turned to the discomfort of scrutiny. Now she thought, how queerly people stare. Was it age? she wondered. Or was it that they perceived something different, not English, something foreign to their sensibilities and tastes perhaps? Or was it something in her expression? Impossible surely. No one knew: no one *living*.

She was pondering all of this when Jack appeared, looking hot and exhausted in his cricket whites. And the shape of him, his gait, and those familiar dark features pulled her back and made her smile. He bent down, kissed her cheek, and then fell into the chair next to her with a sigh. He told her about the match, inquired after her day.

She said, 'And did you see your friends?'

He stared out over the manicured lawn in front of them. Yes, he told her, he had seen his friends.

He was distracted, she could tell. And she knew it was not the cricket.

'If there's someone you'd like to invite here . . . to tea, or to dine with us . . .' she ventured.

He turned to her. 'Someone?'

'Someone in particular . . . a girl, perhaps.'

'There's no girl.'

'I was thinking of Sonia Brownlow, or perhaps Cecily.'

He tried to laugh. Repeated Sonia's name and rolled his eyes.

'Or Cecily?' she said again.

He stood up, pushed his hands into his pockets and swivelled round on his feet.

'This is your home now. It's *our* home. I want

you to know you can invite your friends here,' she said, reaching out to him, placing her hand on his bare forearm.

He looked down at the ground. 'Her name's Cecily Chadwick . . . she's our neighbour. But I don't suppose we've much in common, not really.'

'I'd rather like to meet her.'

He shrugged his shoulders. 'I'm not sure when I'll see her again.'

Cora laughed. 'She's our neighbour, you said. I'm quite sure it's not beyond you to walk a few hundred yards and invite her here. You can tell her that I'd like to meet her.'

He pulled away. 'I can't say that! It sounds perfectly dreadful, as though we've discussed her, which we have now, but . . .'

'Jack, you simply say that your grandmother is keen to meet her new neighbours. That's all. I'm sure she's not a mind-reader, not yet.'

He looked down at her. 'What do you mean by that?'

She smiled. 'I simply mean that I'm quite certain she isn't able to read your thoughts.'

'Can you?' he asked.

'Perhaps . . . but that's because you, your heart, are so very precious to me. You're all I have.'

'I should go inside, clean myself up,' he said, moving away from her.

She smiled as she listened to his footsteps fade, lifted her glass to her lips. The liquid, like the air, was syrupy and warm. She thought about Jack and the girl from next door, tried to picture them together, and wondered what they had spoken of. She wondered how her grandson appeared to a young, innocent village girl. Handsome surely. Burdened? Damaged? She closed her eyes. No. He was neither burdened nor damaged, she told herself, firmly, silently. Poised on the brink of magnificent manhood, Jack was her legacy to the world, the embodiment of everything good in her life, its sum total, distilled to one. And she lifted her face to the sun once more.

But it was in such moments she was catapulted back. For there was no forward, her life lay behind her. Anamnesis: when the journey ended, this was all one was left with, memories. Of foolishness, pride, rapture, pain, sorrow, and regret. Sweet and bitter and bittersweet, they floated about the ether like thistledown in the wind, difficult to catch hold of and, once caught, never quite as lovely.

It was impossible for her to remember what she had said to whom and when. Had she ever told Sylvia the truth? She could not recall what, exactly, she had told her all those years ago in Rome, though she knew she had told her something – something of the truth. That's what had whetted Sylvia's appetite, surely, that glimpse, the glimpse of a story. Oh yes.

The problem, she realised, one of the problems, stemmed from the fact that history had been over-written, and not just once, and not just by herself. Now, it seemed increasingly hard to unravel the facts, the truth of events and circumstances. Could history change its shape with time? Had her subconscious mind intervened and run rampant, editing and rewriting her own story? Memories did indeed change shape with time, she knew and understood this. The conscious mind followed instruction, could be controlled. By reason and logic, and survival? Yes, survival. It could even override the heart, sometimes, for a while. But the heart was infinitely powerful. It could be ignored – to an extent; it could be restrained, repressed, but it could never be controlled. One could never control one's heart.

But now there were gaps and missing links, for seasons and, sometimes, entire years had been erased, people discarded, abandoned along the way, left standing at a dusty crossroads without so much as an adieu. Distant recollections were worn-out flimsy things that only occasionally had resonance, the ring of truth about them. And that once sharp mind, the very foundation on which her life had been built, had slowly come to let her down.

Old age. It was frustrating and yet queerly liberating at the same time. Made frustrating by the obvious and anticipated limitations, both physical and mental, and made liberating by those very same things as well: not being able to remember, not being expected to know or get things right. What does it matter, she thought, if I make a mistake? No one will know. Everyone is gone.

She heard a door close behind her.

'Good gracious,' Sylvia began, sitting down with her notebook and pencil. 'I do believe the air is hotter now than it was this afternoon.'

Cora said nothing. She smiled as she watched Sylvia open her notebook, flick a few pages, scanning the pencilled scrawl: *so childlike.*

And why would she not be? Nothing had occurred to induce her to leave that state, to make her grow up. Sylvia's entire life had been an uninterrupted, solitary affair, without claim to either requited or unrequited love. No lovers, no children, no husbands, Cora thought, continuing to watch her. Had her lips ever once been kissed? No. She would die a virgin. And yet, she had known passion, of a sort, for had she not spent a lifetime imagining it, picturing it, writing it? But dear Sylvia's novels were so very naive, so clichéd, and they were all the same. Sylvia had admitted as much herself. 'It's my formula,' she had said only the previous day, looking quite put out.

In truth, Sylvia had assumed Cora too busy to notice the coincidences, the synchronicity. But Cora had always known, always been aware that she had been the source of inspiration; that it was her experience, her unique perspective, that had expanded Sylvia's understanding of the universe, and of men. And Sylvia was not the only artist whose vision had been inspired, for the soft contours of Cora's once youthful shape were frozen in tinted marble, the symmetry of her young face captured in oils.

'You know, it astounds me how you find so much to write about,' Cora said now.

'Words, dear, just words.'

'Words,' Cora repeated, fiddling with the locket about her neck. 'And how many of those, I wonder, have been spoken and written only to be rued. We have too many words now, too many words for too many things. And new ones being invented all the time.'

'But that's the beauty of language, dear. Man's need for expression is, I think, the most powerful urge of all, the need to say who we are, how we feel, what we think, hmm?'

'And perhaps also to shock, to inspire reaction,' she shrugged, 'instil fear?'

Sylvia appeared pensive for a moment. 'Yes, they can be powerful tools.'

'Indeed. And illuminating. One can, if one is so inclined, identify one's friends and one's enemies simply by examining their choice of words. Even one word, a name . . .' Cora said, staring at her.

Sylvia nodded but made no reply. And Cora watched her as she peered through her spectacles at a particular page, then lifted her pencil to her mouth.

'You really oughtn't do that, you know. I read somewhere recently that lead is not good for one to ingest.'

Sylvia glanced up at her. 'Oh?'

'Poisonous, I presume.'

'Really?'

'Yes, but don't look so worried. I hardly think one can take one's own life in the lick of a pencil.'

'Unlike arsenic,' Sylvia said.

'Or carbolic acid . . .'

They stared each other.

'I meant to ask you, does he know? Have you ever told him *how*?'

'Of course he knows,' Cora replied sharply. 'It was in the wretched newspapers, though I did my best to stop it. I imagine everyone knows, or knew at the time. But I've never discussed it with him, and neither do I intend to.' She paused for a moment, exhaled loudly, and then added, 'Hopefully he does not allow himself to dwell on it. Any of it.'

'Well, yes, and he seems so . . .'

'Fine?' Cora suggested.

Sylvia tapped her pencil on her lip, then nodded. 'Yes, fine.'

'Well, I rather think he is. He's not like her, you know? Good gracious no, nothing like her. He's like his father, and like . . .'

'George?'

Cora turned to her. 'Like his grandfather,' she said.

'You know, the timing of it has always struck me as a queer thing,' Sylvia began again.

'The timing of it?'

'Yes. The fact that it happened immediately after the government's census . . . that she recorded herself and then, almost the very next day, was no more.'

'They're abominable things,' Cora said, raising a hand dismissively.

Sylvia smiled. 'But you've never had to do one, dear.'

'No, and nor would I!'

Sylvia shook her head. 'It's the law, I'm afraid. Everyone has to.'

'The law is an ass.'

'You know, you'd have had to give them your *full* name' Sylvia went on. 'Yes, and oh my, that *would* confound them!' she said, clapping her hands, and then intentionally mispronouncing Cora's full name. 'And 'ow you spellin' that, ma'am?' she added, in a mock cockney accent, Cora presumed, and giggling.

'I do not use Lawson, Sylvia, as you very well know. My name is quite long enough without it. And anyway, the name proved . . . problematic. I have no desire to raise my head above the parapet again.'

'No . . . no, of course not,' Sylvia replied, gathering herself. 'And you're right, censuses are awful things and ask all manner of questions: what one's occupation is, how many children one has given birth to. Oh, it goes on and on. And for the life of me I do wonder why. Wonder who all this information is for.'

'Statistics,' Cora said, with great emphasis. 'Statistics and pigeonholing, placing us all into tidy identifiable groups. The modern world is becoming obsessed by statistics . . . utterly intrusive and condemnable, I think.'

'Well, I can't help but wonder if all those questions were simply too much for her. For Cassandra, I mean.'

'I don't think it was the census, Sylvia. Cassandra had always been fragile, always of a melancholic nature. No, I think she'd teetered on a brink for years, and but for Jack, who knows? Perhaps she'd have taken her own life many years ago. But she waited, she waited until . . . until he was an adult.'

'Unfathomable . . . and I don't imagine she ever thought you'd come back,' Sylvia mused aloud. 'I suppose that's why she waited until he was grown up, had finished his studies. But,' she gasped, shaking her head, 'such a dreadful thing to do to him, poor dear.'

'Best not spoken of, I think, Sylvia. 'Twas a wicked and selfish act and I have nothing more to say on the matter.'

'Well, we have had rather a lovely day to ourselves, have we not?' said Sylvia, after a moment or two. 'And certainly, everyone considered it a great honour to have *you* there to judge and present the prizes today. Oh yes, it's quite clear that they hold you in very high esteem. In fact, you appear to be something of a celebrity, my dear.'

'I don't think so. A foreigner, perhaps, an outsider.'

'But you're not. And you really mustn't say such things. People will take you at your word, especially country folk.'

'Perhaps not but I feel like one, and I'm never

entirely sure where my allegiance lies . . . Though dear Bertie used to laugh at me whenever I said such things.' She paused, smiling, remembering. '"My dear," he would say, "you are as English as I." Of course he was being ironic because he was a Saxe-Coburg-Gotha, and his mother a Hanoverian.'

'The King was fond of you, wasn't he?'

'Oh yes, he was a dear friend, and of course a very dear friend to . . .'

'George?'

'Mm, yes, George,' Cora replied vaguely.

George. His face had haunted her dreams and waking hours for half a century. And yet it was hard to fathom the passing of time and nearness of him, the years between then and now. George. Each and every day of her life she remembered him. His face stared back at her through open doorways and panes of glass, through seasons and years, across a continent and a sea. All of her imaginings led her back to him: the what ifs, the whys, the silent conversations stretching through time. And sometimes, alone, she spoke his name out loud, lengthening that one adored syllable. But what would he think of her situation now? she wondered. *He never knew, never knew any of it, I never told him . . .*

'And would he have loved me any the less?' she murmured.

'What's that, dear?'

Cora started. 'Oh, nothing . . . nothing at all.'

'You know, you quite put me to shame today,' Sylvia began again. 'I'd never realised that you had such an understanding and knowledge of flowers and plants.'

'Not really, my dear, I just know a little about many things – and don't they say a little knowledge is a dangerous thing?'

'But it always seems to me that you know a great deal about *everything*,' Sylvia replied. 'And I insist, you must tell me where this knowledge came from.'

Cora turned to her friend. 'You know, I'm rather beginning to think you'd be better employing your investigative talents in writing crime thrillers instead of silly romances that . . . that have no bearing on real life!'

For some minutes the two women sat in silence.

'I'm sorry', Cora said, 'I've a great deal on my mind.'

'Is it about Jack?' Sylvia asked, leaning forward.

'No, not entirely . . .' She paused, looking at her friend with newly anxious eyes.

'Then what is it, dear? Please tell me what it is that's troubling you so.'

Cora reached over, placed her hand upon Sylvia's. 'I'm not sure I've ever told you how much your friendship means to me,' she said, her eyes on their hands. 'You've been the best, the very best.'

'We've been good friends to each other, dear. And you've been more than a friend to me, you have been family to me. But I can't bear to see you like this, not now. We're both much too old for any more drama.'

Cora tried to smile, shook her head. 'Oh, it's nothing . . . nothing sinister. Complications to do with the trust estates, that's all.'

'Ah, I thought as much. But you know, you really mustn't worry so. All will be well. Edward was a good man, a good husband. I'm quite certain he'll have made sure that you're looked after, provided for.'

'Well, I'm not destitute, not yet.'

'Nor will you ever be, not whilst I'm alive. But it's a scandal,' Sylvia shook her head, 'for you to be so fretful at this stage in your life. Dear Edward would turn in his grave!'

'It is what it is, we all have our crosses to bear . . . and I have spent too much of my life creating heroes and villains out of mere mortals.'

She saw Sylvia open her notebook once more and scribble something down. And Cora smiled. '*Dolce far niente*,' she said, closing her eyes.

'Ah yes, *dolce far niente*,' Sylvia repeated, without looking up.

'You know, I close my eyes and I'm back there.'

'It's this blessed heat. Easily as hot as Rome in August, and to think . . .'

Cora could hear Sylvia's voice, but she could no longer make out the words, and she had no wish to. She wanted to go back there, to that time, always that time, always that place.

Weeks away from England, isolated and

undisturbed, Rome had been a small city then, shrivelled within its walls. A place of lopsided crucifixes and littered shrines, and scattered ruins tangled up in weeds and undergrowth, and centuries of rubble and dust, where cows and sheep grazed about the tumbled pillars of ancient palaces and ragged clothes lay out to dry upon their scorching stones. Where animal carcases, flasks of oil and balls of cheese dangled against the crumbling plaster of windowless shops; where tailors, milliners, shoemakers and carpenters huddled in doorways, a shrine to the Madonna and a candle flickering in the dimness behind them. And in the summer months, when the Tiber exposed her yellow banks and a fetid air hung over the city's ruins, the place languished in that sweet idleness the Romans called '*dolce far niente*'.

'Never look back,' her aunt had told her. 'Your life . . . *our* life began here in Rome.' And for so long, so very long, she had not looked back. She had only ever looked ahead, always ahead. But that *other* time, that time before Rome – for so long pushed away, denied, so much so that it had almost been forgotten – seemed determined to be acknowledged. And names for so long unuttered, buried in the past, had been written down for her to see: *John Abel*.

She opened her eyes. Sylvia was watching her, and she smiled. Now, a new secret hung between them, an invisible pendulum swinging between each and every glance. And Sylvia's constant surveillance, that seemingly relentless albeit well-meaning scrutiny was awaiting answers, waiting for her to elucidate upon then and now, and everything in between.

But no, she couldn't. How could she? She would have to introduce Sylvia to new words – words even she found hard to say. And it would mean going back to the beginning, the beginning of everything. It would mean unravelling seven decades of careful arrangement. She thought of her aunt, of all the times she had warned her about any permanent return to England. But she had had no choice in the matter. After all, the boy had no one, and she had nowhere else to go.

Such a tawdry business, blackmail.

CHAPTER 4

'**A** French cook, I ask you!'
Rosetta was rolling out pastry once more, sprinkling flour across the pine table, wiping her brow between every roll. The kitchen was airless and hot. Cecily sat watching her, only half engaged in their desultory conversation which had meandered from shortcrust pastry to the shortcomings of the soon-to-be-appointed cook at Temple Hill.

'How's she going to find a French cook round here? And what do the French know about English food? It'll all be foreign, oh yes, you mark my words, and then she'll have to eat humble pie, advertise again,' Rosetta went on, oblivious of any pun. 'Never trusted the Frenchies, never would – look at what they did to their own King . . . wouldn't want one in the house, rob you as soon as look at you. And she's half-French – at least.'

'Actually, I think she's English,' Cecily said without looking up. 'Her grandson's certainly English.'

'Hmm. He might be,' Rosetta said, sceptically. 'But there's been stuff said, hasn't there? And there's no smoke without fire.' She glanced over at Cecily. 'But that's not to say he's got her ways.'

'Her ways?'

'All them marriages, that life abroad. It's not normal, is it?'

Cecily didn't answer. What was normal? Was Rosetta's life normal? Was her mother's? Normal was surely whatever was normal; normal was subjective. Normal meant nothing, she concluded swiftly. There was little point in debating semantics with Rosetta.

'I'm not altogether sure what you mean,' she said.

'Well, seems to me she's had a *pecular* sort of a life. Moving about all the time, marrying willy-nilly. It smacks of one thing . . .'

'Mm, what's that?'

Rosetta put down the rolling pin and leaned towards Cecily, her broad hands flat on the table. 'Lustfulness.'

'Lustfulness!' Cecily repeated.

'You may well smirk, my girl, but it's what robs men of what little sense they're born with and sends women to the county asylum.'

Lustfulness. It was not a word Cecily had heard spoken out loud before, or not that she could recall. Lustfulness: is that what had driven their new neighbour from one country to another, one man to another?

'And it all comes from the French . . .' Rosetta was saying, stuck on her theme now. 'I don't want to know what they get up to over there, and I don't want them bringing it over here neither.'

Diminutive, dark, and comfortingly round, Rosetta, Cecily thought, would have made a brilliant actress. She understood drama, knew how to deliver lines. But her talent had been wasted – in service, and in a kitchen, someone else's kitchen. For that was where she had spent her life. She had never been married and Cecily couldn't be sure how old she was. Like so many others, she appeared to be ageing and old at the same time. She was suspicious of any written word apart from those in the Bible, which she read most evenings, and she took enormous comfort in prayer. 'I'll make sure I include him/her/them/it in my prayers,' was one of her stock replies, and to almost anything. And though she liked to complain about the rector – his choice of hymns, his sermons, and his fondness for the New Testament – she was an ardent churchgoer, attending all three services on a Sunday in her waist-length cape and tiny bonnet tied tightly under her fat chin.

The only thing Cecily knew for sure, the only thing she could relate to, was that Rosetta had loved and lost. She had only mentioned him once: someone named Wilf. He had been killed in the Boer War.

'But if she has known great love over and over, is it so very wrong for her to have accepted it? How many hearts could have been broken? How many tears shed? And which is nobler, to take love and cherish it, or to throw it back because one has already known it?'

But Rosetta appeared not to hear her. She continued with her rolling pin, eyes cast downwards, and said, 'And who knows where she's come from . . . could be anyone at all . . . anyone at all . . . I've read about folk who go overseas and come back all la-di-da, oh yes . . . could be anyone at all. Makes you wonder what happened to all them husbands,' she added, glancing up at Cecily with wide eyes.

Cecily laughed. She said, 'Oh Rosetta, only *you* would suspect the poor old lady of murder!'

Rosetta made no reply. She pursed her lips and stretched her short neck as though trying to swallow words. Then she said, 'You should go and tidy yourself up, missy. The Foxes are due here at seven.'

Cecily Chadwick had been born towards the end of a century, and towards the end of a life. Her first proper word, whispered – as she'd been taught – was 'Daddy'; her first sentence, with a finger to her lips, 'Daddy not well.' She had taken her first steps the day of a great earthquake in Japan, but there had been no tremor of excitement in her small hushed world. And then, at the end, it had gone quieter still and all black and white as her ashen-faced mother, already in mourning, with the nurse and the rector by her side, explained, 'Daddy has gone.'

Since that time there had been little physical alteration in Cecily's life. She had stayed on at the village school teaching the infants, and continued to live with her mother and sister in the house her father had built. But lately she had begun to feel a suffocating tightness about the village, like a gown she had outgrown but was still forced to wear. The sameness of each and every day was inescapable, the prospect of change remote. A yearning for excitement, she had been told, was the ambition of a shallow and idle mind, the ambition of *pleasure-seekers*.

Then, early in the spring of that year, the Countess From Abroad had moved into the house on the hill, the place known as Temple Hill. For days before her arrival all manner of vehicles had come and gone, struggling up the steep track, knocking branches from trees, churning up rocks and sand and dried mud. One wagon had failed to make it up at all, had stopped right there in front of Cecily's garden gate. The men had had to carry each piece of furniture up the track, resting halfway, upon tables and in chairs, for a smoke. She had watched them disappear over the brow of the hill, stepped out through the gate and peered inside the wagon at the ornate antiques, rolls of carpets, tapestries, paintings, cabinets, settees and chairs. Stacked high at the back were crates and tea chests, a marble sculpture of a naked woman and, immediately in front of her, uncovered and gazing out into the sunshine, the bronze head of a Roman-nosed bearded man.

In the weeks that followed, as news of the countess's arrival gathered pace, Cecily heard many things: the lady had lived in exile for almost all of her life, the lady was of foreign blood; her manner was unusually forthright, her manner was curiously reticent; she was Catholic, she was Protestant; she was penniless, she was rich. There was, however, consensus on one thing: the countess's style was universally acknowledged as *cosmopolitan*.

It was the rector, Mr Fox, who first alluded to royal connections, and there was talk of lineage and ancestry, albeit unspecific and somewhat vague, linking her to Louis Philippe, the last King of France. To Cecily, Mr Fox appeared to know more than anyone, and certainly more than he was prepared to divulge. But once, over tea and cake, he slipped up and offered Cecily another tantalising scrap, a chink into that rare knowledge. Oh yes, she had indeed been *someone* in her day, he said. 'But the dear lady has come here in search of privacy and peace . . . and we must grant her that.'

As time went on, a selected few had been invited to the house for tea, always at a quarter past four. These, the chosen ones, had seen for themselves the fine French and Italian antique furnishings, paintings, sculptures and souvenirs; the paraphernalia of a life spent in a far more sophisticated milieu than their village. They spoke of the countess's knowledge of Italian and French art and architecture, her apparent fluency in both languages. And when they learned that she had grown up in Paris, well, it came as no surprise.

But there was also talk of lost children, and husbands long since deceased, and though some appeared to consider this careless, almost wanton behaviour, Cecily began to sense something of unutterable tragedy lying at the heart of the story. She pictured marble tombstones scattered across the desolate hillsides of foreign countries, and she could not help but view the countess as the sole survivor of an epic adventure. That the lady's Grand Tour – gone horribly wrong perhaps – had finally, albeit inexplicably, led her to Bramley seemed a curious fluke of fate. And meaningful? Perhaps.

That the countess had had a remarkable life Cecily was in no doubt, for already she knew that her neighbour had lived in a way others had not. But Cecily's mother remained unconvinced. She appeared, to Cecily at least, somewhat piqued by the rector's unquestioning predisposition towards their new neighbour; said he appeared 'a little star struck'. But yes, she had conceded, smiling, the lady had undoubtedly led a colourful life. 'But then, what goes on abroad, what's acceptable on the continent, is different. Quite different.'

'You mean the husbands, the marriages?' Cecily had asked.

'I mean everything.'

For weeks Cecily had been desperate for a glimpse of the Countess From Abroad. And once, driven by that desperation, that need to know, to see for herself, she had ventured up the track, and then further still into the tangled hollow of rhododendrons bordering the driveway to Temple Hill. Like a spy on a mission, gathering intelligence, she had crouched there, waiting. But nothing happened. No one emerged from the house and no one arrived. And to Cecily there appeared to be no signs of life within it.

'But does she never go anywhere?' she had later asked her mother.

'I believe she's quite old, dear. So no, I imagine she doesn't go far. Not now.'

'It must be strange,' Cecily continued, 'to have travelled so much, so far, and then come to a stop. A stop *here*.'

Madeline Chadwick looked at her daughter: 'But she might not be stopping, dear. I heard talk that she's only here for the summer, is returning to the continent for the winter.'

'Only here for the summer?' Cecily repeated. 'But all that . . . stuff – surely she can't be thinking of moving again?'

And then her sister, Ethne, said, 'I don't know why you're so fascinated. Is it the title, dear? Because you know they're two a penny on the continent.'

Encouraged by Cecily, Annie Gamben had made it her business to try and learn more. As village postmaster, Annie's father was privy to almost every-thing that took place within the scattered parish:

births, deaths, engagements, marriages, and scandals (though there were few); who was writing to whom, who despatched and who was the recipient of a telegram; and, crucially, what those telegrams spoke of.

It had been Annie's mother who had first mentioned the *young man*: a relation, she presumed, and from what she had heard – judging by his looks – foreign, possibly Italian. Then Mrs Gamben mentioned the *companion*: a lady only recently arrived by train from London. The companion had been into the post office twice, once to buy a packet of birdseed and some buttons, and once to despatch a large brown paper package to a gentleman in north London.

On the first occasion Mrs Gamben had not taken much notice of the bespectacled lady. It had been a Wednesday and the post office had been busy, as it always was on half-day closing. Realising the lady to be a visitor to the village, and assuming her to be staying with one or other of her customers, Mrs Gamben had been courteous but not overly so. But after the lady had thanked Mrs Gamben and left the shop, Mrs Moody, standing to one side beside the brooms and trugs and baskets, emerged from the shadows and told Mrs G exactly whose guest her previous customer had been. On the second occasion, when the lady arrived with the brown paper parcel, Mrs Gamben had been prepared. She had noted the absence of a wedding band on the lady's left hand, a distinct lack of eye contact, and what she described as a 'rather shifty manner'. Mrs Gamben had politely inquired after the countess, been reassured to hear she was in very good health, and that Miss Appleby – who came to the post office each Tuesday to cut and dress hair – was expected up at the house that very afternoon. The countess, Mrs Gamben surmised, was still very particular about her hair.

Rosetta had been the first to use the word 'orphan'. She had bumped into the gardener, Mr Cordery, 'had it from the horse's mouth', she said, that the boy was quite without parents *and* that there were 'suspicious circumstances.'

Everyone was curious. Everyone wanted to know more.

It was Cecily's mother, Madeline, who raised the subject later that evening at dinner, saying, 'Do tell me, Mr Fox, how is our new neighbour, the countess, settling in?' And Cecily looked up and sat forward.

True to form, Mr Fox appeared delighted to be offered the opportunity to speak about *the dear lady*. Oh yes, he began, she was settling in well, and delighted with the modernisations made to her new home. 'Of course, she's used to continental ways, and finds English sanitation a trifle primitive, to say the least,' he added. And Cecily saw Rosetta – standing behind Mrs Fox, waiting to remove plates – roll her eyes.

That evening, Rosetta had changed into the dark

gown, long white apron and cap Madeline had made for her and liked her to wear on the rare occasions they had visitors to dine with them. But the dress had become a tad too tight around her waist, causing her to tug and pull at it, and the cap, secured with elastic about her head, too loose. It slipped this way and that, and at one point, as she leaned forward to serve the rector, it slowly slid down her forehead until it entirely covered one eye before she managed to free a hand and push it back in place. Cecily knew these evenings to be enough of an ordeal for her, standing about, waiting at table and managing the kitchen on her own, without the added encumbrance of a faulty cap. Also, despite every window in the house standing open, the place was uncomfortably hot. And permeating the smell of meat and pastry and stewed vegetables, like the top note of a cheap perfume that catches the back of one's throat, was the malodorous reek of Mr Fox.

'And do remind me of her full name,' Madeline continued. 'I've been told, of course, but it's some-what unusual. French, I think, isn't it?'

Cecily turned to the rector.

He smiled, nodded. 'You are correct, Mrs Chadwick. It is the name of one of the most ancient and noble families in all of France, de Chevalier de Saint Léger. Thus the dear lady is la Comtesse de Chevalier de Saint Léger.'

'The Countess de Chevalier . . . de Saint Léger . . .' Madeline repeated hesitantly, as Cecily said it silently.

81

'And there were how many husbands?' Madeline asked.

'Someone told me there had been five,' Cecily broke in, without thinking, and she heard her mother and Mrs Fox both gasp.

The rector cleared his throat. He picked up his glass of wine, studied the liquid for a moment. 'It is unfortunate but perhaps understandable,' he said, glancing at Madeline, 'for there to be conjecture of that nature. I can tell you only the *facts*. Facts I am certain the countess would be happy enough for me to share with the assembled company.' He paused again, took a sip of wine. 'The first marriage was to a gentleman by the name of Staunton, in Rome, many years ago . . . perhaps as many as fifty years ago.'

'Fifty,' Cecily repeated.

'I would estimate so . . . yes, I would estimate so. But that union, that *first* marriage, was cut tragically short when Mr Staunton was killed.'

There was a loud clank from the sideboard. Madeline jumped. 'Killed?' she repeated.

'An accident, I believe,' said Mr Fox, without elaborating further. Cecily caught Rosetta's eye and quickly looked away as he continued. 'And thus, the countess – little more than a girl at that time – was left to raise her sons alone.'

'Ah, so she *does* have children,' Madeline said, smiling, sounding relieved.

'Sadly, no longer. I'm afraid her children, like her husbands, are all deceased. Her grandson is the only one left . . . all she has left,' he replied, newly baritone.

'What about the count?' Cecily asked. 'What happened to him?'

He shook his head. 'It was another short-lived union. They were married but a brief time before he was killed.'

'*Killed?*' Cecily said, at that moment conscious only of the repetition of this word, its connotations, and Rosetta's steady gaze.

'Killed in battle during the Franco-Prussian war, and buried there in the battlefield, at Servigny, near Metz.'

'The Franco-Prussian war. That was forty years ago.'

'Bravo, Cecily, it was indeed. Forty-one years ago, to be precise. And so our dear lady was tragically widowed once more, cruelly robbed of another husband, her children robbed of another father. At that time la comtesse,' continued the rector, warming to his theme, 'divided her time between France and Italy, between her fine chateau nestling in the glorious Loire Valley and her home in Rome, where her aunt, the dear lady into whose care she'd been placed as a very young girl, continued to reside. And of course she also kept an apartment in Paris, off the rue du Faubourg Saint-Honoré,' he added gutturally. 'Paris, like Rome, is I think very dear to her heart. For thither she was sent as a child, to live with her aunt . . .' He paused, glancing about the table, his eyes twinkling, smiling, 'who was none other than the Contessa Francesca Cansacchi di Amelia!'

Cecily looked at the others; was this a name she was meant to know?

'Gracious!' said Madeline.

'Indeed, indeed,' said the rector, lifting a napkin to his whiskers.

'Golly,' said Ethne, who'd remained silent until now. 'So she's true aristocracy.'

The rector looked at Ethne, narrowing his eyes. 'Almost more than that,' he said, enigmatically.

Cecily felt her heart shiver. More than that? What did he mean? And she wanted to say, 'Do tell us, please tell us more,' but for some reason, right at that moment it seemed inappropriate. The rector had stopped his story at a very specific point, and quite obviously for a reason. There was more, she realised, much more. She glanced to her mother and Madeline smiled back at her; but now with tightly sealed lips, as if to say, no more questions. Did her mother know something? she wondered. Was her mother familiar with the aunt, the Italian contessa? Did everyone know something she did not? She looked over to Ethne, who appeared more engrossed by the summer pudding in front of her. No, Ethne would not know. She turned to Mrs Fox, seated on her left, but she too appeared more interested in fruit and cream than the unfolding roll call of European nobility. And then she couldn't help herself.

'Is she descended from royalty, Mr Fox?'

He smiled at Cecily, raised a finger to his face and tapped his nose.

'Well,' said Madeline, lifting her glass of watered wine, 'what a life . . . what a life she has had. But it must be hard for an expatriate to settle,' she added. 'She must find Bramley awfully quiet after Rome and Paris and . . . all that,' she petered out.

The rector shuffled in his chair, clearing his throat, and Cecily knew another instalment was on its way.

'I believe the dear lady was ready for a change,' he began. 'The daughter-in-law's tragic demise served to propel that need for change, and here we are, with her and her beloved grandson in our midst. I think we're honoured, Mrs Chadwick, truly honoured, don't you?'

'She must find everyone here pretty dull,' Ethne broke in, sucking raspberry seeds from her teeth. 'I don't mean that in a derogatory way, of course. I don't think Bramley's dull at all, I'd far rather live here than in some horrid smelly city like Rome. But why on earth did she come here?'

Hallelujah! Cecily thought, at last she's managed to spit out one pertinent question.

'Because Temple Hill is her home,' Mrs Fox piped up, soft and sweet, like the pudding in front of her. 'It belongs to her, was built for her, I believe,' she added, glancing along the table to her husband.

'But surely it's much too old,' Cecily said. 'And it's been standing empty for years, hasn't it?'

'That is correct,' Mr Fox quickly replied, silencing his wife, who was about to continue. 'The place has never been lived in, certainly not in my time. Though I've heard tell that it was for a while rented out to a succession of tenants, and then no one. Of course, when I first arrived here, almost twenty years ago—'

'Good gracious, Mr Fox, is it really that long?' Madeline interrupted.

Cecily sighed and Mr Fox smiled. 'Yes, indeed it is, Mrs Chadwick. And oh, what changes I have seen in that time . . .'

Diverted, the rector began to speak about the village and surrounding area as it had once been. Cecily pushed the congealing ruby-coloured mess about her plate. Had her mother changed the subject on purpose? Who in their right mind, apart from her mother, would want to hear about Bramley as it once was rather than Rome and Paris? It was beyond frustrating. All Cecily could do was wait. He'd get back to it, eventually. She knew he'd only just begun.

Bramley had always struck Cecily as an untidy, straggling sort of place. The roads passing through it rose and dipped and rose once more before heading out through tunnel-like lanes to the outlying farms, scattered cottages and huts of the parish. The village had no railway station or market, but it had carpenters, builders, blacksmiths and wheelwrights; saddlers, farriers and millers; broom makers, shoemakers, coal merchants and drapers; grocers, bakers and butchers. The surrounding heathland provided for the broom-squires and thatchers, the bees for honey, hop fields for beer, and the meadows for milk and butter and cheese. It had three public houses, a school, an undertaker and a post office. And there were regular 'entertainments': evenings of poetry, music and amateur dramatics in the village hall. The lending library was administered by the rector's wife, Mrs Fox, who checked and monitored exactly who was reading what each Thursday afternoon.

For hundreds of years those who had been baptised at St Luke's – and then, against the odds, survived infancy – had been wedded there, and later buried there. No one left, no one moved. Bramley had always been self-sufficient, able to supply and occupy its inhabitants' hands and heads and hearts and stomachs.

In her final year at school Cecily had written about 'The History and Times of Bramley'. Most of what she had learned had come from Old Meg, who may have been Young Meg, once. Meg had been the village midwife and had, she reckoned, delivered over one hundred babies and laid out almost as many corpses. But by that time Old Meg confined her activities to the reading of tea leaves – and knitting. She told Cecily that in times not so long gone by *runagates* had skulked about the mist-shrouded wilderness surrounding the village. Yes, it had been a place for fugitives then, she said; a place to hide away, a no-man's-land people travelled through at their peril due to the vagabonds and highwaymen who preyed upon those journeying between London and the coast. She told Cecily that the unplanned ragged lines of the village probably owed something to those lawless folk and squatters, who had erected cottages by night, depositing children in them by dawn so the bailiffs could not remove the heather-thatched roofs above their heads. Then, the railway came to Linford, bringing rich city folk and consumptives from London. Yes, Cecily thought: Daddy.

Daddy – Cecil Chadwick – lay next to the ancient yew tree on the western side of the churchyard. Cecily had grown up knowing him only as a name chiselled on a tombstone. When she was young, she had been taken to his grave twice each week. Then it fell back to once a week, on Sunday afternoons. Now it was as and when – high days and holidays and special occasions, and Madeline alone each wedding anniversary. But sometimes Cecily took a walk through the churchyard on her own. She thought of the dead beneath her feet and pondered on all those long unspoken, long forgotten names: someone's daughter, someone's son, someone's father: hers. In Loving Memory . . . Sacred to . . . Beloveds one and all.

In the churchyard, history – his story and her story – was condensed to names and dates. Nothing more. Lifetimes, no matter how extraordinary, had no narrative, no triumphs or defeats. There were no clues, no achievements listed. And yet there, just below Cecily's feet, lay hundreds of untold stories, stories spanning centuries, bridging generations, linking then and now. Tales of derring-do and recklessness, wisdom and folly, passion and pride and honour, stories Cecily could only wonder at and imagine. The names themselves often conjured an image, the date adding context and detail. So much so that she could often see them, not as bones beneath the sandy earth but in the flesh, alive and animated once more.

Cecily's allegiance with the dead had started at an early age, reinforced by all those visits to the cemetery and bound up in a fascination with Loss. And most particularly, Love and Loss.

Finally, and after some confusion about the point of his lengthy monologue (of which Cecily had heard not a word), the rector found his thread again. Yes, his wife was correct, Temple Hill, as far as he understood, had always belonged to the countess. The rector leaned towards Madeline. 'But you must know,' he whispered loudly, 'the land this very house sits upon was once part of the gardens of Temple Hill.'

Madeline shook her head and, glancing at Rosetta who stood by the sideboard, a dish in her hands, mouth open and cap askew, she said, 'You can clear away now, thank you.' And the maid bustled out of the room.

Madeline then quietly explained to the rector that she had not been involved in her late husband's business affairs. She had no recollection of him ever having mentioned from whom he had purchased their plot of land. But then, after some thought, she admitted she couldn't be sure he had not; he had been ill, her attention focused entirely upon him, his comfort and well-being. And then, as though still taking in what the rector had told her, she said, 'So, our house, the land this house is built upon, actually belonged to *her*, the countess?'

He nodded.

'Well I never,' she said.

Cecily listened as the rector explained that Temple Hill had originally had some one hundred acres of gardens and paddocks and woodland. But slowly, he said, over the past twenty years or so, parcels of land had been sold off for development, mainly on the other side of the hill. Now, he estimated the house would have only a fraction of those original acres; certainly less than ten, he thought.

The evening, Cecily realised, was producing answers to questions even she had not thought of. And as the conversation altered its course, touching briefly on the strikes and unrest spreading through the country, before turning to the recent and not so recent changes to the village, and Mr Fox to his favourite subject – the loss of the old country ways – Cecily sat in quiet contemplation.

So, she was right, she thought, the countess was indeed the survivor of an epic adventure, one that had cost her dearly, robbing her of husbands, children and, it seemed, money. But how had it started? she wondered. She knew the end of the story – or almost, because the countess had arrived there, possibly penniless, and with no family to speak of apart from Jack – but where, exactly, had it begun? And why had she not returned to this country before? After all, she mused, having done the calculation earlier, she was a great age, and had had a house standing empty, waiting for her. If her only family had been in England, why had she chosen to stay overseas? It was incomprehensible. Something didn't make sense. Was she so very selfish that she had allowed Jack's poor widowed mother to sink further and further into her loneliness, her melancholia, while she continued her gallivanting across Europe? No, surely not. She had come here eventually, yes, but that, it seemed from what Cecily had heard, had been after Jack's mother's suicide. Then it dawned on her: the countess had had no plans to come back, ever.

Later, in the room Madeline Chadwick referred to as the parlour to her daughters and the drawing room to her guests, Cecily sat down next to the elderly rector. She wanted to ask him more about the countess. She had obviously led a fascinating life, she said, smiling brightly, eagerly, knowing he'd be flattered by her continued interest. 'And what stories she must have . . .'

'Indeed! What stories,' he repeated. 'But like any noble lady – all old nobility – she is in possession of discretion, Cecily. She is a very private person, without inclination to divulge her credentials or esteemed connections to all and sundry. Oh no, *la comtesse* chooses whom to confide in with great discernment, great care. After all, she has no need to impress the likes of we humble country folk.'

'She has confided in you then?'

The rector smiled, closing his eyes momentarily. 'To an extent,' he replied, nodding his head slowly. 'And thus it falls upon me to be prudent in my judgement of any disclosure. You see, Cecily, the dear lady has no desire to court fame or publicity, in fact quite the opposite. She has come to this parish in search of solitude, perhaps one could even say anonymity.'

'Anonymity? But why? Why would she wish for anonymity?'

'I imagine that if one has lived one's entire life under the glare of public scrutiny, even adulation, one eventually craves the luxury of invisibility.'

A tiny moth fluttered above the oil lamp on the table next to the rector, dipping down towards the yellow light, then back up, round and round, up and down.

'Of course, many of those she was once on intimate terms with have passed away,' he continued, raising a hand to wave the moth from his face, stretching out his breeched legs. 'At one time she knew everyone, in Rome, Paris, and in London: royalty, dignitaries, aristocracy; writers, sculptors, poets . . . and some very famous painters as well,' he added, turning to Cecily with a smile.

'Such as?'

'George Lawson, for one.'

'George Lawson? *The* George Lawson? Lord George Lawson?'

The rector shuffled along the settee towards Cecily. She noticed the silver hairs sprouting from the tips of his lobes, could smell his body odour, and his rancid breath – alcohol, rotting gums, and that evening's dinner. 'I believe they met in Rome, many years ago,' he said, turning to her, breathing full into her face. 'He was there as a young man, before he became famous. It's where he painted his "Madonna", which of course the Queen herself later bought.'

'So they knew each other?'

He nodded. 'I believe so. He was a regular visitor to Paris and often travelled to Vichy to take the cure. Yes, Vichy . . .' he said, drifting. 'It's a place Mrs Fox and I have often contemplated visiting ourselves, but I fear we've left it too late.' He looked down at his empty glass, and Cecily quickly took it and rose to her feet.

Seconds later, handing the rector his replenished wine, Cecily sat down and said, 'But you know I do wonder, Mr Fox, why she didn't return to this country before now. Particularly in view of the fact that she was on her own, and her family, her only family – Jack and his poor mother – here in England.'

The rector pondered, stroking his whiskers. 'Let me say this: I believe the dear lady had good reason to stay away and, unprotected as she was, and is, no wish to rouse her enemies.' He turned to Cecily. 'Jealousy and envy can poison the heart and inspire untruths and wickedness. It is down to all of us here in Bramley to protect her now. I'm afraid I am not at liberty to say any more, but I know you to be an intelligent young woman, Cecily, and I hope I can rely on your discretion.'

Bewildered, Cecily nodded. 'Of course.'

CHAPTER 5

He slaps her face and says, 'You little bitch, you told her . . . you told her, didn't you?' She shakes her head. 'No . . . no, I didn't, I promise.' She places her palm to her cheek and she can feel the heat, the burning stain he has left on her.

It was another sultry evening, with no movement, no breath of wind. The hillside lay quiet in the warmth of the setting sun, and in its reflected glory appeared brighter than ever, the tops of the pine trees ablaze, illuminated by a light that spoke of the perfection of that day.

Inside the house, Cora had finally given in to exhaustion. Her head rested to one side, slowly rising and falling in time with her breathing, a stray curl across her brow. Her still brilliant blue eyes were shut, and her lips, the crinkled curve of a Cupid's bow, occasionally twitched and moved without sound. Her hands lay upturned and open in her lap, in a simple pleading gesture, as if to say, here I am.

She sat in a modern English wingback armchair, a token to English taste in a room boasting

European style. In front of her, an ottoman, upholstered in deep red velvet, piled with books and magazines; adjacent to her, a Louis XV settee and matching chairs; and against the wall opposite, an Italian black walnut bookcase, bowing under the weight of volumes of English, French and Italian literature. Scattered about the long room were various chairs and side tables, another settee, a desk in front of a tall window overlooking the garden, and, hanging from picture rails, framed oil paintings, watercolours and drawings of all sizes. Within the recess of an arched alcove to one side of the fireplace stood an almost life-size marble sculpture of a naked woman, and at the other side, in another alcove and standing upon a plinth, the bronze head of a bearded man.

That evening, she, Sylvia and Jack had dined early once again. Though she preferred to take a light supper later in the evening, this was not the custom in England and had proved something of a problem with Mrs Davey, her housekeeper, who was standing in as cook until a permanent one was appointed. Nine o'clock was much too late to be busying on in the kitchen, Mrs Davey had told the countess; her day was long enough.

After dinner, Jack had disappeared upstairs to his room, to read, he said. She and Sylvia had remained seated at the dining table, lingering over their coffee. But Sylvia had annoyed Cora with her persistent questions. The memoirs, which Cora was quietly beginning to have second thoughts about, seemed to be coming between Sylvia and her wits. To Cora's mind, Sylvia was becoming possessed with an unhealthy obsession about her life. And she had told her so.

Sylvia had abruptly risen to her feet, saying she wished to take a stroll about the garden, and Cora had retired to the drawing room. She sat by the window on the western side of the house, flicking through the dog-eared pages of one of Sylvia's *Lady's Pictorial* magazines, peering through her old lorgnette at murky images and out-of-date advertisements, keeping thoughts at bay. But as daylight dwindled her eyes had grown heavy, and as the sun slipped down behind the trees she put the magazine to one side, allowed herself to sit back in her chair and closed her eyes.

Now she was lost in her dreams. But her dreams, like her memories, had fused, muddling people and chronology, muddling everything. Nameless yet familiar faces spoke the wrong words, borrowing sentences; people were not what they seemed, not who they appeared to be, and places were unreliable, altering their shape and form to a different city, a different country, taking her back to where she had started . . .

She feels sick, the ship is listing, but she does as she is told, placing her hand upon soft leather and promising, 'No one.' She repeats words over and over: this is what she must say. Yes, yes, she knows, she says, she will not forget.

When she walks down the plank and steps ashore,

97

she stands amidst rubble and ruins and dust, and stone columns stretching all the way up to the heavens. The sky is brighter here . . . but she must not forget, she must remember the words . . . and the name.

Cora asked for dreams. She asked for them to refresh her memory. But chaos was her recurring nightmare. And in this chaos her overriding desire was to find George, to get back to him. And sometimes she did, and sometimes she did not. But when she did, in those rare dreams when she finally found him – waiting for her, beside the steps – he held out his arms to her, wrapped them around her so tightly she could feel the warmth of his breath upon her forehead, the softness of his velvet jacket against her cheek. And when she awoke, fresh from his embrace, she remembered, remembered it all: the heady sensation, the hunger for another's touch, the rise and fall of each wave, and that feeling of complete abandonment, where only the senses were alive, and yet lost at the same time.

Lately, she had begun to enjoy that blurred landscape which often bridges slumber and wakefulness, that place of semi-consciousness. She liked to linger there, in that glow, aware it would come to her with more substance if she remained within it. Hoping *they* would come to her if she remained within it. For it was then, in that place, she could hear them: cherished voices, whispering and murmuring from another century. Occasionally she heard music – a piano, someone singing

– beyond the open window, drifting across the garden, in the next room or upstairs, faint and impossible to place. And once or twice of late she had known with absolute certainty that he was there, standing so close to her she could sense his presence with all of her being. Close enough for her to feel that frisson once more.

When Sylvia, Jack or one of the maids entered the room, she kept her eyes firmly shut, as though in defiance of her own physical decrepitude as much as her circumstances. And perhaps because when she finally opened them nothing ever looked quite as it should. Things were all wrong, she was all wrong, like a sole survivor washed up on a foreign land with the material contents of her life tipped out around her, sad mementos, conspicuous and out of place.

In conscious moments, she revisited her most favourite times, working through them slowly and in detail, backwards and forwards, forwards and backwards, savouring each second of a moment again and again. And there was Lucca. No longer a place, but a memory, a time. Sacrosanct. Fortified.

She was careful never to near unhappy memories, or venture back too far. Once, it had been easy, or easier, to steer clear of those dark places and difficult times. But now, like coming to the end of a road, a place where there is no further way forward, she had no choice, she had to turn and look back upon her path. She saw herself at different stages as different people: the young woman of almost twenty in Rome; the woman of thirty, mistress of a castle in France; the woman of forty, part of the beau monde of Paris; mother of two sons, wife of three men, lover of one: all different people with different lives. And that time before Rome, the place her journey started, obscured from view by those people she had become, had once been.

Numbness had come with old age, but to her bones, not to her heart. And though in public she was careful to keep her emotions in check, to maintain – or try to maintain – a ready smile, a relaxed countenance, in quiet, solitary moments, moments of reflection, and often when least expecting it, she was sometimes plunged under, submerged, left gasping for breath; drowning in a great swell of sorrow and joy and pain and rapture. And it was this, the memory of senses and sensations, that made her weep. She wept for lost children, she wept for lost love; she wept for a life slowly ebbing, and for things still inexplicable to her.

And now, at this great age, she wept for her mother too. Not simply in sorrow at her distant passing, or the loss of her, but in need of her. The child within the aged body and creaking bones, the little girl who had not been allowed to say goodbye, finally wanted to be heard. Mother. The word itself had piercing resonance. For she, too, had been robbed of that particular title.

'. . . mother, . . . mother? Grandmother?'

She opened her eyes.

'You're in darkness,' he said, lighting the lamp on the table beside her.

'I must have drifted off.'

'You were talking about your mother.'

She blinked, staring at the shape of him, allowing her eyes to adjust to the new light. 'I was dreaming,' she said.

He sat down on the chair opposite her. 'And what were you dreaming of? Your mother, obviously.'

'I'm not sure. This and that. It was all a muddle, it always is.' She glanced about the room. 'Is Sylvia back indoors?'

'Yes, and retired for the night. She said she didn't wish to disturb you. Actually, she was rather upset.'

'She gets upset too easily, far too easily. Always has. It's part and parcel of having had so little in her life.'

He smiled. 'Perhaps we need to remember that,' he suggested. 'That she has had so little.'

'You're right, of course you're right. I was sharp with her. I shall apologise in the morning.'

'I know we've had very little time together,' he began, staring down at the floor. 'Growing up . . . well, you were overseas, I couldn't see you, but now we have the opportunity . . . I'd like to know more about everyone: Father, Grandfather, Fanny, and you, your family, your parents. You see, it strikes me I know nothing about my own family. Mother,' and he paused after he said the word,

'Mother was unable, or perhaps not inclined, to tell me anything about the Staunton side of my family. She always claimed she knew little about you.'

Cora smiled, looked at the clock on the mantelshelf. 'Good gracious, half past ten. I've been asleep for two whole hours. I rather think it's time that I, too, went to my bed.' She struggled forward in her chair. He rose up, took hold of her hand and helped her to her feet. He looks so like him, she thought, observing his features in the lamplight; so like him.

'Will you tell me sometime? Will you tell me about the family, *your* family? I'd like to hear about them all,' he said, holding her hand in his.

'Yes, yes, of course I shall, but not tonight, my darling,' she said, trying to smile, placing her hand upon his cheek.

As she moved away from him, towards the door, he said, 'Oh, and I was thinking of inviting Cecily Chadwick to tea on Tuesday . . . You said you'd like to meet her.'

She turned to him. 'Yes, I would, and that's a splendid idea. Goodnight, dear.'

As she closed the door and moved across the hallway, she felt a constriction about her chest. She grasped the handrail, began to climb the stairs, and the rustle of her petticoats momentarily distracted her: that swish-swish-swishing sound that had accompanied her every movement, all of her life. A fleeting image of her younger self dashing up steps two at a time flashed through her mind's eye, and she caught that sensation once more: the weightlessness of youth. Whalebone, she thought, can't really be good for one's breathing. But lodged deep in her breast was an ever-tightening dilemma, and one name playing on a loop inside her head: John Abel . . . John Abel . . . John Abel.

After Cora retired to her bed, Jack sat alone for a while, cogitating. He reflected on the conversation he had had with Sylvia, earlier, in the garden, and it concerned and perplexed him in equal measure.

'Of course, it could be the heat,' Sylvia had said. And he knew she was being polite, as any good friend would be.

'I'm sorry,' he said. 'I can only apologise.'

She had recounted Cora's harsh words, had been tearful, and understandably so.

'That she thinks I'm *possessed* . . . with an obsession about her . . . her life, and after she invited me here, asked me to record her memories . . .' She shook her head, removed her spectacles and dabbed at her eyes. 'I don't know what I've done, Jack, to make her turn on me like that.' She raised her head, staring straight ahead. 'I fear for her,' she continued, 'that she can turn on *me*, her oldest, most devoted friend, and with such . . . such venom, such passion. Hatred, that's what it was. Pure hatred.'

'No, no, she doesn't hate you. You mustn't for

one moment think that. She's very fond of you, I know.'

But he was at a loss. Why had Cora turned on Sylvia? Sylvia, who wouldn't say boo to a goose. Sylvia, whom Cora herself had claimed was such a dear friend. After a while he said, 'You may be right. It may be the heat. I know she was used to it once, but we must bear in mind she's a good deal older now.'

Sylvia sniffed, tucked her handkerchief inside her sleeve, and for a while they sat in silence, side by side, looking out over the garden.

'I only hope she comes back to us soon,' she said. 'That we haven't lost her.'

'Lost her?'

'It happened in Rome . . . in the summer. July and August. The heat brought it on, the delusions, the fever . . . paranoia . . . madness,' she said, so quietly that he had had to lean forward to catch the last two words.

Now, he thought Sylvia had overreacted. His grandmother was right: she had had so little in her life, was as unsused to drama as Cora was used to it. Poor Sylvia. But as he rose to his feet and moved towards the lamp, something surfaced. At first, a mere sensation, a glimpse and flash of yellow. Then, slowly, more: his mother, another lady, unrecognisable, faceless; a yellow-walled room, long forgotten, unidentifiable; and a small dog – sweet little thing, grey – rolling about on the rug in front of him. His mother and the other lady are behind him, talking. They don't say the name but he knows that the 'she' they speak of refers to his grandmother.

His mother says, 'She'll never come back here to live, not permanently. She's too afraid.'

'But afraid of what?' the faceless woman asks.

'Being discovered . . . being found out. Oh, she'll come back for a drawing room at the palace . . . spend a week or so gadding about. But she's terrified of any of *them* finding her. She thinks I don't know, but I do.'

The faceless woman says, 'Did *he* know?'

'No,' his mother replies, and she almost laughs as she says, 'My husband adored her.'

Upstairs, Sylvia lay awake in her bed. Too hot to sleep, too distressed to write.

It had all started with the blessed letter, another letter. It had arrived in the afternoon post, and it had been she, Sylvia, who had taken it in to Cora. Sylvia had noted the pale yellow paper, the name and address typed in red ink . . . but perhaps only because of the somewhat clashing colours. Never could she have foreseen that she would later be attacked as the messenger.

Cora took the envelope from her, and as Sylvia spoke of something else – she couldn't now recall what – Cora glanced at it and then simply placed it to one side, upon her desk. She was dealing with bills, settling accounts. There was no reason for Sylvia to suppose the yellow envelope contained anything more than another invoice. But even then, Cora had been dismissive, sharp with her.

'Is there anything else?' she had asked, interrupting Sylvia, and just as though she was a wittering servant.

'No, nothing else,' Sylvia had replied, and far too meekly she thought now.

Cora had stayed in that room, at her desk, for the remainder of the afternoon, which was odd, because she had told Sylvia at luncheon that she would take no more than an hour over her correspondence and accounts, and then, she said, they would take a walk. So Sylvia had sat on the veranda, waiting. She had used the time productively enough, making a new list of questions to ask Cora, and pondering an idea for a short story. But by four o'clock, and with no sight or sound of Cora, Sylvia had crept along the terrace and peered in through the south window. She could clearly see Cora, in profile, doing absolutely nothing at all but gazing out through another window – the one immediately in front of her desk. She could also see that there were no papers, invoices or even pens out upon the desk.

She had been pressed up against the climbing hydrangea for some minutes, watching her friend daydream, for that was how it appeared, when she noticed Cora's lips moving and realised that she was in fact speaking. And so she tiptoed quietly along the wall of the house to the open window, on the other side of which sat Cora. At first, it was impossible to make out what, exactly, Cora was saying. She spoke in a strange, low, monotone voice but, after a little while, Sylvia recognised the words, and listened to her as she continued: 'The dew of the morning, sunk chill on my brow . . . it felt like the warning, of what I feel now. Thy vows are all broken, and light is thy fame: I hear thy name spoken, and share . . . in its shame.'

Byron. Sylvia almost said the name out loud. She had been there the very first time Cora recited it – 'When We Two Parted' – at her aunt's soirée, in Rome. And he had been there, too: George. Had he known the lines were for him? Had she ever told him? But yes, he must have known. For it had all been for him; even then, everything was for him. The two of them had crossed paths a number of times by then, and Cora had already visited his studio – in secret and alone – once, or was it twice? Sylvia could not recall.

But Cora had told her, certainly, of that first visit. He had been nervous, fumbling and awkward. They had spent time looking at the sketches and studies from which he was working, and he had talked her through his vision, his 'Madonna'. He had explained to her how he would use only one or two models for the multitude of minor characters, but would add detail to their dress so that they would appear different. The painting would tell a story, he said, but each section of the vast canvas was as important as the whole, with a separate story to it. Cora said he talked with such

107

conviction and passion, such intensity in his eyes that it made her feel as feeble as a child and yet more alive than ever before. And then he had said to her, 'And I want you, Cora, to be my Madonna.'

Sylvia closed her eyes. Cora continued to murmur.

Even then, after that first visit to George's studio, Cora claimed they had confided in each other. She said she had told him things she had never told anyone, which Sylvia found hard to believe. And yet, wasn't that when Cora had begun to drift away from *her*? Wasn't that when Cora had begun to change, altering her story, telling Sylvia she had made mistakes in her recollection of events? But Sylvia had already written things down. And he knew nothing. How could he love her if he knew nothing about her?

Silence. Sylvia stood perfectly still, hardly daring to breathe. Then Cora began again. She seemed to be in some sort of trance-like state, reciting the poem over and over. What on earth was she doing? Trying to summon him from the grave?

It was after Sylvia returned to the veranda and had pondered on this bizarre occurrence that she began to think the worst, began to wonder if Cora was in fact losing her senses.

Later, at dinner, Cora had been unusually quiet. And afterwards, as the two women sat alone together, Sylvia had tentatively mentioned the memoirs; had suggested that perhaps they could make a fresh start on it the next day. Cora appeared to be in agreement. She had smiled and nodded, with a degree of magnanimity. But then, when Sylvia very gently said, 'I heard you reciting your poem earlier today, dear,' she had flown off the handle, accused Sylvia of spying on her. That was when she had also said Sylvia was obsessed, obsessed with her life. And it was a ridiculous accusation in view of the circumstances.

'Ridiculous,' she said out loud, wiping her nose. I have simply loved her, loved her and been a loyal and true friend . . . for all of these years, all of these years . . . and she's never appreciated me, all I have done for her . . . never appreciated.

Sylvia had made no mention of the letter to Jack, or the queer poetry recital. She had no wish to burden the poor boy further. He had already been through enough. Quite enough. But, if Cora would not tell him the truth, it would, in time, surely fall upon her to do so.

CHAPTER 6

The door slams shut. Neither one of them moves. The woman lies crumpled, motionless on the floor, the girl sits in petrified silence, waiting, listening, hardly daring to breathe. Only after his footsteps have faded, only when there is complete quiet does the girl slide down from the chair and run across the room. The woman reaches out, tries to speak, but her mouth is filled with blood, her teeth coated red, and the girl can't distinguish the words in the gurgling, swelled sound. And so she says, 'It's all right . . . he's gone now.'

At one time in her life Cora had been a brilliant listener. She had asked a great many questions, keen to hear about the minutiae of others' lives. Long anecdotes, digressions tedious to anyone else, had been met with an unerring patience and attentiveness. And this skill alone had won her many friends. But now Cora liked to talk. Not necessarily about herself, but of those she had once known, the places she had once lived or visited.

She had made Tuesdays her 'at home' day but

other days, too, had seen a steady stream of callers. Once or twice, as many as ten had sat down to take tea with her, glancing about her drawing room with eager eyes and a seemingly endless list of questions, some surprisingly intelligent, others less so. What had Rome been like before the reunification? Had she met Garibaldi? (Of course, she had.) And the Pope? (Yes, many times.) Had she been in Paris during the Commune of '71? (No, thankfully not. She had been residing in Rome at that time.) Did they still speak Latin in Rome? Was it true that they made the Jews race in bare feet through the streets and locked them up at night?

The fact that she was able to answer these questions, that she could enlighten, educate and inform her new neighbours had given her a sense of satisfaction, and pride, even a raison d'être for the short time they were in her midst. She was flattered by their interest in her, in her life and her possessions. She pointed to paintings – a watercolour of her former home, the Chateau de Chazelles in France, a portrait of her at twenty-one years of age, and another of the count in uniform. She spoke of her early days in Rome, pronouncing the unpronounceable, rolling her Rs and slipping into Italian here and there. She explained to them that the English expatriate community, then, had been strong, with an English quarter situated around the Piazza di Spagna – yes, where the famous steps are – and with English shops selling English produce, English tea rooms serving English tea, English hotels,

English banks, even English employment bureaus offering English servants. 'Well,' someone said, 'that is a relief!'

Rome, she told them, had had no fewer than thirty-five thousand foreigners living within its walls when she first arrived. 'Of course, many of them were visitors, there for only the season. And it is without doubt the perfect place to spend the winter months. The light is altogether different then,' she went on, staring out of the window. 'I'm not sure how I shall cope with winter in England. I haven't spent a winter here since—' She stopped. 'Since I was a girl.'

'And, if I may ask, where was that, ma'am? Whereabouts did you grow up?'

'Gracious, now you are testing me!' she said, affecting a laugh. A few followed suit, and she added, 'I rather think I grew up in some distant county that no longer exists, for the world has changed and the place of my childhood is no more.' Heads turned and nodded. 'Like many of us here,' she continued, gauging a consensus, 'I grew up in a different world.' She turned to the gentleman. 'I'm afraid my early life is very dim and distant to me now. And, I fear, decidedly dull by comparison to my life overseas,' she said, smiling.

She was long used to navigating difficult conversations. It was easy enough, or had been, to chart a course. Deflection was a useful tool, to turn the tables, ask the same question back, and then another, and another, so that that the original question, addressed to her, was abandoned, forgotten. She imagined it similar to driving a motorcar and avoiding the potholes on the road ahead. The driver sees them coming and swiftly takes action. The passengers remain oblivious, distracted by a newly pointed out vista. But it would, she thought, be nice not to *have* to drive the blessed motor every time, to be able to be a passenger, be able to sit back and simply take in the view.

Thus, motoring on, across the Channel and back to Rome, she spoke of glittering entertainments and tableaux vivants, of the torch-lit parties and moonlit charades within the walls of the Coliseum, and casually sprinkled a few famous names. She spoke of a vibrant hubbub of noise and colour, and they could almost hear the carriages, carts and wagons, the thunderous clatter of hoofs and wheels. They sat in spellbound silence as she led them down dark and narrow streets, across sunlit piazzas to fountains and churches; they followed her up ancient steps, through vast doorways into cool, candlelit basilicas where saints lay at their feet beneath a marble floor. And they could see it, see it all; hear the fountains gently flowing, smell the incense within the church.

She chose not to tell them of the eight o'clock curfew, which locked up the poor Jews *Pio Nono* called 'dogs'; she chose not to mention the dead cart, which crossed the piazza beneath her bedroom late at night, swaying this way and that, heavy with lifelessness, and bound for a pit in the Sacred Field beyond the city walls. She chose not to tell them about the city's lepers and beggars, who slept in filth on the streets and sat outside the bakers each morning, waiting for crumbs to be thrown. These poor souls, and others, she kept to herself.

And what about that first journey, someone asked, that must have taken some time? Indeed it had. It had taken over twenty-five days to reach Rome. She tried to recall the route: 'From Le Havre by public coach to Nevers, across the mountains to . . . Chalon-sur-Saône . . . down the Saône to Lyon . . . then another steamer, to Avignon . . . from there, overland to Marseilles, and thence onwards to Civitavecchia.'

Yes, that was the route, she thought, staring through a shaft of light at a memory . . . *a place so far away no one will ever find us.*

She watched the light break through the small porthole, splintering into a myriad of dust-filled rays. She stepped down from her bed and moved over to the window. 'We are here,' she said, turning to her aunt. 'We're in Italy.'

They had originally expected to sail upriver to Rome, but the captain advised them to continue their journey overland. The French government steamers, which commuted between Rome and the coastal port, transporting the French army and supplies to its protectorate, did so only on appointed days, and this day was not one of them, he explained. He mentioned Palo, some Etruscan tombs at Cerveteri, and though Cora was keen, Fanny said she had no desire to see Palo or to visit any ancient tombs. They needed to get to Rome before nightfall.

Sidestepping horse dung and beggars, amidst the cacophony of street vendors, soldiers, sailors, horses, dogs, carts and barrows, the two women moved along the quayside towards the carriage office. Italian men, women and children of all ages vied for their attention, desperate to sell their wares, and filthy barefoot children with eyes as black as coal stretched out grubby hands and tugged at their skirts. 'Don't worry, dear, Rome will be quite different,' Fanny said, taking hold of Cora's arm and guiding her through the quagmire.

A group of young Italian men attached themselves to the women, walking alongside them. 'Inglese? Inglese? *Benvenuta!*' One pushed forward. 'Good day, fine ladies, I speak the English . . . and I will be your guide, yes?'

'No, thank you, you will not,' Fanny replied, grasping Cora's hand.

'But signora, please, we are your friends . . .'

Cora knew their lack of chaperone made Fanny more nervous than ever, and it had been the same in Marseilles. There, a Monsieur Saint Léger had kindly offered to act as their guide and chaperone, and for a while Fanny appeared quite taken by the attentive Frenchman. Her attempts at his country's language, as well as her knowledge of Paris, seemed to have impressed him too. However, when he became what Fanny described as 'uncommonly interested' in them, asking too many questions, she had had no alternative but to abruptly end their arrangement. 'We can't afford to make any mistakes now,' she had told Cora.

Two more young Italian men were now walking alongside them, gesticulating and speaking effusively to Cora in Italian, and then English. 'I love you!'

When Cora's broad smile began to erupt, Fanny halted. 'Please!' she hissed. 'You're encouraging them, and I have already warned you about Italian men – they need no encouragement.'

Before arriving at the carriage office the women found the apothecary the captain had recommended, and there, with the help of Cora's book, its section 'Useful Phrases and Words for the Traveller in Italy', they purchased a foul-smelling concoction which Fanny was assured would settle her stomach. Cora had wanted to browse the shops and stalls – the drapers, with its bundles of exotic coloured silks propped up outside, the milliners, housed in no more than a cupboard, but Fanny said not. They must make haste. 'And we must remain on our guard, Cora,' she said, sitting down inside the carriage and pulling the blanket over her lap.

'Of course.'

The palette of the landscape glowed in the late morning sun. The air was fresh and cool, and the light very different to the thin midwinter veil of England. As the carriage creaked and swayed, Cora tried not to think back but forwards. Italy was her home now. And for a while she kept her eyes closed, knowing that if she opened them tears would escape. For her aunt's sake, she had for the most part been animated on their journey, pretending to be excited about their new life in Rome, and she was, in a way. But then and there all she could think of was her mother, weeks away and lost to her. For how would she ever find her again?

Through the lonely meadows and pastures of the campagna the carriage stumbled on, occasionally passing another heading back to the port, or a cart, piled high and swaying perilously from side to side. Abandoned houses languished at deserted crossroads, and scattered about the desolate wilderness were the ruins of a temple, the fallen arches of an aqueduct or the shell of a dilapidated church.

Late in the afternoon, as the air grew cooler and colours faded, the hazy outline of the city's rooftops finally came into view. And as the carriage passed by the lopsided tombstones and broken pedestals of the Protestant Cemetery, and entered the gate of Saint Paul, Fanny turned to her niece and smiled. 'Now we *are* here.'

But the city the women had anticipated had shrivelled and shrunken with age. For within its crumbling walls lay only more scattered ruins, tangled up in stunted trees and grass, and wide-open fields, woodland and empty space, with no signs of life. Then, slowly, the inhabited city began to emerge: dilapidated buildings, half built and unfinished, weathered by time and neglect, with tattered shutters of flaking paint, festooned in ragged garments hanging out to dry in the winter sun. The noxious aroma of sewers and festering rubbish permeated the bouquet of cedar, cypress and pine, and the two women sat in silence, each one afraid to speak. Rome was not as they had expected.

Twisting and turning, the carriage continued, in and out of shadows, shaving doorways, grazing peasants and statues and littered shrines, scraping off plaster and paint. Cora took in her new home. Was it really any different to where they had come from? And those suspicious dark eyes staring back at her, what did they say, what did they ask? *Who are you? Why are you here?*

Then, turning on to a wide avenue, Cora gasped. The splendour of the city spread out before her in ruins she recognised from pictures, white marble fountains, sculptures and pillars, columns stretching up to the sky, pink in the twilight. Rome became Rome, ancient and grand, rising up from the muddle of her unruly young buildings and capturing one heart, one imagination.

It had been upon her arrival in Rome that Cora had made decisions about her life: how it could be, how it would be, and how it would end. She had decided then that she would never suffer the ignominy of being passed over by life and discarded in death. She had decided then that she would have a rich and full life. It lay ahead of her, a blank canvas simply waiting to have colour and texture added. She would live, love and die in Rome, and be buried amongst England's lost poets in the Protestant Cemetery, where a white marble angel would stand guard and a carpet of violets would cover her grave. This was what she decided when she became intoxicated by possibilities, and fell in love for the first and last time.

'The photographer from Linford is coming today and I rather think we should be outside, on the lawn,' said Cora, standing by the window, her back to Mrs Davey. 'Yes, the light will be better for him . . . perhaps by the horse chestnut,' she added, turning to the housekeeper. 'It's a little cooler and more shaded there. If you and Sally can erect the gazebo, and perhaps induce Mr Cordery to help you, that would be perfect. We shall take tea there.'

'I'll see what can be arranged, ma'am,' Mrs Davey said, sounding less than enamoured by the idea.

'Tea in the garden, how delightful,' said Sylvia as the door closed. 'I've always loved taking tea in an English garden at the height of summer. Tea and scones, and white linen . . . and green, green grass and buttercups, and daisies and butterflies and sunshine,' she went on, quietly, whimsically. 'It all fits together so beautifully, don't you agree?'

Cora glanced towards her and sat down.

'Like tea and crumpets toasted over a roaring fire in winter, when it's dark and stormy and snowing outside, hmm?'

Cora nodded. 'But the grass is hardly green, and I fear we, too, may wither and perish in this heat.'

'Oh, but we'll be fine in the shade. You have your fan, and you're more used than any of us to a torrid climate.'

The two women had made up their differences the previous day, after Cora had apologised. Sylvia had assured her that she had not been spying, would never dream of doing such a thing. Cora had shaken her head. 'Please,' she said, 'let's not speak of it. I was out of sorts. You know me well enough by now, I think, to know it meant nothing.'

Too hot to be outside, they had spent the day together indoors, comparing notes on specific times; lost for the entire afternoon in their shared recollections, almost laughing at their younger selves. But Sylvia could see that her friend was still troubled, deeply troubled. She knew it would only irritate Cora if she asked again what the matter was so instead she attempted to distract her friend with prompts beginning, do you remember when . . .

Whilst Cora spoke, Sylvia took copious notes, and then later, in the evening, read them back to Cora, who nodded her head all through, and seemed perfectly happy with what was recorded. Before retiring to bed, Cora had thanked Sylvia for her patience, told her that she had enjoyed their day together. And Sylvia had gone to bed satisfied, happy. At last they had made a start. They had begun at Rome but Cora had assured her that they would 'deal with' the beginning – Paris, and even Suffolk – all in good time. And Sylvia, keen to cement their new understanding, had said, 'There's no rush. We have plenty of time, dear.'

Shortly after they had first met in Rome, Cora had mentioned her family – her parents and siblings – to Sylvia. 'All gone,' was all she could say as a tear rolled down her cheek. Later, she had elaborated on this, telling Sylvia the story of her poor family's demise. Her mother, a renowned beauty, feted by society and despised by other women, had died in childbirth, leaving her heartbroken father to bring up their four children alone. At that time, she, her father and siblings had lived with their grandparents on their vast estate in Suffolk. But in the aftermath of this tragedy her father had taken to drink and gambling, and within twelve months of her mother's death he had shot himself. It was then that Cora had been placed in the care of her mama's sister, Fanny, who was living in Paris at the time with a distant French relation. Her younger brothers and sister had continued to live with their grandparents, but in the course of the following two years all three of her siblings died: one of pneumonia and two in the cholera epidemic.

But the very next day Cora appeared to regret telling Sylvia this version of events, for she had

called on her and said, 'What I told you yesterday
. . . about my family, you haven't repeated it to
anyone, have you? You see, it's not necessarily the
truth . . . not the whole truth. I am not allowed to
tell anyone . . . but I'll tell you one day, I promise.'

The mystery had been compelling enough for
Sylvia thereafter to be vigilant. But as she listened
to Cora, and to others, rather than be able to piece
together what might have happened, she had only
become more confused. Locations changed, names
altered, and siblings were unborn. Then, not long
before George left Rome, and in an angry and
highly strung state after an argument with her
aunt, Cora blurted out another version of events,
one that Sylvia, to her everlasting and eternal
regret, *would* repeat.

Now, Cora said, 'By the way, Jack has invited a
girl to tea.'

'Well, how lovely, how marvellous.'

'Cecily . . . Cecily Chadwick.'

'Cecily Chadwick,' Sylvia repeated, whispering
the name, as though it were a secret in itself. Then
she opened her eyes wide: 'Aha! Quelle surprise!
Le Double Cs.'

'Yes, a queer coincidence.'

'He's quite taken with her, don't you think?' Sylvia
said, tilting her head, peering over her spectacles at
Cora.

'He barely knows her,' Cora replied. 'But it
would seem he likes her enough to invite her here
to tea, to meet me,' she added.

'How exciting!'

Never having been married, never having had children, never having known pain and heartache or love and loss other than the deaths of her parents at ripe ages, and after calm and orderly lives, Cora believed that Sylvia viewed the world through a child's eyes, with a child's propensity for emotion. Life to Sylvia was exciting, splendid and marvellous, or perplexing and unfathomably queer, or sad. No two states, no two emotions, co-existed, for there had been no dichotomy, no duality in Sylvia's world. She remained, Cora thought, oblivious to the complexities of the human heart, the nearness and sometimes overlap of love and hate. She had had no reference to, no real understanding of the characteristics of a passionate nature: that a woman could both laugh and cry with grief, or hate the man she loved, or be driven to madness, and even murder, by a thing as sweet and tender as love.

Sylvia had written about love, of course, and continued to do so. But her stories were about a particular type of love, a certain sort of character: the requited type, the fathomable sort, leading to a happy ending. Cora knew that as far as Sylvia was concerned, her life had been rich and filled with love: the love of her husbands, the love of her children and friends. Each seemingly unhappy ending had reshaped itself, altering to a happy one. And, even now, Sylvia determined a glorious sunset on Cora's life. Oh yes, she kept saying, it would all turn out fine in the end. But would it?

The memoirs remained an issue, and in truth Cora regretted ever having agreed to it. There were ways round it, she had decided, though she was not yet entirely sure how to navigate them. In the meantime, the focus of their attention would be Rome: her first years there, meeting George, his early work. She could not let Sylvia down. The book seemed to be her raison d'être. And Cora had promised her, promised her years ago, that she would be the one, the only one, to tell her story.

Earlier that morning, alone in the temple, she had stared at the name once more. Typewritten in capitals and red ink, it was designed to shock her, warn her, she knew. But what was she to do? There was no demand for money, not yet. That would come later, perhaps. No, this was simply to let her know that the past – her past, her secret – was not forgotten.

She would just have to bide her time. After all, what was the worst that could happen? The man in question was long dead. No one would remember; no one would be interested. Any self-respecting newspaper editor would throw the story out. But as she rose to her feet her resolve sank. She had come too far to allow anyone to besmirch her name, the Lawson name, or jeopardise Jack's future.

CHAPTER 7

By noon, the thermometer outside read eighty-seven degrees Fahrenheit. By three o'clock it had risen to eighty-nine. Rosetta predicted another of her turns if the heat did not abate, and sat holding a damp towel to her head at the kitchen table, from time to time muttering expletives. Madeline was in her workroom, as usual, wrestling with swathes of green velvet: the Brownlows' new winter curtains. And Ethne was noisily, laboriously, practising – what sounded to Cecily like one long, thumping dirge – on the pianoforte.

In a white cotton dress with broad blue sash, Cecily descended the stairs. The dress, once her mother's, had never appealed to Ethne and thus had come direct to her. Originally, in Madeline's day, it had had a profusion of lace ruffles running from its high neckline down over the bodice, but Madeline had altered it to fit Cecily's specifications: a narrower skirt, a flat sailor-style neckline and collar, no lace and a shortened hemline.

'You look very pretty, dear,' said Madeline, raising her head. She stood at the cutting table, scissors in hand. The room smelled of lavender and camphor and newly cut fabric. 'Enjoy your tea party.'

Cecily walked across the hallway and picked up her straw hat. Earlier, after lunch, she had managed to find a few roses in the garden, a few the drought had not yet killed off, and had pinned them to the ribbon round the hat's crown. She placed her hat on her head, checked her appearance in the mirror, and walked on, to the kitchen.

Rosetta removed the towel from her forehead and looked up as she entered. 'My, you do look a picture . . . you look like a bride . . . on her wedding day!' she said, tearfully, red-faced.

Poor Rosetta. Her face, her hands – even her body – appeared to have swollen in the heat. She had dispensed with her stockings and her strangely misshapen shoes, which lay on the floor next to where she sat, and her feet were resting in a large pail of water.

'Poor Rosetta,' said Cecily, bending down and kissing Rosetta's thick warm hair.

'My little angel, that's what you are. My little angel, sent from him above . . . the only one who cares about poor old Rosetta.'

Cecily moved swiftly through the darkened scullery, where flies buzzed at the mesh-covered window and crawled about the leftover ham lying out on the slate bench. She stepped out into an incandescent day. Nothing moved, nothing stirred. The air was still and silent, heavy with the weight of an oppressive heat. Even in the last hour the temperature seemed to have risen. And as she walked down the pathway and turned on to the track, she felt that weight, a pressure upon her head and in her chest, and with it, a strange sense of foreboding. Not nervousness, exactly, but the queerest sense of some future sadness, like the fluttering of an ill-conceived notion, or the fleeting scent of misfortune. For a moment, even the track ahead appeared portentous, darker. As though the arching branches had eyes, fixed on her, watching her. As though they knew a secret not from the past but from the future.

Breathing in deeply, dispelling doubt and moving on, she wondered who else might be at the house, and she hoped that Sonia Brownlow would not be there. 'Sycophant,' she said out loud. Oh, how she wished Annie had been invited too. But the invitation had been for her alone.

It had been Jack who had invited her. He had called at the house himself. But he had been rather offhand, she thought, flippant. 'You're very welcome to drop by for tea on Tuesday, if you fancy,' he had said, staring towards the gate to the orchard.

'That would be nice. At what time?'

'Quarter past four.'

Then he turned and marched off down the path.

As she walked down the driveway towards the house, Cecily could hear voices drifting over the bank of rhododendrons on her right. She could hear Mr Fox quite distinctly, too loudly, speaking about the falling attendance at church. Then another voice, unrecognisable and vaguely apologetic, saying something about faith being carried in the heat . . . or was it in the heart?

She wasn't sure how, exactly, to announce her arrival: should she go towards the voices, take a pathway and wander through bushes, then emerge, unannounced, in front of them all; or should she go to the front door?

She walked on, towards the shadowed north-facing front of the house, where the gritted driveway merged with a large circular space big enough for carriages to turn. At its centre was a bed of tall grasses and a small oriental-looking tree. Immediately in front of the house, defining its lines, emphasising its symmetry, was a neatly trimmed box hedge. She slowed her pace as she passed two shaded windows, noting her reflection in each, and trying to see beyond the glass; but the blind within one was drawn down and the shapes within the other too indistinct to make anything out.

The front door stood open and, next to a substantial boot-scraper firmly fixed to the ground, a coconut mat said 'Welcome'. Ahead of Cecily was a small anteroom with a highly polished black and white marble tiled floor, another boot-scraper with brushes, a mirrored coat stand to the wall on the right, draped in a variety of cloaks and coats, and a pair of discarded galoshes beneath; directly opposite her another half glass-panelled door remained closed. Cecily stared into the glass, straightening her hat, checking and smoothing her dress, then pulled on the bell.

It took a while for the young maid to emerge from the shadows and open the door, but as soon as she did, and before Cecily could speak, she said, 'Good day, do come in, please follow me, miss,' and beckoned her into the darkened hallway. She led Cecily past a long ancient-looking table, where a red leather frame announced 'IN' and where an arrangement of wilting flowers had shed petals and pollen on to letters and papers scattered beneath. Above the table hung a large oil painting: a Pre-Raphaelite-looking woman with golden flowing hair, standing by a pillar and staring back at Cecily over a bare shoulder. They passed a settee of chipped gilt, faded pink velvet and tattered brocade, a stairway of threadbare carpet leading up to a half-landing where light flooded in through a tall arched window, illuminating dust motes and cobwebs. She followed the maid down a passageway, past a marble sculpture of a naked man, to another glass-panelled door, and then out on to a canopied veranda. Here stood two more sculptures, some aged wickerwork chairs and a table, and a passion flower, thick and rampant and twisted around posts. They stepped out on to a wide stone-flagged terrace, which looked out over flowerbeds and lawns, beyond the formal terraced gardens to a wilderness of trees. The maid lifted her arm, pointing to a green and white striped gazebo set out on the grass. 'Her ladyship's yonder. Tea's to be served outside today,' she said, bobbing her head and turning away.

As Cecily descended the steps leading down to the lawn, she heard the rector say, 'Aha, and here she is!' Ahead, under the canvas and seated in a variety of chairs, were the rector, Sonia Brownlow and her sister, Marjorie, Miss Combe, and a bespectacled lady with thinning grey hair and a book in her lap, whom Cecily immediately and instinctively knew to be the lady novelist.

In the centre of the huddle, majestically upright and watching Cecily as she crossed the lawn, was an elderly lady in an old-fashioned rigid ensemble of navy blue and white striped silk with lace cuffs, and a broad-brimmed navy blue hat atop a cloud of white hair. She wore an inscrutable expression, her eyes almost closed, her mouth unsmiling. Even if Cecily had not known who she was – and she knew exactly who she was – her eyes would have been drawn to this one person. Wherever she had seen her, whether in some busy city street, on a train, in a painting or photograph, she would have noticed her, been drawn to her. For her presence was compelling, without need of name or identity. Cecily felt a new sense of trepidation.

The rector rose to his feet: 'Allow me to introduce you to Miss Cecily Chadwick, ma'am,' he said, with a nod to Cecily and a half-bow towards the lady. And without thinking, completely spontaneously, for she had not planned it, and had never in her life made such a gesture before, Cecily placed one foot forward and lowered her body in a deep curtsy. As soon as she raised her head she caught Sonia's pinkish smirk, and felt her own face tingle. But the countess's demeanour shifted; she opened up her bright blue eyes and smiled.

'Cecily. How lovely to meet you. Do sit down, my dear,' she said, gesturing to the empty chair at her side. 'I imagine you know everyone here.'

Cecily glanced about and nodded as the others said hello.

'And this is my dear friend, Miss Dorland,' she went on. 'Miss Dorland and I grew up together in Rome. Miss Dorland writes novellas,' she added, with a sudden and definite emphasis on the last word.

'Novels,' the bespectacled lady said quietly. 'I write novels.' And she smiled at Cecily.

'I thought we'd take tea outside today, Cecily. I do hope it's not too much for you, dear, this heat.'

'No, no, it's—'

'One so loathes abandoning summer, peering out at it like a sick child from beyond a window, never being able to step out into this glorious light,' she said, gesturing bejewelled hands upwards. And then she tilted her head back, closed her eyes and breathed in deeply.

Cecily watched her. She saw that her skin was tanned, more tanned than any one else's she knew, though she had seen people – even women of a

131

similar age – at the fair with that same sort of colouring and had always thought it attractive. But the countess was nothing like any woman at any fair. In fact, the countess was nothing like any other woman. The combination and contrast between the colour of her skin, her eyes, and the whiteness of her hair was striking and, despite her age, quite beautiful. In repose, the corners of her mouth slipped downward, lending age and an air of sadness to a face that still had something of the glow of youth about it, in spite of its lines. And that mouth . . . the mouth was – or certainly had been – a very pretty mouth, Cecily thought. But it was impossible to put an age – a definite age – on the lady. To Cecily, the countess appeared settled in that ill-defined place women reach, eventually, sometime after forty. A place her mother had happily, voluntarily – and prematurely – entered; a place where white hair alone did not necessarily denote years. She glanced at the novelist: girlish in demeanour, ancient in looks, she surmised. Confusing. She looked back at the countess: ancient in demeanour, but something still girlish around that mouth, puckering, pursing, smiling and pouting in turn. Then, as though sensing the scrutiny, the countess opened her eyes and turned to Cecily with a curious smile.

'Sunlight!' she said, dramatically. 'It's what feeble bodies crave, what troubled souls hunger for.'

'I just adore sunshine,' said Sonia, emulating the countess and tilting her head upwards. 'I think it's perhaps something to do with having been born in the tropics.'

'You should be careful, it can make folk feverish. Look at the deaths in the newspaper, and one here in Linford only last week. It's taken its toll, that's for sure,' Miss Combe said, ever the voice of sobriety and caution, and tucking her chin into a froth of lace. 'And it's been proven it can make people go quite mad.'

'It is not the heat which makes one go mad, Miss Combe,' the countess said, 'though it is, I grant you, a contributory factor. No, it's the lack of sleep, the broken nights . . . the nightmares. The lack of peace our consciences need and require in order for us to face each and every new day.'

'Hear, hear!' boomed Mr Fox.

Cecily noticed Miss Dorland open the notebook in her lap, lick her pencil, and then scribble something down. She heard Marjorie whisper loudly to Sonia, 'That doesn't make any sense. Why do babies need so much sleep then? Surely they have clear consciences.'

'It's always so refreshing to have the young amongst us, wouldn't you agree, Mr Fox?' the countess continued, ignoring Marjorie and turning to the rector. 'One always feels invigorated by their . . . sheer zest and joie de vivre.'

'Ah, yes, indeed, ma'am,' he said, nodding, his eyes fluttering shut.

She turned to Cecily. 'So, my dear, do tell me

a little more about yourself. I hear that you've lived in Bramley all of your life.'

'Yes, that's right. And in the same house too . . . the place my father built.'

The countess released a short gasp. 'Mr Chadwick, such a talented man!'

'You knew him?'

'No, my dear, sadly I did not. But I'm always impressed by men who build, design or make things. What gifted, talented souls they are, as all artists are. But such a great loss to you and your poor mama . . .' She shuddered. 'Oh, to be robbed of a father, that paternal, guiding force, that fountain of knowledge and wisdom. 'Tis arguably the second greatest loss for our sex to endure.'

The countess did not appear to notice Cecily's blush, or Miss Dorland's nervous glance towards the rector.

'Yes, indeed,' she continued, 'far worse, I think, than the loss of a spouse, a husband, but of course not as great as the loss of a child,' she added quietly. 'No, that is the greatest loss for any woman to endure.'

Minutes later, as two maids came across the lawn towards them, carrying the tea paraphernalia, and whilst the others talked amongst themselves, the countess turned to Cecily. For a moment she did not speak, but simply smiled at Cecily, studying her face. Her blue gaze moved across Cecily's features, her nose, her mouth, then back to her eyes. And it was intoxicating, a scrutiny that made

Cecily feel light-headed, quite dizzy. The countess said, 'You know, we have the same intials, you and I. The double Cs.' She leaned closer. 'My name is Cora, Cora de Chevalier,' she said, lifting her arm, stretching out her hand. On her little finger was a heavy gold ring engraved with two intertwined Cs. 'So you see, already, we have a great deal in common.'

As tea was served and sipped, and plates of scones and queen cakes, and shortbread and small triangular sandwiches passed about, the conversation meandered from this to that and back again. There was no sign of Jack, and the countess made no reference to him, offered no apology for his absence. Cecily watched Miss Dorland, noted how quietly she sat. An observer, she concluded. And from time to time she caught the novelist's eye, and they smiled at each other.

Mr Fox spoke at some length about Lady Agatha Withenshaw (she had recently donated substantial monies to the clock tower and war widows funds). And then Miss Combe interjected, stretching her neck from a sea of ruffles and white lace to say that Lady Agatha had a vested interest: she was a war widow herself. Mr Fox smiled, said that was not the point, but then failed to elaborate further, and Miss Combe, glancing away, tucking in an already receding chin, murmured something, and Cecily heard the word 'gold-digger'.

There were debates on the temperature, reckonings – and a tally – on local deaths the heat had caused, and then discussion of the growing unrest across the country. The countess spoke about the trouble in the Balkans, about Germany's egotism, and then, shaking her head and genuflecting, said something in French. At which point, Mr Fox tried to laugh but it came out all wrong, and the countess threw him a withering glance. Cecily made a mental note to read up on foreign news, and to look up the Balkans in the atlas when she returned home. The countess appeared to know about everything: history, art, empires, civilisation, science and social order; the future of India, the future of Germany, the future of mankind; and wars. Listening to her, it seemed as though the whole world was in turmoil, standing on the edge of the abyss, looking down into the void. She told Mr Fox that he and all of England needed to wake up, and Cecily heard Miss Combe gasp. Then she proclaimed that England itself was on the verge of civil war, to which the rector responded with mirth, and teased her, saying, 'You have spent too long, ma'am, in countries not your own. We are civilised here.'

'Civilised?' she repeated. 'Someone once told me England was filled with civilised philistines and cultured barbarians.' She paused, smiling coquettishly, and perhaps more to herself and a memory than to anyone present. 'London, I was told – and yes, it was a very long time ago – was a capricious city dressed up in finery, pretending to like art without ever knowing what art is. London, I was

136

told, was a place of ignorant snobbery! No, I'm not sure the English are civilised, not yet, Mr Fox.'

'I'm afraid I have to disagree,' he replied. 'We may have lost some dignity . . . certainly since the eighties and nineties, but this country remains the most civilised of the Western world. Our culture, our manners, our society – and our Empire – are envied the world over.'

'Pffsh,' she cried, with a rapid gesture of her hand. 'We *have* lost our dignity, Mr Fox, and we have lost our way: morally, spiritually and culturally. What made us great has made us arrogant and will surely pull us down. Look at Liverpool, and London for that matter. How can we speak of civilisation, what pride can there be in our Empire when people here are starving? Such poverty is the direct result of that insatiable appetite for Empire. Imperialism, profit, expansion – it all comes at a cost. And I have seen the squalid tenements and courts and alleys that are also a part of our Empire, Mr Fox. They are nothing to be proud of.'

For a moment Cecily wondered if the countess had been poor-peopling, like Sonia's mother – visiting those desperate families who lived in only one room. She saw Mr Fox smile, close his eyes, and then heard him say something quietly about history. But the countess interrupted him again, saying that history could never record the truth, or any individual stories. They would be lost, gone forever. It would take an overview, it would generalise, she said, diminishing real stories and identities, personal perspectives, and within them truths, turning triumph, defeat and tragedy into something else: popular entertainment, she suggested.

The rector made no reply, and for a minute or two no one spoke.

Then Miss Combe began: she was considering electricity, canvassing opinion on its safety. Someone had told her that it was not compatible with long hot summers, which seemed prevalent nowadays. (And there was a brief exchange about English summers of the past, whether they had in fact been hotter, longer, better.) Mr Fox advocated that electricity, the sort that travelled through wires, was quite unnecessary. Wires, he said, were the problem. Wires were not compatible with the British way of life and should not be tolerated. It was the countess's turn to laugh. And she did. Then she mentioned someone named Marconi, a friend of hers, Cecily presumed. Yes, the rector conceded, the Italians were good with wires. Or rather, that's what he seemed to be saying.

And thus, like the ebb and flow of waves upon a shore, the tide drifted back to Italy, to Rome. The countess spoke of people whose names Cecily knew she really ought to know, but the countess seemed to know so many. For every name she mentioned was followed swiftly by another, and then another. And Mr Fox in particular – in fact, alone – turned quite giddy and began to rub his thighs, like one of Cecily's infant schoolboys when they were allowed to clean the blackboard. And Cecily, embarrassed for him, for a moment distracted by him, missed the beginning of another story: about a doll in Rome, a doll that performed miracles.

'The Piazza d'Ara Coeli,' the countess was saying, 'lies at the heart of medieval Rome, close to Monte Palatino and the Roman Forum. Like all piazzas, it has a fountain at its centre, and a church: the church of Santa Maria d'Ara Coeli. Situated on the Capitoline hill, overlooking the piazza, it is built upon the site of the ancient Roman Temple of Jupiter, where Augustus heard the sibyl announce the birth of Christ. It houses the Santissimo Bambino, a wooden doll carved from a tree that grew on the Mount of Olives, and said to have been painted by Saint Luke himself. There are many stories about how the Santissimo Bambino found its way to Rome, and each one includes a miracle. Romans believe the doll has divine powers and is able to heal the sick. And, up until quite recently, it was often carried from Maria d'Ara Coeli and transported through the city's streets in its own carriage – with footmen and priests in attendance – to visit those sick and infirm. In return, grateful Romans continue to bring the Bambino gifts – money, jewels and gold. And each Christmas the children of Rome visit the doll, to sing to it, and offer up prayers and thanks. It is an ugly, macabre thing,' she added, wrinkling her nose. 'Though I've oft enough prayed to it myself.'

'I was always frightened of it,' the novelist said quietly. 'I never liked its face, never liked to look into its eyes.'

'Did it really perform miracles?' Marjorie asked.

But the countess suddenly appeared distracted. She gazed towards some steps at the edge of the lawn, smiling and frowning at the same time, as though she had just noticed an old friend.

Miss Dorland said, 'So the Romans believe.'

There was something childlike about the novelist's voice, something innocent and tremulous and sweet. And just as one could see that the countess had been a great beauty, one could also see that Miss Dorland had not. Her looks accommodated themselves well to age, and Cecily imagined she possibly hadn't altered very much in appearance since her youth. Her face was unexceptional, unremarkable, like so many others – forgettable. And yet there was an innate softness to her, in her manner, and genuine warmth in her unforced smile. She deferred to the countess in all things, it seemed, and watched her closely, her eyes constantly moving back to her. And the countess for her part appeared to treat Miss Dorland like a younger sister, or perhaps a daughter. She looked down at the grass and up at the sky as she listened to her friend speak, occasionally correcting her on a detail, or on her pronunciation. 'No, dear, it wasn't actually then . . . the D is silent, dear . . .

no, Sylvia, she was his aunt, not his mother,' and so on. But it was clear, to Cecily at least, that the two women knew each other very well, and had known each other for many years. Like an old married couple (rather like Mr and Mrs Fox, Cecily thought), they finished each other's sentences and corroborated each other's anecdotes with nods and murmurings; and when one could not remember – a detail, name, time or place – the other swiftly stepped in.

Cecily noted the elderly novelist's hands, fidgeting and busy all the while, playing tunes between fingertips, tapping a beat on an invisible machine. She spoke in short precise sentences, and, every so often, lifted a hand and touched the small gold-framed spectacles perched upon the bridge of her nose.

To look at, the two women were the antithesis of each other: one still voluptuous, with a shape Cecily imagined to have been envied in youth and that extravagant cloud of white-white hair; the other angular and flat, with dull grey hair scraped back into an impoverished bun. Unlikely friends. And yet, Miss Dorland was – and must always have been – a calm presence in the countess's turbulent life, Cecily supposed.

Cecily could have listened to the countess all day, particularly when she became caught up in a reminiscence, for there was something, then, in her style, the mellifluous sound of her voice, her enunciation and consideration of each and every syllable, as

141

though she was reciting poetry. She paused, pursed her mouth, and sometimes pouted; she sighed mid-sentence, looked heaven-ward, closed her eyes, opened them, leaned forward, raised her hands, breathed in deeply, then stared into the distance, ponderously, as everyone waited for her next word, next sentence, next exhalation.

There was one queer moment though, when Miss Combe mentioned a story that had appeared in the newspaper about a local woman who had been sent to prison for bigamy. A name was mentioned, and Mr Fox nodded solemnly; yes, he knew the woman in question. Had he married her? Cecily wondered. But Miss Combe went on to say that the woman had had no fewer than three biga-mous marriages, and that the variety of children from each totalled thirteen. The countess listened to all of this, and to Mr Fox's murmurings, then, with a great intake of breath, she said that bigamy was a very complex issue and, in many cases, an understandable course of action. It had been common enough, she said, in times gone by; indeed, she herself had known bigamists, both male and female, who were quite respectable people as well. She cited a number of hypothetical cases, reasons why it could not, perhaps should not, be viewed as a crime, and she spoke – seem-ingly with some authority – about the archaic divorce laws. Mr Fox then leaned forward, wide-eyed, and spluttered, 'But you sound as though you're advocating it, ma'am.'

She smiled at him, closed her eyes and shook her head. 'No, not advocating it, Mr Fox. Rather, trying to *understand*. This woman has been locked away, her family broken up, her children farmed out to strangers. The law refuses to look at the reasons for the action, it simply sees the crime and punishes the perpetrator. But, like self-defence, a crime is not a crime if it can be justified, understood . . . and then, perhaps, forgiven.'

Mr Fox sat back in his chair. No one spoke.

When the photographer, Mr Trigg, appeared, Cecily at first thought that he, too, was there as a guest. Then the countess raised her hand to him and said, 'Dear Mr Trigg, do please say if you require anything. I'm afraid my grandson is not yet back from his motor excursion and we can't possibly go ahead until he is here.'

Sonia said, 'Ooh, are we to have our photograph taken, ma'am?'

'Mr Trigg is here to photograph some of my paintings, but I thought it rather a nice idea for him to capture us as well,' she replied, as the photographer quietly busied himself, arranging his equipment on the lawn.

By the time Jack finally appeared – leaping over a small box hedge and striding across the lawn towards them – Miss Combe was on her feet saying she felt rather queer about having her photograph taken; she had not expected it. He wore no jacket, no necktie, and the waistcoat of his suit was unbuttoned. He apologised for his tardiness, explaining to them that his motorcycle had had a puncture somewhere south of Linford, and his soiled white shirt – as the countess pointed out – seemed to verify this. Miss Combe sat back down; Sonia sat up; and Cecily stared down at the grass. Mr Fox laughed. 'Motorcycles indeed!'

'Well, my darling, I'm afraid you've missed tea but I'm sure Mrs Davey will bring out a fresh pot soon enough.'

'I'm fine,' he said, catching Cecily's eye.

He moved forward, hovering over the plates on the linen-covered table, picked up a handful of sandwiches, and then sat down on the grass. The rector spoke to him about his new motorcycle, and Cecily heard him say, yes, he was running it in, but had taken it up to almost forty on the Linford straight. And she pictured him, flying along that road she knew so well, with the wind in his hair, looking out at the world through goggles. Speed, she thought, he likes speed.

Mr Trigg announced that he was set up and ready, if it was convenient to her ladyship. Chairs were moved about. Sonia put on her gloves, Miss Combe dispensed with her parasol, and Jack and Mr Fox took their places, standing behind the ladies. Then Mr Trigg told them all to remain perfectly still until he gave the word . . .

And it was all over in a flash.

The countess clapped her hands. 'Bravo! Well done, Mr Trigg!'

Shuffling and smiling done, conversation

resumed. Sonia asked Miss Dorland about her next novel. It was to be titled *Lord of Nivernais* and set in France, the lady novelist replied. Then the countess explained that Nivernais was a region of France where she had once lived. She laughed. 'I don't believe I'm being too immodest when I say I suspect the book owes something to me.' Miss Dorland replied, 'Well of course, they all owe something to you, dear.' Sonia said she would love someone to write a book about her one day, Miss Combe said she could think of nothing worse, and Marjorie quietly helped herself to another queen cake. Mr Fox and Jack continued to talk about motorbikes, and motorcars, and aeroplanes. And Cecily heard Jack telling him, too, that one day soon enough people would be travelling all over the world by air.

'How about that, Mr Fox?' the countess interrupted. 'You and Mrs Fox could fly to Rome!' she said.

He shook his head. 'Mrs Fox would never entertain such a notion. And I certainly shan't be volunteering. The modern world is unsettled, in a state of flux, I fear, and this need for continual change, invention, reinvention!' he shouted, to make his point, Cecily presumed, 'is too much for me. But I must admit, I do rather like the idea of a motorcar,' he went on, turning his attention back to Jack, seated at his feet. 'Yes, Mrs Fox and I were discussing the possibilities only this morning and—'

'I think you've been rather neglectful of your guest, Jack,' the countess broke in, waving a hand in Cecily's direction. 'Perhaps you'd like to show Cecily around the place . . . the gardens?'

'Of course,' he replied, rising to his feet. 'Would you like to to see around the gardens?'

Sonia stood up. 'I'd love to see the gardens,' she said, oblivious of any faux pas. 'You know, we never did get to see them last time,' she added, turning to the countess.

'Ah, your enthusiasm is to be commended. But I was looking forward to having a little conversation with you, Sonia. I've barely spoken to you, my dear.'

Sonia looked from the countess to Jack and then back at the countess, and then sat down.

The countess turned to Cecily. 'Allow Jack to take you on a little tour. It's hardly Versailles, but I think we're making progress,' she said, smiling beguilingly at Cecily.

They walked across the lawn to steps leading down to another, fringed by wide herbaceous borders and swathes of overgrown wilting rose-bushes. A gritted pathway crossed the second at right angles in the centre, where an ancient-looking sundial stood, and, beyond it, a long pergola, festooned in creepers and trailers, and dangling tentacles like cobweb-covered hands. At the end of the pergola, next to an arbour, a tall, black, wrought-iron gate stood open on to the wooded hillside, where centuries of fallen leaves had made a thick carpet of the earth. Here, under towering beeches and pines, the brightness was diffused, the air cooler.

He said, 'I'm sorry I was so late. I hope it wasn't too much of an ordeal for you.'

'No, it wasn't an ordeal,' she replied, walking on. The sound of a motorcar's engine drifted over from the other side of the valley, its horn honking loudly as it approached the last hairpin bend before the village. And when its noise finally abated the voices on the lawn were no longer audible. But the sound of the fair on the village green – a brass band and children shrieking – drifted up through the wooded dell.

'You know, when the house was first built there were very few trees here, on this part of the hill. Apparently one could see Linford and beyond, almost as far as the coast on a fine day.'

'This place was built for her, for your grand-mother?' Cecily asked, glancing towards him.

'I believe so. I suppose she wanted to have some-where to come back to, eventually. And all these pine trees,' he added, looking upwards, 'are a nod to Rome. She'd have no doubt moved the Roman Forum here if she could've done.'

'But she never lived here, until now.'

'No. She preferred to live in Rome, and Paris. It's where all her friends are . . . or were. And,' he looked at her and smiled, 'she's not overly fond of England.'

'Why is that?'

He shrugged his shoulders, ran a hand through his hair. 'She considers herself European, and having been an expatriate for so long, I think she feels somewhat estranged from English ways and customs. She finds people here . . .' he paused, pondering, searching for the words, 'perhaps a tad judgemental, narrow-minded. She abhors snobbery, says England invented it,' he added, amusement in his voice.

He stepped from the pathway, pulling back overgrown laurel and waist-high ferns to reveal stone steps leading down to another path. And as he held back the branches and Cecily moved down the steps, she caught the pungent musky scent of fox.

'She's had a such an interesting life,' she said, ducking cobwebs, stepping from the hard stone on to a deep brown carpet of pine needles and leaves.

He leapt down the last few steps, landing in front of her. 'Yes,' he said, breathlessly, looking back at her. 'Though bizarrely I don't know a great deal about it. You see, we've not seen an awful lot of each other. She was always overseas and, well, I was here with my mother. I'm only just getting to know her . . . and about her life.'

'Must be queer,' Cecily said, glancing away, 'to only now be getting to know each other.'

'I suppose it is,' he replied, turning and walking on. 'She loves to speak about Rome, as I'm sure you've gathered this afternoon. And she loves to talk about Paris, and the old chateau, but she's not too fond – seems almost reluctant – to speak of her childhood and early life. I imagine it was a sad time for her. She lost both of her parents so young, was left with no one apart from her aunt, who was more like a mother to her. Watch out for the holly,' he added, over his shoulder.

'Did you ever visit her in Rome?'

'No, sadly not. I saw her on the rare occasions she came to London, but she and my mother never saw eye to eye, and there was always . . . always a strained atmosphere. I used to think she blamed my mother for my father's death.' He reached down, picked up a stone and, just as though it were a cricket ball, ran forward, described an arc and hurled it out across the valley.

'But that was an accident, surely?'

'Yes, of course it was. But I'm not sure my mother was my grandmother's ideal choice of wife for my father. Her background was so different. Her father – my maternal grandfather – was South American, Argentinian.'

'I thought you said she hated snobbery?'

He laughed. 'She's contradictory, if nothing else,' he said, shaking his head. 'No, my mother, or perhaps more specifically her father, were not the match my grandmother had in mind. He was an opera singer, or wanted to be. He had no money when he arrived here in this country, sang for pennies, by all accounts. His name was Virdeon Cazabon. Rather a good name for an opera singer, don't you agree?' he said.

'That's where you get your dark looks from.'

'Both of my parents were dark. I'll show you a photograph later, if you'd like.'

She nodded. 'Yes, I'd like to see.'

'I was born there, in Argentina . . . Buenos Aires. My mother for some reason decided that I should be born there and not in England.' He paused. 'It was shortly after we returned here that my father died.'

'He fell from his horse?'

He stopped. 'Yes, and not very far from here, as it happens. He was out hunting . . . it was January, the earth was hard . . . and his horse took a tumble. A rabbit hole, I believe. He was thrown . . . landed on his head . . . died hours later.' He turned to her. 'Fate, eh?'

Cecily shook her head. 'Fate . . .'

They continued on in silence down the steep path, deep into the valley and taller woods, zigzagging briars, thickets of holly, bracken and ferns. When they reached the dried-up mud of a stream, he said, 'This was flowing quite magnificently at Whitsun.' And he kicked at the hard earth with the toe of his shoe. All around them, high above them, the great beeches loomed, cathedral-like, majestic and timeless, effulgent in the sunshine. Magical, Cecily thought.

They followed the path of the stream, spoke of incidental things: the new bridge planned for the ford; the cricket teams' fixtures for the forthcoming weeks; and the entertainments planned in the village hall. Then Cecily told him of her wish to travel, to visit far-flung places, see cities and live in them, perhaps. And he told her of his wish to live in the country, in a place such as Bramley, and be settled and happy. 'It must be marvellous to belong somewhere. To live in a place where everyone knows who you are,' he said.

She spoke of her father, the last time she had seen him, or the last time she could recall. And he told her a little more of his, adding, 'My grandmother speaks very highly of him, of course . . . And now there's only me.' He shrugged. 'I have no relations, no cousins, you see. Quite a responsibility . . .' He spoke of his mother, briefly. She had, he said, suffered from melancholia all of her life, had had that artistic temperament. But with each year her depression had grown worse. He knew, he said, but he was away at school. 'What could I have done?' he asked. 'She longed for someone who had gone. She became more and more reclusive, hardly venturing anywhere towards the end. She wanted to go back in time . . . to sleep, that was all.'

Eventually, they turned and slowly climbed back up the hill. And as he held back the branches on the steps once again, as she passed by him, he said, 'I'm pleased you came today.'

The countess appeared to be dozing. Mr Fox and Miss Combe – who had been on the point of leaving for at least an hour – were discussing a recent drowning in a nearby pond: the perils of bathers. Miss Dorland was quietly reading her notebook, and Sonia and Marjorie were nowhere to be seen. As Jack and Cecily sat down, the countess opened her eyes and smiled. 'I'm afraid the Brownlow girls had to leave,' she said. 'Their father's chauffeur came to collect them.' She turned to Jack and said something to him in French.

He replied in English. 'No, we went the other way, took the path down through the woods.'

The countess turned to Cecily. 'You didn't get to see my temple?'

Cecily shook her head. 'Temple? No, I've not seen it.'

'I shall show it to you next time,' she said. She leaned forward and whispered, 'It's a very special place, a memorial to—' She stopped, turned towards the rector. 'I'm sorry, what was that, the name you just mentioned?'

Mr Fox appeared momentarily confused. He had been speaking about some new tenants at the farm on the edge of the village. 'Ah, John Abel!' he said, remembering. 'Yes, he and his family moved into Meadow Farm two weeks ago. Nice people, from somewhere in Suffolk, I believe. I was there earlier today and—'

'John Abel? Are you quite certain that was the name?'

'Oh yes, absolutely.'

'And you say they're from Suffolk?'

'Yes, that's what he said, that's what he told me,'

the rector replied, a little mystified. 'A name you're familiar with, ma'am?'

'I believe my aunt once knew someone of that name. But that was many, many years ago,' she replied, glancing away. And then she reached to the table and picked up her mother-of-pearl cigarette case. 'Would anyone care for a small sherry?' she asked.

CHAPTER 8

That night, Cecily dreamt of the Bambino Santissimo. She dreamt it came to Bramley, carried through the lanes and up the track to her house in a sedan chair, waited on by Mr Fox and Jack Staunton, who said, 'We have to get it back to Rome by teatime.' But the chair became stuck in the garden gate, and her mother said, 'Expatriates always require a wide gate.' And when Cecily peered inside the chair, she saw that the doll was not a doll at all, for it was smoking a cigarette, and appeared to be . . . the countess.

When she awoke, she dismissed the dream, and then lay in her bed for some time, remembering the events of the previous day, working through it all once again, trying to recall the exact words and sequence of conversations. Had he said he was pleased that she came? Or had she dreamt that? No. He'd definitely said it: I'm pleased that you came. She could remember exactly where they were, could walk back to the very spot. And hadn't he looked at her in a certain way? Had he not had that rather serious, concentrated look in his eyes? The same expression Walter had worn when he told her that she always made him laugh? She pictured Jack once again, standing in his white shirt, with that black smear across the front, holding back a branch. She could see the shadow of his beard, the line of his mouth, beads of perspiration glistening above his top lip. That beautiful lip . . . had it ever been kissed? she wondered.

She turned on to her side. The room was warm, already bathed in sunlight. A somenolent coo drifted in through the open window. She closed her eyes, took herself back twelve hours.

She had bid the countess goodbye at around six o'clock. Mr Fox and Miss Combe had finally left, together, and the countess wished to go indoors, saying she felt the air becoming cool, though how – at around eighty degrees Fahrenheit – Cecily could not fathom. Jack said he would walk her home, and they had come by way of the eastern side of the house so that he could show her his motorcycle.

Around a gritted yard was a row of little cottages, a coach house and some stables; and connecting the main house to the coach house, another entire wing, less grand but easily as big as her own home, that Cecily had never seen.

'What's in there?' she had asked, pointing.

'There? The game larder and pastry larder, lamp room and scullery, the china closet, and Mrs Davey's bedroom and sitting room. And the servants' hall, of course,' he replied.

The yard led on to a lane, bordered on one side

by a paddock, where a few rabbits sat about on the grass, and rotting hen coops and hutches butted up against a fence. On the other side was a pink brick wall, which Cecily already knew to be the wall of the kitchen gardens.

'And where does the lane lead to?' she asked.

'The cinder track? Down to the main road, eventually, at the very bottom of the valley,' he replied, pulling open the coach-house door.

Then he began talking about his motorcycle, mentioning all sorts of numbers and letters, and then more numbers, none of which meant anything to Cecily. Well, yes, she said, it looks marvellous. She had not known what else to say. I'll take you out on it, he said, again. 'But please don't ask your mother, she's bound to say no.'

They walked back by way of the house and the main driveway, and lingered there, at the top of the drive, before turning out on to the track. He said, 'I meant to say to you earlier, I rather like your hat, what you've done with it – the flowers,' he added, gesturing to it in her hand. She had been embarrassed. But why? If anyone else, even Walter, had commented on any hat she'd worn it would not have made her feel anything other than pleased to receive the compliment. She'd have smiled, said, 'Thank you.' But instead, with him, she was momentarily speechless, quite unable to put together any words that made sense. She had stammered, said something disjointed and nonsensical about it being one of her sister's hats, that it was Ethne who had attached the flowers, and that she didn't particularly like it. And, just to prove it, she had pulled one of the roses out and thrown it into the rhododendrons behind her. He had stood back, hands in pockets, smiling, as though he knew, realised; so she had pulled out another and flung it across the driveway.

She shuddered as she recalled it.

They had sauntered down the track, stopping every once in a while, extending minutes . . . or had they? Had she been extending each minute while he had been wondering why she walked quite so slowly?

She turned over on her bed, her head in her hands.

'You know, you've hardly told me anything at all about yourself,' he said. 'I've spoken about me and my family, added to which you've had to listen patiently to my grandmother, and to Mr Fox's ramblings – when he could get a word in edgeways – and to that awful Combe woman.'

She laughed. 'There's nothing much to tell,' she said. 'I was born, I grew up, and here I am. That's it, so far.'

He nodded. 'Hmm. I like that. And it's actually the from here I'm interested in.'

Had he said that? Was that what he said?

She turned on to her back, looked up at the sloping ceiling. And she could see them, there on the track, walking down the hill together, beneath that tunnel of branches.

'Where would you like to go from here, Cecily Chadwick? What do you wish for?'

She had pulled the last wilting rose from her hat and thrown it into the hedgerow. 'I wish for happiness, of course. I wish for fulfilment, to do more with my life than simply marry, have children, grow old and then die. I want to see other places . . .' She stopped, looked at him. 'And I want to write.'

She turned on to her stomach, buried her face in the pillow, moaning. 'I want to write! Ugh! I can't believe I told him that . . . I've never told anyone . . . no one knows.'

But what had he said? She turned on to her side once more.

'You want to write? You write?'

'Yes, I try to. It's what I want to do, all I've ever wanted to do.'

It *was* what she wanted to do. It was what she wished for. She wanted to be remembered for being more than just someone's wife, someone's mother, or someone's daughter. She didn't want to have to marry simply in order to validate her existence upon this planet. What good had that done her mother, or anyone else? Husbands made decisions, yes; they offered respectability, safety and, usually, a home, a lifestyle. But they also went away, they also died, leaving pale-faced widows and confused children, bereft and adrift; leaving a gap far bigger than if they had never been there. Marriage brought status, she knew that, but it also brought a sort of invisibility, anonymity.

'Do you allow anyone to read what you write?' he asked.

She shook her head, already rueful.

'Well, you must allow Sylvia to. It'd be good for you to get her opinion, wouldn't it? She's had perhaps as many as a dozen books published, I think.'

They reached the gate, and she hadn't wanted to look at him, hadn't wanted to in case he was quietly laughing at her. But she had – and he hadn't been. He'd stood quite close to her, his eyes cast downwards, flicking the peeling paint from the gatepost. Then he'd looked up at her and said, 'You know, you could call by tomorrow, bring some of your writing for Sylvia to read . . .'

'I'm not sure.'

'No, perhaps not . . . But you could call by anyway, if you'd like to.'

'Or you could call here,' she said, feeling bold.

'I could,' he replied, smiling back at her. 'Should I?'

She nodded.

'Then I shall.'

They had stood there in silence, staring at each other, smiling. Neither of them had spoken for some time. And the queerest thing was she couldn't now be sure whether that silence had lasted only a few seconds or some minutes. In her mind it was interminable. In her mind, it went on and on. And yes, she had been bold, forward in that look, which said, quite simply, she thought now, 'I like you.' For surely that particular smile couldn't have said anything more, could it?

She rose quickly from her bed, reached to the window and drew back the curtains.

'He started it . . .'

Yes, he started it. He had looked into her eyes, smiled, glanced away, glanced back, smiled some more; and then, finally, as she'd pushed on the gate, as the latch had dropped – clickety-click – he had slowly backed away.

It had been later that evening, as she sat with her mother and sister, that she said, 'I've invited Jack Staunton to call on us tomorrow.'

And Ethne had smirked but said nothing.

'For tea?' Madeline asked, a note of mild alarm in her voice.

'Yes, I suppose so. I think I said around four . . .'

'I see.' Madeline put down her sewing, cast her eyes about the room, as if reckoning it from another's perspective. Then she said, 'I think perhaps it impolite not to also invite the countess. You said she's very nice . . .'

Nice: it was not the best-chosen or most accurate word to describe the countess, Cecily realised. Nice meant . . . unthreatening, well-intentioned, amiable. The countess was amiable, but as for well-intentioned, Cecily wasn't altogether sure, and unthreatening? The lady was formidable. She smoked cigarettes, took sherry in the garden, possessed ardent opinions on almost everything, and used words like *sex* without even noticing.

What on earth would her mother make of it all, of her? But it was decided that Rosetta would deliver a note to Temple Hill the following morning, formally inviting all three – the countess, Miss Dorland and Jack – to tea, but not that day. It would appear a little hasty and ill-conceived to send an invitation for the very same day, Madeline said.

'But I've already asked him, told him to call by tomorrow.'

'That's fine, dear. I shall explain in my note.'

'You must admit, it would be rather strange if he came to call here alone,' Ethne began. 'People would assume you were courting,' she added, glancing at Madeline.

By mid-afternoon a date had been set, but not for tea at the Chadwicks'.

Rosetta had begrudgingly taken the note, and returned with another – a counter-offer. 'I can't be doing with going back up that track, not again, not in this heat. It's a hundred degrees out there, and there's about to be an almightly storm,' she said, handing over the sealed envelope and falling into a chair. She fanned herself with her hat. 'Just look at my feet,' she added, lifting her skirts.

Madeline opened the cream envelope, unfolded the paper. Cecily could see two elaborate gold letter Cs at the top of the page. Madeline read the note in silence, reflected, and then reread it, aloud: 'My dear Mrs Chadwick, thank you so very much for your kind invitation to tea. I was however on the very point of extending an invitation to you and your daughters to dine with me here on Saturday evening. I know from dear Cecily how busy you are, and I am quite sure dinner is perhaps less of an interruption to your day, and it will be such a treat for me to have you all here and to meet you at last.' Madeline paused, reflective once more. 'Shall we say seven p.m.? I do hope this isn't too early but I know people here prefer to dine earlier in the evening.'

She turned to Cecily, a furrow of wariness about her brow. 'Well, would you like to go to dinner? Ethne, you won't be able to come of course, you agreed to go with the Foxes to the concert at the Jubilee Hall,' she reminded her elder daughter. 'So it would only be you and me,' she said, smiling at Cecily.

And thus Cecily found herself under an ominous sky, clutching another note from her mother to the countess. As she walked up the hill she recalled the time, years before, when she and Annie had ventured there together. 'You do know that we're trespassing,' Annie had said, making it all the more thrilling, all the more frightening.

Perched high on the hill and surrounded by woodland, the only way to see the place was to trespass. With their hands pressed up against dusty panes, they had peered in at empty rooms, and then wandered about the gardens, traipsing across overgrown lawns and down mossy pathways, through tangled woods and bracken, ducking branches. When they stumbled upon the temple – almost lost in holly, its pillars covered in ivy – they quickly concluded that it pre-dated the house, had been built centuries before, an ancient relic. And the word 'sacrifice' had been enough for them to run back up the hillside, out of the shadows and on to the track.

The house had struck Cecily then as the perfect place to hide away from the world, to be invisible. Mothballed and forgotten, it had felt to her like a sleeping place; a place waiting for someone to come and rescue it and bring it back to life.

Cecily's own home, the brick house her father had built, though considerably smaller and less secluded, was – she had thought then – much prettier. It had a low-pitched roof with exposed rafters, a number of unusual stained-glass windows, and, inside, panelled walls, a parquet floor and built-in shelves, cabinets and window seats, all in the same honey-hued oak. It had been his idea of home, his and her mother's vision, where they would grow old together. And Cecily knew this because her mother had told her, and told her when she was still in mourning. It was one of Cecily's monochrome memories, a flashback to that other time, before her mother finally discarded her widow's weeds and brought colour back into their lives. And though that colour had always been muted, for Madeline was not overly fond of brights, there was, Cecily knew, something intrinsically safe in those indefinite shades.

Like all bright things, money had never been a topic of discussion with Madeline. Its vice or virtue, surplus or lack were never addressed. It was a blessing, she had said, to have a roof over one's head, food on the table, a bed to sleep in; and they must count themselves lucky. Growing up, Cecily had come to realise that their own situation veered more towards lack than surplus; that her mother's frugality was not born of idiosyncrasy of character but of necessity. Gowns, blouses, skirts and coats were patched and mended, Ethne's old dresses adapted and taken in to fit Cecily. Nothing was discarded or thrown away, every remnant – every hem from every shortened gown, every frayed cuff and sleeve and collar – was kept and stored, and used again, ingeniously. Then Madeline bought her Singer sewing machine and began to take in work: altering waistlines and hems, removing collars and stitching new ones, adapting fashions and tastes. She made quilts, cushions and curtains, loose covers and bedspreads. And spent each evening darning linen, embroidering table napkins and antimacassars. She worked hard, built a reputation, and became known as the best seamstress in the area, receiving commissions from local gentry, including the Brownlows, whose bespoke curtains and blinds she had laboriously finished by hand.

But to Cecily, there was something else, something born of loneliness – and perhaps denial – driving her mother's industry. Why else would each and every single moment be spent cutting, stitching and sewing, as though her whole being depended upon it? As though to stop would allow her time to think, to remember. Rosetta had said, 'When you've loved, truly loved, and then lost, you can never again give yourself to another.' And Cecily had immediately thought of her mother, and not of Rosetta. She thought of the love between her parents, the woman she lived with, who had given birth to her, and the man she had never known. How had their love been? She tried to imagine them together, the couple in the silver-framed wedding photograph. She imagined her mother bright and young in her father's arms, imagined them looking into each other's eyes, dancing towards the future, laughing. And she began to feel that sense of loss, that feeling of the world being not quite complete, not whole; that feeling of something – someone – missing, a future taken. No, there could be no brightness in Madeline's world, not now, not ever. But would there be brightness in hers?

By the time Cecily arrived at Temple Hill, the sky had darkened further. The maid glanced upwards at the heavens, then ushered Cecily inside, slamming the front door behind her, shutting out all dwindling light. She asked Cecily to 'please wait there a moment' and disappeared into the shadows, then re-emerged and led Cecily to a room. The countess was alone and sat by a window, rather formally attired, Cecily thought, in a stiff costume of pale lemon and white lace. Perhaps she was going out, or perhaps she had just returned. She did not rise from her chair but reached out and took hold of Cecily's hand, saying, 'I think you're just in time . . . we're hoping for a deluge,' and then asked her to take a seat. Cecily handed over the note, at the same time informing her that although Ethne had a prior engagement, she and her mother would be delighted to come to dinner on Saturday evening.

'*Perfetto!*' said the countess. She glanced down at the small brown envelope in her hand, and Cecily saw her momentarily frown. Then, without opening it, she placed the envelope on the table next to her, beside a small red leatherbound book, and went on to explain that *darling* Jack and Miss Dorland had gone to Linford with Mr Cotton. They were both catching the train to London, she said, Jack to visit a school friend, where he would be staying for a night or two, and Miss Dorland to meet with her publisher and sort out various matters at her flat. And Cecily felt the sting of disappointment, for she had hoped to see Jack, if only to explain the altered arrangements. The countess said, 'Of course, he'll be back by Saturday, when you come to dine,' and offered Cecily a smile.

Outside, daylight shrivelled. The room shrank into dimness. And as the first crack of thunder took hold of the house, shaking chimneys and timber and glass, the countess gazed out through the window and said, 'So desperate . . . desperate for relief.'

But the storm rumbled on without any relief. There was no deluge.

They spoke about the village, the school in particular. And the countess told Cecily that she herself had once, when young, taught at a Sunday school in Rome, a place called the Granary Chapel which had for a while improvised as a church for the English expatriates there. And Cecily immediately wondered if she had lost her faith; if something had happened in her life which had caused her to question and then denounce God. The countess had not been to any service at Saint Luke's, the village church.

'Children,' the countess said, dreamily, as though thinking aloud, 'are not simply the future, they're the light in all our lives.'

She looked away, shook her head and raised a hand dismissively. At first, it was as though a new thought – contradictory or conflicting – had come to her at that very same moment. But as she continued to stare across the room, seemingly at something fixed, Cecily turned, half-expecting to see someone, a figure, even a ghost. But there was no one there. Seconds after this, the countess glanced at the clock on the mantelshelf and pulled on the bell by her side. 'I find a small glass of wine at this time of day reinvigorates the senses, opens one's heart, prepares one for . . . for evening.'

So Cecily took a glass of sherry with the countess.

And when the countess opened the small mother-of-pearl cigarette case and held it out to her, Cecily took a cigarette. It burned her throat and she coughed. The countess told her they were 'Best Venetians'. A count – with a strange-sounding unpronounceable name – sent them to her, she said; she'd never smoke English cigarettes, 'but these are actually very good for one'.

When the clock chimed six, Cecily said she really should be going soon. But she didn't want to. And the countess, turning her head away, glancing out through the window, said, 'Had we but world enough, and time . . .' She looked at Cecily. 'Time's winged chariot . . . to his coy mistress? Andrew Marvell?'

'The metaphysical poets.'

The countess smiled, nodded. 'You remind me a great deal of myself when I was young. Seems but a moment ago.' She lifted her glass to her lips, and Cecily noticed her hands: bejewelled fingers, still slender. She watched her sip from the glass, place it down upon the table next to her, and then glance about the room, her hooded eyes moving swiftly from one object to another, as though checking it was all there, in place. Each surface, every table and shelf, was littered with memorabilia: china and glass and photographs and, Cecily noticed, on the table immediately next to her, two framed black silhouette cameos of cherubic infants with tousled hair.

The countess said, 'Freddie and Georgie. My babies, my boys . . . gone now.'

'Freddie?'

'My firstborn, my eldest, taken from me when he was barely six years old. He is in Rome . . . left there now.'

Sadness slipped down her face. She reached to the locket about her neck, mouthing silent, inexpressible words, struggling perhaps with the need to remember, something, someone, all of them. Wishing perhaps to say their names again, Cecily thought, watching her. Then sunlight broke into the room, under the sash, under the blind, bouncing off china and glass and mirror, and Cecily heard a thin mournful sigh, like the tail-end vibration of a sad song. The clock on the mantelpiece chimed the quarter hour and the countess dissolved into the light, spectral with her white hair and pale gown.

'They're all there,' she said. 'Freddie, my aunt, Jack and—'

'Jack?'

'My first husband. He passed away when . . . before Georgie was born.' She raised a hand to her eyes. 'Do draw down the blind a little, will you, my dear.'

Cecily rose to her feet, moved over to the window and lowered the blind. She wanted to ask questions: were there only two children, two sons, or had others, too, been lost along the way? What about the daughter Mr Fox had mentioned? And how many husbands had there actually been? And which children were born to which husbands? And how had the first husband died?

'My family is rather a muddle,' she said, as if able to hear Cecily's thoughts. 'Perhaps all families are . . . my first husband was also my aunt's stepson.' She paused as Cecily sat back down, and then continued. 'My aunt married a man named James Staunton. He lived in Rome with his son, Jack, whom I later married.'

James Staunton had been contracted by the papal government to set up the Anglo Romano Gas Company and begin the long process of installing gas in the city, she told Cecily. 'When I first arrived, the new gas works were still in the process of being built – on the banks of the Tiber. They were ugly, something of a deformity, particularly there, surrounded by such antiquated beauty. But Mr Staunton was an *industrialist*,' she said with emphasis. 'He and my aunt fell in love so very quickly. It was rather a whirlwind courtship. She was an intelligent woman, calm and measured, a remarkable woman . . .' she petered out, and remained silent for a moment or two. 'She and I had been living in Paris,' she began again, remembering, 'and it was there, in the room of Roman Antiquities at the Louvre, that I first became acquainted with Rome, fascinated by its relics . . . And then, lo and behold, my aunt married Mr Staunton, and there I was *living* in Rome!' she said, smiling at Cecily.

But the story was too fast; there were gaps. How

had they come to be in Paris? Why had they gone there? And how, exactly, had her aunt met Mr Staunton? And what about Jack? What happened to him?

Her early days in Rome were spent just as any other tourist, the countess said, moving on again swiftly, 'visiting and revisting the ancient sites, piazzas, picture galleries and churches, so that within a very short time, I needed no map or guidebook. And I did not care what anyone said, to me it was heaven, *heaven*!'

'What anyone said?'

'Oh well, in comparison to other European cities, Rome was still considered by many to be backward and shabby, third rate; a place to visit, to stay for a while, but not to live, not permanently,' she replied. 'And it had something of a reputation . . .' She glanced at Cecily, 'for fugitives, all sorts of shady characters.'

'Not unlike here then.'

She laughed. 'No, possibly not,' she replied. 'And yet, for those of us who chose to live there, it offered a kind of freedom, and the chance to be whoever one wished to be,' she added wistfully.

'Yes,' said Cecily, imagining.

'And behind every doorway, no matter how humble, were masterpieces, friezes depicting ancient stories, magnificent frescoes, statues, intricate mosaics and richly marbled floors. Every window and balcony overlooked the antiquities, like one's own museum, one's very own art gallery.

It felt to me like the centre of the world. And of course it had been, once. Everywhere one looked were relics, history and art, stupendous art. How could one fail to be inspired in such a place? All of it shaped me, who I am, and like those I have loved, it remains here,' she said, placing her palm flat upon her chest. 'It lives within me . . . that place.'

And how could it not? Cecily thought. To have spent one's formative years in such a place was indeed an extraordinary privilege.

The countess gazed out of the window. 'I would like to go back there,' she said, 'just once more.' And she began to describe a vista in such extra-ordinary detail that Cecily too could see it: a view across jumbled terracotta rooftops, across a sea of steeples and domes, across scattered ruins and pillars to crumbling walls, and beyond those walls to wide empty pastures and distant hills.

This was what had awakened the countess to beauty, Cecily thought, what fed her senses and continued to nourish her soul.

'And your first husband, Jack . . . he died there?' Cecily ventured at last.

'Yes, that is where he rests, where they all rest.'

'But not George?'

She flinched. 'George? Why, George is in Rome . . .'

'Oh, I'm sorry. I was sure Jack said his father had fallen from his horse somewhere near here.'

'Ah yes,' the countess said, closing her eyes,

nodding. 'Forgive me. I sometimes get a little confused with names. You are correct. Georgie,' she said, with emphasis on the 'ie' sound, 'did fall from his horse, and not far from this place. He was so dashingly handsome,' she said, smiling, remembering, 'invincible to his fellow officers and to everyone else . . . and much too brave to suffer the ignominy of an accidental death. He always thought he'd die a heroic death on the battlefield – if any at all. And he made me think that too. But . . .' she paused, shook her head, 'he was mortal. Mortal like his father.'

'So sad.'

'Yes, it was a difficult, painful time, for me – for all of us. He left a young wife, Cassandra, and of course little Jack, only weeks old. I was in Rome . . . I returned here, of course. As soon as I received the telegram I left Rome and returned here as fast as I could. But I was too late.' She lowered her head. 'We buried him in the snow . . .' she said quietly, 'we buried him in the snow as his father passed away.'

'His father?'

She looked up at Cecily. 'Godfather,' she said. And then she glanced once more across the room, towards the bronze head in the alcove. 'They stay with us, of course. Departure from this life, death of the physical body, is not an end. We merely cast off the trappings of this realm for another. The soul is immortal. I know this now.'

Cecily nodded.

'And yet, 'tis the queerest thing,' she began again, quietly, 'to find myself here, at this age, in this place. Peculiar to find oneself anywhere, to still be here, when those one has known are all gone.' She turned to Cecily. 'But of course I have Jack to think of,' she said, in a louder, firmer voice, and picked up her glass. 'He is the future and all that matters to me now. And he's a darling, darling boy, so very like his grandfather in looks and thought and deed. And that is my comfort. It's what we leave behind us that defines who we have been, not our birth date, or death date, nor whom we married or where we were born. Those are the facts, of course, the details, but they're minor details, they mean nothing on their own, tell nothing of the story of a person's life. What made one's heart quicken, what one saw, how one felt; the decisions made, the regrets: all of this is lost, forgotten. And when one reaches my age, 'tis hard to recall one's early life and first impressions.'

Without thinking, Cecily said, 'And what *are* your earliest memories?'

The countess tilted her head to one side. 'My earliest memories . . .' she said, turning away with eyes half-closed, 'my earliest memories are of a place called Standen Hall, a place in Suffolk. It is where I lived before I went to Paris, before my mother . . .' she paused, 'before my mother departed.'

'What was it like?' Cecily asked, leaning forward in her chair.

'It lies a few miles to the west of Woodbridge, off the old London road. And you know, I can picture it now, the view from a carriage window. One passed through an immense gated entrance with a towered gatehouse to the right and headed down a long, long winding driveway, through breathtaking woodland and gardens, and then the vast red-brick Tudor sprawl came into view – the tallest chimneys you ever saw. There was an enormous front door, easily as large as any of the grand doorways in Rome, which opened directly into the oak-panelled medieval great hall. I recall suits of armour, stag's heads mounted high up upon the walls, and a vast wooden staircase rising up to galleried landings lined with portraits. It was truly a splendid place.'

Cecily smiled. 'Home.'

The countess nodded and smiled.

'And you never went back?'

'No. Never. Once my parents were gone . . . well, there was nothing left for me there, no one left. And my life had moved on. I was in Paris, and then Rome, and then married with children. It was impossible to go back, and there was no reason to go back. Life moves on and we must move with it,' she added, smiling, weary.

'Sad. Sad for you, ma'am, to have had to leave everything behind.'

'Please, no more "ma'am". Cora. My name is Cora.'

★   ★   ★

Later, as Cecily strolled back down the track, she felt quite different to the person who had marched up the hill only hours earlier. The fortified wine had undoubtedly mellowed her senses, but it was more than this: there was something new and altered in everything around her, and within her. As though the world – and herself with it – had passed through a spectrum. She knew that nothing would ever be the same; nothing could ever be or seem as it had earlier that day, or before that day. And though the ground felt softer, like a cushion beneath her feet, and the sun, now exposed and still high in the sky, spilled out upon that dark umber carpet in soft slanting rays, something inexplicably sad had attached itself to her, and she felt its burden.

The atmosphere within the room she had just left had been peculiarly insulated, and not just from the heat and light of the day, but from everything, almost from time itself. Three whole hours had passed by in a flash, and in those three hours she had had a glimpse of a life, a different life. A door had opened – an inch, no more – and she had been allowed to step forward and look through it – for a moment, no more. But in that moment, in that glimpse, how much she had seen. Time had slipped away, and she and the countess had been equals, had spoken as friends.

And before Cecily left they had made a pact.

'I'm a very private person, Cecily. I would prefer

you to keep these things we've discussed to yourself. I'd like to think I could trust you.'

'Of course, I wouldn't dream of betraying your
trust, Cora.'

'I knew . . . knew we were going to be good
friends, you and I. And there's something else,
something I'd like you to do for me, Cecily, a small
favour.'

Cecily nodded.

'You must mention this to no one, no one at all,'
she said, 'not even to Jack. In fact, most especially
not to Jack. It's to do with the man at Meadow
Farm,' she began.

CHAPTER 9

It was late Saturday morning. The village was busier than usual, and noisy. And temperatures were running high. The horse-drawn van of the baker, the butcher's bang-tailed cob and the omnibus to Linford – already running ten minutes late – were locked in dispute and remained stationary, surrounded by bleating sheep being moved from one parched field to another by way of the main street. As the bus driver – coerced, Sylvia presumed, by his hot and impatient passengers – honked on his horn and shouted, she and others had spilled out from the post office to watch tempers fly.

Sylvia had already been to the Sale of Work at the village hall, but when she spotted Cecily emerge from the festooned doorway of the hall into the maelstrom she had waved her hand. But Cecily appeared to see nothing, least of all Sylvia. She marched off at some speed, weaving her way through the livestock which was running this way and that and up the wrong lane. As Cecily disappeared, Sylvia too had moved on, through the stupid animals, holding her bag aloft. Once clear, on the decline to the ford and with Cecily in sight once more, Sylvia quickened her pace. She called out, twice, and both times Cecily stopped, just as though she had heard her name. But she failed to turn and simply marched on. And when, eventually, Sylvia caught up with her, Cecily had been unusually abrupt.

'Oh, hello, Miss Dorland,' she said flatly, and sounding quite put out, Sylvia thought.

They had stood for a while in one spot, while Sylvia caught her breath.

'I hear . . . I hear you're to dine with us . . . later,' Sylvia said, fanning her face with her hand.

'We're supposed to be, yes,' Cecily replied, in the same cold voice.

She had not reckoned on Cecily Chadwick being a moody sort, not at all. Something must have happened, Sylvia thought, for her to be so . . . so rude.

'Is anything the matter, dear? You seem a little out of sorts, if I may say.'

Cecily shook her head. 'It's nothing,' she said, without meeting Sylvia's eyes.

As they began to walk, Sylvia told her that she, too, had been to the sale earlier, and they stopped again as Sylvia produced the woven bookmark and bag of pot-pourri she had bought for her friend.

'Oh yes, I'm sure Cora will like them,' Cecily said, barely looking at the things.

At first, Sylvia thought she had imagined Cecily saying the name.

'Cora?' she repeated.

'Mm. I'm sure she'll like them.'

Cecily moved on, but Sylvia remained fixed, the bookmark and muslin bag in her outstretched hands, and a strange giddy feeling, which tilted the pathway ahead. For a moment she thought she might faint. And when Cecily turned, looking back down the hill at her with a queer smile, she appeared to Sylvia rather smug, even triumphant.

She put away her gifts and continued up the hill towards Cecily. 'So, you've been up to the house . . . been to call on her?' she asked.

But Cecily appeared not to hear her. She stared straight ahead, a look of concentration furrowing her brow. And so Sylvia rephrased the question: 'I take it you've seen the countess recently?'

'Oh yes,' Cecily said, and then added – a little defensively, Sylvia thought – '*You* were in London.'

'Ah, when Mr Fox was also there?'

'No. There was only me,' Cecily replied.

But Cora had made no mention to Sylvia of Cecily's visit. She had mentioned only that the rector had called on her. And Sylvia had become increasingly suspicious of that man. To Sylvia's mind, he seemd uncommonly interested in Cora's life. She was worried that her friend, troubled as she was and, perhaps, in need of succour, might feel inclined to unburden herself to him. He had taken to calling at the house almost daily, and had arrived, quite out of the blue, earlier that very morning, before Sylvia set off for the village. It was most irregular. People did not make calls in the morning, and Cora usually refused any callers at all before 3p.m. But then, when Cora informed her that she wished to speak to the rector alone, in private, Sylvia suspected that they had had a prearranged appointment, that Cora had in fact been expecting him. Sylvia loitered in the hallway, tidying papers and adjusting an arrangement of flowers, but not a sound had permeated the closed door.

Now she heard Cecily say, 'I spent quite a while with her. She told me about her boys . . . Jack's father, George, or Georgie as I think she calls him. And also about her childhood, where she grew up.'

'Her childhood, where she grew up?' Sylvia repeated.

'Don't worry,' Cecily said, turning to her, 'I promised I'd not breathe a word to anyone, and I shan't.'

'I see.'

They walked on in silence and when they reached the privet hedge bordering Cecily's garden, Sylvia said, 'I must tell you something, Cecily.'

She then explained how worried she was about Cora, about her friend's recent outburst, the sitting alone in the temple. 'I know that Jack, too, is concerned . . . very concerned,' she added, grimly. 'Recently, she seems . . . she seems to be more confused than ever, almost delusional.'

'It's the heat,' Cecily said, with a shrug of her shoulders, and quite dismissive to Sylvia's mind.

'No, it is not the heat. She's long used to that. No, there's something else. I know it. And my worry is . . .' she turned her head away and sighed. 'She's become so muddled about everything, her past, the details of her birth, her childhood. I'm not sure what, exactly, she told you, Cecily . . .'

Cecily stared back at her but said not a word.

'But the chances are it was fantasy. Fantasy,' she repeated.

'I see, and yet she didn't appear muddled to me, not about *that*, anyway. She remembered it all in great detail. But don't worry. I shan't break my promise. You have my word on that.'

At that moment Madeline appeared at the garden gate. Sylvia said hello, Cecily said goodbye, and Madeline said how much they were looking forward to dinner later.

Sylvia moved away, newly troubled.

It was not that she did not trust Cecily, not exactly. It was perfectly clear Cecily Chadwick could keep a secret. But her manner had been strange. She had been abrupt and decidedly reticent when Sylvia first caught up with her, almost as though she had been trying to get away from her. Is that why she had rushed from the hall? Had she in fact seen Sylvia before Sylvia had seen her? And why had Cora made no mention of Cecily's visit?

As she continued up the track, a sensation of estrangement enveloped her, and she paused at the top of the hill and caught her breath in a loud gasp. She was being sidelined, excluded, left out and cut out of Cora's story. And that Cora had spoken to Cecily – Cecily Chadwick, a nobody, a young slip of a thing she barely knew – about her life, her childhood, was incomprehensible. But the facts of the matter were simple enough: Cora had elected to confide in another the one thing she herself had been waiting a lifetime to hear, to have confirmed. 'And after everything I've done for her, everything she's promised me,' she whispered, walking on, her heart pounding. 'Does my loyalty and love count for nothing?'

She stopped. Questions sprang up in profusion, like the nettles on the side of the path, stinging her mind. *What* had Cora told Cecily? *Why* had she told Cecily? Was it possible that Cecily Chadwick knew more about Cora than she? What on earth was Cora playing at? After all, Cora had invited her down here for that very reason, to tell *her*! To once and for all explain the truth of events before she arrived in Rome.

She walked on. One thing was clear, an alliance had been formed, memories annexed, and Cora was now a protectorate of Cecily's.

'Cecily Chadwick!'

She stopped again. She needed to compose herself, needed to think things through. But the sense of betrayal was agony, *like a dagger plunged into my heart* she thought. Oh, but it was not her who was adrift, she reasoned, it was Cora who was adrift; drifting away from reason and sanity, away from a lifelong and tested friendship. Had I known, she thought, I should never have come . . . never have come.

She moved off the track, through the long grass towards the rotting timber of an old gate, placed her arms along its length and allowed her head to fall forward. The world was spinning and she with it. 'It's not jealousy . . . not jealousy,' she whispered, eyeing a spider weaving a silvery web around a wasp twice its size. Then she raised her head, wiped her mildew-covered hands on the skirt of her gown, and as she crouched down to reach through the gate for her hat, she heard a voice. 'Miss Dorland, is everything quite all right there?'

It was Mrs Moody, walking her goat.

'Yes, fine. I was just admiring the foliage and lost my hat,' she replied, pulling the boater through a gap in the gate and rising to her feet.

'Beautiful day for it,' Mrs Moody said, staring at the skirt of Sylvia's dark gown.

'Indeed . . . yet another.'

'Bernard and I always have a little stop here. You're standing on his grass,' she said, and laughed.

'And I must away. Cor— my friend will be waiting for me.'

'Oh, and how is her lay-ay-dyship?' Mrs Moody asked, jerked forward, towards the grass, by Bernard. 'The rector mentioned that she's not been herself of late. Troubled by the heat, he said. Well, I said, that doesn't make sense, not being that she lived abroad for so many years, but he said it takes a while to *climatise* and I suppose it's true enough. It happened to me when I went to Brighton, you know, and it was enough to—'

'I really must get on,' Sylvia interrupted, and as she turned away, Mrs Moody called after her.

'Do give her my regards . . . And tell her I know what it's like.'

Sylvia closed her eyes: *Mrs Moody sends you her best, and wishes you to know that she, too, has suffered climatisation.*

No, of course it wasn't the heat that was troubling Cora; it was laughable that anyone would think so. It was the situation she found herself in: having to come back to England and confront her past.

By the time Sylvia reached the laurel-lined driveway, she had made one decision. There was nothing else for it, she would have to speak to Jack.

Cora was in the garden. She sat upon a bench by an herbaceous border clutching the red, leather-bound volume of Byron's poems: the one George had given her, still with the dust of a pressed violet marking the page. She watched butterflies: tortoise-shells, peacocks, chalk-blues, and a single red admiral. It was safer to love these ephemeral things, she thought, than humans. Their lives were brief and fleeting but when they died there was no pain, no need for grief. They always came back, came back each year . . .

If only he could come back . . . if only I could go back.

185

She glanced about the garden. To think it had all been excavated and planted for her. And yet, how queer it was to be sitting in it, in England. That had never been her plan. Her plan had been to die in Rome, to be buried there, alongside George. But she had had to leave him, had had no choice, just as he had had no choice all those years before.

So many parallels . . .

'So many parallels,' she said out loud and sighed. She liked to think of the path of their lives – criss-crossing and overlapping – as synchronistic, and the events within them mirroring. But the only parallel had been each of their liaisons with people old enough to be their parents, although Cora had trumped his sixteen years with her thirty, and then trumped him again in her choice of third husband. If it had been a contest, Cora had certainly won, and by much more than a mile.

She thought his name, heard his voice: 'I have to go. It's a tremendous opportunity for me.'

Yes, it *had* been a tremendous opportunity, history had proved it so. And yet . . . and yet . . . George's opportunity had been the undoing of *them*, and the undoing of her. But fate had also conspired in the form of that wretched woman, Mrs Hillier. Without her, who knows what might have happened.

She glanced up to the heavens, wondering briefly, fleetingly, if dear George and Mrs H were reconciled there. *No, it was a . . . a business arrangement, a commercial partnership. There was nothing more to it. He told me so, told me so himself.*

And John Clifford had also told her, or had tried to, once, all those years ago. A pupil of Canova, Clifford had been considered Rome's finest sculptor, and his studio the liveliest in the city, a Mecca for all visiting English artists. It was the place Cora had first been exposed to long philosophical discussions and passionate political debate, which had in turn educated and informed her thinking. The gentle and paternalistic Clifford had taught her how to draw and, in quieter months when the city's many visitors returned home and only those who had no desire to be anywhere else remained within its walls, Cora had spent hours listening to his anecdotes and reminiscences of how Rome 'used to be'.

Cora's aunt had, initially, been concerned at the amount of time Cora spent in the company of artists. She had been agitated about the morality of a *mal entourée* whose sole occupation seemed to be the pursuit of pleasure. But Clifford had reassured her, told her not to worry, that he would keep an eye on young Cora.

In his self-deprecating way Clifford liked to allude to a vague and unrequited love in his life but it was commonly accepted that he had no great desire for requited love; he appeared ambivalent in matters of the heart, indifferent to the opposite sex. But for Cora, his position as unattached observer gave him an advantage others could not possibly have.

187

'My dear, George is not the man for you,' he said. 'He is simply not a man for marrying, or for belonging to anyone. He is married to his art.'

'And what of Mrs Hillier?' she asked.

'Mrs Hillier? Mrs Hillier is a married woman, and almost old enough to be his mother.'

'But George spends so much of his time with her.'

Even then, she was aware that she sounded like a lovestruck jealous child, but she did not care. Clifford was a dear and trusted friend, and she knew he would not repeat their conversation. She also knew that what he so enjoyed was the knowledge that he was trusted with such tender secrets.

'Yes, but she is his advocate and patron now. Thanks to Mrs Hillier, dear George has made some fine connections, and will have some worthwhile commissions, of that I'm sure.' He looked from Cora to his easel. 'He knows it's perfectly safe to spend time with her. She is married, unavailable, but more importantly, perhaps, he knows there is no danger of falling in love with her.'

Cora stepped down from the upturned crate and, wrapping a sheet around her body, moved towards Clifford, looking over his shoulder at the sketches for his 'Tinted Venus'.

He went on; 'Mrs Hillier's a delightful lady, a sophisticate, and undoubtedly accomplished, but the relationship she and George share is platonic, I'm quite certain of that. They share passions but not for each other, and their . . . their friendship is mutually advantageous. George needs

Mrs Hillier to be his champion, and she needs him for . . . reflected glory. She has the contacts and the influence, not only in London but here in Rome and in Paris, too. Think about it. George is a very clever fellow. By Jupiter, he is!'

'But you're inferring that George is using Mrs Hillier to promote himself, to further his career.'

'He's ambitious, Cora, very ambitious, and determined to prove himself, particularly to his father. And that means being successful and selling pictures! Dear George, perhaps more than any of us, feels a need – nay, a pressure – to be accepted and successful, to make money. And, sadly for you, my dear, his compass directs him to Mrs Hillier.'

George had already spoken to her about his father, and at some length. Mr Lawson Senior had wanted George to follow in his footsteps and study architecture. He had told his son that only a very tiny proportion of painters, only the most God-given talented ones, ever made any money at it. 'All he cares about, or seems to care about, is that I have a profession, a noble profession – oh, and that I marry well,' George told her.

'Marry well?'

'Yes, marry someone of standing, someone *known*, someone he approves of.' He glanced to Cora and added, 'But if I really cared what *he* thought, would I be here in Rome, would I be painting?'

'He does not care what his father thinks,' Cora said to Clifford. 'I know, he's told me.'

Clifford smiled at her. 'But what he says and what he does may differ. Particularly where you're concerned.'

Despite her misgivings, despite Clifford's words – was it a warning? – Cora held on to her fantasy. John Clifford was an old man and love had passed him by. She and George shared something – something different, something private, something no one else would understand. They were going to travel together, live like gypsies, and while he produced art, she would produce his sons and daughters. They might never be rich, but they would have enough, he said, and that *enough* was more than enough for Cora.

Cora winced. She did not wish to recall that time, nor what came immediately after. She preferred to remember those last few months together. How perfect it had been, despite the ticking of the clock. 'How it could have been, how it should have been.'

He had said, 'Tell me you love me, and kiss me . . . kiss me goodbye.'

Yes, that was what he said.

'I love you but I shall never ever say goodbye to you, George.'

'Not even after I am gone?'

'No, not even then . . . not ever.'

She had held on to his hand, listening to his breathing, watching his eyes flicker and close, and open and close.

'I shall bring you violets,' she had said, 'every

day. I shall sit with you, talk to you . . . tell you all the things I never told you. And then, at the end, I'll be there. I shall be there with you for all eternity.'

'For all eternity,' she heard him say now, and repeated it with him.

But in the distance she could hear another voice, and through a pathway in the rhododendrons she spotted Sylvia on the driveway, talking – it seemed – to herself. She smiled. Always busy on a new plot, she thought. She called out and Sylvia stopped, and then looked about her with an expression of panic. She appeared rather flushed, quite wrung out, Cora thought. But when Sylvia finally located Cora, her expression altered, and she smiled as though in relief and waved back. She then made her way through the bushes, lowering her head as she passed under a tangled archway. And as she stepped down on to the grass, Cora thought she heard her mutter something about a ditch.

'There is no ditch, dear, not there.'

In her room, Cecily was still seething.

She lay upon her bed staring up at the sloping ceiling, unable to stop the sequence of images of *them*, together, larking about in boats, motoring down wide city streets, posing for the camera. Like picture postcards, they laughed and smiled back at her from each one, with Sonia in the foreground, smiling broadly and calling out to her, 'Hell-o-o, Cecily, look who I am with!'

Oh God, the agony! How could he? How could he have been with *her*?

It had been at the Sale of Work in the village hall that Sonia had told her about London. She had only just returned, she said, had been there for a few days, helping her mother select furnishings for their new Knightsbridge apartment.

'And so we came back on the train with him,' she said, glancing at Cecily. 'Well, we bumped into him travelling up there, you see, so I saw quite a bit of him, and his friend, Noel . . . so charming. And the coincidence is, Noel's parents keep an apartment in the same building as mine! Can you imagine? I'm sure you'll meet him at some stage. I rather think he said he might drive down here sometime. He has his own motorcar . . . Oh, it was a hoot! We motored all over London, up the Mall, through Trafalgar Square, with Noel and Jack pretending we were tourists and calling out to people in French . . .'

She went on and on. Then she said, 'And yesterday evening, Millie Compton – my oldest, bestest friend from school – Noel, Jack and I took a boat out on the Serpentine. Oh, it was heavenly! We had a picnic, and naughty Noel brought along two bottles of champagne! Can you imagine? I was almost blotto!'

'Real champagne?' Annie asked, and Cecily could have kicked her.

'Oh my dear, the best, the very best *real* champagne. And rather potent stuff too, I can tell you.'

She threw her head back and affected a laugh. Then she leaned over the table in front of them and whispered, 'Poor Jack was quite fuddled by the end of the evening, he had something of a sore head this morning.' And then she did another of her silent laughs.

Cecily had picked up her basket, turned to Annie and said she hadn't realised the time, and before either girl could speak, she marched off out of the hall.

She could barely remember the walk home, so angry had she been. Then Sylvia Dorland had appeared out of nowhere, wittering on about the sale and some silly bookmark she had bought for Cora. At first, she had not listened to a word Sylvia said. She had been picturing the London foursome, lounging on rugs and sipping champagne, and Sonia tossing her head about in that way she did. She had been wondering who was paired with whom: Jack and Sonia, or Jack and Miss Millie Compton? Wondering if Jack Staunton had wrapped his fuddled arms around Sonia, for she had freely admitted that she had been blotto.

But then Sylvia said something about Cora being muddled, and had given her such a queer look; and she realised almost immediately Sylvia's concern. So she had quietly reassured Sylvia, and given her word. Now she wondered if Sylvia had actually come looking for her on Cora's instruction. For it seemed odd to her that Sylvia would say such things about her friend, almost disloyal.

More likely, she mused, that Cora regretted their conversation of earlier that week, and had asked Sylvia, devoted as she undoubtedly was, to ensure that she, Cecily, kept to her promise. But what about the people at Meadow Farm? Was she still to pursue her line of enquiry and find out who they were and where they hailed from? Why on earth does she want to know about them anyway?

'What does it matter?' she said out loud. 'We're simply the poor neighbours, briefly dazzled – like everyone else.'

She sat up on her bed. She would not let Jack Staunton know. No, she must not give away so much as an inkling that she knew or cared about his sojourn in London. It would be so obvious, so cheap. And jealousy was a low emotion, possibly the lowest, along with envy and greed. And pride? Hmm. She was not sure about pride. But now was not the time to ponder upon pride, she decided. The facts of the matter were simple enough: if Sonia Brownlow was his cup of tea, she had misjudged him, overestimated him.

No, she would not give away anything to anyone from now on.

She rose to her feet feeling resolute and strong. Tonight was definitely the night to wear the turquoise silk chiffon.

CHAPTER 10

Cecily stood with her mother and Sylvia in Cora's drawing room.

'Oh yes, a remarkable life,' Sylvia was saying, addressing Madeline Chadwick but with her gaze fixed on Cecily, 'and we've known each other *almost* our entire lives.'

She had been explaining to Madeline that she was to write the final part of the countess's memoirs, and, in case Madeline was in any doubt, that this was indeed a great honour.

Minutes earlier, the maid had led Cecily and her mother through the hallway, past the painting, which Cecily saw Madeline raise her eyebrows at, telling them that the countess would be 'down shortly'. She had shown them into the room, moved to a table and, without asking, poured each of them a small glass of sherry from a decanter. Madeline, who rarely drank alcohol, took the glass and said thank you. Cecily could tell that her mother was nervous, apprehensive. For Madeline glanced about the room like a hungry animal, keen to take it all in before the countess or anyone else appeared, and sipping perhaps too frequently from her glass. Cecily had watched her mother's eyes move from the polished curves of one sculpture to another, and across the walls from one naked breast to another.

'And these are the countess's sons,' Cecily said, pointing out the cameos to her mother. 'And that is the Comte de Chevalier de Saint Léger,' she added, gesturing to a portrait. 'And that one is Cora when she was young.'

'Cora?' Madeline blinked, taking another sip.

'Oh yes, she asked me to call her by her given name.'

Sylvia appeared, wearing the same dark grey dress they had seen her in earlier, and just as though she had heard Cecily's last words, she requested that they dispense with formalities, abandon the Miss Dorland, and simply address her as Sylvia.

Looking at Cecily, who had pinned up her hair and wore a gown of pale turquoise silk chiffon, Sylvia went on, 'We have no secrets, of course, dearest Cora and I. When two people have known each other as long as we have, well . . .' she shrugged.

Seconds later, Jack entered the room. He wore a tuxedo, with a wing-collared shirt and white bow tie, and was more dashing than any man Cecily could recall ever having seen. Still busy fastening a cufflink at his wrist, he smiled at Cecily. 'Good evening, ladies,' he said, moving into the room. His hair was damp and slicked back, and his face more tanned than it had been earlier that week when Cecily had last seen him, when they had loitered at the garden gate in silence, exchanging smiles.

Cecily introduced her mother. He shook her hand, said he was honoured to meet her, and Madeline flushed. 'Please, do sit down,' he said.

'I'm sure Sylvia's already explained, my grand-mother sometimes takes quite a while to dress for dinner. It's a ritual, a lifelong ritual,' he said, looking from Cecily to her mother and then back to Cecily. Madeline drained her glass, and he sprang to his feet, took the glass and refilled it.

'I heard you weren't feeling awfully well earlier,' Cecily said, looking towards a sculpture upon a plinth in an alcove.

He frowned, shook his head. 'No, I'm feeling tip-top, actually.'

She turned to him. 'Not too much champagne then?'

'Cecily!' Madeline gasped.

'Sonia seems to think you were quite fuddled by it.'

'Cecily!'

'You and naughty Noel and silly Millie . . .'

'Really, dear, whatever's come over you?'

'I'm just ragging Jack, Mother. Aren't I, Jack?'

He smiled. 'It would seem so.'

Cecily turned to her mother: 'Jack and a few others, including dear Sonia, were partying up in London yesterday. I saw Sonia earlier and she was telling me *all* about it,' she added, forcing a smile and glancing at Jack. Then she put down her glass and stood up. 'Do please excuse me a moment.'

She walked out into the hallway, her head spinning, angry with herself, and then continued on down the passage to the veranda. The sherry made her feel hotter than ever and she stood in the open doorway fanning herself with her hand. Nothing ever went as she planned; she had certainly not planned that. The plan had simply been to look as lovely as possible whilst appearing as indifferent as possible. 'Stupid, stupid girl,' she whispered. She moved out on to the veranda and glanced about in the vain hope that Cora might have been there earlier and left her packet of Best Venetians lying out. Then, like a miracle from above, she saw a plume of smoke rise up from behind a hedge.

'Yoo-hoo! Hello, excuse me,' she said, moving across the terrace.

A man's head appeared.

'You're Mr Cordery, aren't you?'

'That I am, miss.'

'You don't happen to have a spare cigarette, do you?'

'Yer not really a smoker, are you?' he said, holding the match to her, watching her.

'No, I'm a beginner,' she said flatly, finally getting the thing alight.

She walked back to the veranda and stood on

the steps, picking bits of tobacco from her lips. The cigarette made her head spin more, made her feel more out of control.

'Bloody stupid!'

'What's that?'

It was Jack.

'I hadn't realised you smoked,' he said, moving alongside her.

'I don't.'

'I see.'

She caught his smile.

'It's gone out,' he said. 'Would you like me to fetch you another?'

'No. No, thank you,' she replied, tossing the thing into a nearby shrub. And as she turned to him, she saw him quickly look away. 'Is it funny?' she asked.

'Are you angry about something?'

'You don't answer a question with a question, Jack. Anyhow, we'd better go back inside, we've left my mother on her own with Sylvia.'

'My grandmother's with them, and they'll be fine. Probably best for them to have a moment without us.'

She looked away, across the terrace, across the tops of the trees.

He said, 'You're looking very nice tonight.'

'Thank you.'

'But you seem different . . . different to how you were on Tuesday.'

'Hmm, well, a lot can happen in four days.'

She felt his hand on her arm, her bare arm, his skin touching hers. 'What's happened? Tell me?'

She pulled her arm away, moved along the step. 'It's not . . . it's not about me and Sonia . . . or silly Noel or whatever it was you were referring to just now, is it?'

There was nothing for it; she had crossed a point, a point of no return, and she would have to ask. She turned to face him, took a deep breath . . .

'Please, tell me what it is?' he said, now frowning, looking into her eyes.

Oh dear, it was tempting, so tempting. *He* was tempting. And right at that moment she wished she could tell him everything – all of it, everything about her – from beginning to end; for him to know and understand her . . .

'And this is the veranda . . . ah, hello, children.'

It was Cora, leading Madeline, obviously giving her a guided tour of the place.

Cecily exhaled, loudly; and Jack swiftly stepped down from the step, on to the terrace.

'Dear Cecily!' said Cora, reaching out to her, taking hold of her hands, and then kissing her upon each cheek. 'And my word, what a vision!' she gasped, stepping back. She turned to Cecily's mother. 'Madeline, you must be very proud to have a daughter like Cecily . . .'

Madeline, Cecily thought: that hadn't taken long. No one called her mother by her first name. How had that happened so fast? She glanced towards her mother, who looked a little pink in the face and was shrugging her shoulders like a bashful schoolgirl. And then she turned to Jack, who smiled back at her knowingly.

'I'm giving your mama a little tour, Cecily dear, and then we shall dine,' Cora said, turning away. And as she disappeared back through the doorway and into the house, she said in a loud whisper, 'No wonder poor darling Jack's so distracted.' And Cecily saw him close his eyes and bite his lip.

For a moment he didn't speak, and neither did she. They could hear the two women's voices echoing down the long passageway. And as they slowly faded, he sighed.

'Madeline!' Cecily said.

'Mm. I knew it was best to let them get on with it. My grandmother has a way with people.'

She caught his gaze stray from her face to her body. But as he turned away, his awkwardness struck her, and she felt guilty. For hadn't she pushed him? And wasn't he lovely? Wasn't he perfect?

She stepped down from the veranda, sat on the step and looked up at him. 'Did you get drunk in London then?'

He ran a hand over his hair. 'A little,' he replied.

'Was that why you were angry?'

She tried to laugh. 'No. Of course not!'

He sat down next to her. 'So, are you going to tell me? I think you were about to – a moment ago.'

She shuffled, fiddling with the soft fabric of her gown, and as she leaned forward, flicking at the dust on the toes of her satin shoes, she said, 'I . . . well, I . . .'

'Yes?'

'Yes,' she repeated, absently.

Then she heard the smile in his voice as he said, 'Come on, you've got to tell me now.'

'Now, I'm not sure.'

'Not sure of what?'

She turned her head towards him, his knees. 'Did you . . . did you . . .'

He leaned forward, tilting his head, levelling his gaze with hers. 'Did I get drunk? Yes, a little. Did I flirt with Sonia Brownlow? No. Did I flirt with Millie Compton? No. Would I ever want to? No.'

She stared back at him and didn't speak.

'Does that answer everything?' he asked.

She nodded.

'Is that what it was all about – in there, out here, is that it?'

For a moment she wished she wasn't there, wished she were invisible. She shut her eyes, opened them again, and he was still smiling at her, a different sort of smile, one she hadn't seen before.

'How could you possibly think I'd be remotely attracted to someone like Sonia Brownlow? Do I appear desperate?'

She laughed. 'No, no. But she, Sonia, has,' she shrugged, 'her ways.'

'*Her ways*? Short of wearing a placard, I'm not

sure what else she could do to advertise her ways.' He paused and Cecily laughed again. 'And let me tell you, her friend Millie is rather a knockout too. But perhaps slightly thicker built – in brain *and* body.'

And at last she unfolded herself and sat up, smiling now at the spectacle of the London four-some. 'But why did you go about with them, you and your friend, if they were so ghastly?'

'It was all set up by the delightful Mrs Brownlow and Noel's mother – you know how they do. Let's get the young people together, sort of thing. Anyway, as it turned out, it was quite a laugh. I don't suppose Sonia told you that she fell into the Serpentine.'

'No!' Cecily shrieked.

'Yes, truly,' he said, beginning to laugh. 'She was trying to step out of the boat – and I don't think Noel did it on purpose, he swears he didn't – but the boat suddenly moved away from the pier and Sonia . . .' he was laughing, struggling to get the words out, 'Sonia almost did the splits before going in!' He wiped away tears. 'It was so funny . . . you'd have died. She managed to keep her hair dry, but she wasn't at all happy when we finally dragged her out . . .'

They sat giggling for some minutes, and every so often he added to the story, offering Cecily another comic detail. Then he said, 'I so wished you'd been there. Noel and I were fit to explode by the time we dropped her home. Every time she moved about the leather seat in Noel's motor, there was a squelching sound, and she apologised!'

She felt his hand graze the middle of her back, his palm rest flat there. He said, 'So you see, you have nothing to be angry about. There's only one girl I'm interested in.'

And though she said nothing, did not look at him and made no reply, she wanted to. She wanted to hear him say her name. She wanted confirmation. But the moment passed. He moved his hand away and moved on. He asked her if she had been writing, and she told him that she had. She told him of her idea for a novel, inspired, she said, by Cora's life overseas. Then the gong sounded. And as he rose to his feet, he offered her his hand. 'Cecily.'

In years to come, Cecily would return to that evening, his words, his smile – and even the sound of the gong. She would relive it again and again, because it was a beginning, *the beginning*. Everything that had happened in her life up until that point had been a prelude to that moment, moving her forward, leading her to that touch, that smile, those words. Her life had arrived. She could see the future, the possibilities, and she could see Jack Staunton walking towards her from each and every horizon.

Dinner was a success, Cora charm itself, if a little distracted from time to time. It was, Cecily thought, as though the past was still with her; as though those she spoke of were there, in that room. Once or twice Cecily followed her gaze, turning her head towards the baize door, the wall, the salamander, as though she, too, would be able to see something, someone standing there. At one point she was sure she had seen Cora nod and then raise her hand, just as if she was dismissing someone from the room. But no one was there.

Cora spoke of Rome and Paris, relishing a few well-worn anecdotes that Cecily had heard once and Jack and Sylvia perhaps tenfold but that Madeline had not yet heard. They all laughed at her reminiscences of the mischievous antics of her young sons, specifically Jack's father, Georgie. And she spoke once more of her aunt, a woman of impossible glamour and style, it seemed, who had been such an influence over her life – a mother to her, she said. But when Madeline enquired about her mother, her real mother, Cecily saw that veil of melancholy descend once more. She had simply been too beautiful for this life, Cora replied.

All through dinner Cecily and Jack exchanged smiles as though they had a secret, which they did. For hadn't he said there was only one girl for him? And so, though Cecily heard the conversation and joined in from time to time, and though she ate some of the hors d'oeuvres and a little of the clear velouté, the roast pigeon and then the meringues with fruit and whipped cream were barely tasted. All she could think of were those words, that *one girl*.

But when Sylvia leaned towards her and said,

'It's awfully nice that you and Jack have become friends,' and then added, 'But it's such a shame that he won't be here for very much longer,' she felt her heart sink, and knew Sylvia was reminding her. And at the end of dinner, as they all filed out of the dining room, when Cora stood in the doorway, saying, 'Oh Cecily, do please wait here with me a moment,' Cecily was sure it was going to be about Jack; that Cora, too, perhaps wished to remind her of the opportunity he had ahead of him; that nothing should stand in his way; that attachments were superfluous at this stage in his life. And as the others disappeared from the room, she was already practising one line: *I understand everything.*

So when Cora whispered to her, barely audible, and beginning, 'I don't wish to put you under any pressure, dear, but I need to warn you about *him*,' Cecily was already nodding, already saying, 'I understand everything.' She failed to hear the last two words of Cora's sentence: *John Abel*. And, intoxicated by the evening, the wine, the words, the possibilities, and the giddy feeling that others – in their concern and warnings – had her best interests at heart, she went on, adding, 'Sylvia has already spoken to me about him and I understand.'

'Sylvia?' Cora sounded surprised.

'Yes. She didn't need to say a lot, and neither do you.'

'I see,' said Cora. 'Well, it seems dear Sylvia is ahead of me – in all things.'

'And don't worry, I shan't say anything to him.'

Cora appeared aghast. 'I should hope *not*. He must know nothing. Nothing at all!'

It was then, at that moment, Cecily noticed her eyes – intense and glistening, bright with tears. And so she reached out and took hold of Cora's hands. She said, 'I was not expecting . . .' then she paused, searching for the right words. 'You must remember that up until quite recently I had no idea of his or your existence . . .' she shrugged. 'Neither of you were here, in Bramley. And yet, you and he and all of this has changed me, and changed the way I see the world. But I know, I understand, the timing. I *do* understand.'

Cora closed her eyes. 'Well then, we should perhaps leave it be.'

'But there's one thing, one thing I must tell you,' Cecily said. 'He'd quite like to know more about you, simply in order to understand who he is.'

'Who *he* is?' Cora repeated. 'No,' she said emphatically. She shook her head. 'I'm afraid it cannot be.' Then she released Cecily's hands and walked away, into the hallway and then on into the drawing room. Cecily followed her. As she entered the room, Jack stood up. He helped himself to two of Cora's Venetian cigarettes and asked Cecily if she'd care to join him. And so they returned to the veranda and sat down side by side in wicker chairs, looking out over the pale evening sky.

He smiled as he asked her, 'So, are you going

to tell me what it was my grandmother wished to speak to you about?'

She turned and smiled at him when she said, 'No.'

He sighed. 'Secrets, eh? Do all women keep secrets?'

'Hmm, possibly . . . probably, but I imagine men do too.'

He laughed. 'Well, I don't but I suppose there's still time for me to accumulate a few.'

'Plenty of time.'

'And no doubt at Cambridge . . .'

'No doubt.'

'I'll be going off there in a matter of weeks.'

'Yes, I know.'

'I have to go up before term starts to sort out lodgings, that sort of thing.'

She nodded.

'Will you go back to the school? Continue teaching?' he asked.

She shrugged. 'I suppose so.' Then she said, 'Oh well, it'll be Christmas before we know it.'

He looked down at the ground. 'I'm not sure I'll be here at Christmas. I've been invited to Neufchatel. Noel's parents have a place there . . . and I've sort of said yes.'

'How wonderful.'

He turned to her. 'But I'll definitely be back here next Easter.'

She stared ahead. 'I may be travelling then.'

'Really? You're going away?'

'Oh yes. Did I not tell you? I'm going away with my aunt.'

'No,' he shook his head. 'You never said.'

'Yes. France, Germany, Austria, Switzerland . . . and Italy, too, I think.'

'So you'll be away for some time?'

'Mm.'

After a while he said, 'Will you come out for a spin with me? You really must, you know. Not tonight, of course, but perhaps tomorrow, or . . . Monday?'

'Monday . . . I'm not sure.'

'Well, think about it. I'll take you out from here, we can go down the cinder track.'

When they returned to the drawing room, Madeline was already on her feet. The light was fading, she said, and they must get home before darkness fell. Then they all shook hands, and a maid appeared to show them to the door.

Cecily did not hear a word her mother said as they walked home. In the space of a few hours she had been raised up into that pink and orange sky – then dropped. Or that's how it felt. For now she saw only the long winter ahead. She saw time stretching out – the months, seasons and years to come – and herself slowly shrivelling, shrinking, drying up; withering in Bramley. And she saw Jack Staunton in a place called Cambridge, surrounded by impossibly glamorous and erudite young people, and beautiful young women. She felt such a fool. What on earth had made her think that he could ever be interested in someone who had been nowhere and done nothing?

As her mother closed the front door, she said, 'Oh, Ethne must be back,' but already Cecily was halfway up the stairs pulling the pins from her hair; already she saw herself as the *one girl* who had gone overdressed to dinner.

CHAPTER 11

When Sylvia found the small brown envelope on the table in the drawing room, the first thing that struck her was that it was in the wrong place. Unopened post belonged on the silver salver on the hallway table. Cora only moved letters from there when she was ready to open them, and then always at her desk. This letter, Sylvia could see, remained sealed, unopened. Picking it up, she noted the hand, small and somewhat malnourished, and the strange spelling. But people had forever been confounded by the name, and Cora was used to being addressed in a variety of fashions (once, Sylvia could recall Cora telling her, even 'Her Royal Highness' had prefixed the misspelt name). But this was a brown envelope which, upon feeling it, contained nothing more than a flimsy, insubstantial sheet. A bill? Perhaps. Turning the envelope, Sylvia could see that it was not properly sealed, easy enough to open. But as she lifted it up to the lamp, leaning forward to examine it further, the door opened.

To Sylvia's mind Cora overreacted. She was not snooping, not at all. She was simply concerned that this was yet another of those wretched letters. And she wished nothing more than to protect her friend. But oh, how Cora had gone on, saying that Sylvia had no right to be 'prowling' about the place, rifling through her papers and letters. What was it, exactly, that she was looking for? she asked, sounding angrier than Sylvia had ever heard her. But she gave Sylvia no opportunity to reply, for she went on, saying, 'Had I known you wished to play detective whilst here I should never have invited you.'

Sylvia tried a number of times to speak, to explain, but Cora would not stop. 'You were about to open that envelope, Sylvia, I saw you. No, don't even try to deny it. I was here, standing right here in the doorway, watching you. Do you wish me to read it to you? Do you wish me to read every one of my letters to you? Is that what you want? Must I show you every single part of me, my life? Am I to be allowed no privacy at all? And all of you . . . all of you crowding in on me, demanding answers . . . wanting to know everything, every tiny detail!'

Her breathing, always a problem, had become quite rapid and she raised a hand to her chest as the words tumbled forth. Her face was flushed, shining, and strands of her white hair stuck flat to her brow, wet and dark. When she finally sat down, breathless and still clearly agitated, she grimaced as though in pain, and Sylvia rushed to her side and laid her hand upon her forehead.

'You have a temperature, dear. A fever,' she said, reaching for the bell on the wall. 'We must get you to your bed.'

Cora remained silent as Sylvia led her upstairs to her room, cooing words of contrition. 'You should know by now I'd never do any thing to hurt you . . . only your best interests at heart . . . always have . . . always have.'

When Cora's maid appeared, Sylvia moved aside and stepped out of the room into the lobby. She could hear Cora saying something about it all being too much for her, and the maid softly hushing and fussing. When the maid finally emerged through the doorway, Sylvia stepped back into the lamplit room to say goodnight.

'Don't think I don't know . . . I know everything,' Cora said, without looking at Sylvia. She was not lying flat and not quite upright, but propped by a multitude of white linen pillows, against which her hair, now plaited in two thick ropes, all but disappeared. In the great galleon of a bed she suddenly appeared very small, Sylvia thought, small and frightened. And it was the same fearful look Sylvia recalled having seen before, a very long time ago.

'You've been talking about me to Cecily . . . talking about *him*.'

'Him?' Sylvia repeated. She presumed Cora meant George. 'I most certainly have not,' she replied. 'But that girl is determined, oh yes, you mark my words.'

'You're all determined . . . won't be satisfied until I've lost my senses and been committed . . . like her, and like John Abel.'

Sylvia stood at the end of the bed. She ran her hands over the sheet. 'Hush now, you must rest, dear. I shall tell Jack that—'

'You shall tell Jack nothing,' Cora said, fixing her eyes on Sylvia.

'All I meant was—'

'You shall tell Jack nothing,' she said again.

Sylvia hovered, watching Cora's hands plucking at the bedcover.

'You were always there for me, weren't you, Sylvia?'

'Yes, indeed I was, and I still am.'

'Yes, always there for me . . . always able to tell me about George's new lover, the very latest rumour.'

'Aha, so that's what this is all about. You've been remembering Evie Dip—'

'No! Don't say it! I don't want that name uttered in this room! I don't want to hear that name now or ever again.'

Sylvia had been the one to tell Cora, the one who had written to her in Paris of the Dipple Affair. She wrote to Cora that she had heard from various 'reliable' sources that George had become *quite obsessed* with his latest sitter. She had mentioned the girl's age, telling Cora that it was *the talk of all London*.

'But I had no intention of . . .' Sylvia began and

then stopped. There was no point. Cora was, Sylvia thought, delirious, quite delirious. So she simply bid her friend goodnight. But as she turned to close the bedroom door she heard Cora mutter something about *revenge*.

'I'm sorry, I didn't quite catch that,' she said.

'It wasn't revenge . . . my marriage, it was never about revenge . . .'

'Of course,' she replied. 'Goodnight, dear.'

Minutes later, when Sylvia eventually located Jack, sitting on the candlelit veranda, doing nothing but staring out into the dusk, she stopped in her tracks and stood perfectly still for a moment, struck once again by the likeness. The profile could be him, she thought: George, before he grew his beard. And she could not help but wonder if it was in fact Jack's presence that was tipping Cora. For how must it feel to have him there? The only one left, all she had left: a constant reminder.

She sat down beside him, explained to him that Cora had retired for the evening and that she was not at all well. She was concerned, she said, for her well-being and for her state of mind. But like all young people, it seemed to her, he was distracted, and spoke only in short sentences containing those ubiquitous words – *age* and *heat*.

'She has a fever, Jack. She was quite delirious. I wasn't going to mention it to you, I don't want to worry you, but . . . she accused me of spying, snooping on her.'

He turned to her. 'Do you think we should send for the doctor first thing in the morning?'

'I'm not sure. She hates doctors, has never had any time for them. I told her that she should remain in her bed tomorrow. Her room is cool . . . I think she needs to rest.'

'You're a very good friend to her, Sylvia,' he said.

She could have told him things then, could have told him how betrayed and hurt she felt, how very odd Cecily Chadwick had been with her the other day, her suspicions about that girl, and about Mr Fox. And she could have told him about the letters, and about George Lawson, and Edward. But when he yawned, stretched out his legs, then turned to her and said, 'You know, Cecily writes. She's working on a novel,' Sylvia simply smiled.

He sat up in his chair. 'She wants to write a book based on Cora's life.'

She stared ahead. 'Oh, really? I rather thought that was my role.'

'Ah, no, nothing like a memoir. A sort of mix of fact and fiction, I suppose, something *loosely* based on her life. I think she's made quite a few notes, has begun working on it.'

'Well, well.'

'I thought you might take a look. I told her I'd ask you . . .'

Sylvia rose to her feet.

She was not a violent person, had never struck or been struck by anyone, but right at that moment, had Cecily Chadwick been there, she thought she might very well have slapped her. She said, 'Oh, I shall have to see, Jack. I'm rather busy, as you know, with your grandmother's memoirs, and finishing off my own novel.'

Jack nodded.

He was not to know, she thought. He was innocent in all of this. But as she moved towards the doorway back into the house, another thought came to her, and she stopped and turned to him. 'As a special favour to you, I shall take a look at Cecily's book, the one she's writing about Cora's life. It makes sense for me to see it. After all, I *was* there.'

'Thank you, Sylvia,' he said, smiling.

Upstairs, Cora had returned to Italy.

She dreamt of that time so long ago, when George announced, 'I have to go. It's a tremendous opportunity for me.' And she was young and she was desperate, and she was begging him to stay in Rome with her. He said, 'I'll be back, I promise. I'll be back in the autumn.'

It was shortly after George's departure that Cora married Jack Staunton, her aunt's stepson. She gave birth to Freddie five months later. George did not return to Rome; already, by then, he was famous and much in demand. The Queen had bought his 'Madonna', Cora read in the English newspapers. And it was via those newspapers she caught up on the events in his life, often weeks after they had happened. From time to time she received first-hand reports: he had attended some party, been present at someone's wedding, been in Paris, or Florence, or Munich, but not Rome, never Rome. She heard that he moved within the highest echelons of English society, was a regular dinner guest at Buckingham Palace, counted dukes and duchesses amongst his closest friends, was courted and feted, and hailed as 'England's greatest living painter'. Royal patronage, it seemed, had catapulted him into a different stratosphere.

And she had heard the gossip, the rumours about the women in his life. But those whom he chose to escort and appear in public with, and those he allegedly entertained in private were quite different.

She pictured him, then, in glittering company, and wondered if he ever thought of her, ever wished her by his side. And sometimes, lost in a daydream, she allowed herself to indulge in fantasy once more. She imagined herself with him, standing under a bright chandelier. 'Your Grace,' he would say, holding on to her hand, 'I don't believe you've met my wife . . .'

She had not been angry, could never be angry with him. He had not known. And he could not know, not then, not ever, that she had given birth to his son. Aunt Fanny had said so, and had dealt with the crisis swiftly. She had spoken to her husband, and the marriage had been arranged within weeks. Freddie came early, Fanny told everyone, though Cora knew there was gossip.

And the gossip continued about George, also.

His relationship with his patron, Mrs Hillier, the woman who had introduced him to society in Rome and was his most devoted advocate and champion, had come under scrutiny. It was reported that the two were inseparable, that the married lady, some years George's senior, was always at his side, and that her husband turned a blind eye. It was reported that the two travelled together frequently to Paris, and that Mrs Hillier, a former opera singer, acted as hostess at the many dinners and musical soirees at George's home in London. Some suggested that George Lawson was using the well-connected older lady, that his ambition knew no bounds, and that his success was in no small way due to Mrs H's introductions.

But Amy Hillier had long dazzled everyone in Rome, particularly Cora's aunt. An invitation to one of her musical soirees had become a highly sought-after ticket of entry to the exclusive expatriate set. It had been at Mrs Hillier's sumptuous home on the Pincio Hill, with its long windows and sunset-coloured walls, that Cora had first met George, though she had heard his name before that day, heard that George Lawson, the most promising English painter in a lifetime, had come to Rome.

She and George had spoken together only briefly that night, although they had exchanged many glances. Mrs Hillier barely left his side. It was just as Cora's aunt had predicted when she said, 'Mrs Hillier has a new raison d'être: his name is George

Lawson.' That evening Cora had been introduced to any number of people: various English aristocrats wintering in Rome, politicians, Austrian and Italian counts and countesses, and a coterie of English and American artists and writers. And she was introduced to George's father as well, who had been passing through Rome on his way to Greece. It was also the first time Cora had heard the famous diva, Mrs Hillier, sing, though she had heard tell of the exquisiteness of her voice, and would later say that it was Mrs Hillier's *bel canto* that finally stirred her from an adolescent slumber.

Some years later, when Mrs Hillier returned to Rome with her husband, Cora found herself once more on the Pincio Hill, when she and her aunt were invited to tea. She learnt that George was working in Florence. Mrs Hillier had visited him en route to Rome and spoke of him at some length, saying that she was worried about his health; that he worked much too hard and had had such problems with his eyes. Cora's aunt nodded sympathetically throughout, then asked, 'And will we see him here in Rome?' But Mrs Hillier said not. He would be returning to London from Florence, she said, glancing at Cora.

It was in fact Cora's aunt who insisted she take up Mrs Hillier's invitation to join her house party at Lucca. And the doctor had already suggested that a change of environment would be good for her. He told Cora that her melancholia was due to nothing more than a sensitive disposition. And he suggested to her that another baby would set things right.

But how could there be another baby? Jack never touched her, had no desire to touch her. He was sometimes kind and affectionate, and he undoubtedly loved little Freddie, but he was not and never had been her lover. Their marriage had been arranged, hastily arranged. It was not what a marriage should be. And she told him so, in their increasingly frequent whispered arguments. He said, 'But what more do you want? I've given you my name.'

She was – she had known from the start – simply the wrong sex for Jack's tastes. And yet she was grateful to him, for though the marriage was a sham, a respectable sham, he had married her and given her son his name. Whilst Jack's father remained in denial, oblivious to his daughter-in-law's predicament, Cora's aunt knew. 'One can't have everything,' she told Cora, alluding vaguely to her niece's circumstances. 'And you should consider yourself fortunate, very fortunate. You have a husband *and* a child you love.' A passionless life was, it seemed, the price to be paid for a youthful intoxication, the penalty for having loved outside convention.

When Cora spoke of the excursion to Lucca to her husband, he had been his usual distracted and dismissive self. 'Yes, why not? You should go,' he said, without looking up from the *Giornale di Roma*.

There had been no mention of George when Mrs Hillier first suggested the trip, though Cora had privately wondered if he would be there, if he would join the party. Two days before she was due to leave Rome, she discovered that George was to meet up with them at Florence and come on with them to Lucca.

It would be their first meeting in almost four years.

CHAPTER 12

She wishes he were dead, hopes he'll catch the consumption or the cholera, or step out in front of a carriage and be trampled to death by horses. He calls her 'my pretty' and she turns away. He says, 'Don't be like that now . . . come here.' And because she's alone with him, she has to go to him and sit on his lap. 'My pretty,' he says, stroking her hair . . .

The sun rose early over Temple Hill, breaking through a narrow gap of pale chintz, throwing a searchlight over Cora's bed, her pillow, her face. She had had another difficult night of interrupted sleep and broken dreams and was exhausted. Now, the effort of another day – and within it another lifetime – seemed almost too much. For what would she remember this day? How many times would she be confronted and challenged by her own memory?

She lay still for some time, cogitating, deliberating, pushing away, reordering people and events, sequences and words. She was used to the heat, used to the light, but she was not, and never would be, used to the weight of years, or that unyielding inflexibility that had become so much a part of her body. Resistance, she thought, had made her like this, for she knew that the mind and body were inextricably linked, and that much – perhaps all – of the weight of her burden was due to her fight against it. And hadn't it started when she was still young? Hadn't it started with George? With that need to be someone unstained, without blemish, or past or future? But no, it was not right to blame him. Too easy, too easy, she thought.

The situation she found herself in was her fault and no one else's. She had returned there knowing that she would perhaps be found. 'A place where no one will find me . . .' she said out loud, and then closed her eyes. She had wanted to speak to Cecily about the letters, had wanted to tell her – and she had had the opportunity, after dinner, when Cecily freely admitted she had been *changed* by what she knew. But what did Cecily know? And how could she, Cora, tell her anything without knowing what, exactly, she knew? It had been a perplexing conversation. He was desperate, Cecily had said. Yes, of course he would be. But was it him? Was it really the farmer, John Abel, sending the letters, reminding her?

'It could be any one of them . . .'

She turned her face to the window. The light was quite different, not of the same quality as Italy. She could hear someone outside beneath her window, the sound of sweeping, whistling, and then song. And the light and the song, and the sudden and fleeting sensation of another time momentarily lifted her spirits. If she closed her eyes she could be back there in a split second. One of the benefits, the very few benefits, of old age was having that menu of moments: moments to return to and relive, over and over. This was control. And one had to control one's memories, otherwise . . . otherwise they could run rampant, leading one to places and times best forgotten. But oh how they seemed to be running amok on her now. The way to do it, she thought, the way to stop all of this is to train the mind, restore one's history. *I must take control and focus my mind . . . I must remember, I must forget.*

She had never been an early riser and there seemed little to rise for now. Ten o'clock was quite early enough to greet the day, take breakfast – always coffee and rolls – and plan, yes, plan what was to happen. But what was there to plan? What was there to happen? Lunch, and tea, and dinner, a walk about the garden, perhaps. Nothing more arduous. Accounts to be settled, bills to be paid, correspondence to be dealt with – and what would the post bring today?

She wondered what time it was, but the numbers on the clock were blurred. Was that one o'clock? No, Sylvia would have come in by now, come to check on her. Someone would, surely. They would not leave her there, sleeping, dozing, drifting. Perhaps she had been asleep for days, sailing through time. But it was rather nice, to be left alone, to not know the time, not know the day . . . not know.

Sylvia had said not to get up, said that she would see to things. She could remember that. Yes, she could remember that. Sylvia had helped her upstairs to her bedroom . . . But they had had words, harsh words, and it pained her now to think of them. Had she overreacted? Sylvia *had* been snooping, there was no doubt at all about that. She had seen her, holding the little envelope from Mrs Chadwick up to the lamp. And later, when Sylvia had loitered at the end of her bed, guiltily, awkwardly, what was it she had said? Something about Edward?

'Edward,' she said, and sighed.

For a moment she could hear music, a distant serenade, swept over countries and rooftops and into her room. And she closed her eyes once more, drifting back to a wedding in Paris . . .

She can see George standing in a huddle at the other side of the room. He has not spoken to her and he does not look at her. She moves about the palatial room holding on to the arm of her new husband. She smiles, says hello, kisses people and takes hold of their hands. She turns to her husband and listens to him as he speaks. From time to time he places his hand over hers resting on his arm, and he says her name. But it's not the same. Can never be the same. And yet, what was she expected to do?

'You've been dreaming,' Sylvia said, smiling at her.

The windows in Cora's room were open wide, but the air was thick and hot, and when she tried to speak her words were syrupy and stuck in her mouth. She tried to move, tried to sit up. Sylvia quickly rose to her feet, leaned over her, adjusting the pillows behind her head. She said, 'I've told Jack you're not feeling quite yourself. He's gone off out, said to give you his love, and tell you that he'll see you later.'

She nodded, tried to smile and closed her eyes. She saw Jack and Cecily, and herself and George; he was there, he was not there; and Jack and he were one and the same. She felt a touch, a hand upon her forehead, and in her dream it was him pushing back her hair, stroking her brow. She heard herself say his name and then a female voice, 'No, it's me, dear.' But when she opened her eyes and glanced down, she fleetingly but clearly saw his hand resting upon her own. She saw the lines of his knuckles, his fingernails – the smudges of paint beneath; his gold rings glinting yellow and white, bright white, in the sunshine.

The female voice said, 'But you do look a little better . . . more like yourself. And I've asked Mrs Davey to bring up a tray. Just a scone and some tea, I said.'

She turned to Sylvia. 'What time is it?'

'Half past three . . . and I know you abhor tea being served before four, but you must have something. You've missed breakfast and luncheon.'

She raised herself up, and as Sylvia pushed and

pulled at the pillows behind her she wanted to say, 'Please don't . . . please let me be . . . I'd like to be on my own.' She watched Sylvia sit back down, saw her pick up her notebook, then make that kissing noise with her mouth and tap her pencil on the page. Here they come, she thought, more questions. She can't leave it alone, can't let me be.

Questions, once eagerly anticipated and enjoyed, now seemed relentless, intrusive. And she was certainly in no mood for them today. It felt too close, too raw. As though the intervening years had been peeled back and the past was there, in that room with her. As though everyone was in that room with her, standing about the bed, waiting . . . but what were they waiting for? She was not about to die. Not yet.

Then, Sylvia spoke again. She asked if she could go over the details of a landscape, said it would help her describe the setting for a particular chapter in her novel, *Lord of Nivernais*.

'I've gone back to it,' Sylvia said. 'Seeing as we're not making much headway on *your* book.'

'Aren't they *all* my books?' Cora asked. 'And anyway, you visited France enough times yourself.'

'No, no, not France, Lucca.'

Cora narrowed her eyes. 'Lucca? You've gone to Lucca?'

'Yes,' Sylvia replied. 'I hope you don't mind. It's where Harriett, my protagonist, and Armand—

'I can't believe you've gone to Lucca. Why

228

Lucca? You could have gone anywhere, taken them anywhere. Why there?'

'Oh Cora, really,' Sylvia stammered, 'it's just a place . . . the place I've put them for their reconciliation. You see, Harriett is returning to Rome, and Armand is now back from the war. I wanted to—'

'But why Lucca? It's not on the way anywhere, and which war? You never mentioned any war to me. And you know how I feel about Lucca.'

'Well, I suppose I could move them, place them in Siena, perhaps, but really, I wanted somewhere quiet. And it has to be Italy, you see, because . . .'

Cora did not hear any more. In a split second she had been thrown back half a century, to Lucca.

They had lain entwined as dawn broke through the shuttered window, casting golden stripes across their bodies. He said, 'I never want to leave you.'

'But you will, you will . . . you have to.'

He had to . . .

Cora travelled by train to Florence. The party headed out on foot from the hotel for luncheon with George. But when the moment came, 'Hello, George,' was all she could summon. He asked after her aunt, and Jack, and then he said, 'And your boy? How is Freddie?'

She smiled. 'He is well.'

He sat with Mrs Hillier at lunch and, though as attentive as ever to *her* needs, Cora was aware from his gaze, his frequent glances, that something of the chemistry remained. Towards the end of lunch, when everyone decided to return to the hotel for a siesta, he leaned forward and invited her to take a walk with him, to Santa Croce. As they strolled through the streets arm in arm, he told her about the Italian sculptor with whom he was working, and Cora listened, slowly coming alive for the first time in four years.

Within the Gothic splendour of Santa Croce, and with her arm linked through his, they walked along the monumental walls, surveying the marble tombs of Dante, Galileo, Vasari and Michelangelo. They lit candles and sat down, side by side, in contemplative silence in a shaft of warm light.

'Not homesick for your beloved Rome, I hope?' he whispered.

'No, I needed to get away – you have no idea how much.'

'Oh, but I do. It's why I asked Amy to invite you.'

She turned to him. '*You*? You asked Mrs Hillier to invite me?'

He looked back at her, frowning. 'I heard . . . that you've been unhappy.'

She glanced away. 'A little,' she said.

'I don't like to think of you unhappy. I always imagine you smiling, always smiling. And I wanted to see you . . . It's been a long time.'

Even then, she had wanted to wrap her arms around him, to tell him about Freddie and explain her marriage to Jack. She wanted to tell him

230

everything. But she simply smiled at him and said, 'Yes, too long.'

Early the following morning the party set off in two carriages, travelling from Florence to Prato, then on via Montecatini to the house, three miles east of Lucca, arriving as night fell. But that evening, on a terrace ablaze with torches, candles and brightly coloured paper lanterns, Cora felt awkward, in awe of the assembled company and, in particular, of their hostess, Mrs Hillier. Dinner was served late in the large but simply furnished dining room, where four ostentatious silver candelabras lined the long table. Cora sat between George and an American, named Grant Duvall.

'Alicia and I just adore Florence, but Rome . . . Rome was a disappointment. I'm not sure what we expected but it's a mess of a place. It needs tidying up; and it needs a different government! And you know, there's no mention in any guidebook about the smell, the aroma di Roma! Anyway, we won't be going back, not unless all those pretentious English expatriates and fugitives move out!'

When the conversation moved on to politics, Garibaldi and the supposed imminent reunification of the Italian states, Mrs Hillier held everyone's attention. She knew Giuseppe Garibaldi, knew everyone, and spoke with authority on the very latest political developments. And George, Cora noted, sat in spellbound silence as he listened to her speak. He respects her, she thought; he loves and respects her.

The following morning, afraid she had overslept, Cora hurriedly dressed and went downstairs, but the place was quiet, no one stirred. She walked out on to the terrace, where the hum of cicadas and sound of a nearby stream soothed her haste. Here and there, the mist of night lingered, clinging to the curves and sloping vineyards beneath her. A valley of pale umber and myrtle, the shapes of cypress and pine, and high up in the distance the walls of an ancient fortification glinted in the morning sun.

Somewhere beyond it all is Rome, she thought. And she imagined her son asleep in his bed, and wished she were there, at home in Rome.

Those first few days had been spent idly. There were walks and picnics. Mrs Hillier was carried across the bumpy terrain in her *chaise à porteur*, while Cora and the others walked on ahead in search of the perfect location for lunch. Each evening there were *tableaux vivants*, readings, poetry recitals and charades on the terrace. Cora adopted the role of observer, and learnt much from watching the dynamics at play. She was able to see how Amy Hillier orchestrated proceedings, commanding the attention of her guests with an obvious need to be centre stage, and yet at no time appearing overbearing or insensitive to her friends. But Mrs Hillier was a seasoned hostess, and a performer, Cora concluded.

She was able to see for herself the intimate bond between George and his patron. But she was no longer jealous. She realised that her friend John Clifford had been right all those years ago when he had told her that George's relationship with the older woman was based upon mutual need. And it was obvious, obvious to her, that George respected and admired Mrs Hillier. And he was undoubtedly grateful for her support. After all, it was she who had launched him on his path to success. His talent, good manners, his educated background and love of music had enthralled Mrs Hillier from the start, even before he officially became her protégé. But now Cora realised that George and Amy Hillier had a great deal in common: they were both perfectionists, and egotists, absorbed in a private, mutual admiration.

It had been towards the end of that first week at Lucca that George asked Cora if she would sit for him. He wanted her to pose outside, on the loggia, and at first she was not sure. She had sat for him before, years before. But her shape had altered, become fuller, more curvaceous, and that confidence of youth and lack of inhibition had been replaced by the modesty of a mother, and a respectable married woman. She knew Jack would be furious, knew she should refuse.

'No. I don't think so.'

'Please?'

'But I'm too old to sit for any painter now, especially you, George.'

'No. You're perfect. Please?'

He wished to paint her in a Grecian-style robe, and it had been Lottie Davenport, the retired American actress, who had insisted that she should be the one to style Cora, taking her upstairs to see what they could find. And so, in a white muslin sheet with an ornate brooch pinned to her shoulder, and a belt of twisted silk tied around her still slender waist, Cora had returned to the loggia, where George, with Clifford's help, had arranged the scene already set in his mind's eye. Lottie then suggested to George that Cora's hair be loose and flowing, something which embarrassed Cora more than the frayed sheet she had been bullied by Lottie into wearing.

'Really? Why does my hair need to be down?' Cora asked.

'Because no one in ancient Greece wore their hair in a modern up-do!' Lottie replied.

'That's not strictly true, Lottie. I've seen paintings of Grecian women – goddesses – with their hair taken up,' Amy Hillier interjected, before looking at Cora and adding, 'But it would certainly be a more romantic vision if you were to have your hair down, Cora.'

George said nothing but smiled at Cora, appealingly. And so, with Lottie's help once again, she disappeared upstairs to unpin her hair.

'I'm not sure my husband would be pleased,' she said, as Lottie unpinned her hair.

'Does he not like you to be admired?' Lottie asked, but Cora made no reply.

'You're a beautiful woman,' Lottie went on, 'and your husband need never know. Secrets are quite often beautiful in themselves, you know,' she said as she brushed Cora's hair. 'We should all keep a part of ourselves for only us to own. We must never share the essence of who we truly are, for then we are lost, well and truly lost.'

'But that means one can never give oneself completely . . . never truly love.'

'I suppose it does. But true love is a curse as much as a blessing, you must know that.'

'I'm not sure I've ever truly loved anyone, apart from my son.'

'Oh, I think you have; I think you know how to love deeply, profoundly, passionately, but you have not been loved back like that, yet.'

She felt Lottie's hand upon her bare shoulder. 'I think that's George calling. We'd better go back down,' she said, moving away.

Downstairs, the tension evaporated when Lottie blew an imaginary trumpet and then called out, 'My lords, ladies and gentlemen, her Serene Highness Queen Cora of Lucca!'

George smiled. Clifford, pipe in mouth, broke into riotous applause. And Amy Hillier looked from Cora to George but remained silent.

Over the next three hours George made what appeared to Cora to be dozens of sketches, some discarded in crumpled balls upon the floor, others placed on a marble table next to his easel. Eventually, and despite Cora's complaints that her bare feet were cold and that her back ached, George at last began to put paint upon the canvas. Unlike Clifford, he worked silently, lost in the execution of his work, studying each fold of material, each shadow; perfecting the lines and shape of his model's features; scraping off paint with a palette knife, adjusting his composition, perfecting the balance and harmony of his vision.

The others had long since left the makeshift studio and moved inside, and Cora could hear them, arguing and laughing over card games. Part of her longed to go inside so she could sit in a chair, be comfortable and warm. And yet she savoured each moment alone with him, knowing his attention on her was so intense, so complete, his dark eyes moving from her to the canvas and back to her. From time to time, he spoke, asking her to straighten up, move a finger or raise her head, but there was no conversation, and the silence between them seemed only to heighten the atmosphere of intimacy.

He walked towards her, adjusted the sheet where it was knotted at her shoulder, his warm flesh brushing against her bare skin. He lifted the back of his hand to her jaw, gently raising her face, his eyes upon her mouth, her nose, and then her eyes. He touched her hair, arranging it down her back, the tips of his fingers grazing her spine. He stepped away, casting his eyes over her, her body, and smiled. '*Perfetto*,' he said, then returned to his easel and picked up his palette and brush. She could hear his breathing, each grunt and sigh, his tongue in his mouth as it opened and closed in varying degrees of concentration.

And looking back at him over her shoulder, she watched him as he watched her. She studied his face once more: the hooded eyes, the Roman nose, that so familiar high forehead and tousled hair, now greying at the temples. The lips, a mouth she knew so well, and a beard, from time to time tugged and pulled at. The crumpled collar of his velvet jacket, the ruffled silk of his necktie. The concentration in his eyes: the perfectionist at work.

Finally, as the afternoon light began to fade and the air grew noticeably cooler, he looked up at her and said, 'Shall we continue tomorrow?'

'You said an hour or two, George, not a day or two!' she replied, stretching her arms out in front of her, and then up over her head.

'But you're a vision, my perfect vision . . .'

The following morning, as everyone was about to depart on an expedition to the town, Mrs Hillier asked Cora if she would mind staying there with her to keep her company. She had had a headache the previous evening, retiring to her bed early and requesting supper on a tray, which George had taken up to her. But she still felt 'under the weather', she said.

'George enjoys your company very much, Cora. I'm so pleased that you decided to join us here. As you know, I'm sure, he gets bored so easily, can never be in one place for too long,' she said, as the two of them walked slowly down the hillside. 'It's good for him, I think, to see old friends, people his own age . . .' She stopped. 'Though age itself is no barrier to friendship, of course, and really means nothing at all.' She smiled at Cora. 'One person may take a lifetime, fifty, sixty, seventy years to reach the wisdom another attains in thirty. We are all different in our ability to acquire knowledge, to mature and learn; it is not dependent upon a number. The ability and rate at which one learns from experiences is in itself fascinating. There are those who take a lifetime and learn very little, and others whose hunger to learn the lessons of life enables them to gain wisdom from a tender age. I have met idiotic and immature old men, no more than little boys, devoid of any wisdom or clarity, and I have known exceptionally wise young men, custodians of great knowledge. Dear George falls into the latter category of course.' She paused and smiled. 'And happily, he does not see my age, only my wisdom. We are kindred spirits, you see, and have probably shared many lifetimes together before this one.'

'Do you truly believe that?' Cora asked, remembering her aunt's word for people who held such views: 'pagans' she called them.

'Yes I do. There are people we meet who are so familiar to us, not in their physical appearance perhaps, but in their aura. Instinctively we recognise them and feel an inexplicable but deeply powerful connection. It is the recognition of a kindred soul. You see, Cora, the soul is immortal. Have you never felt that rush of familiarity upon a first meeting?'

'Yes, indeed I have, but I've never been able to understand it, and I'm not sure I'm able to believe in reincarnation. It would be nice to think we are reborn, but where does that put heaven and God?' she asked, looking up at the cloudless sky.

'Does one have to be exclusive of the other?' Mrs Hillier asked.

'No, perhaps not, but if we keep on returning to a physical body, at what stage do we ascend to heaven?'

'When we have acquired wisdom; when we have learnt all there is to know about ourselves. What did Socrates say? "Know thyself"? I think we have to know ourselves, and that is the most difficult thing. The most difficult thing!'

When the women reached the bench by the stream, they simultaneously closed their parasols and sat down. Cora could hear the older woman breathing in deeply, as though savouring each sensation, and she felt mildly irritated by her own inability to clear her mind. It seemed a cluttered untidy mess over which she had no control. And yet she knew that beyond that mess of unanswered questions lay vast pools of wisdom.

'I think you know how very dear and precious George is to me,' Mrs Hillier began again after some minutes. 'It is my mission to nurture his talent, to support him in any way I'm able. His well-being is of the utmost importance to me . . . indeed, to the world.'

'Of course.'

Mrs Hillier sighed. 'His art is God-given, a gift from the Almighty. He is not like ordinary men. He cannot allow himself to be encumbered by attachments that will burden him and stifle his creativity. He must have peace – peace of mind, space, freedom from the ordinary and mundane activities which the rest of us are unfortunately so taken up with. No, he cannot be burdened. And it is why he will never marry, why he prefers celibacy.'

Cora stared ahead and said nothing.

'Passion, lust, romantic notions, he knows these things are fleeting, that they will rob him of what he so desperately needs in order to fulfil his life's purpose. Oh yes, he knows this, he knows this now.'

Later, that evening, after the others retired one by one to their beds, Cora and George were left alone on the terrace. As the candles around them flickered and burnt out, they sat in silence watching fireflies in the blackness. Then Cora said, 'Do you believe in reincarnation, George?'

He turned to her. 'What a question to spring on me! Why do you ask that?'

'Because Mrs Hillier told me today that she believes we have all lived more than one lifetime.'

'Ah, well, Amy has such notions.' He looked

away and smiled, obviously familiar with Mrs Hillier's view of the universe. 'I'm not sure,' he said, hesitantly. 'Based on what I've read recently, no, I do not. Science has taken over our theories and seems to be challenging all of our beliefs. And yet it cannot answer all of our questions. But reincarnation? Well, it's a fanciful and rather egotistical notion, is it not? That we are given another chance? That we go on and on. No, I'm not sure I can subscribe to that. But what do you think? You've obviously been pondering this.'

Cora shrugged. 'Of course I would rather like to think I had at least a few more lifetimes ahead of me – one is definitely not enough. But then I am greedy by nature and wish for too much.' She paused. 'It's just that Mrs Hillier, well, she believes you and she have known each other before . . . in other lifetimes.'

He laughed, shook his head. 'She's testing you, sounding you out.'

'But why? Why do that?'

He shrugged his shoulders: 'Perhaps because she's intrigued,' he said, a smile in his voice.

'Intrigued? By me? How ridiculous!'

He turned to her. 'But why does it astound you?'

'Because I am nothing by comparison.'

'You have youth. You have physical beauty. And you know yourself, I think.'

Cora turned to him, her face clearly visible in the moonlight. 'But I am hardly youthful, and as for knowing myself . . .'

'Does your husband know you?' he asked, staring ahead, into the night.

'Marriage is no guarantee of knowledge, George.'

'I always thought marriage, commitment, meant *truth*, opening up one's heart.'

'Opening up one's heart . . . Is that why you've not married yet? Are you afraid to open up *your* heart?'

'Perhaps. But I tell my dear father it's because I've not yet met the right woman, lest I appear a coward . . . which of course is the truth of the matter. The one unalterable truth.' He turned to her. 'I fear I am destined to be on my own now. And that is my sadness. I have everything I ever wished for and nothing at all; no one to share with; no one waiting for me at home; no sons or daughters to climb up on to my lap and tease me and love me; no wife who knew me before my success, who loves me for me, for who I am. And why? Because I chose for it to be so. I chose, didn't I? So, now tell me, how brave am I?'

She rose to her feet. 'I think we should go inside. It's getting cold,' she said.

He reached out, grabbed hold of her hand. 'Tell me you love me . . . tell me you still love me. Tell me you forgive me.'

'George, please.' She pulled her hand free. 'I can't tell you that. I can't, it's too late.' And then she turned and walked quickly towards the house, and as she moved through the open doors she heard someone call out her name: an unfamiliar, broken voice.

Upstairs, in her room, she slammed the door shut and stood perfectly still for a moment. I must leave here, she thought; I should never have come. I must leave here . . . go home. She moved across the room to the wardrobe, began pulling out her gowns, letting them fall in a heap at her feet then sat down amongst them. 'I must go home,' she repeated through tears.

She did not notice the door swing open, or hear it close. And as he fell on to his knees by her side, she whispered, 'I must go, I must go home.'

'My darling, my own dearest . . .'

He took hold of her hands, lowered his head and kissed her palms. 'Forgive me,' he said, and she felt the wetness of his tears slip between her fingers.

'We cannot do this, I cannot . . .' she began, but then his mouth was over hers, his hands cradling her head. And as he ran his fingers through her hair, pulling it loose between breathless sobs, kissing her lips, her face, her neck, repeating her name over and over, she felt his hands move down her body, his fingers untying the lace of her gown, against her skin, exploring, tracing. And with his tears in her mouth, she pulled him closer.

'Who's sad to see you in England, dear?' Sylvia was saying, leaning over her, over the bed. Daylight had faded. It was late in the afternoon, or perhaps early evening, Cora thought. And then she heard herself say the name, 'Edward.' She had not meant to say it; she had heard Sylvia's question and thought it, merely thought it.

'Edward? I don't think Edward was ever sad to see you back here. Was he?' Sylvia asked.

'No, no, sad about George . . . about George and me,' she replied.

'But did he know? I thought he'd never known . . . hadn't realised.'

She raised her hand. 'Sylvia, you must stop. You don't understand.'

'Oh, but I do. You see, I never listened to anyone else, only you. And so I . . . I believe you, and I know it was *not* revenge . . .'

She turned to Sylvia. 'I'm sorry, but I must ask you to leave, Sylvia,' she said, clearly and calmly, with complete clarity. 'I want you to leave now.'

CHAPTER 13

The lanes were bathed in a soft dappled light, and the air, gliding over Cecily's arms and face and through her hair, blissfully cool. The hedgerows, arching branches and trees and fields flashed by in a blur of colour, and the engine throbbed and roared. And sometimes, as they slowed, as they tilted, rounded a corner and changed gear, the machine made a strange and unnerving put-put sound. From time to time they came to a junction and stopped, briefly, then moved on, accelerating down the straight and into the sunshine. And once or twice, when the engine cut out and he had to restart it, he turned to her, smiling, his face half covered by goggles. 'Hold on! Hold on tight!'

Speed: it was, quite simply, intoxicating. Too thrilling for words. He was right. It made her heart thump and made her feel alive. She closed her eyes, savouring the new sensations: the light and shadow swiftly moving over her, over them, light shadow light shadow light shadow; the feel of the air, warm summer air, brushing her skin, moving her hair, her clothes; the sound of the engine, the thrust of its power; and even the spine-tingling, heart-wrenching, nerve-wracking threat of danger.

Speed. It was modern and daring and brave. It was the Future.

Or that's how it felt to Cecily that day.

When they reached the Bracken Pond, he pulled over, on to a gritted pathway under the trees. He turned off the engine and pulled off his goggles as he climbed from the bike. He stared at her, smiling broadly, and then laughed. She said, 'Please, don't laugh, don't say anything. I can well imagine what I look like.'

He stepped forward, took her hand. 'But you look wonderful. You look . . . wild and exciting.'

She had received his first note, in a sealed envelope, on the Sunday morning, the day after dinner at Temple Hill. It had been delivered by hand; her reply and the others were posted.

Cecily,
    Did we part as friends yesterday evening? I am not sure and this bothers me more than perhaps it should. I sincerely hope that I have not offended you . . . & that we are still friends.
    JS

Dear Jack,
    Of course we are friends! I was, I admit, a little tired, and rather hot. Perhaps it was that . . .

In haste,
CMC

Dear Cecily,
   I think you are perhaps being disingenuous
. . . but that may be your prerogative. Either
way, I hope that we ARE still friends, and
that you are well.
   Jack
   PS. What is the M in your name?

Dear Jack,
   I am very well, thank you, & assure you
that I was most definitely not being 'disin-
genuous'. This misunderstanding has arisen,
I believe, simply from an absence of knowl-
edge of each other & of our respective
characters.
   As ever,
   Cecily
   PS. The M is for Madeline, after my mother.
   PPS. Do you have a middle name/names?

Dear Cecily,
   I think you are right with regard to the not
knowing, & so, though I am unable to furnish
you with any detailed (objective) observations on my own character (and though I
could perhaps provide you with names for
'character references'), I can, in the absence
of said knowledge, offer the following:

Middle name: George (after my father, of course)

Birthday: December 2nd

Favourite place: the top of a hill near the Bracken Pond

Hobbies: hate the word. Makes me think of a children's toy horse . . . & suggests solitary model-making et cetera.

Ambitions: to learn to fly, and to have an outrageously long & blissfully happy life.

Likes: ski-ing, cricket, the English countryside (about here); Sherlock Holmes & anything else by Conan Doyle; the theatre, the pictures, Lily Elsie; music, my gramophone, Bach, Beethoven, ragtime; meringues, and very cold beer.

Dislikes: Shakespeare, Chaucer, jelly (a pointless food), pomposity & lies.

Enough for now, I think. But I would be grateful for similar from you . . .

Yours,

Jack

PS. I wonder what you are doing at this very minute. I am in the garden, lying under the horse chestnut – writing to you!

Dear Jack,

Yes, I too was in the garden, reading (Far From the Madding Crowd, if you really wish to know).

So, here goes:

Likes: reading (Austen, Hardy, Dickens, George Eliot and almost every English poet), writing, daydreaming (& quite extraordinarily good at the latter); jelly (definitely NOT a pointless food), blackberries (picked fresh from the hedgerow & popped straight into one's mouth), wild strawberries and CREAM; sunsets, long twilights, & storms, wild skies and moonlit starry nights; music . . . Beethoven and Debussy. Honeysuckle, snowdrops, four-leaf clover and forget-me-nots. My bicycle. The smell of hay, the greenness of the beeches, and breezes. (Yes, breezes!) Breathing in the world. Here & now . . . and everything this very minute. And the future – what is to come!

Dislikes: people who pretend to be something other than what they are; cruelty, inequality, and spitefulness; Mr Fox's long sermons, Rosetta's (our maid) stew and dumplings, Ethne's incessant piano practice, and Sonia B's silent, head-throwing laugh. Gossip, supposition and small-mindedness.

Ambitions: to LEAVE Bramley and travel, to write, live in a city, & to attend the opera at least once in my life. And of course to be 'blissfully' happy (surely that goes without saying?)

Favourite colour: violet.

Favourite place: . . . not yet discovered!

Favourite sound: possibly the wood pigeon that I am listening to now . . .
That's about it. I think.
Cecily

Cecily,
Show off! I had already surmised that you are without doubt cleverer than me. Did you perchance see the sunset yesterday evening? I wondered if you were outside . . . was half tempted to come over.
Jack

Jack,
Ha! I was not showing off . . . I was doing my very best to be honest! Yes, I did see the sunset. Mother says it means a storm . . . & almost 100 degrees today. Hard to believe we're in England.
C

Cecily,
Are you free tomorrow? I thought you might like to come out . . . a picnic? Just a thought . . . if you are we could meet here . . . 11 o'clock?
J

Hitherto, the only letters Cecily had received had been from her cousins or Aunt Kitty. And so Madeline, witnessing the arrival of at least two of

Jack's letters, had asked, 'Who are your letters from, dear?' And Cecily said, 'Oh, just Annie. She's testing the service for her father.'

'How very enterprising!' Madeline replied.

The first note had made Cecily tremble, more than was warranted by its sentiments, she thought. And she had spent hours thinking of her reply, then penning it, perhaps ten times over, before finally reducing it to little more than a sentence. But after that, it had been easy: a written rather than spoken conversation. Was he flirting? Possibly. But that possibility was the most exciting thing about it all. Jack Staunton was corresponding with her. He was not only writing sentences *to* her, he was thinking about her, and that thought alone altered her world, and her consciousness of it.

The evening she had written about her likes and dislikes – outside in the garden – she had felt as though she was sharing something of herself for the very first time. Because no one had ever asked before, because no one had ever focused her mind in that way. What did she want? What did she like? He wanted to know. He wanted to know about her, her thoughts, how she felt, what she saw, how she saw. He wanted to know.

And everything around her – the garden, its colours, the sounds, lack of sound, even the fly-filled air – suddenly seemed more real than ever, and inexorably linked to him: linking her to him, yards away, minutes away. It was an inevitability; it was fate. All of it. Everything. She saw her life flash before her, and she saw him, Jack Staunton, with her throughout. Yes, it would be; it had to be.

That night she had fallen asleep smiling, blissfully happy in the knowledge that she was worthy of his interest, inebriated by the possibilities ahead.

He organised the picnic, telling her he had put it together himself (this, she could believe): hard-boiled eggs, pork pie, cheese, bread and butter, apples, and ginger beer (non-alcoholic, he'd assured her, but after one mouthful she realised he'd lied).

They had lounged about on the rug on the sand, watching ill-clad bathers, the rigmarole of families and children and dogs. At one point Cecily thought she spotted Mrs Moody paddling at the water's edge and ducked down, lying flat upon the rug on her stomach. But no, it was not the village gossip, just someone who resembled her.

'So, what did you tell your mother? Where did you say you were going?' he asked.

'With Annie, of course – to Linford. She's a brick, won't say a thing,' she replied, turning over, sitting up, wrapping her arms around her knees.

'I don't imagine you lie to her often – your mother, I mean.'

'Oh yes I do. Well, not often, but sometimes.'

He lay with his arms behind his head, staring up at the sky. 'It's a rotten business, isn't it? Having to lie, especially when there's no reason. But sometimes . . . sometimes it's so much easier than telling the truth.'

She glanced at his legs, stretched out next to her, the shape of his bony kneecaps and slender calves through the fawn-coloured fabric. His shoes looked expensive, and new; and she wondered if Cora had bought them for him. Above one navy blue sock was a patch of bare, pale skin covered in a down of dark hair. And she had an impulse to reach out and touch that patch of skin – which shocked her.

'I rather think my grandmother lies,' he said, pensive.

'No, surely not,' she replied. 'She might not wish to divulge things about herself, her life, but that's quite different to lying.'

She remembered Cora's words of the week before: 'I have never been a person to place too much store on truth,' she had said, as if declaring it to the world and not just to Cecily. 'The truth is an enigma. I may say that I've never known truth. I have known great love, great pain and loss, but not necessarily truth.'

'You mean withholding the truth?' Jack asked her.

'Gracious, no. I didn't say that. I really don't know . . .'

He sat up. 'But you see, I think you're right, I think that's exactly what she does. I think she offers people a rather sanitised, edited version of events in her life. The only one left to corroborate her version is Sylvia, and she appears to be sworn to secrecy on all things.' He paused. 'I imagine

Sylvia could tell me so much, but of course she daren't; she worships the ground my grandmother walks on.'

Cecily smiled. 'She is awfully fond of her, isn't she?'

'Irritatingly so. I rather think poor Sylvia has spent her entire life hanging on my grandmother's every word. She's like a devoted pet, or some lady-in-waiting,' he added, kicking at the sand. 'I've asked her, of course, about my father . . . and about the others.' He turned to her. 'She knew them all, you see, she's been around forever.'

'What did she tell you, what did she say?'

He looked out across the water. 'Nothing. She answers each question with a question: what has your grandmother told you? Don't you think you should ask her? And so it goes on. Good luck to her with the memoirs, that's all I can say. I don't imagine my grandmother has any intention of collaborating on that particular project, which may explain the tension between them,' he added.

'Tension? What do you mean?'

'I can tell that my grandmother's becoming irritated by Sylvia's presence. She's been avoiding her. Yesterday, I found her in the garden, at the temple, and it seemed to me as though she was hiding. She asked, "Where's Sylvia?"' He mimicked his grandmother's clipped voice, and an exaggerated wide-eyed stare. 'And then, later,' he continued, 'Sylvia came up to me and implied that my grandmother was going potty.'

Cecily laughed. 'What did she say?'

'That she was worried, *deeply worried*,' he said with exaggerated emphasis, 'about my grandmother's state of mind. She talks in riddles, that woman. She told me that *it* had happened before, and I had not a clue what she meant, whether she was referring to some former madness in the family or something else. I suppose I should sit down and have it out with her.'

'With Sylvia?'

He turned to her. 'With my grandmother. I should just ask her outright about everything. You see, I'd rather like to know who I am. Does that make sense?'

'Yes, of course,' she replied. 'And I'm sure she'll tell you everything you want to know, if you explain.'

He looked down, shook his head. 'It's a queer thing not to know about one's family, where one comes from.'

'I'm sure there's no great mystery, nothing scandalous.'

He moved forward, resting his chin on his knees. 'But perhaps there was. Perhaps there was a scandal. Perhaps my grandfather's death was not an accident.' He ran his hands through his hair and sighed again. 'And I know – am very much aware – that the only reason she came back here is because of me, my situation. But I have this feeling . . . this . . .' He paused, staring down at the ground, then turned to her. 'She talks around

255

everything. Haven't you noticed? She talks in anec-dotes, the same stories over and over, but none of it's real, not to me at any rate. Don't get me wrong, I'm very fond of her, and I recognise that she's . . . elderly, forgetful perhaps, eccentric most defi-nitely,' he added, smiling. 'But there are too many things she won't discuss with me, so what am I expected to think?'

She nodded. What was he expected to think? It was perfectly reasonable that he should want to know about his family, his father and grandfather. Already, perhaps she, Cecily, knew more than he did. But Cora was wise; she would choose her time, know when it was best.

'I don't suppose it's anything sinister, you know. I imagine she's simply being cautious, protective of you.'

'I'm not a child.'

'No.'

They had been there for an hour, no more, when he rose to his feet and said, 'I'm bored of this place. Let's move on.' His mood had changed. He was quieter, reflective, and Cecily wished she could tell him, tell him something. But she had promised Cora. So they gathered up the rug and half-eaten picnic in silence. As they walked back to the bike, Cecily yearned to reach out, to take hold of his hand, his arm, to offer a touch. She said, 'It doesn't really matter who our families were or are. I like to think we can be whoever we want to be.'

He glanced to her and smiled. 'A romantic notion, I think.'

As he pulled on his goggles, he said, 'I want to show you a place. It's not far from here, only ten or so minutes away.' He climbed on to the bike, averting his gaze as she carefully climbed up behind him. Seconds later, they roared off down the road circling the perimeter of the pond.

They climbed up the sandy track hand in hand, through waist-high heather to the top of the hill. And all around them, as far as the eye could see, was heathland: an undulating purple landscape broken only by the shapes of birch and pine. In the distance was the small looking-glass pond, its bathers now almost invisible to the eye, its sailboats tiny white dots upon its sky-filled surface.

'This is where I wanted to bring you, where I've wanted to bring you for some time. Isn't it glorious?' he added, staring up at the sky.

She watched him, his head thrown back, his pale throat exposed, his hand to his brow, as if searching for something above. 'Glorious,' she said.

And then he lowered his head, and staring into her eyes, he moved closer. 'I like to come here and look up,' he said, 'look up at the sky and imagine I'm up there, looking down. Looking down on the world.'

'And what do you see?'

'Sometimes I see you. In fact quite often I see you, sitting alone, reading in your garden, writing your stories,' he replied. 'I see Cecily, and I wonder what she's thinking.'

She smiled. 'Perhaps she's thinking of someone called Jack Staunton, wondering what he makes of her.'

He lifted his hand to her cheek and moved closer. 'What he makes of her . . .' he repeated, but his sentence petered out as his lips touched hers.

His kiss was achingly tender. So gentle at first that Cecily was the one to move forward, pressing her lips more firmly against his. And as he wrapped his arms around her, drawing her to him, she could feel the world spinning, that vibration, and his heart, her own heart, their lips, that kiss: the moment. He spoke her name as no one had ever before said it, and she knew then and there that no one ever again would express it so.

'I didn't plan that,' he said, looking at her with smiling eyes. 'I didn't bring you here to . . . to kiss you.'

And she couldn't speak. Words deserted her. But she could feel a trembling. A wobbling sensation rising up from the ground through her feet to her legs, and up her legs to her body, her stomach, her chest, her arms and hands and fingers, and neck and head. Even her eyelids seemed to be not completely fixed. And her mouth, lips – still parted, but soundless, wordless – seemed to be caught in that vibration: quivering. For a moment she thought she might cry. She felt tears sting her eyes, as every-thing around her, already spinning, blurred more.

He reached out, took hold of her hand, lifted it to his mouth and placed his lips there, softly, lingering. And she thought she might fall over. For the earth seemed to be moving quite rapidly now, the sand on which she stood slipping away from under her feet. It must be heatstroke . . . must be the ginger beer, she thought, focusing on a tree, a single tree, trying to steady herself.

'I don't want you to think I'm taking advantage. It's not why I brought you out today . . .'

And she couldn't look at him, couldn't look at his face, his eyes. But she could hear herself breathing, breathing loudly; or was it him? Everything seemed muddled, blended, too connected . . .

She felt him pull her towards him once more, his arms around her, his hands upon her spine, and she closed her eyes, lifted her face – her lips – to his again. And then her head spun, upside down and all around, and up and down again. And she thought, if he releases me I will surely fall. But he didn't. And even when he moved his mouth away from hers, gently grazing her jaw, he kept his arms around her, and through half-closed eyes she saw his mouth curve upwards at each side.

In time to come Cecily would revisit that moment; that perfect moment. She'd return to that place, that day, reversing the world on its axis, spinning it backwards through sunsets and dawns, and sunsets and dawns and seasons. Sometimes she'd look down from the sky, see two small figures, together, entwined; feel his arms about her once more. And she'd see everything and everyone else, too: the bathers stepping out of the water, shivering and wet; the picnickers on the shore, gathering up rugs and baskets and children and dogs; and the lanes, sleepy and silent and dappled in light, waiting for them to pass through. Waiting for them to pass through once more, young and with hearts fit to burst; young and with lives still ahead; young and with kisses still wet on their lips. And their lips still trembling and damp from kisses; racing through lanes with lips damp from kisses; racing though lanes with skin still warm: his skin still warm.

CHAPTER 14

The earth is hard. Dampness has permeated the rug beneath them. Jemima is asleep, cocooned within the quilt they share. High above are infinitesimal stars: glistening, eternal. Her father has promised her some shoes when they get to Colchester. There's work there, he says, moneyed folk there, he says. Suffolk's no good, no good now the farmers are all poor. They'll be able to get a room there, have a bed and perhaps a fire, too. And she pictures the room, the bed and that fire . . . and she tries to imagine the warmth. But the soles of her feet are blistered and torn, and her back aches from carrying little Johnny.

Sylvia waited in the garden for Jack. Her bags were packed. She would go, if that were Cora's wish. It had been the mention of *that* marriage, of course, and the word revenge, she knew that. And yet, hadn't she said that she knew it *wasn't* revenge? That she did not care what others had said, that she had only ever listened to Cora? And she had, almost.

Truth was, it had been impossible to ignore the

261

gossip, impossible to ignore the facts. Oh, she could understand it, understand why Cora did it, but there was bound to be talk. George was renowned, famous by then. But he had treated her badly, very badly. That was undeniable. And he had had his chance, and often enough. He had used her. He had slipped in and out of Cora's life as and when it suited him, and never, not once, offered to marry her. In Sylvia's mind he was nothing more than a selfish – albeit talented – bounder. And Cora deserved better, much better.

As soon as Sylvia heard the sound of the motorcycle coming up the hillside she made her way through the bushes on to the driveway, and flagged down Jack. Her words spilled out before he had time to pull off his goggles, and, turning off the motor, he asked her to repeat them. He was shocked, she could see. And she was tearful. He took hold of her hand, told her not to worry; his grandmother quite obviously did not know what she was saying. He would go and speak with her, go and speak with her immediately, he said.

So Sylvia sat in the arbour by the sundial, as agreed; for she would not set foot inside the house until Cora had taken back her words. Her bags were packed, she had told Jack. Cotton could easily be sent for. There was a train at 6.46 p.m.

It took Jack almost half an hour to return to the garden, to Sylvia. But he was full of assurances and told Sylvia that of course Cora did not *really* wish her to leave, particularly not on such bad

262

terms. It was all a misunderstanding, he said, more than once. But he was noticeably perplexed by the escalated quarrel, and, once Sylvia had agreed that she would stay on, at least for another day, he asked how the whole thing started.

'I am in a most difficult situation, Jack,' Sylvia began, 'because your grandmother does not wish me to speak to you . . . about anything at all.'

He shook his head. 'I don't understand.'

'There are matters to be resolved, things I am not at liberty to tell you, things that she herself is unable to speak about, even now after so many years, even to me. Unfortunately, *others* are forcing the situation.'

'Others?' he repeated. None of it made any sense.

She nodded. 'It may surprise you, but I have been quietly noting Mr Fox's, and your friend Cecily Chadwick's, keen interest in your grandmother's life. I believe their questions, their scrutiny, at a time when Cora is struggling, grappling with deeply personal dilemmas, have simply been too much for her. This, I fear, is why she turned on me. There is no other explanation for her . . . her paranoia.'

Jack, who had smiled as Sylvia said Cecily's name, now looked away, frowning.

'Oh, but there is one other matter that I should perhaps mention.'

Jack turned to her and, after a moment's hesitation, Sylvia made him promise with his hand upon his heart that he would never breathe a word to Cora; would never disclose to anyone her suspicions about the nature of Cora's recent correspondence.

A letter had in fact arrived late that very afternoon. Sylvia had found it lying on the silver salver in the hallway shortly after she had packed her bags. It was in a strange childish hand, not typewritten, and bore a London postmark. It was plain to see that the sender did not know Cora, for the name was not quite right. Had she not been quite so upset, she might have been tempted to take it, tear it up or burn it, Sylvia told Jack. For these letters, she believed, were at the root of Cora's agitated state of mind. She did not tell Jack that this particular letter was different to the others. It was not her place, she decided. But when he rose up from the bench, saying he would fetch and open the damned thing himself, she did not stop him. Minutes later, he returned, empty-handed. The letter had gone. It had been taken up to Cora.

The following morning, heeding Jack's advice to carry on as normal, as though nothing had happened, Sylvia simply smiled and said, 'Good morning,' when Cora appeared and sat down to breakfast. She and Jack had agreed, in view of the circumstances, that Cora needed their patience and protection more than anything else. So Sylvia had tried to make conversation. She said, 'You know, you really should have stayed in your bed. After all, there's nothing happening today.'

Cora stared straight ahead. 'I spent yesterday in

bed. I've never been a malingerer and I don't intend to become one now,' she replied.

'Can I get cook to do you some eggs?' Sylvia asked.

She shook her head. 'No, thank you, I'm not hungry. I think I might take a walk.'

'A walk?' Sylvia repeated. 'To where?'

'About the garden. I need a change of air . . . fresh air.'

'I'll get my hat.'

'If you don't mind, I'd rather like to take a walk on my own.' She rose awkwardly from the table, and Sylvia quickly disappeared from the room into the hallway and returned with her cane.

'Thank you,' Cora said, taking the cane, without looking at Sylvia.

Cora knew that Sylvia had spoken to Jack, despite her plea. She knew an allegiance had been formed. She knew that Sylvia would say she was going mad, losing her senses. And perhaps she was. Beneath her clothing she could feel the heat of a fever, still there upon her skin. She felt weak, unsteady on her feet, and in her heart. And her sense of loneliness was more acute than ever.

As she stood on the terrace, looking south, directly into the sun, she closed her eyes: I have outlived them all, and outlived any purpose, she thought. Am I to spend the remainder of my days in hiding, in fear? Will I ever know freedom, be able to breathe?

She moved on, carefully descending the steps to

265

the lawn, nodding to one of Mr Cordery's men as he raised his cap to her. The garden was quiet and a cloudless sky promised another languorous hot day. She walked slowly across the grass, pausing every few steps to look about or upwards, preoccupied. If only there was someone she could talk to. If only she could tell someone the truth. But what was the truth? What were the facts?

'Really, what does it matter?' she said out loud.

'Beg your pardon, ma'am?'

'Another glorious day!' she called out, without turning.

She descended more stone steps, standing still for a moment on the last to look out across the garden. Put things in order . . . I must put things in order for him, for Jack. Perhaps write it down . . . yes, that would be sensible. She stepped on to a gritted pathway. I can only be as honest as I recall . . . what more can I do? She walked under the shade of the pergola, already vaguely aware of a presence – a shadow on the periphery of her vision – flickering amidst the tangle of jasmine and clematis. She emerged from beneath the pergola, sat down on the bench inside the arbour, and looked back across the lawn.

She had seen him there before, conspicuous, incongruous, entirely out of place. This morning he was standing by the sundial, with one hand flat upon the lichen-covered stone surface. He looked so very out of date, over-dressed and old-fashioned, she thought, watching him watching her.

They did not speak. Not in audible words. Their conversations – the few they had had – had been conducted almost entirely in silence. He seemed to prefer that.

She took him in: his hair, a single curl hanging down upon his forehead, his beard, greying, his crumpled trousers, well-worn burgundy velvet jacket and usual necktie. He was, she supposed, about forty. Forever forty.

'You should never have left me,' she said, in barely a whisper.

'I never wished to leave you,' he replied, without moving his lips.

'But you did. You always went back to her.'

'No. There was only ever you.'

'You say that now, but it's too late. It's all gone. Over.'

'I'm here, aren't I?'

She looked away for a moment, irritated. 'No, I am here. I'm here without you, and I don't know what to do, how to be. And I'm no good at being old.'

She saw him throw his head back in a noisy silent laugh. Then he fixed his gaze back upon her. 'You'll never be old. Not to me. Look at you now. How old are you? Twenty? Twenty-one?'

'I was when you first met me. But you've been gone these past twenty years . . . and gone from me long before that.'

She saw him look away, shake his head.

'But I have Jack,' she added. 'You never saw him, never knew him.'

He glanced back at her, frowning, perplexed.

'Not that Jack. That Jack passed away years ago, in Rome, remember? I have another Jack . . . our grandson.'

'Our grandson,' he repeated, silently, smiling. He lifted his hand from the sundial and held it out to her.

'No. No, not yet.'

And she watched him dissolve into the sunshine.

She had had numerous conversations with him like this, and could never be sure when or where he would turn up. Once or twice he had appeared at the most inconvenient times, and she had been forced to ignore him, shushing him off in a glance, lest anyone else should see. Later, she had inevitably felt guilty, had had to apologise to him, explain that she couldn't always be at his beck and call. Life goes on, she had told him. I am back in England now, and the English do not like unannounced callers. She could always make him laugh.

It bothered her, somewhat, that he never quite seemed to know who Jack was and always appeared confused. But it was understandable, she supposed. The only Jack he would recall would be her first husband. And neither one of them ever mentioned him, or the others. They had an understanding, and had never needed names, or indeed words. They shared a telepathy that went beyond the grave and was integral to the force that bound them to each other; she had never needed to confirm or deny anything to him. He knew, had always known . . . surely?

But now she reminded herself, he had lived in ignorance about so much – and for so long.

After Lucca, and weeks after Jack's death, Cora had given birth to another George: George*ie*. Despite letters, one 'in sympathy', the next promising a visit, and another proclaiming delight at being asked to be godfather and stating that he was 'honoured' she had chosen his name, George did not visit Rome after Jack's untimely death, or for the christening of his godson.

As etiquette decreed, Cora spent two years in mourning. Dressed in black parramatta silk and bombazine gowns, she lived her life quietly and rarely ventured out. She was still young, people told her; she would, perhaps one day, have another husband, more children. But she had had her children by the man she loved and the man she loved had gone. Her two boys, she decided, would be her life; she would be a mother first and foremost.

When Freddie became ill, Cora and her aunt took it in turns to nurse the five-year-old. It was a fever, nothing more. For two days and nights they sat by his bed, watching him doze, bathing his body with cold compresses. But on the morning of the third day, as dawn broke across the city, and as her aunt finally gave in to sleep, Cora noticed her boy's breathing become more laboured. She climbed up on to the bed, folding his small body into her arms, holding him close; willing his heart on. She ran her fingers over the curves of his face – his cheeks, his nose, his mouth – memorising the softness, each rise and fall, each undulation; those pale purple-veined eyelids fringed with long lashes; that high brow and dark chestnut hair. And in that final hour, she prayed to every saint whose name she could recall, and to every god of every creed; she bargained with them, made promises to them all.

The sun had set by the time Dr Small convinced her to release the dead boy from her arms – still rocking. 'He cannot hear your lullaby now. He is gone, my dear. You must let him go . . .'

Two days later, Cora watched her son's tiny coffin as it was lowered into the ground outside the city walls. And that night, after she had been found, and after Dr Small had been called once again, she lay on her bed and quietly told her aunt that she knew with certainty that there was no God. 'Look at me, what has he done for me? Everything I love he takes away, everything I beg him for he snatches from me . . .'

From that day onwards Cora rarely, if ever, spoke of Freddie. And thus, over time, people forgot; forgot that she had in fact had two sons, not one. But in the locket round her neck she kept a curl of dark chestnut, five-year-old hair.

Freddie's death swept away the last remnants of girlish fantasies, certainly any girlish fantasy of a romantic hero. No one, it seemed to Cora, was going to rescue *her*. Happy-ever-after endings belonged to novels and, perhaps, to those her aunt referred to as 'people of quality'. For their journey had not started as hers had, they had not had to flee from anything. Sometimes, in quiet moments, she would unravel the thread of her life and work backwards, revisiting that season when she and George had first met. If he had married me, she thought, how different my life would be, how different I would be. And if I had been *someone* . . . he would have married me.

But there was so much George did not know, had never known. How could he love her? He did not know her. And how could she love a man who had turned his back on her in order to pursue ambition, success?

As Cora's life continued quietly in Rome, George's soared noisily in England, and echoed across the continent. His name appeared more often than ever in the newspaper. It was by then a name everyone knew. And though a few continued to speculate on the nature of his relationship with his patron and constant companion, Mrs Hillier, most in Rome and back in England assumed the bachelor artist and married lady – sixteen years his senior – to be dear friends.

It was the year after Freddie's death, at a ball at the Palazzo Ruspoli, that Cora was introduced to an officer in the French army named Antonin de Chevalier. Dashingly handsome, stationed in Rome, he was younger than Cora by five years.

And later, that same winter, three years after he had bid adieu to Cora at Lucca, George Lawson returned to Rome – with Amy Hillier.

In the carriage en route to Mrs Hillier's soiree, Cora tried to explain to Antonin the nature of the relationship between George and the older married lady. But he laughed and simply said, 'Darling, I am not a baby. I know about these things.' Minutes later, after Mrs Hillier had greeted them both in the lobby, he whispered, 'No, I think I am a baby. I do not understand.'

'Not all love is bound by physical attraction, Antonin. I used to think it was, and I used to think it was simply Mrs Hillier's patronage that drew him to her, but now I'm not so sure. Yes, George was always ambitious, but their relationship is . . . is more complex than that. She has a hold upon him I've never been able to fathom. She's not beautiful, not in the traditional sense, but perhaps her soul radiates a beauty for him. I think George became bored by physical beauty long ago; there had to be something more enduring than mere physical beauty.'

'Perhaps, but I hear he is, as you English like to say, a *snub*, and she has good connections, no?'

'The word is snob, Antonin. But no, I don't think so. George is not a calculating man. He would not use someone in such a way, and has no need to. He's a creative soul, an artist.'

'Aha! They are the worst. And Rome is full of them, aristocratic creative English souls, rich and idle and sitting in the Greco putting France, Italy and the whole entire world to rights.'

She moved away from him with obvious irritation.

'Why are you so defensive about the painter and the aged singer?' he asked in a whisper, following her through the room.

She stopped. 'I'm not defensive, Antonin. But when you refer to my friend as a snob, I am *slightly* offended. It is no compliment. You're implying that he assumes some sort of superiority, and I happen to know he's not like that. People misunderstand him, that's all.'

'And you, my darling, do you understand him?'

'Yes, I think I do.'

'He is an old love of yours, yes?' he asked, smiling.

'No, he is not an old love in the way that you mean, but he is an old and dear friend of mine.' She looked up at him and smiled in a conciliatory way.

'*Il est bien beau?*' he said after a moment, looking across the room at George.

'He used to be compared to a Greek god – Jupiter Olympus, I think . . .'

That evening, Amy Hillier's apartment looked as grand and opulent as ever, like the backdrop to a painting or the stage set of an opera. Everything in her home appeared to be an *objet de beauté*; each and every item carefully and thoughtfully placed to afford harmony and symmetry. Panelled walls, painted dark pink and gold, were adorned with the work of her many painter friends. And a portrait by George now hung above the fireplace, though it often took guests a moment or two to realise that the attractive woman in the painting was in fact their hostess.

Finally out of mourning, Cora wore a gown of deepest burgundy silk, made for her by the latest French dressmaker to arrive in Rome. It showed off her figure to perfection and complemented the rubies adorning her throat: a gift from Antonin.

George stood with his back to Cora, talking to other guests, but as she walked towards him, something of her presence must have stirred him, for he turned as she approached. He took her hands in his, stepped back to look at her and for a moment, neither one of them spoke – or seemed sure how to navigate their conversation. But the moment passed, and it was Cora who charted their territory. It had been a long time since she had attended such a party or been dressed as she was that evening; a long time since she had sipped fine champagne, and a long time since she had stood in front of George, his full attention upon her. She felt exhilarated and bold, and something in her wanted to toy with him and his safely guarded emotions.

'You know, George, I'm so pleased that we've caught up with each other at last.'

'As am I.'

She smiled. 'It's been a while.'

'Too long.'

'Yes, too long . . . feels like a lifetime . . .'

'You've been through a great deal. And I want you to know that I'm sorry, so sorry that I've not been able to visit until now. But I've thought of you, often, and I must say you look remarkably well.'

'Older, wiser,' she replied, glancing about the room.

'I'm sure.' He nodded. 'He was a good man, Jack. I . . . I,' he stumbled, 'I wish I'd had the chance to know him better, and little Freddie, too. I never met him.'

She stared at him. 'No, you never met him.'

'I can't imagine—'

'No, you can't,' she said quickly. 'There's so much you don't understand, George. You're like a child, a cosseted little boy, protected from the truth.'

He looked away and made no reply.

'And there's something I've been pondering for quite some time. It's a secret, but one I may need to explain to you at some stage,' she continued, turning her head, looking about her and sipping her champagne. And as she ran the tip of her tongue along her unpainted lip, she felt his eyes upon her.

'You're angry with me, again . . . and as intriguing as ever,' he said. 'But tell me this secret.'

'I did not say that I would tell you, George dear,' she said, turning to him. 'You see, I wonder *if* and how I should tell you. It might capsize you,' she added, wide-eyed. 'God forbid, it might quell your creativity . . .' She gasped. 'Or even tarnish your reputation!'

'You're mocking me, teasing me, Mrs Staunton.'

'Certainly not, Mr Lawson,' she replied, already giddy from the mix of champagne and sensation of power. 'I know how much you cherish secrets. Didn't you once say to me that a secretive nature is the most alluring, most intoxicating thing in a woman?'

'Did I really?' he answered, playing nervously with his beard. 'Perhaps I did.' He shrugged. 'It was a foolish thing to say and I'm not altogether sure what I meant by it. The foundation of friendship, true friendship, should always be honesty. I'd like to think that I've been a true friend to you and in turn I hope that you can be candid with me.'

For some minutes they stood in silence. She was aware of George's eyes upon her, and she was determined not to look at him.

'You're playing games with me. Why mention your secret if you have no intention of telling me?' he said, moving closer, beginning to enjoy the clandestine nature of their conversation.

'Perhaps because it's about you.'

'About me?' he repeated. 'Well, it could be so many things, and I would be a fool to venture—'

'Then I don't suppose you shall ever know,' she said, altering tempo and turning to him. 'But I want you to know this, when I stood up and spoke those lines from Byron, all those years ago, they were for you, George, only for you . . . it was all for you, everything.'

For a moment he seemed unable to speak. He stared down at the floor, frowning. Then he whispered, 'I don't know what you want from me . . . I don't understand. I can't—'

'I want nothing from you, not now, other than your friendship.'

'But of course, you have that, and more, much more.'

At that moment the piano stopped and they looked away from each other to clap for a performance neither one of them had heard.

As Amy advanced towards them, Cora said, 'Don't worry, I would never do anything to compromise or embarrass you,' and she placed her hand upon his arm.

'You two are always to be found in a corner together. So what are the secrets you share? Please, do tell,' Amy asked, standing in front of them.

'No secrets, simply catching up on idle gossip,' Cora replied. 'Do please excuse me, I must find Antonin,' she added. And as she walked away she heard Amy say, 'Are you quite all right, my dear? You look as though you're in pain.'

Amy Hillier had watched Cora closely that night. But what had she seen? Amy advocated beauty, like youth, too transient to admire on its own merit. Real beauty, she said, radiated from the soul and found its expression in music, art, literature and poetry; it did not wither or age. Later, many years later, Cora realised that Amy Hillier had seen what she herself could not possibly have seen then: that she, Cora, had altered and matured; that the blandness of youth and inexperience had given way to something else. And that life – pain and heartache – had not taken away but had added. And perhaps Amy Hillier had realised then, that night, that there was only one woman able to wield power over George's tightly guarded emotions and upset his equilibrium.

'I was cruel . . . I wanted him to suffer . . . I wanted him to feel my pain, my loss. I wanted him to feel regret,' Cora said now. She stared down at the lawn in front of her, parched and dry; thirsty, she thought, like Chazelles. The grass had always been thirsty there, too, would never grow like English grass . . .

No, she had never told him, she thought, returning to that memory. But she supposed he knew, had always supposed he knew. And then, at the end, hadn't she told him? Hadn't she raced to him to tell him that *their son* had died, and hadn't he placed his hands over his head and wept like a baby? 'But how could he not have known? I tried to tell him, tried so many times. And they looked so alike . . .'

It was then, at that time, she thought, that she had finally told George about Freddie, too. Freddie, who had died so long ago; Freddie, whom he had never met. Yes, she had told him on his deathbed that he had fathered not one but two sons. But it was not to hurt him, not then. She told him because she wanted him to know that she had loved him enough to raise his sons alone, without him. Because she wanted him to know how much she had loved him. She wanted him to know and understand.

She looked up, saw her younger self running barefoot across French grass chasing a small boy, and he, standing under the shade of trees, watching them, laughing. He had flitted in and out of their lives, Uncle George, famous Uncle George. She had not been his wife, had not been his mistress, not the acknowledged one, at any rate. She had been the mother of his children, kept in the shadows, overseas.

For years Cora had hoped – indeed, longed – for George to return to her, to declare his love to her. But his life, always a complex, compartmentalised world, became even more so. His talent, his fame and, more importantly it seemed, his reputation had trapped him. He inhabited another world, was part of an establishment foreign to Cora in every way, and the respectable public image of the English aristocratic painter, the image on which his commercial success had been built, served only to force his deeply private nature further into hiding. He carefully nurtured his public persona and vehemently guarded his private life. And as a close friend of the Prince of Wales, he lived at the very epicentre of fashionable London society. But there had always been gossip about him. He had once been rumoured to be having an affair with a notable duchess and, before that, embroiled with a former mistress of the Prince of Wales. He had moved on, and then on again.

There had still been Mrs Hillier, of course, and Cora had had no doubt that there were others, younger and prettier, and hidden away from public view. Once, over dinner in Paris, George had confided to her that he was neither inspired by nor attracted to the respectable eligible women of his class. And she had wondered if the rumours were true about the 'sitters' with whom he was reputed to have affairs.

But Cora made no demands. How could she? Clifford had been right all those years ago when he told her that George could never be owned; that he was owned only by his art, his vocation. So, instead, she had valued their friendship, and took comfort in *it* and her knowledge of him, the years that they had known each other. And she had her son; she had Georgie.

She raised her head to the sky. Hard to believe it was an English sky. Hard to believe it was the twentieth century. 'Nineteen eleven,' she said out loud, and she shook her head. It sounded absurdly futuristic. For she wasn't yet used to the twentieth century, the sound of it, its dates and strange fashions and new-fangled gadgets, and the year nineteen hundred seemed but a moment ago, or still in the future. But it had come and gone, and then, another decade. And I am here, she thought, in nineteen eleven, in England.

He had always said, 'You're too vibrant and colourful for England, too much of a free spirit, they won't be able to let themselves trust you . . .' And hadn't Edward warned her, too, all those years ago, that the dream would end, that it had to? That she would, eventually, leave Rome and return to England?

Edward . . .

But she did not wish to think about him, not now. 'It was a mistake . . . a mistake,' she said, rising up from the bench.

She walked towards the wrought-iron gate. A jackdaw flew up from the trees overhead, squawking as it rose into the blue. She could hear Mr Cordery's voice in the distance, the hum of a mowing machine. She stood by the gate for a moment, then turned and looked back across the garden, tapping at the earth with her cane. Had I done things differently, if I could have done things differently . . .

Then she heard them, the voices, all talking at once, still desperate to be heard.

'He was always so *ambitious*.'

'A snob!'

'A social climber!'

'And so fond of a title.'

'You simply weren't good enough for him – in his eyes.'

'Enough! Enough!' she called out, moving on along the path.

It wasn't like that. He had no choice . . . he had an opportunity, here in England, he had to return. He had no idea, he did not know . . .

'Yes he did. He had a responsibility to you and to—'

And she called out, 'No! I will not have it. Do you hear me? I will not have it . . .'

Then no one spoke. And the only thing she heard was the beating of her heart, the rushing of her blood through her narrowing veins, and his name, always his name.

CHAPTER 15

Her father has gone. She knows not where. But two whole days and nights have passed since he left. He told her to be good and look after the others. That was all. And it seems queer to her now that he didn't say more, and so she wonders if he has gone to look for her mother. But she has run out of stories, and the penny he gave her is gone. If he has not returned by morning she will take the others and walk back to the big house.

The sun continued to burn down, bleaching colour from the landscape. By the end of July the pastures around Bramley had turned brown; local farmers had been forced to raise the price of milk, and wells were running dry. The dock workers' dispute, which had begun in Southampton in June, had gathered momentum and spread to the north, and the threat of strikes erupted again. But now women were joining the fight for better pay, better working conditions, with jam-makers, pickle-makers, biscuit-makers and tea-packers all threatening to take action. And whilst the countryside lay in deep torpor, the cities in turmoil, an oppressive haze hung over Temple Hill.

Cora wondered if she, and perhaps the whole country with her, was going mad in the heat, and if it would ever abate. Sleep had never been easy and now it seemed impossible, apart from those daytime exhaustion-induced nightmares, and journeys into the past. Each one seemed so real. It was as though in returning to England she was having her life, that journey, forced back on her – to review, to reckon with, to atone. And she could not tell anyone. Could not say, 'I am afraid, afraid to close my eyes, afraid to remember.'

But Sylvia knew.

When Cora said, 'I need to talk to you,' Sylvia's heart leapt with joy. It did not matter to Sylvia what her friend was about to tell her, whether a confession, an anecdote, an apology, or nonsense. The fact was, Cora wished to speak to her again. Cora had barely uttered a word to her, had barely looked at her or spent any time with her since their fracas. Instead, she had chosen to spend an inordinate amount of time sitting about the garden, in her temple, alone, contemplating goodness knows what. And though Sylvia had tried to reach out to her, to offer the proverbial olive branch and words of comfort, Cora's isolation was such that she might as well have been in another country, Sylvia thought.

'You know I'm here for you, always,' Sylvia said, shuffling forward in her chair.

Cora nodded, glanced away momentarily, and then took a deep breath. 'The thing is, I appear to be the victim of some sort of blackmail attempt, again.'

'No!'

'It's a queer affair, and I'm not altogether sure what to do.'

Though the two women spoke at some length about the letters, Cora was careful not to divulge to Sylvia the exact nature of the contents of these missives. She told Sylvia that she suspected she had more than one blackmailer. For she had thought about the letters long and hard, she said, and there were obvious differences and discrepancies: in the hand, the spelling of her name, and the demands. Whilst one demanded money, and a paltry amount at that, the other seemed to want nothing more than confirmation of her identity.

'You must not give in to any of their demands,' said Sylvia.

Cora turned to her. 'But your advice, as I recall, was to cooperate.'

Sylvia looked blank, shook her head. 'No. You've never spoken to me about any of this, dear. I never said that. When did I say that?'

'The other day, in my room. I was sure I heard you tell me to *cooperate* with whoever is sending me the letters. I thought you knew about them.'

Sylvia almost laughed. 'My dear, you were delirious, imagining all sorts of things.'

'Hmm. Well, I'm thinking of dealing with it

differently this time. I'm contemplating bringing in the police.'

'Really? I thought you said you'd never do that. And what about the publicity? What about Jack? You have to think of him now. I'm quite sure if you ignore them, they will eventually realise the futility of their actions.'

'You may be right,' Cora replied, nodding, pensive. 'I shall deliberate.'

'I really think you should,' Sylvia said quickly. 'I think any haste on your part – in any sort of response – could be counter-productive and have damaging consequences. You said so yourself, the last time.'

'That was almost thirty years ago and, if you remember, the circumstances were very different. I was not residing here . . . was here only very briefly. This time,' she paused, staring at Sylvia, 'this time, I can't escape to another country.'

Sylvia shook her head. 'Astonishing that they've managed to keep track – of you, I mean, after all these years.'

'It's all because of that wretched business with Cassandra, I suppose, my name being in the news-papers again.'

'But which name?' Sylvia asked.

Cora smiled. 'De Chevalier de Saint Léger, but people have long memories, particularly those with . . . tawdry motivations.'

Sylvia reached out, placed her hand upon Cora's, and said again, 'I'm sure if you ignore them, offer

286

no response at all, they will stop. They have to stop. What else can they do?'

Cora lowered her eyes. 'They can carry out their threats, go to those publications who appear to take such delight in printing cheap gossip. And I can't allow that. I can't take that risk. Not now.'

'You know, and I've told you so before, if we finish your memoirs, tell the truth, the whole story, it will once and for all silence your critics. You need to be open and honest about that time before you went to Rome, you need to record the facts.'

'Yes. I have been thinking this too. We must get to it, Sylvia. After all, it's what you came down here to do,' she added, looking up at her friend and attempting a smile.

And Sylvia suddenly felt quite emotional. It had been a trying few days but now, despite the gravity of the situation, despite that painful exchange, it seemed reason and friendship were restored. At last they could get to work on the book that would, in Sylvia's mind, once and for all quell any festering rumours and innuendo about Cora's past and her marriage to Edward. There was not a moment to lose, Sylvia said, and now was as good a time as any to make a start.

For the next few days the two women worked in harmony. They sat together each afternoon, sometimes in the house, sometimes outside in the garden, and as Cora reminisced, Sylvia took it all down. They were, once again, covering ground already recorded, but Sylvia decided to keep quiet and allow Cora to lead the way. At the end of each session Sylvia read back to Cora what she had written, and Cora would nod, say yes or no, offer amendments and sometimes check Sylvia's spelling. Occasionally, Cora had second thoughts and asked Sylvia to omit a name or event for unspecified reasons. But Sylvia was happy enough to strike a line through a page or a name.

They were sitting on the bench by the pergola when Sylvia said, 'Oh, I must make a note of Antonin's medals and honours.'

Cora shook her head. 'There's no need.'

The war that claimed Antonin de Chevalier's life was a short war, over in a matter of weeks. After his death, Cora and her son left France and returned to Rome, where they remained as those that had been part of the Commune were rounded up and executed in their thousands. Paris was no place to be, France was no place to be, and Cora, not yet forty, was a widow once more.

She had no desire to return to the Chateau de Chazelles, she said. There, weeks passed by without any visitors, and she knew the slow passing of time and sense of isolation would compound her melancholia and sense of loss. With Antonin so often away, she had lived there alone but for the servants and her young son for almost two years. There was little to do other than walk and read, or ride out across the empty fields and rolling hillsides. Her time had been punctuated by regular trips to Paris, to visit her dressmaker and select new gowns, and catch up with friends, including George, once.

He had written to her to tell her he would be passing through Paris, en route to Vichy with Mrs Hillier. But when Cora and her son went to meet them for tea at their hotel, Mrs Hillier was indisposed; 'understandably exhausted by our long journey', George said.

At first he seemed distracted, twitchy, and after only five minutes excused himself to go upstairs and check on his companion. Like a devoted pet, Cora thought. It was late summer and they sat outside in the hotel's private garden, watching Georgie chase pigeons. He told Cora he was astounded by how much his godson had grown, and when Georgie ran up to him and jumped on to his lap, Cora had had to look away, so shocking was the likeness. 'He's adorable,' George said minutes later, watching the child gallop across the parterre in front of them, 'quite adorable.'

They made polite, if somewhat stilted, conversation, mainly about his work and his recent exhibition in London. And from time to time one of them asked the other, 'And do you ever hear anything of . . .' But when, eventually, Cora picked up her purse and said, 'It's getting late and I must not keep you,' he reached over and grabbed hold of her hand. 'I hear things, you know, even in London. I hear you have a new lover . . . a *young* lover.'

Cora smiled. So, word *had* got back to him. Sylvia could always be relied on. 'And what if I do?' she asked, pulling her hand free.

He looked away and said nothing for a moment. But as she rose to her feet, he said, 'Don't go yet. Stay a little while longer.'

'A little while longer?' she repeated, staring at him. 'That's what you used to say to me . . . stay a little while longer Cora, and I did. But you did not stay a little while longer for me. I think you should go and check on Amy,' she added, pulling on her gloves. 'You haven't been up to look in on her for over an hour.'

And then she called out to her son and bid him adieu.

'What about your aunt's marriage to Prospero?' Sylvia was saying.

'Hmm?'

'What would you like to have recorded about that?'

'Oh, well, one must include that, and all the changes at that time. It was, I suppose, the beginning of the end . . . in Rome.'

The year after Antonin's death, and months after the death of James Staunton in Rome, Cora returned to France, to an apartment situated off the Rue du Faubourg Saint-Honoré, in Paris. It was an area she knew well. She had given the matter considerable thought and could think of no better place to live. Expatriate Rome, she had decided, was too small, too confined, and she had no wish to live permanently with her newly widowed aunt. In Paris she would be free, without any need to look over her shoulder. And where better to be a widow?

A trust set up by James Staunton ensured that her son's educational and personal expenses were more than adequately provided for, and with a small income from investments she was at last 'of independent means'. Georgie was to be despatched to boarding school in England, her aunt resided in another country, and she had no husband to curtail her activities. She also knew that George made regular trips to Paris.

At that time reminders of the city's recent struggle were visible everywhere, but for Cora nowhere was more poignant than the burnt-out ruin of the Tuileries Palace. The opulent, lavishly furnished rooms, built by Catherine de Medici and home to the sovereigns of France for hundreds of years, had perished, and all that remained was the charred façade. But Paris, like Cora, was about to go through a process of reinvigoration and reinvention. New wide streets and boulevards, pleasure gardens, squares and fountains would give the city an altogether bright and modern feel. Paris reawakened Cora to her love of city life, and the bustling cafés, thronged streets, constant movement of people and vehicles, the daily spectacle of the city's wealthy fashion-conscious residents, made her feel as though she was living at the very hub of the universe, the capital not just of France, but of the world.

For a number of years Cora's routine remained unchanged. She spent her mornings idly shopping, buying brocades, feathers and lace to add to hats and costumes, visiting her seamstress, or passing through the endless rooms of paintings and marbles in the Musée du Louvre galleries. Each afternoon she pulled on her riding habit and bowler, ordered her horse to be brought round, and set off side-saddle for the Bois de Boulogne. Evenings were filled with the opera, theatre, and endless dinners where she indulged in her love of conversation, updating herself on the political swirls and rumbles from Rome and London.

Cora's aunt was by now a formidable force in Rome, and, at the age of seventy-one, had remarried. A colonel in the Noble Guards of his Holiness the Pope, Prospero Cansacchi was a decade younger than Fanny Staunton, with an ancient lineage, a palazzo, and a title.

Fanny's marriage pleased Cora greatly, and she wasted no time in placing an announcement in the London *Times: Mrs Francesca Staunton, widow of the late James Staunton of Rome, aunt of the Countess de Chevalier de Saint Léger, was married to Count Prospero Cansacchi di Amelia, at Amelia, Italy, on Saturday last.*

The newly styled Contessa Cansacchi visited her niece in Paris, but whilst Cora relished the relentless merry-go-round of the French capital's

292

colourful nightlife, her aunt still preferred the cosiness of expatriate Rome. The world of her stylish niece was exciting and glamorous, but it was much too fast and modern for the old contessa. But Rome, too, was changing, and the medieval town inside the ancient city walls had been all but swept away. The narrow streets and ramshackle buildings of Cora's early days had been replaced with grand civic buildings and fine hotels, and the construction of a vast monument to Victor Emmanuel had commenced on the ancient site at Capitoline hill, overshadowing the old Piazza d'Ara Coeli and dwarfing its tiny, crumbling fountain.

Many of the English expatriates, rattled by the changes and upheaval, had returned home, knowing that an era had ended. But each winter continued to deliver a few familiar if tired faces, as well as a steady stream of seemingly deliriously happy new ones, enjoying their first Grand Tour. Hungry for souvenirs, artefacts and paintings, the new visitors were different to the old ones: they were rich. And though Cora's aunt and others considered their seasonal guests to be rather insensitive, vulgar and brash, Cora had no issue with new money. Privately, she preferred many of the jolly new arrivals to the somewhat pessimistic and impoverished expatriates. She was enthralled by their bravado as much as their wealth, for where the expatriate set were able to exude a collective artistic sensibility and an appreciation for the antiquated beauty in their midst, their bejewelled visitors were able to purchase it.

Invitations to the elderly Contessa Cansacchi's soirees were highly sought after by visitors to Rome. Her apartment, though a little overcrowded with ornamentation, seemed to them to bear all the hallmarks of old money, with a distinctly continental style. And her soirees were invariably a mix of the old and new crowd, as well as Italian and French nobility. New arrivals, who had visited Paris en route to Rome, were told, 'Ah, so you were in Paris . . . you may have met my niece, the Countess de Chevalier de Saint Léger?' It was heady stuff for many of them, and partly what they had come to Europe for: to be educated, purchase art and make interesting connections. And when the Countess de Chevalier de Saint Léger was in residence, staying with her aunt, she only added to the array of foreign titles on offer. She was altogether different to anyone back in England.

As knowledgeable as she was fashionable, her gowns – all from Paris – were of exquisite taste, something money alone could not buy. Yet it was also noted that the younger countess had an easy ability to relate to the common man. Her manner was as of much interest and note as the size of her bustle or the height of her hair, the way in which she used her hands or held her glass or fork; the subjects she chose to speak about and those she preferred to remain silent on. She appeared to encapsulate all that was glamorous in a modern cosmopolitan society, and yet – and without offending anyone – she also broke any number of rules. She held opinions and challenged men quite openly, displaying a confidence that was rare and exciting and frightening at the same time. Her once golden hair had a silver hue, and was worn in a fashionable up-knot, usually adorned with an encrusted comb or exotic plume. Her face, everyone noted, had an uncommon youthfulness about it, and her usual expression of aloof detachment was softened by the teasing suggestion of a smile about her mouth, which men – and in particular the man who would be her next husband – found quite beguiling.

CHAPTER 16

'*If you touch her again I'll kill you,*' *she says, in a new voice, and holding the knife out in front of them.*

'*Whores,*' *he says, and spits on the floor. '*Bloody whores, both of you.*'

And then he turns and leaves the room.

'Paris! That was my zenith,' Cora said to Sylvia.

But they had already *done* Paris. Sylvia knew all about Paris. She knew full well that the *happiest days* of her life had been spent there, where he was – where George was – so often, so easily. It had been their place of rendezvous, and for so many years. Wasn't that why she had moved there, to be able to see him? Oh, Cora always claimed she had lived there because she loved the place, particularly at that time. But Sylvia knew better.

'I rather think we've covered Paris,' Sylvia said.

'It was his favourite city, you know?' Cora went on. 'The one place we could meet and . . . just *be*. The one place people didn't bother him, make demands on him, his time. Where he was able to be himself, able to relax.'

Sylvia nodded. 'But didn't Mrs Hillier keep a house there?'

Cora jerked. 'What has that to do with anything? I hope you're not including *her* in the book. I want no mention of her. None at all. Yes, she kept a house in Paris, as you well know, but she was in very poor health by then, bedridden, and quite unable to leave England. And anyway, she and George's friendship had long since ended.'

Sylvia chose not to mention Evie Dipple, George's muse and sitter at that time, reputed to keep house for him in London. Cora had turned a blind eye to it, so she would too.

'And I want absolutely no mention of that awful Evie Dipple woman either,' Cora suddenly said, as though reading Sylvia's thoughts. 'Or any of the others.'

'Of course not.'

After a few minutes, Sylvia – who had been silently practising, building up to it – said, 'Shall we make a few notes about your early life?'

'Fine,' Cora said, looking away, across the garden.

But as soon as Cora mentioned Standen Hall, Sylvia shook her head and put down her pencil. 'You need to be truthful, Cora. You're not being truthful *enough*.' She closed her notebook. 'But we can ponder on it, return to it tomorrow. It will allow you a little time to think things through.'

'Think things through,' Cora repeated vaguely.

Yes, she needed to think things through, she thought; unravel fact from fiction. The truth, the glimpses she had had of it of late, was hazy and blurred, and dreamlike. Had she dreamt her life? she wondered. If only her aunt were still alive, she would tell her what to do. For hadn't she always told her what to do, how to be, *who* to be?

But Sylvia's words – suspended about the ether *and* in print – had confused her further. Stories based on her life, inspired by *her version* of her life, had been recorded, over and over, with differing permutations and endings, and always without any beginning. She glanced about the garden, back to her friend and away again.

Then, out of the blue, Sylvia said, 'Actually, if we aren't going to work on the memoirs, do you mind if we *do* talk about Paris again? Harriett is back there, you see, she has returned to Armand and I need to immerse myself – set the scene.'

'I thought they were at Lucca?'

Sylvia laughed. 'Really, dear, that was chapter fifteen; this is chapter twenty-four! Possibly the penultimate chapter.'

'Possibly? Dependent upon what?'

'Well, whether Armand takes her back, of course.'

'Of course? But haven't you decided? One would have thought as their creator you have *some* say in their fate.'

Sylvia raised her eyes, pensive for a moment, then said, 'Yes, to a certain extent I do. But I never decide my endings until I arrive there. And I chose Paris because you've always told me that it is the most romantic city, a city for lovers.'

Cora's head throbbed. The heat was stifling. A storm was forecast. Sylvia had read it out to her. And the whalebone, holding her in, holding everything in, made it almost impossible for her to breathe. Sylvia meant well, she knew that, but her constant fussing and need to please had become irksome, and almost as intolerable as the heat. She felt no sense of peace, or space, and that feeling of claustrophobia only added to her discomfiture. And the questions: always asking, wanting to know something about something – a date, person, place, who was who, who had said what to whom. She hadn't meant to snap, and had no wish to be discourteous or unkind, but really, surely Sylvia could see it was too much. And after all, it was her wretched story.

When she said, 'I may as well write the blessed thing myself,' she had meant it. But Sylvia had looked crestfallen, quite tearful, and so she had apologised, again. Then she said, 'I must take a walk. I need to think about things.'

'My dear, you need to settle yourself.'

'No . . . no. I have to sort . . . my head, my heart.'

Sylvia rose to her feet, laid the back of her hand across Cora's brow. 'Oh, but you feel feverish again, dear. Perhaps I should send for Dr Parsons.'

'I do not need a doctor.'

'Then stay where you are and allow me to read to you.'

'He's here, Sylvia. He's with us.'

'Who is here, dear? Who do you think is here?'

'He is. I've seen him, more than once, here in the garden, and in the house. He wishes to speak to me, I think, he wishes to tell me.'

'Tell you?'

'Yes. There must be a reason why he's come to me, here, now. You see, I think he knows . . . knows what is happening.' She looked at Sylvia. 'Oh, I know, I know what you're thinking, you're thinking I'm going mad with the heat, that I'm suffering delusions. But I'm not. I saw him as clearly as I see you now. He's here, Sylvia, he's waiting for me,' she added, and smiled. 'He still loves me.'

'Well, of course. Of course he's here with you, and of course he still loves you. He always did, always.'

Sylvia had seen Cora mouthing words to herself in the garden days before. She had followed her outside and, from behind the pergola, had watched her as she sat muttering and mumbling – presumably to George. She saw and made out enough to know that Cora believed she was speaking directly to him. It was beyond sad. For there was no one there – how could there be? He had been gone two decades. And yet, watching her, straining to hear her, Sylvia found herself turning time and again towards the sundial, looking for him, almost longing to see him.

Many of Cora's words had been silent, others mere sounds, melting into the air. But Sylvia distinctly heard her say George's name, and mention 'our grandson'. A few minutes after that, when Cora had yelled out, 'No', and appeared to look towards the pergola, Sylvia had swiftly moved off up a pathway through the woodland, towards the driveway back to the house.

It was late in the evening when the storm arrived, rattling windows and doors and glass panes, whistling down every chimney. It had been anticipated for days, but came with a force so great that rather than quell any delusions it took them a stage further.

Cora had been at sea. Somewhere between Southampton and Le Havre, or Marseilles and Civitavecchia. She had woken to pitch-blackness, a small cabin rocking, the great roar of a swell outside. She felt hot and sick, feverish once again. She had clung to her bed, wondering what year it was, to which port she was headed, and whether or not she was married, and to whom. Everything was muddled, tossed about by the roll and sway and hidden in the darkness. And thus she drifted in and out of slumber, and in and out of that first journey to Rome, glancing through carriage windows and tiny portholes, across a sea vast and deep and dark. Sailing away from England, away from them . . . and away from *him*, the man she had called 'Uncle John'.

When she heard the footsteps, felt someone climb upon the bed, arms reach around her, she could not be sure if it was not part of another dream. But when she heard herself speak, say his name, it seemed to her to be real . . .

'George?'

'I'm here.'

'I'm frightened.'

'There's nothing to be afraid of, my love.'

'But we might drown . . .'

'No, we shan't drown.'

'Don't leave me.'

'I shan't leave you.'

'I don't know what to do. What shall I do?'

He did not reply. And so she asked him again, without words, in silence: *what shall I do?*

You must do nothing.

You knew, didn't you?

Yes, I knew.

But how did you know? Who told you?

Someone. Someone told me . . .

I wasn't allowed to say anything, wasn't allowed to speak about any of it. Fanny said I must never speak about it, no one could ever know.

Hush now, you must sleep, must rest.

Then she felt his hand upon her hair, heard herself breathing, in and out, in and out.

CHAPTER 17

*I*f it happened again she would kill him. She had heard her say it. And if she didn't kill him then someone else would have to. Someone else would have to do it. If only her mother would come back and take her away from this place. Come back and gather them all up.

Summer wilted. Frogs and minnows shrivelled and dried and died in the sun-baked mud of ditches and ponds and streams. Lawns long yellow turned brown, and birds stopped singing. No sigh of nature could be heard, no breath of wind moved the trees and no petal stirred. But the out-of-towners and motor enthusiasts continued to flee to the country, honking horns on silent lanes, searching for a picture-postcard church, an open tea shop, and cooler air.

At Temple Hill, Cora waited for Cecily.

When she heard Sylvia mutter, 'That girl can't seem to stay away,' she said, 'Jack invited her, and *I* happen to like her calling in.'

Sylvia said, 'Are you aware she's planning to write a book about you?'

Cora laughed. 'Well, it's not the first, is it?'

'So long as you know what she's up to. It's none of my business, of course, my only concern is protecting you.'

'I hardly think I need protecting from Cecily.'

Sylvia's antipathy towards Cecily Chadwick was, Cora thought, like some queer jealousy. Every time her name cropped up, Sylvia's back straightened, face crumpled. She was suspicious of Cecily, Cora understood that, but it was surely unfounded. The previous day Sylvia had gone so far as to say she thought Cecily might be a gold-digger. She told Cora that she had seen Cecily more than once examining her possessions, looking beneath bits of china, scrutinising artwork for a signature, 'just as though she were placing a monetary value on them'.

But Sylvia had always suffered from jealousy. Not of Cora, but of anyone close to Cora. She had been jealous of George from the start. Had wasted no time in telling Cora of rumours, many of which Cora later discovered to have been incubated and hatched by Sylvia herself. And she had been the first, the very first to explain George's relationship with Mrs Hillier, and then later, for years, agree with Cora that he would never in a month of Sundays give up the older woman, that it was hopeless, that he simply did not love Cora *enough*.

'They visited the Academy yesterday,' Sylvia said. 'Have you told Jack? Does he know?'

She stared at Sylvia. 'Know what?'

'Well . . . that you are there, dear.'

Cora flinched, shook her head. 'No. And I don't intend to.'

John Clifford's sculpture 'Tinted Venus' was now at the Academy. She was there, on display and naked for all to see. It was easy enough to pass off the painting in the hallway; 'It was a gift,' she liked to say, 'from a dear old friend.' It had been Mr Fox who had used the word 'erotic'. She had been shocked by his choice of adjective and had laughed at the time, saying, 'Gracious, I shall have to have it burned, else the people of Bramley will burn me!' He had laughed, but hadn't he given her a queer look?

Sometime later Jack had asked, 'It's not you, is it, in that painting in the hallway? It's just that it rather looks like you, or how I imagine you once looked.'

She had laughed again. 'I *am* flattered! I have no idea who the sitter was but I can assure you that it was not me, my dear.'

And Sylvia, too, did not know. Oh, she knew about Clifford's 'Venus', and about George's 'Madonna', but she did not know what had happened at Lucca. Though she liked to think she did. She did not know that George had painted her there, and years later presented her with the painting. Cora had given Sylvia a synopsis, an edited synopsis of those weeks at Lucca, and she, Sylvia, had added to it, as she always did. And yet it amused Cora. For so many clues were there, hanging in the hallway of her home. But even Edward had failed to realise that it was in fact herself as Aphrodite.

It had been some years after her marriage to Edward, during that first summer's visit to England, when George arrived by cab carrying a large canvas covered in brown paper. It was, he insisted, a gift, and he looked at Cora as he said, 'Consider it my belated wedding present to you both. I should have given it to you when you were married but I could not bring myself to part with it.' And she had been embarrassed, as much by his attachment to the canvas as the image upon it.

Edward had later commented to her that it was not, in his opinion, 'entirely suitable' as a wedding gift. But had he not realised then that it was her? For he had stared at it for some time, perplexed, before having it removed to the attic of his home.

Now she wished she were able to tell Cecily about the painting, the story that went with it, the child conceived during its execution. Cecily, she thought, understood art and would not be shocked. But no, it was too complicated, would mean explaining so much, which would only lead on to more. 'And then she would judge me . . . she would not understand,' she concluded.

And yet Cora could not help but smile whenever she thought of Cecily, because she inevitably thought of her grandson as well. She had watched them together, seen Jack's fumbling attempts to be indifferent, seen that look in his eyes, even when he glanced at Cecily for a second or two. And it had catapulted her back. So familiar was his look, his aura. Oh yes, he was smitten, in love. But they were both so young, and he was ambitious, had already told her that he had no wish to settle down until he was at least thirty. And Cecily? Cecily had informed her that she wanted to travel, see the world, and not be encumbered by family, and expectations and obligations. She was a modern woman in a modern world. It was all so very different now.

Sylvia was saying, 'I wonder what they'd make of it if they knew about you being there, in the Academy.'

'I'd rather not think about it, if you don't mind.'

There were no two ways about it: Sylvia would have to go, and soon. She was becoming a liability and knew far too much, Cora decided. She had not properly considered, had not properly thought through the implications of having Sylvia there, with Jack.

'John Clifford,' Sylvia said, wistfully. 'He was such a kind, dear little man.'

'Yes, he was,' Cora replied. She could still picture the elderly sculptor, standing in his dusty smock, surrounded by his tinted marble goddesses and nymphs. And hadn't he been the one to first warn her? Hadn't he been the one to tell her that 'dear George' was not the marrying sort; that he was married to his art, his vocation? But she had dismissed Clifford's words, had continued her fantasy, for so many years – a lifetime.

When Sylvia announced that she was going out for a walk, Cora said, 'But you'll miss Cecily.'

'She has no wish to see me . . . and I'm quite sure you'd prefer me not to be here,' she added – newly cryptic, Cora thought.

When Cecily arrived she brought apples and raspberries, and some eggs. And, for a while, Jack loitered about in the doorway, looking nonchalant, or trying to, and saying things like, 'I'm just popping out to the courtyard', or, 'I need to have a quick word with Mr Cordery . . .' and then disappeared for five minutes and came back, twitchy, nervous, hands in pockets. But Cora was keen to catch up with Cecily alone. And so, eventually, she asked Jack if he'd be so kind as to run an errand for her, delivering a remittance to the shop in the village.

Cora did not particularly wish to hear about the Academy. It had once been George's domain, the world he had presided over without her. But she had to ask. It would have been impolite not to.

'And so, what did you see at the Academy, dear?'

'Golly, we saw so much, I hardly know where to begin.'

And then she did, she began a roll call of familiar names and old friends, and Cora stared at her, impassive, occasionally raising an eyebrow in recognition or nodding.

'Oh, and we saw quite a few of Lord Lawson's paintings as well.'

Cora smiled. And as Cecily reeled off famous

titles, each one – still vivid – flashed through Cora's mind's eye. 'And Sylvia happened to mention that you were once his sitter,' Cecily added.

Cora closed her eyes. 'Dear Sylvia, she does get a little confused about certain things, and this is one of them!' she said and tried to laugh.

'But you knew him?'

Cora glanced away. 'Yes, yes, I knew him. I met him in Rome, when I was very young – when we were all very young.'

'He was President of the Academy,' Cecily said, as though Cora needed to be reminded.

'That is correct, he was. And a supremely gifted and talented painter.'

Happily, the conversation moved on.

'. . . and then we took an omnibus and sat up on the top, and went the whole way round Hyde Park, and Jack pointed out where he lived with his mother . . . You never lived in London?' she asked.

Cora shook her head. 'No, though I know it well, and have stayed there often enough.'

'I'd like to live in London one day, I'd like to experience life in a city.'

'Paris is the best city to experience life when one is young.'

'Do you ever wish you were still there?'

'Oh, sometimes, but only if I could be young again also,' Cora said, smiling.

'Hmm. I can imagine you there, in Paris. It suits you more than Bramley!'

It suits you more . . .

The words threw her back: they were the very words Edward had used in Paris, when George brought them together again, after so many years.

'It suits you more, more than Rome or London. Yes, Paris suits you!' Edward had exclaimed, and all three of them laughed.

They were dining at the Café Anglais on the Boulevard des Italiens. She and George had recently travelled together from Rome via the Riviera to Paris. And back in the French capital, they had attended the opera and theatre, and dined out together each evening. At that time George made frequent visits to the city and they had seen more of each other. To many in Paris they were a fixture, a couple like any other. So much so, that many there – none the wiser – simply assumed them to be *Monsieur et Madame*. And Cora, now styled the Countess de Chevalier de Saint Léger, had begun to think this was the way it would be. And she could live with it, she thought. She could live with George coming back to her once a month, perhaps, telling her there was no one but her, that he loved her, adored her. Such passion, she told herself, would only be diluted by a contract, a contract of marriage.

But that evening at the Café Anglais, Edward had overshadowed George. For his presence was commanding, his seniority unquestionable. And he had been charming, effusive; telling Cora he simply could not believe how little she had aged, or that the young English girl he remembered so well from Rome was now such a renowned society figure, a feted hostess. Like a fine wine, he said, she had only improved with age. But Edward's broad smiles and attentiveness had had a debilitating effect upon George's spirit, he had grown quieter and more sullen as the evening progressed. He sent back his steak, complained about the service, and made such a fuss about a draught from the door that they moved tables, twice.

Only years later did Cora learn of George's anguish that night. That after escorting her home and returning to his hotel with Edward, he had been unable to sleep and had come to her.

At two o'clock in the morning he had walked out from his hotel on the Rue de Rivoli into a seedy mix of nocturnal human debris littering the street corners and alleyways of the French capital. He told her that his body seemed decided upon a route without any consultation with his mind. Eventually, he had found himself in front of the stone steps leading up to the doorway of her apartment building. And through the closed shutters he thought he could make out a light within her room. He had stood there for some time, wondering what he should do. With his hands thrust deep into the pockets of his overcoat, he had shuffled and paced, up and down and up and down in front of the building, berating himself out loud and muttering expletives in any number of languages. At one point, he ran up the steps and held his hand over the cord of the bell, only to pull it away and run back down the steps. Then a light had gone on inside the ground-floor apartment. A window opened. 'Who is there? What do you want?' a female voice called out. And George quickly marched off back up the street, into the night.

Now Cora thought, if only he had pulled on that damned cord. Why hadn't he? What stopped him? She felt the dull ache of regret and longing, and years gone by. And she thought of her marriage, her final marriage, there in Paris the very next year. But it was not revenge. It had never been about revenge. Or had it?

There had always been gossip about George's affairs, and there had been so many by then. He had grown more handsome with age, his silvering hair and beard lending him a distinguished look which seemed only to emphasise his success. And what had once been his 'perfect vision' had aged, aged beautifully, as he repeatedly told her, but aged nonetheless. The waist had thickened, the pert chin had softened, and the hair, like his, had silvered and lost its sheen. Oh, Cora still had her admirers, George included, but she could not compete with youth. She was by then the mother of a young man, and had, everyone knew, been widowed twice, and the map of her life showed on her face.

The final agony came only a few months after that fateful dinner at the Café Anglais, when Cora received a letter from Sylvia informing her that George had recently returned to London from

Paris – with Evie Dipple. Had Cora seen them together? Did she know? Sylvia asked. She went on to say that she had heard he was 'smitten, quite besotted by the girl, and she – young enough to be his daughter! But I imagine you saw them, crossed paths, or perhaps heard that they were in town? I'm longing to know if you met them, and what you made of it all & of her. I understand she is an actress as well as an artist's model, & from somewhere in the East End, I believe. Quite something when one bears in mind what a snob George once was. Such hypocrisy!'

That George had elected to bring his young lover to Paris cut as deep as any goodbye. They could so easily have crossed paths and yet she had been kept in the dark; he had not even had the decency to warn her. The irony of her name, her title, and the fact his new love hailed from the East End of London was not lost on her either. And if we had met, if we had bumped into each other, she thought at the time, what would I have done? How should I have been? Am I nothing more to him than a former and occasional lover, an old friend? 'I am the mother of his children . . . the mother of his son.'

'Does it still feel strange to be here, back in England?' Cecily was asking, leaning forward, elbows on her knees, chin cupped in her hands.

'Sometimes. Sometimes I think I might wake up and discover that I have dreamed this . . . this

313

particular part of my life, my dotage. Wishful thinking, perhaps,' she added, raising her eyebrows. 'You know, when I was young, when I was your age and first in Rome, everything felt *too* real . . . too vivid and alive.'

'Maybe it was that place.'

'Mm, that place, that time. It was all new to me, still foreign, exotic,' she smiled, 'and I, like a newborn baby, opening up my eyes for the very first time, dazzled by the splendour, the magnificence, the mystery of it all. Life is so intoxicating when one is young.'

It was Clifford who had said to her, 'We all lose our senses here, for a while at least. It's an inevitable though heady infatuation. We're made to fall in love – by history, the romance of the place. The possibilities seem limitless, and for a time we think we are immortal, like the ancient ruins surrounding us. You're simply infatuated, my dear. No more or less. It will pass.'

But it never passed.

Later that afternoon Jack came to Cora and asked if he could speak with her. And she guessed what was coming, had been anticipating it for weeks, but she was still unprepared. Now, he too sat with a notebook and pencil, saying he wished to record it, 'get it all down'.

'There's really no need, Sylvia is recording my memories.'

He told her he wished to know more about Jack, his namesake; his grandfather, he called him.

'Oh well, he was a good man, a very good man, kind, discerning . . . gentle. Very like his father.'

'And I look like him, or so Sylvia said.'

'Mm, somewhat.'

They spoke about her aunt, and Cora described the palazzo apartment where they had lived with James Staunton and his son, Jack; pointing to various paintings and items of furniture that had once been there. Oh, how she wished he could have seen it, and seen Rome, as it used to be. They had been so happy there, a close family, she said. Herself, Aunt Fanny, James Staunton and Jack: a family of four. And she and Jack like brother and sister.

He frowned. 'But then you married him . . . Jack.'

She smiled, nodded.

'But was it not odd for one's uncle to become one's father-in-law? One's brother one's husband?' he asked. 'Must be queer to marry within one's family.'

Her heart shivered. 'Well, we were, for a time, like brother and sister.'

'And then?'

'And then we fell in love and were married,' she said, looking down, smoothing out the skirt of her gown. She glanced up, caught his eye. 'Not all marriages are born of passion, and I'm not sure it's a necessary foundation for an *enduring* marriage,' she said.

'And were you happy together?' he asked, staring directly at her.

She glanced away. 'Well, yes,' she replied, 'as happy as it was possible to be then . . . as happy as I knew how to be then.'

'You never speak about him.'

She shrugged. 'It was a long time ago, we were married for a very short time.'

'And his death, it was an accident?'

She nodded. 'Yes,' she said, 'an accident. He slipped and fell.'

It had been early autumn, she told him, barely a month before the birth of his father, Georgie. An English banker – a friend of the family – had arrived at the apartment in a state of great distress, followed by two men, carrying Jack. He was already unconscious, covered in blood from a gaping wound to his head. There was nothing Dr Small could do. He died hours later. 'I thought at the time I was dreaming, having a nightmare, that I would wake up and discover . . . something else. It's all a blur now, that time. I was nearing the end of my confinement and I think I slept all through those final weeks.' She shook her head. 'Hard to recall . . . hard to recall.'

For a few minutes his questions stopped. He sat pondering, cogitating, jutting out his jaw, hand to his chin in that way he did – like George, like Georgie. Then he said, 'I always feel as though there's something you're not telling me. Please, don't take this the wrong way. I just have this . . . this feeling that . . .'

'Yes?' she said, looking up at him, her heart trembling.

'Oh, I don't know. I imagine it's all because, well, because I've not known anything about you, not properly, not up until now. You know, for a while you were almost a myth to me. I hardly believed you existed!'

She laughed.

'Mother always said you were . . . a little difficult, impossibly grand and rather . . . too beautiful. She said that she'd always suspected you had a few dark secrets. I think she thought you held things back, weren't completely honest with Father.' He paused, looked away. 'I think she almost resented you for the love you had for him.'

'Well, of course I loved him – I loved him very much. He was my baby, and the most loving and affectionate son. He always seemed to sense how I was feeling, whether I was sad or happy, or lonely. And he never had Ge— ack in his life. He was born in the midst of tragedy. Rather like you.'

He lowered his head. 'Yes, it would seem we were both jinxed.'

'Don't say that. You had a father who, had he been here now, would have loved you, oh so much. And a grandfather who would have adored you.'

He looked up at her. 'And what about *your* father?'

'I'm afraid I never really knew him,' she replied.

'But what was his name?'

'His name was Samuel . . . Samuel Stopher.'

'So you were born Cora Stopher?'

It was the first time anyone had put those two names together, but she simply smiled and nodded.

'And what did he do? Did he have an occupation?'

'He was a gentleman . . . a rentier.'

'A rentier?'

'He owned land . . . property.'

'In Suffolk?'

She nodded. 'Woodbridge, or thereabouts.'

'We should go and visit, you and I. I'd be interested to see it, where you grew up, where you hail from.' Then he laughed. 'I can't very easily visit South America, but Suffolk is within reach.'

After a little while, he put the notebook to one side, sat back in his chair and said, 'So, tell me about the great Antonin.'

And she was relieved, for she could speak about Antonin, her time at Chazelles, without any sense of trepidation. She could tell him how a dashing French officer had wooed her in Rome, married her and taken her to live in his castle. She could speak about a distinguished military career, a noble death and medals and honours. She could tell him of that short-lived but fortuitous union, and just as it had moved her on, so it moved them on.

Eventually, he said, 'And you never wished to marry again?'

She shook her head, glanced away. 'No, twice was enough. Quite enough.'

CHAPTER 18

What she needs is a weapon, something weighty, something to knock him out with. He would be slow, would be drunk; was always drunk at night. And her aunt was frightened; she could see that, had seen and heard enough to know that husbands are not always tender and loving.

Yes, a weapon.

For three days Cora barely uttered a word to Sylvia. She was angry, angry at Sylvia's snooping, and at her ridiculous claims and insinuations. The only person she could rely on was Cecily, who had reported everything back to her, confirming her suspicions once and for all that Sylvia could not be trusted. The final straw – though there had by that time been enough to line a stable floor, she thought – had been her discovery of Sylvia's visit to Meadow Farm. And it had been Mr Fox who had reported that particular excursion back to Cora, having passed by on his bicycle.

She had hoped that Sylvia would take the hint, would voluntarily depart and return to London. She had hoped that she would not have to ask her to leave. The former would perhaps allow them to salvage some scrap of friendship, in time; the latter would most definitely end it forever.

When she finally summoned Sylvia to the drawing room and said, 'I wish to speak to you, Sylvia, please sit down,' Sylvia had not smiled, and Cora suspected she knew what was coming. She produced her own notebook and quietly read out from it. Then she looked up at Sylvia and said, 'Well, do you have anything to say?'

Sylvia said, 'A litany of charges, it would seem, and no doubt all Cecily Chadwick's doing. But I have to tell you that I think you're being foolish, very foolish to listen to and trust that girl. In fact, I've been holding back my suspicions about her and her mother for some time.' She paused. 'I fear your blackmailers are closer to home than you realise.'

Cora laughed. 'The Chadwicks! Oh, Cecily and Madeline are not my blackmailers, Sylvia. I know exactly who—'

'You've always been naive,' Sylvia interrupted, 'always trusted the wrong people. It's why you're in the situation you're in today. Had you thought more, been more discerning in your judgement,' she continued, her voice now trembling, 'your life might have been different . . . and perhaps you would not have lost *him*!'

'How dare you. How dare you say that to me, after *everything*. You know nothing, nothing at all about real life. You've spent half a century lost in your own imaginings, making up stories that have no bearing whatsoever on real life, real love. You don't know what real love is.'

'I know what it's not – it's not what you did to him. That was unforgivable, and it will make you go mad – mad like her before you. It was revenge, pure and simple, and you know it.'

Cora stared at her. 'I think you've said enough, more than enough. I've already sent for Cotton, he'll be here any minute. There will be a train back to London sometime soon, I'm sure,' she added, pulling on the bell by her side.

Sylvia rose to her feet. 'You can banish me and you can hide away here, but you can't escape, not now. Jack wants to know the truth, he wants to know who he is, and he's going to find out, he's going to discover *everything* about you . . . and about that awful aunt of yours,' she said. And then she turned and left the room.

The overcast sky and silent drizzle seemed appropriate weather for a departure. She sat down in the wagonette and glanced back at the house. No one had anticipated her arrival and no one had come out to wave her off. The door was already closed.

Goodbye.

It was her lack of status, lack of husband, she thought, that allowed people to treat her thus. And it had always been so. Had she been married, been a widow, the world would have viewed her differently. She would have been elevated to *belonging*, worthy of respect, protected by the love and esteem of a man, living or deceased. Without it, without that status, the world had been dismissive – of her, of her feelings. At best, it smiled at her politely. At worst, it simply ignored her. And, perhaps born from that invisibility, and from her immersion in fiction and a focus on other people, she too had often forgotten her own existence, had had to remind herself.

Mr Cotton slammed his door. 'All aboard!' he shouted and laughed. The vehicle turned, headed up the driveway, and Sylvia did not look back. As the motor bumped down the track, past the Chadwicks' privet hedge and white gate, through the trickling ford and up the hill on the other side, she kept her eyes fixed ahead. Passing through the village she saw Mrs Gamben standing in the doorway of the post office, a shawl wrapped about her head; the butcher – all waxed moustache and boater – standing next to his bang-tailed cob; and coming up by the village green she saw Jack and Cecily on the road ahead, his jacket spread over their heads. They stopped and stood aside as the motor passed by. Sylvia looked straight ahead.

She would not cry, could not cry. She would be back in London soon, home, to her meagre life, her tiny flat, and her safe habits for one. No one would say 'how dare you', no one would say 'that will be all'. She would catch a taxicab from Waterloo, and stop at the shop on the corner for milk and bread, and something for supper. They'd say, 'You've been away a while, Miss Dorland. Been anywhere special . . . had a nice time?' And she would smile, and tell them, yes, wonderful.

She would climb the five flights to her landing, pull out the key and open the coffee-brown door to her own small world. And everything would be just as she had left it. She would carry her bag to the bedroom, place it down upon a neatly made single bed, and then – only then – would she allow herself to cry.

A fire had been lit. They were drenched through, and Jack's jacket in a sorry state. But when Mrs Davey brought in the tea tray, she said she would see to it and took it away.

Jack said, 'We saw Sylvia, with Cotton . . .'

Cora smiled. 'Yes, she's had to get back to London . . . had a telegram earlier. Something to do with her publishers, I believe.'

'Has she gone for long?' he asked.

'I'm not entirely sure,' Cora replied. 'But I don't expect her back this summer.'

He glanced over to Cecily, raising his eyebrows. He said, 'Well, that is a shame . . . she never got to have a look at your story.'

'I shall take a look . . . if you'd like me to. I have an eye for a good story,' said Cora.

Cecily looked from Cora to Jack and then back to Cora. 'Yes, thank you, perhaps when it's finished,' she said, and Cora smiled and nodded.

It was not until later, when Jack walked Cecily home, that Cora had a chance to ponder the contretemps of earlier, Sylvia's parting words. She had managed, she thought, to mask any shock in front of her grandson and Cecily at tea, but she was still aghast, had hardly thought her friend capable. And really, none of it made sense. For what was there for Sylvia to be angry about? After all, she had been the one in the wrong, the one snooping and spying, tiptoeing about the place, *investigating*, determined to have her answers, desperate for a story.

. . . that awful aunt of yours . . .

Cora winced, shook her head. It was all her own fault, she thought. She had been naive, had trusted Sylvia and told her far too much too early on. And what had been said could never be unsaid, that was the problem. If she had never in the first place mentioned that wretched man, John Abel, all those years ago in Rome, Sylvia's appetite would never have been whetted.

She closed her eyes, shook her head. 'Such a foolish thing to do, and all for added drama, as if there wasn't enough!'

But one thing was patently clear: Sylvia had been jealous, and jealous for a lifetime. But jealous of whom, what, and why? Jealous of the drama, perhaps, envious of the action. Then another thought came to her: was it George? Had Sylvia, too, been in love with George? Had she, for all these years – and as she watched and read and listened to

Cora – been in love with the very same man? But no, it was more complex than this, Cora mused. For there seemed to be another dynamic at play, lingering on the outermost periphery, confounding her, confusing her, whispering too quietly for her to hear.

And that parting diatribe, she thought, moving away from a vague suggestion, spewed out like a bile-filled held-back torrent . . .

. . . *had you thought more, been more discerning in your judgement, your life might have been different . . . and you would not have lost him.*

She closed her eyes. Love . . . *I know what it's not . . . it's not what you did to him . . .* But what did I *do* to him? Cora thought. My only crime was to love him. Sylvia was right, she conceded, she had lost George, and more than once . . . and for a long while after her marriage to Edward. And yet that was also what had brought him back to her.

How could she have said no to Edward? He had asked her to marry him any number of times, and he would not give up, had pursued her with letters and visits and such declarations. She frowned now at the remembrance of that time, his courtship of her. He had said he would take care of her, and of her son; he would make sure she had property of her own, and an income, too. She would be secure for the rest of her days.

It had been the news that George had been in Paris with Evie Dipple that made her realise she had waited long enough, that George Lawson was never going to marry her, or anyone else.

When she wrote to Edward to accept his offer of marriage she stipulated a number of preconditions: she would not be able live in England, she would not be able to run his house; she would prefer not to use his name, but retain her French name and title; and they would not be able to spend Christmases together. 'However, we shall be able to enjoy one another's company here on the continent, as and when your work permits . . . Regarding your very kind offer of a property, I have a hankering for somewhere quiet, a secluded place, the sort of place where one might never be found, and with enough space for my son and any family he might have in the future.'

Days later, she received a reply from Edward: he agreed to every condition. 'You have made me the happiest man in all of England,' he wrote. 'As to your house, I believe I have found the perfect location!'

In the end the marriage had been an arrangement that suited them both. Edward had continued to live and work in England whilst she continued with her life between Paris and Rome. She had returned to this country, to England, once or twice in the summer months, and Edward had visited her on the continent each winter. They had travelled together, touring France and Germany, Switzerland and Austria, and Italy as well.

And he had been true to his word. Shortly before

they were married he purchased some one hundred acres of heathland, on the very edge of a quiet village, where he would build Cora her home. And though she did not see the place until a year after its completion, she had instructed him on some of the detail: the need for 'a south-facing canopied veranda, high ceilings and tall windows, well-stocked pleasure gardens, and pine trees'.

He was a good husband, and she had made him happy, very happy, for he had told her so, often. They had been married for almost six years by the time he passed away in his sleep at his home in London. She returned for the funeral, and for the reading of his will.

'They've quite clearly had some sort of bust-up,' Jack was saying. 'I don't believe for one moment Sylvia had a telegram from her publisher, do you?'

'Well,' Cecily began, relishing the feel of her hand in his, 'it's not entirely outside the realms of possibility. She is a writer, she does have a publisher . . .'

'Ah yes, I can just see it . . . Miss Dorland needed urgently, stop, *the end* not acceptable, stop, more words needed, stop, forthwith, stop . . .'

'Who knows, maybe she has to attend some sort of meeting, something important.'

'Rot! She and Cora have had a fall-out. You saw Sylvia in the car, she wouldn't look at us, didn't wave. And it's been building up for weeks, since Sylvia first arrived. I told you about the last time, when Sylvia came running out of the bushes and flagged me down on the drive like an escaped lunatic. And that wasn't their first upset either. It's quite obviously something to do with the stupid memoirs, and you know what? I knew it would happen. I warned Sylvia, told her the day she arrived that she had one almighty task on her hands.'

'I feel sorry for them both, but perhaps more for Cora than Sylvia,' Cecily said.

'Why's that?'

'Perhaps because she's a kinder person than Sylvia.'

They had reached the bottom of the hill and they stopped. They were yards from the garden gate but it was shaded here, private. He moved closer to her. 'Do you really think that?' he asked. She could tell from his eyes that he wasn't remotely interested in her answer. But she smiled and nodded as he moved his mouth to hers.

CHAPTER 19

*S*he knows the broken brick is there, under her bed, because she put it there. It had been left lying by the wall of the tanner's yard, and she knew as soon as she saw it that it was meant for her, meant as her weapon. She had carried it all the way back through the lanes and up the stairs to their rooms in her apron; and then placed it under the tiny bedframe. Next time he came, she would use it. She would. She would hit him over the head with it.

Within a week the temperature had fallen, the brightness faded. Clouds returned to their usual place. Autumn was in the air. Everyone said so, and everyone shared in the relief. It was over, at last. Things could return to normal now, they said.

At Temple Hill, windows and doors were firmly shut, fires were lit and blankets returned to beds. And Jack's trunk, brought down from the attic, now lay open in his room.

Cora dreaded his departure. She had no wish to be alone again. She had grown used to his company, used to him and Cecily about the place, coming and going, noisily, giggling and laughing, as though

329

all of life was amusing. And sometimes it was, for they made it so.

There had been trips to Linford to order books and purchase stationery; and a trip to London, to Gamages, and to a tailor where Jack was measured for a new suit. He had protested, telling Cora that he did not need another suit, but she had insisted, saying it was important, the sign of a gentleman, to be well-dressed. Cecily went with them and they dined at Simpsons in the Strand before returning home. On the train, Cora had quietly watched them: the glances and smiles and not-meant-to-be-noticed gestures. Jack was in love, and in love for the very first time. Nothing, no other love, would be quite the same, she knew. But he was so young; they were both so young. They had their whole lives ahead of them. And she told him this, later that evening.

'I know that you're very fond of her, as am I, but you can't allow yourself to be *too* attached . . . and you must not allow her to have too many hopes,' she said. 'It would be cruel.'

He adopted that demeanour she had become accustomed to: he looked away, shrugged and said, 'I know. I do know this.'

'I imagine I'll see a good deal less of her once you have gone . . .'

But Cecily had no intention of abandoning Cora. She remained enthralled by her faded beauty and dusty treasures, by her stories and her life. She was, to Cecily, cultured and worldly, and possessed with an attitude quite different to others of her generation or to anyone else in Bramley. And yet so much of her life remained an enigma, even to Jack. But perhaps it was this, Cecily thought, perhaps it was the not knowing which allowed others, including herself, to imagine and fill in the gaps. Oh, Cora had confided to an extent, she had told Cecily a few of her secrets, but without any context or chronology these things meant little. In fact, they only added to the intrigue.

One day shortly after Sylvia left, when Cecily arrived at the house and Jack had been out on his motorcycle, Cora invited her to join her in a stroll about the gardens. She seemed agitated, distracted, and as they walked across the lawn, she said, 'One thing you will unfortunately learn in time, my dear, is that not everyone wishes for your happiness . . . or good fortune.'

It was another one of her cryptic comments and meant nothing to Cecily at the time, because once again it was random, without context. Cecily said nothing, and they walked on in silence towards the arbour.

'There's to be a military display on the green tomorrow – soldiers from Aldershot. The Wiltshire regiment, and a band,' Cecily said, trying to lighten the atmosphere.

Cora shuddered. 'Why people want to watch soldiers perform acrobatics with guns and ugly machinery I don't for the life of me know.'

'I suppose it's rather exciting to some,' Cecily offered.

'Exciting? One would have thought life was exciting enough without any reenactments of war.'

'Not everyone's life has been like yours, Cora.'

'Hmm,' she murmured, resting her cane to one side, and drawing in her skirts for Cecily to sit down. 'The problem with the British is that they have not seen war at close quarters, not here, not on their own soil, not for generations.' She turned to Cecily, 'No one is alive to remind them of the futility – the carnage, the waste. No, the British go off and fight in other countries. It's very different when it's happening around you. I pray that I never see another war, that your generation – you and Jack – never see any war.'

For a few minutes they sat in silence. The garden was quiet, sleepy in the morning sun, the air cool.

'You must forgive me, Cecily. I'm a little out of sorts today,' she said, placing a bejewelled hand upon Cecily's. She wore a number of rings on her wedding finger and Cecily wanted to ask her which was from whom: which ring went with which man. 'In old age one's thoughts crowd in on one day after day,' Cora went on. 'It's an exhausting business,' and she turned to Cecily with a nervous smile.

She seemed troubled. Her eyes were tearful. And Cecily said, 'Is it Sylvia? Are you missing her?'

She looked away, shook her head. 'No, it is not Sylvia, and no, I am not missing her, as it happens. But I am not relishing the months ahead. I am not looking forward to . . .' She stopped, her lip trembled and for a moment she took on the countenance of a little girl, lost and frightened. 'I have spent so much of my life alone, one would have thought I'd be used to it by now. I've lived in foreign cities, foreign countries, on my own, and yet this country, England, is more foreign to me than any other place.'

'That's because you've been away for so long. It's understandable.'

She nodded. 'But enough of me, I want to talk to you about Jack.'

'Oh . . .'

'It's not easy, for you or for me, to see him go. I understand this,' she began. 'You are . . . attached, fond of each other, I know. But sometimes one has to relinquish attachments, we have to be selfless and brave.' She turned to look at Cecily. 'Am I making sense?'

Cecily nodded.

'I don't want you – either of you – to be hurt, you see,' she said and paused, looking downwards, breathing in deeply. 'People come into our lives without warning, and for a while they make us forget who we are. Only when they leave us are we reminded; only when they leave us do we have to return to who we were before. And that can be painful because we've been changed, and what fitted before, what seemed at least comfortable, is no longer so.' She raised her head, staring into the distance. 'We think nothing can ever be whole again,' she added in a whisper. Then she turned to Cecily. 'I spent a long time waiting for someone, waiting for someone to come back to me. I don't want you to make that mistake.'

On their last day together, like so many days before, Cecily and Jack went out on his motor-cycle. She had told her mother, had had to tell her – after roaring past Mrs Moody in Linford – that yes, she sometimes rode pillion on Jack's bike, 'sort of side-saddle and on a cushion,' she added, as though it would make a difference. But Madeline was aghast, furious that Cecily had lied to her, astonished that all the times she had presumed her daughter to be up at Temple Hill, perhaps taking tea in the garden, she had in fact been 'speeding about the lanes with a young man. It's not only dangerous, it's improper!'

'There's nothing improper about it, women are buying them as well.'

Madeline shuddered. 'Next, you'll be telling me you're off to London to fight for votes!'

'Yes, I very well might.'

'Really, Cecily, I don't know what's come over you this summer. You've always been such a . . .'

'Good girl?'

'Yes,' said her mother, looking at her, mystified. 'And of course everyone will assume that you're courting now, you and he,' she went on, 'and I'm not entirely sure what I'm supposed to do.'

'I don't care what everyone assumes but I do care what you think, Mother.'

'What I think . . . what I think is that you're both too young.'

'But you were little older than me when you married Father.'

Madeline shook her head. 'That was different. Jack is about to leave for university, Cecily, he's not going to stay here. He has a future mapped out for him, and I can't help but feel . . .'

'Yes?'

'That he'll leave you behind, dear.'

Perhaps he would leave her behind. The notion was one Cecily had certainly pondered, particularly after Cora's words to her in the garden. And she had drawn conclusions: he would leave her behind; he had no choice. He had said to her himself, 'it's a tremendous opportunity'. And it was. A university education could not be passed over, no matter what. It would set him up for life. Oh, that she could have the same path and spend three whole years studying, reading, surrounded by erudite people – people she could learn from, people who spoke about poetry and literature and art, people who had travelled and seen places and been places; people who led interesting lives. Oh, that she could be *someone*.

But there was a chink of light, a hope, flickering at the back of her mind – or the front, depending on her mood. He would return, during holidays and when he was able, and then, at the end, he'd be free. Three years, she concluded. I shall have to wait three years.

Nothing had been said. No words about their future had passed between them, though they had spoken often enough about foreign places, places they had read about, heard about, would like to see. She imagined them strolling along the banks of the Seine, the Danube, the Tiber, arm in arm, a handsome couple. And sometimes she imagined them together at Temple Hill . . .

Three years. I shall wait three years, she told herself. Cora's warning to her had, she thought, been about wasting an entire lifetime waiting, and she would certainly not be doing that. Three years was not a lifetime.

But as his departure date loomed, she became aware of the clock, of the minutes and hours, the slipping away of time and the inevitable goodbye, when he would leave Bramley and move on. And the flicker of hope died.

Jack's life, she imagined, would be as glamorous as his grandmother's. Faster, modern, and not yet abroad, but on a path to somewhere: somewhere far more sophisticated than Bramley. He would, perhaps, remember her – the village girl, that innocent country girl, the one he had been quite fond of at the time. The one he had taken up to London, and rode about with through the lanes. The one he had kissed on a hot day at the top of some hill he couldn't quite remember. In years to come he would return there, to Bramley, at first to visit his grandmother, Cora, and then, after her death, to stay at the place himself from time to time, for he would surely inherit it. And Cecily, too, might be there, might be invited up to Temple Hill for tea. He would take her hand in his and say hello, politely, then step aside to introduce his wife . . .

Oh, the agony!

It would not happen, it could not happen. She could never allow it to.

But the thought, the image, kept coming back to her. She saw herself – rounded, matronly, a brood of noisy, ruddy-faced children and a quiet husband by her side. And him, Jack, lean and dapper, smiling on benignly, sympathetically. But sometimes there were no children or quiet husband, just her: thin and bespectacled and monosyllabic, a spinster of the parish, a schoolmistress, speaking about the weather, the last sermon, and Miss Combe's new electricity.

He would say, 'Cecily Chadwick, well I never. I hardly recognised you . . . still in Bramley, eh?' For she had never gone anywhere, other than that day excursion to the coast each summer. There had been no travelling, no countries visited or cities explored; there had been no great adventure, and no other loves. And she would smile, grateful for the acknowledgement, the remembrance, and then laugh – and make a joke of her lack of a life. 'Oh, but I could never leave Bramley,' she would say. 'After all, I'm settled here, and it is so wonderful to live in a place where everyone knows who you are.'

He would introduce her to his children, all lined up and quite as beautiful as he, and with exotic names and precocious but enchanting demeanours: Nathanial, Atalanta, Theodopholis and Hermione. And they would look at her with pity in their eyes, but not for her but for their father, that he could ever have loved someone so plain and parochial, that their successful and debonair father could have been so short-sighted. And they would not know what to say, or how to be, and so he would intervene and make small talk, until it was time for her to leave. Then they would all heave a sigh of relief, and tease him that he had once had a thing for poor Miss Chadwick.

When he released her hand he said, 'You never know, I might get back at Christmas . . . come and say boo!'

She smiled.

'Otherwise it'll be Easter.'

'Yes, Easter,' she repeated.

'It's not that long.'

'No.'

'We've our whole lives ahead of us, you know.'

'Of course, I know that.'

'Don't be sad . . . please, don't be sad.'

They stood in the fading twilight by the gate and all she could think was that by morning he would be gone. And all she could hear were the whispers of the coming days and weeks: *the poor thing went about with him all summer . . . bound to happen . . . he was hardly going to settle down here*

– *with her.* And she would have to brave it, have to smile through it all as though it had been nothing, a brief flirtation, a passing fancy.

'But we've had a fine old time to ourselves,' he said.

'Yes, we have.'

He looked away. 'I can't promise you anything . . . I can't—'

'It's perfectly fine, Jack. You don't need to say any more. I understand.'

She smiled and turned away. She heard the latch on the gate drop, clickety-click, his feet upon the track, and a door quietly close.

CHAPTER 20

The movement of cold air stirs her. The cover has been pulled back. She can hear the rasping sound in the blackness, smell him as he moves closer. 'Come here my little lovely, come to Uncle John now . . .' She tries to wriggle free, but he has hold of her, is pulling at her nightgown, and as she struggles, as she struggles to reach down beneath the bed, the soft cotton tears, releasing her like a baby from the womb and her hand to the floorboards, the brick . . .

Cora could smell the mustiness of an English winter. It was a smell she vaguely remembered: a mingling of damp plaster, rotting wood and vegetation, the smoke of coal fires, and coldness. Coldness. The house felt newly strange and suddenly much too large for one person. She had no need for so much space. Though she might have had, once, when the place was first built, when she still had a son, anticipated a daughter-in-law, envisaged grandchildren. When Georgie told her that he planned on having a large family, 'to make up for the deficit'.

'Deficit indeed!' Fanny had repeated, laughing. 'That's what he said. I suppose it's because he's grown up alone.'

'Well, he'll have to find himself a wife first, and she'll need to be a robust girl, my goodness yes,' Fanny went on, smiling. 'But at least you have the place, the space for this enormous family he's planning.'

Cora moved to the window, gazing out at the excavations for the new monument in honour of the King. Her aunt had told her that it would take over two decades to build and be so vast it would dominate the city's skyline.

'No one knows who anyone is any more,' Fanny was saying, 'it's all changed, anyone of quality seems to have gone, and instead, we have a constant stream of loud Americans to plague us. Tourists they call themselves. They come for a week and fly about the place with lists and maps and itineraries – such frenzied haste.'

'It's the same in Paris,' Cora replied. 'The Americans are *everywhere*.'

Cora had travelled by train from Paris to Rome, as she did each and every Christmas. Edward remained in England, spending Christmas with his family, as he had done each year since their marriage. It was, as her aunt liked to remind her, an unusual domestic arrangement. Twice a year Edward visited her, and she had returned to England the previous summer, staying for two weeks under the roof of his fine stucco-fronted house in Kensington, only ten minutes' walk from George's London home.

As Cora turned away from the window, Fanny returned to the subject of Georgie. 'And how is your darling boy?' she asked.

'Georgie,' Cora repeated, and immediately felt the warmth of maternal blood run through her veins. Georgie, she thought, and could not help but smile. 'He's hardly a boy, he's a grown man now,' she said. 'He is well, very well, and I believe he's charming everyone in London.' She moved about the room, picking up ornaments, examining them, as if to check that they were the same ones that inhabited a place in her memory; running her fingers along polished marble and mahogany; the velvet pile of a sofa, a chair.

'And does he see much of . . . of his godfather?' Fanny asked.

'Oh yes, he sees him from time to time. But of course George is very busy at the Academy, and still travels a good deal.'

'And you? Do you still see him?'

'I saw him in Paris last . . .' she saw her aunt wince and stopped. 'But why do you ask if you do not wish to hear? Why does it pain you to hear me speak about him?'

'Because it's not right for you to see him, not now you're married. He had his chance – so many chances – and you waited for him . . . waited for him for so long. You simply can't allow him to walk in and out of your life, not now.'

'I have to see him; you know that. It's impossible for me to banish him now.'

'But don't see him alone, Cora, please. There's enough gossip already about you and your marriage . . . and him.'

Cora shook her head. 'I no longer care what the old expatriate wives of Rome are saying about me. And there'll always be gossip about George. There always has been.' She turned away from Fanny. 'But, seeing as you've mentioned it, tell me, what is the gossip?'

Fanny did not immediately reply. Cora turned to her. 'Well?'

'That you and George continue to see each other in Paris, alone, that his breakdown was in no small part due to your marriage and . . .'

'And?'

'Georgie.'

Cora sighed. 'George and I see each other when he is in Paris, of course – we're friends, we'll always be dear friends.'

'Friends? And does your husband know just how friendly you are with . . . the President of the Academy?'

'As for his breakdown,' Cora went on, 'he was simply exhausted. Everyone at the wedding could see that. Everyone knew how hard he'd been working . . .'

Fanny shook her head. 'No, it was a blow and it hit him hard. I saw. I was there, remember?'

Cora said nothing.

'But he leads such a queer life,' Fanny said, changing tone, shifting in her chair.

'Why do you say that?'

'No wife, or family, an older married lady his constant companion. It's not normal. But he was always a little peculiar, I thought. Charming but a little peculiar.'

'George was ambitious, single-minded in his vocation, his art. He's a very private person and requires solitude in which to work. He could not cope with a family, family life. And Mrs Hillier is not his *constant companion*, not any more. She no longer travels and has, I believe, been in poor health for some time.'

'It always seemed to me . . .' Fanny began, then hesitated, choosing her words carefully. 'It always seemed to me as though he was fearful . . . hiding something.'

'Hiding something? Oh, perhaps his emotions. But now I understand that genius, real artistic genius, can take every ounce of passion from a man, so that . . . he's left with little to give, to share with another,' Cora replied, staring at a framed miniature of her son.

'Hmm. Jack knew, didn't he?'

Cora kept her gaze fixed on her son's face. 'Knew?'

'About you and George . . . later, he knew about you and George.'

'I'm not sure what you mean, or what Jack thought . . . about anything. But do not, please, rewrite *that* particular chapter. Jack's death had nothing whatsoever to do with me, or George, as you well know, and if he was concerned he never said. And I married him, didn't I? I did as I was told.' She moved over to her aunt, sat down opposite her. 'You know . . . you know that I loved George. I still do. I can't change that. I can't change what my heart feels.'

'No, you can't say that, not now. You have a good husband, one who cares about you, who loves you.'

'Oh, I know that, of course I do, and I'm immensely fond of him, too. But let me ask you this: did you cease to love your husband, James, when he died?'

'No, of course not.'

'But you love another now?'

'Yes, but that's quite different, he's a different person and this is another stage of my life.'

'Exactly.'

'But James is dead, Cora; George lives and Edward—'

'Edward is my husband,' she interrupted, rising to her feet. 'He understands that George and I were . . . are close, that we remain firm friends.' She walked over to the window. 'And yes, George lives, but so perhaps does another man . . . so perhaps does John Abel.'

And that was it. The name – the unmentionable name – had been uttered, silently shattering three decades of carefully arranged words, and everything between them.

She turned to her aunt. 'I'm sorry, but I'm afraid it's a little late in the day for you to lecture me on the morality and virtues of a faithful marriage.'

Fanny did not look at her, but Cora could hear her breathing as the name ricocheted about the room: impossible to grab hold of and take back. And what she had said was true enough: John Abel might yet be alive. And if so, where did that leave her aunt? There could be no moral high ground. Not then, not ever. They were both guilty.

When Cora asked Mrs Davey to close up various rooms, the housekeeper reminded her that they had never in fact been opened up; that the morning room and a few of the bedrooms were still stacked with crates, yet to be unpacked. Something to do over the winter, Cora thought: unpack and go through it all, sorting. Mr Cordery would have to bring the crates down to the drawing room; she would open them up there, where it would be warm. She would be able to review it *all*, her life. Unravel the knot.

She had not heard from Sylvia and did not expect to. But she would write to her in time, eventually. She would send her a Christmas card, perhaps. And she could rest easy about the people at the farm. Cecily had been to call on them and they had told her that they had never heard of any other John Abel. The name was a coincidence, nothing more. They were perhaps related in some convoluted way to *him*, Cora thought, but it was a common enough name, or had been, once. And the letters had stopped, for now at least.

Yes, she would be able to address things now, without botheration and interruptions. She would have time and peace; space to think. She would be able to work through everything, put it in order; write it all down. Or perhaps Cecily could . . . After all, she was young, part of the modern world. What was once shocking and scandalous was . . . not so unusual now. People were more forgiving, more understanding, surely. And all families had secrets, hidden away somewhere.

She would unravel the knot and work backwards. Go all the way back to the beginning, to that time before, before they had moved on, before new countries and new names, before the inventing and reinventing began. She would go back to where *she* first started. Because she needed to make sense of the start in order to make sense of this end. And there was an end, looming, she knew. It was why she needed to set things in order, why she needed to put things straight. There should be no mess for Jack to have to deal with. Death, she often thought, should be peaceful, any ripples for those left behind soothing. But at other times she was filled with panic, terrified of the dark void ahead, and of meeting those she had – in life – escaped.

I must not think of death, she told herself; otherwise it will surely hear me and come knocking . . .

So she tried to look forward to bleak winter, to

the drawing in of days and long dark nights. She tried to settle herself in autumn, watching clouds and drizzle, and a pale English sun. And she waited for Cecily to call.

She had, she realised, been testing Cecily over the course of the summer, slipping in details here and there, but still not entirely the truth. She had been sounding her out, watching her reactions. And the girl had not once appeared shocked, had not flinched. She had been sympathetic, understanding. She had passed the test.

I shall tell Cecily the truth, she decided; ask her to write it all down. But there remained one problem: which version and for whom? Well, for Jack of course. There was only him. But would he want to know? Perhaps it would be better for her to omit certain details, to leave it to fate and the future to unravel. Yes, perhaps. She had no wish to cause him any unnecessary pain or distress, or to burden him further. No. Her desire was simply to put the record straight – for herself, in her own mind; to release her burden and be in possession of that state generally known as a clear conscience. She would ask Cecily, take her advice. After all, she cared about Jack, and who knew what might happen between them in the future.

Thankfully, Cecily was not going anywhere. They would no doubt spend some of the long winter evenings ahead together, for Cecily had already said, 'Don't worry, Cora, I'm still here.' Yes, so long as she had dear Cecily calling on her, with that sweet open mind and sunny disposition, she would not succumb to loneliness, not give way to *the others*. And she must stay warm, speak to Mrs Davey about the fires; make sure there was enough coal and logs. Oh yes, she must stay warm.

The mere thought of an English winter made Cora shiver. That harsh chill which permeated one's clothing and flesh and bones. She had told people that it would be her first in six decades, but this was not strictly true, because she had come back once, briefly, in the depths of winter.

Standing by an open grave, her face too cold to move, her heart numb, Cora had watched her son's coffin as it was lowered into the frozen earth. But even then, as he was delivered into that cold hard ground, he had become a memory, nothing more than a memory. He was a name, another name, soon to be added to a churchyard of chiselled names. And the realisation that his presence – his face, his voice, all of him – was already dimming and being forgotten, struck her . . .

Those who had known him would remember his laugh, his smile, his humour, and his bravery. They would speak of him for a while, clinging on to those remnants, but slowly, with time, they would forget. In years to come his name might crop up in conversation, someone might say, 'Ah yes, George Staunton, I vaguely remember him. Whatever happened to him?' But the name would fade, the tombstone fall, and, eventually, inevitably, disappear into the undergrowth of that quiet corner of the churchyard.

Perhaps one day someone would notice that leaning tombstone covered in lichen and ivy. They might bend down, pull away the weeds, and then – moving their hands over the stone – say the name out loud once more. And for a moment, just a moment, they might wonder who he had been, George Staunton; whose child, whose husband, whose father. They might try to imagine what someone of that name looked like, how he spoke, what made him laugh or cry. But they would never be able imagine the baby born in Rome, nor the circumstances surrounding his birth. They would never be able to picture the boy who had grown up in France, or envisage the young man who had returned – so dazzlingly handsome and suntanned – from two years in India. His lifetime, the thirty-three years he had walked upon the earth, had ended, abruptly, one Saturday morning in January.

In the years that followed, after her son's death and before her final return to England, visits to old friends – and to acquaintances she had made on her incessant journeys – kept Cora busy. There was little else for her to do at that time, and she was in fact of no fixed abode. Her circle of friends had slowly diminished. Many of them had passed away, others had returned home, to England or America. In Rome, there was a new crowd, a younger crowd, a mix of English, American and European artists, travellers, and new business people, as well as the usual fugitives and misfits.

But Rome was not the same place. The city had changed shape. The antiquated ruins and monuments remained, weathered further by the passing of years, crumbling through ignorance and neglect, and now like gargantuan tombstones strewn haphazardly about the place, randomly interrupting the new order and tidiness of modern Rome. But the small medieval city, the Rome of Cora's youth, had been all but swept away.

On her last visit to the city, she sat each morning outside the Café Santa Maria in the Piazza d'Ara Coeli, and from under the shade of her parasol watched the exotic human traffic pass by like contestants in a fancy dress parade: young Romans strutting like peacocks, elderly peasants cocooned in grubby cloth, and wealthy English tourists in their distinctive upper-class garb for hotter climes. The English tourists, known for their good manners, always smiled and nodded, *'Buon giorno.'* They assumed her to be Italian, Roman, and she never let on. Never said, 'But I am also English.' Instead, she surreptitiously studied them as they studied their maps and guidebooks and discussed their itinerary for that day.

The invisibility of old age allowed her to observe and listen. It enabled her to bestow these unknown friends with detailed identities, so that by the time they moved on she knew them all the better for *not* having spoken with them. Later, as she walked through the shadowed streets off the Corso she often fancied she could hear the revelry of a party from an upstairs window. And sometimes she would stop, stand and listen to sounds that were there but not there: the French military band playing on in the Piazza Colonna, the cheers and thunderous echo of a carnival. But there were times when her loneliness was acute, the sense of singularity suffocating, the absence of familiar voices deafening.

Each afternoon she visited the Protestant Cemetery, arranging flowers or tidying the potted plants within the box-hedged graves. And here, sitting on the old iron bench under the shade of cypresses, silent conversations flowed.

Rome reinvigorated her, body and soul. Paris was simply exhausting. And London, on those rare occasions she had flitted in and out, was jarring and judgemental, too big and brash. And the lack of light, that interminable smog, rendering its streets dank and inhospitable, depressed her spirits. In the cacophony of the English capital she had always felt like an alien, an outsider, for it was the place from which she had fled, and then returned too late in life to be fashionable.

Travelling from city to city, country to country, had for so long been the ebb and flow of her life. And though no one was waiting for her in Rome or Paris, or anywhere now, continuing this movement allowed her to luxuriate in the sensation of busyness. She was able to talk of train times, schedules and itineraries, departure and arrival dates, arrangements and contingencies, as though they mattered; as though her time was valuable, as though others depended upon her punctuality and *were* waiting.

She knew her way to the Eternal City the way anyone knows the path that leads them home. From a train carriage window she checked off the sequence of familiar vistas, counting down landmarks, towns and cities. And later, travelling back over that same landscape, they were checked off again, in reverse order.

On her final journey, returning to England for good, she had been unusually reticent, had no interest in making any new friends. Standing upon the deck of a steamer, taking in England's ragged hemline – quiet, contemplative, inconspicuous, she hoped – she offered little conversation and made no mention of any connections. On that last journey she simply played the part of an elderly lady returning from an indefinite period abroad. And when those standing alongside her turned to her and said, 'Ah, so good to be home,' she simply smiled. 'Yes indeed, so good to be home.'

'. . . We'll live like gypsies . . . divide our time between Rome and Florence, head to Paris in the spring . . . and the south of France perhaps in autumn.'
'But not England?'
'No, not England. Who needs England?'

'And you'll stay with me?'

'Of course, I shall . . . I'll never leave you.'

'Not even if I had done something . . . wicked?'

'Hmm, something wicked . . . If you had done something wicked, well, I rather think I'd love you all the more for it.'

And so she gives in, moves her mouth to his, and seals her fate.

BOOK II

ENGLAND 1923

CHAPTER 21

Sylvia had said it out loud, and silently, too: *Cora is gone . . . Cora is gone . . .* She had to; had to remind herself. It would take time, she told herself, to grow used to the idea. And it was why she had sought out the photograph, why she sat with it in her hands. But it was still queer to think of *her* dead, a person no more. Difficult to accept that she had been mortal, just like everyone else; impossible and too painful to think of her beneath the sandy soil of an English churchyard.

Perhaps it would be easier if she had seen the grave, witnessed the burial and been a part of that ceremonial goodbye. She would, she thought, have been able to say adieu. She would have been able to let her know.

For years Sylvia had pondered a hello and not a goodbye. She had anticipated a reunion, reconciliation, imagined them embracing, forgiving, smiling at one another, herself saying, 'I shall hear none of it; it is all in the past now.' She had imagined returning once more down that sweeping driveway in Mr Cotton's wagonette, and Cora, standing there upon the doorstep – waiting for her, just as she had that sultry summer's day twelve years ago. How pleased Cora had been to see her . . . She had said, 'Here at last!' and then playfully chastised Sylvia for her tardiness, telling her that she had been waiting patiently all morning. And Jack had been there too: eager to finally meet his grandmother's oldest friend. He had said, 'I've been longing to meet you . . . have heard so much about you.' That was how it had been, hadn't it?

Yes, it had been a perfect day. One etched on her memory.

But there could be no reunion, not now, not ever. That indomitable spirit, that indefatigable soul had departed this life and moved on – as she always had.

Sylvia stared at the photograph. She ran a finger over the tear: a scar on her memory, and on her heart. But it was too late, too late to offer Cora her happy ending, too late to assuage her loss or make amends: too late to tell her. And there was an added torment bound up in those few hushed words to a painter, so long ago in Rome.

'But had I known . . . had I known . . .' she whispered, shaking her head.

And then she closed her eyes once more as she relived that bittersweet moment, when Cora had clung to her weeping, saying, 'He says we have no future, no future together . . . he says it cannot be . . . that he cannot marry me . . . will never marry me . . .'

But how wonderful it had felt to hold her, to have Cora in her arms, so weak and fragile, and lost. 'You have me,' she had said. 'You have me, and I shall never ever walk away from you.' And yet she had. For hadn't she walked away that summer, twelve years before? Hadn't she left Cora then, weak and fragile and lost once again, afraid, alone and old?

'I let her down! I walked away . . . just as he did . . . I was no different.'

Sylvia had not been able to attend the funeral, though Cecily had been kind enough to telephone a second time to inform her of the arrangements. The first call, the one to tell her Cora had died, had come out of the blue. And Cecily had been quite cold, Sylvia thought: perfunctory in her approach. But Sylvia was not used to receiving telephone calls. The only telephone at the Windsor was in the arched alcove of the lobby, where, on the rare occasion it was in use, people liked to loiter about, listening. It had a sign above it which read, FOR RESIDENTS' USE & EMERGENCIES ONLY, in red letters upon white. It was a queer, perplexing contraption and Sylvia had no use for it. And that day, when Mrs Halliday came into the dining room and said, 'Do excuse me, Miss Dorland, but you're wanted on the telephone,' Sylvia had been mystified. For who would call her? She had no kin.

Mrs Halliday had handed her the parts, whispering instructions, 'To the ear, dear . . . that's it

. . . now say hello . . .' Sylvia thought she heard a voice: 'Sylvia . . . Miss Dorland, is that you?' But the line had been bad and, not sure what the call was about or to whom the voice belonged, Sylvia had been circumspect, reticent.

'Yes,' she had said, elongating those three letters, phrasing the word as a question.

'It's Cecily.'

'Cecily . . .'

'I hope you remember me . . .'

Cecily Chadwick. 'Yes, yes. I remember you. Of course I remember you. How lovely to hear from you.'

'I'm calling with some . . .'

But Sylvia did not catch the words and had to ask her to speak up.

'*Sad* news,' Cecily said, louder, and with emphasis. 'It's Cora, I'm afraid she passed away on Friday. I thought I should call . . . call and let you know.'

And that was it. Cecily may have said more, Sylvia could not remember. She had been too stunned, too upset to take in anything else. She had said goodbye and then stood for some time clutching the receiver, unsure what to do with it *or* the news. When Mrs Halliday reappeared, she asked, 'Bad news, dear?' She took the receiver from Sylvia's hand, hung it up, and led her back towards the dining room. But Sylvia had said no, she could not face anyone, could not eat now. 'My friend, my dearest friend has passed away.'

She did not cry, not that day. She simply returned

upstairs to her room and sat quietly until it was time for bed.

Perhaps Cecily said something about the funeral during that first call. Perhaps she had told Sylvia she would call again to let her know the arrangements. Either way, Cecily had called again a few days later, and that was when she had also said that she had something for Sylvia from Cora.

'Actually, I've had it in my possession for quite some time,' she said. 'She asked me to make sure that it was passed on to you in the event of her death.'

Cora: ever the planner.

But there was no way Cecily could get up to London, not at that time. Not with the funeral and everything else she had to deal with, she said, but perhaps in a few weeks, when things were calmer.

An obituary in one of the London newspapers was simply titled, 'Death of the Countess de Chevalier de Saint Léger Lawson', and read:

> *We deeply regret to record the death which occurred at her home in Bramley on Friday of last week of the Countess de Chevalier de Saint Léger Lawson, who had been in failing health for some time past . . . The Countess was in her eightieth year and had a very wide circle of friends both here and on the Continent, to whom her passing is a matter of sincere regret. The Countess was thrice married and by her*

first union, to Mr John Staunton, there was a son, Captain George Staunton RHA, who met with his death in a hunting accident many years ago. Her second marriage was to the Count de Chevalier de Saint Léger who was killed in the Franco-German War; while she was wedded on a third occasion to Mr Edward Lawson, late President of the Royal Institute of British Architects, and father of Lord George Lawson, late President of the Academy.

The Countess was born at Standen Hall in Norfolk, and was the niece of the late Contessa Cansacchi di Amelia who passed away some time ago in Rome. A renowned and fashionable figure within Continental society, the Countess resided a great deal abroad, in particular in Rome and Paris, and was noted for her cosmopolitan tastes and for her fine collection of art and antiques . . . The funeral took place at St Luke's Churchyard, Bramley, on Wednesday afternoon, where the remains of the deceased lady were laid to rest . . .

The piece went on to list the chief mourners, and to say that 'the grave had been prettily lined with moss and bunches of violets by Mr Cordery, the head gardener at Temple Hill'. It then listed the floral tributes, and Sylvia was pleased to see her own name.

Of course there were mistakes, inaccuracies. How could there not be? Cora had spent a lifetime confusing and confounding everyone with her story. And she had always lied about her age, was ten years older than the age they quoted. But she would have been satisfied, Sylvia thought, to be a decade younger – even in death. And the obituary recorded most of the official version: almost all of the important names were there. And yet, Sylvia could not help but wonder where the information had come from, for someone had tidied it all up. That someone had to be Cecily.

Sylvia cut out the obituary and pasted it into the scrapbook, the one she kept that charted Cora's life, and now death. It included every announcement – the birth of each of her sons, their deaths, and the deaths of each of her husbands; her marriages; court circulars, drawing-room appearances, and clippings about George. But there had been so many about George, particularly after his death, that she gave up cutting and pasting *him*. Also in the scrapbook were two pencil sketches of Cora by John Clifford, and another by George (all three from Rome, when Cora had been no more than twenty); a ribbon Cora had given her at around that same time, and various notes confirming appointments and rendezvous. Sylvia liked to look at those notes, the handwriting, the young signature long before the loops and swirls of the double C flourish that became her customary abbreviation. There was a lock of pale golden hair, various pressed flowers, and postcards and telegrams, and a small swatch of blue silk Cora had sent her shortly before her marriage to Edward. The photograph, the one taken in the garden that day at Temple Hill, would go in there also, Sylvia decided: at the very end. It was the only one she had of them together.

Some weeks after the obituary, the same newspaper announced a sale at the house:

> *The trustees of the estate of the late Countess de Chevalier de Saint Léger Lawson announce a sale to be held at her home, Temple Hill, including the whole of the antique and modern appointments: Louis XIV and Empire escritoires, secretaires, commodes and tables. Two fine old English mahogany and oak long-case clocks. Beautiful Chinese silk embroidery and antique Italian tapestry. Rare old French trousseau chests, French, Italian and English oil paintings and water colours, Italian carved cabinets, settees and chairs in old English, 890 volumes of books, plate, needlework, tapestries, French linen, clocks, bronzes, Italian marble sculpture, ornamental china and porcelain, Venetian air twist and other glass and crystal, English oak dining furniture, together with the usual indoor and outdoor effects . . .*

So, Cecily was selling it all. Cora's precious cargo, gathered over a lifetime and brought back to England, was to be sold off, flung back across the counties of England, the countries of Europe.

And that announcement, the announcement of the sale at the house, inspired more tears than any obituary. Because all of those things, every item of furniture and glass and linen, each book and painting and each piece of china, were all that was left of her, all that Cora had left to the world of herself. And Sylvia could picture it all, picture it all so vividly, the dismantling of that life.

CHAPTER 22

When Cecily arrived she was not at all as Sylvia remembered her. A glamorous woman, festooned in fur, had replaced the gauche and awkward girl of Sylvia's memory. And she was taller, much taller than Sylvia remembered. She moved across the room with an alarming confidence, leaned forward in a haze of perfume and pressed her lips to Sylvia's cheek. Sylvia released a short, sharp gasp. She could not recall the last time anyone had done such a thing. She watched Cecily place a brown paper parcel on the low table and dispense with her fur, draping it along the back of the armchair. 'Golly,' she said, as she sat down, 'what a day.'

It was stormy outside. Sylvia had noticed. She had watched the weather at the window for most of that day: the constant drizzle interrupted by intermittent downpours, the petrified limbs of the trees in the park opposite against the low sky. Later, she had heard the wind, coming in angry gusts, and then the bells: an ambulance or fire engine, perhaps. And she could only wonder at the drama unfolding somewhere.

'Yes, what a day,' Sylvia said, eyeing Cecily as she opened up her handbag and took out a familiar cigarette case. 'I hope it hasn't been too much trouble for you, coming up to town,' she said.

'No trouble, no trouble at all,' Cecily replied. She flicked a lighter, tilted her head and released a plume of smoke into the dimly lit room; then she placed the handbag on the table in front of them, next to the brown paper parcel. 'Actually, we're up for a few days.'

'Ah, I see,' Sylvia said and nodded.

It made sense. Yes, it made sense. *This* Cecily did not look like a schoolmistress from the country, not at all. This Cecily was undoubtedly used to trips up to town, to hailing and dashing about in taxicabs, in a flurry, in a rush. This Cecily was different to the one before. She wore the new shorter length skirt, her hair was cut fashionably short, too, and, Sylvia noted, she left an imprint of her painted lips at the end of her cigarette.

Sylvia leaned forward, pushing the glass ashtray across the polished wood, and said, 'Oh, I must show you something.' She reached down to the shelf beneath the table and handed Cecily the photograph. 'I'm afraid it got torn . . . caught in an album or some such thing, I can't quite recall now.'

Cecily stared at the image. Yes, she too could remember that day. 'Feels like a lifetime ago,' she said. 'So much has happened since then.'

And it had for her, and for the world, but less so for Sylvia.

Right up until her move to the Windsor Hotel, four years ago, Sylvia had followed a daily routine unchanged and unaltered for over half a century. The move had been disruptive but inevitable. And the Windsor had undoubtedly been the right choice. It was situated round the corner from her former flat, and almost all of the residents were elderly ladies, like herself. Most were widows, who had had a husband, or two, and children, or not. Many of them were colonials who had returned from India and the Far East after the war had ended. It was one of the things Sylvia liked about the Windsor, the class of person. And it made the conversation all the more interesting to hear about places like Bangalore, Kashmir and Calcutta, and verandas and bungalow lifestyles. She had even toyed with the idea of writing a novel set in India, loosely based on her new friend Mrs Evesleigh's life. Oh yes, the Windsor had been the right choice. These women understood expatriate life, and Sylvia had been able to talk about her time in Rome, and about her dear friend, the Countess de Chevalier de Saint Léger Lawson. A few claimed to know or recognise the name, thought they had heard it – or part of it – before, and then usually asked, 'Any relation to *Lord* Lawson?'

'Stepmother,' Sylvia replied, 'and dear friend, as was I.'

Inevitably, there then ensued some discussion

about George Lawson: his life and work, his affairs – and rumoured illegitimate children.

'Well, I really wouldn't know about *that*,' Sylvia responded, running free, but enjoying the debate and that tingle of attention.

Sylvia had had special cards printed to announce her move to the Windsor, and though she had only managed to send out a dozen or so of the fifty, later cutting up the unused ones to use as bookmarks, she *had* sent one to Cora, with a note on the reverse, saying, 'My dear, I do hope that you are well, and that we might be able to catch up one day in the not too distant future. As ever, Sylvia.' She had hoped for a reply, a note to say 'Good luck' or something along the lines of 'Wishing you well in your new home', but nothing came.

The war, Sylvia agreed with the other ladies, had changed everything and everyone. No, nothing would ever be the same. But they had their memories, memories of how things had once been, memories of lost places, lost faces. Even now, four years later, The War consumed a great deal of their time, and energy.

But Sylvia had had no children or grandchildren to lose, and though she had lived through and witnessed the seemingly never-ending horror, and had imagined – or had tried to imagine – circumstances not her own, she had for the most part been buried in the execution of the book she and Cora had begun years before, the book they had worked on during the summer of 1911. It would not be Cora's memoirs, could not be Cora's memoirs, but it could be the story of her life, Sylvia had decided. The story of her life as it could have been. And it was to be Sylvia's peace offering. For she had planned to write to Cora, enclosing the first draft, once it was finished. She would not and could not, she had decided, do anything with it without her friend's blessing.

But time had run out and now the manuscript lay in a drawer, and Sylvia was unsure what to do with it. Unsure, that is, until Cecily's second telephone call. And as soon as Sylvia heard Cecily say the word 'manuscript', her heart leapt. Cora knew, had obviously remembered, and it seemed as though from beyond the grave she was giving it her blessing, sanctioning it.

And it was understandable, commendable, Sylvia reasoned, that Cora wished Cecily to see it first, particularly in view of the circumstances. But she must not be *too* eager. There was an etiquette to be observed, a way of handling these things, just as there was with everything else. She would wait, wait until later, once they had crossed bridges, so to speak. Then she would offer Cecily a sherry and produce the manuscript. She had imagined Cecily's face – though it had been different, younger, and altogether more open – the look of astonishment, surprise, then the tears and smiles; and she had heard her say, 'Oh Sylvia, she would have been so happy, so grateful . . .' And Sylvia would say, 'It's the book I have been writing for over fifty years, my final work.' And they would raise their glasses to—

'. . . Sylvia?'

Cecily was still holding the photograph in her hand and Sylvia thought she had perhaps missed a question. 'Mr Fox died . . . passed away last year,' she said, presumably for a second time, and quite as though Sylvia and he had been close.

'Oh dear, how sad.'

She went on, and Sylvia realised that she was working her way through those in the photograph, and beyond it, to a village, bustling and busy, going about its business. That summer's day – that moment, that second – when they had all smiled at the camera and Mr Trigg had hit a switch, they had been frozen in time, together, forever.

Sonia Brownlow married Jack's friend, Noel, Cecily was saying now. But he had been killed in action only weeks after their wedding. She had married again, another army man, and was living out in India, Cecily thought. 'And did you see Marjorie, Sonia's sister, in the newspapers?' she asked.

Sylvia shook her head. 'No, was she married?'

Cecily laughed. 'No! She was arrested, at a suffragette parade. But I believe she's been released.'

'Arrested,' Sylvia repeated, Gracious.'

It baffled Sylvia why these women did such things, why they wanted to vote. Some things were better left to men, she thought: politics, fighting, voting; making decisions.

'Whatever happened to Miss Combe?' Sylvia asked. 'I rather liked her.'

'Poor Miss Combe,' Cecily said. 'You know, she never got her electricity. She passed away quite suddenly, unexpectedly, during the very first days of the war.'

'And your friend, the one from the shop, the post office, where is she now?'

The farmer – or farm worker, as it turned out – that Annie had been waiting for finally arrived and married her the year before war broke out. They produced three children before he was killed in action in 1917. And though Annie remained a widow, there was someone in her life, Cecily said.

'And your mother . . . your sister?'

Cecily's sister, Ethne, was married to the new rector, a Mr Meredith Ballantyne, and Madeline continued to live at the same house, the one her husband had built. Rosetta had moved in, Cecily said, after Ethne moved out. But Bramley had changed, people had gone, businesses had disappeared. 'It is all different,' she said, 'not at all as you'll remember . . .'

They spoke about various other people in the village. Cecily mentioned a few names Sylvia could not recall, and, bizarrely, Sylvia mentioned names Cecily could not recall.

'I imagine you saw the details of the sale?' Cecily said.

'Yes, I did. But it strikes me as a great shame,' Sylvia replied, noting the 'CC' ring on Cecily's finger. 'I'm not sure she would have wanted it *all* going under the hammer.'

'But we can't keep it,' she shrugged her shoulders, 'we just can't. We don't have the space.'

'But surely if you lived there, at Temple Hill . . .'

Cecily smiled, shook her head. 'No, it has to be sold, I'm afraid. You see, there was little to no money, and we certainly can't afford to run a big house like that, not on the money I earn. I don't think Cora had any idea quite how impoverished she was . . . and probably just as well.'

'She was never very good with money,' said Sylvia. 'It's so sad that the two of you never saw each other again after that . . . that little upset you had.'

'*Upset?* Oh, but we never fell out, not really. I loved her, loved her dearly, and I think, I hope, she knew that . . . but yes, I wish I had seen her again. Just once, once more.'

Cecily looked away. She said, 'I'm afraid she was very confused at the end, had absolutely no idea who anyone was. It was a blessing, really.'

'When did it start, the confusion?'

Cecily shook her head. 'Oh, years ago, during the war. She simply couldn't accept what happened, what was happening around her. It was very hard for her.'

'Yes, of course.'

'But she had become forgetful, a little confused, even before that time.'

'Yes,' Sylvia said, remembering.

'She thought she was back in Rome, thought she was young again . . .' Cecily leaned forward, stubbed out her cigarette. 'It was sad,' she added, closing her eyes for a moment, shaking her head again. 'Because she was so . . . so vulnerable, so . . .' she glanced up at the ceiling and then laughed. 'You know, she began to wear her hair down,' she said, looking directly at Sylvia and wiping away a tear.

'Down?' Sylvia repeated.

'Yes, *down*. And sometimes with a moth-eaten plume or an ancient paste clip in it, but she looked so pretty, quite beautiful with that long white-white hair,' she went on dreamily. 'Yes, very pretty.'

'It's how she wore it when she was young.'

'And right up until the end she was always dressed, always in one of her costumes, as though about to go somewhere, or receive someone.'

'It's how it used to be . . .'

'She was sweet, childlike . . . and very talkative, too. Do you remember her queer accent?'

Sylvia smiled, nodded. How could she forget?

'You know, when I first met her, when she first came to Bramley,' Cecily continued, 'it seemed to me as though she was always . . . delivering a speech, harking back to Rome, to what once had been. I was really quite awestruck – I rather think we all were, then,' she said wistfully. 'She was so intriguing, so enigmatic, and oh, how we all hung on to her every word!'

Yes, Sylvia thought, *how I hung on* . . .

'And she always seemed so . . . so extraordinarily wise . . .'

How people had fawned and courted her, Sylvia thought – even then.

'And forgiving. She was forgiving, wasn't she?'

Sylvia smiled, nodded. Yes, she was forgiving. She forgave *him*; despite everything, she forgave George. And now Sylvia was pleased she had given them that time, those final few months together.

'I was so sorry . . . when I heard, heard about Jack. It must have been hard, very hard for you,' Sylvia said, and not without empathy. 'And you know, I did write. I wrote to Cora at the time,' she added.

Cecily nodded. 'It was hard for us all,' she said and sighed. 'But by then everything had changed. The village had thinned out, altered its shape and character. And so too had she. You see, it was then, during that time, that she dispensed with her title, decided she wanted to be known simply as Mrs Lawson. She didn't go anywhere, hardly ventured outside. And people began to say that she was mad, quite mad. They said that the place was haunted, that she lived amongst ghosts and spoke more with the dead than with the living. And perhaps it was true. But then she lingered on there for so long, for so many years, too long, surrounded by all her statues and bronzes . . . lost in her memories.'

Yes, Sylvia thought, picturing Cora's dust-shrouded paraphernaila, how dark the house must have been: dark and dusty, and filled with things no one would ever dream of having indoors nowadays. How could she *not* have gone back, stuck there, surrounded by it all? But she had the name, the only name she ever wanted, in the end: Mrs Lawson.

Cecily continued. She had called on Cora regularly, she said, but the place – the house and Cora herself – appeared sadder and shabbier on each occasion. Like Dickens' Miss Havisham, it seemed to her as though Cora was trapped in time, 'in a moment – a day, a month, a season, a year – she simply couldn't let go of or release. She became a relic, a relic of a bygone era.' But even before this, Cecily said, she had witnessed Mr Fox and a few others alter tempo. The tide turned, and just as though they – the very same people who had once been mesmerised – had been jilted at the altar, as though they had been wooed and courted and then somehow let down, they turned on her. They began to say that she was and always had been deluded, that she had simply made things up, and that she was nobody special.

By the time the war ended, she had gone, Cecily said, closing her eyes for a moment. 'She was lost . . . and I suppose we were all browbeaten, disenchanted, uninterested in titles and former lifestyles, or any tales that did not involve a Military Cross.' No one associated old Mrs Lawson with any famous names; no one was interested, she said. One decade had altered everyone's perspective, and Cora, the Countess de Chevalier de Saint Léger, her connections and memories of Paris and Rome, had been forgotten. 'No one knew she was there.'

'In these past few years,' Cecily continued, 'since the war, she just seemed to . . . shrivel up, literally shrink. Mrs Davey stayed on with her, of course, and Mr Cordery, too. But she had few if any visitors, apart from yours truly. And she had no idea who anyone was anyhow, no idea what time she was in.'

Cecily told Sylvia that Cora's bed had been moved downstairs, into what had been her drawing room, and a live-in nurse employed to take care of her. The canvas of her life, which had once been epic – in miles and scale and vista – grew smaller and smaller, until it became nothing more than the view from that bed.

'But I'd like to talk to you,' Cecily said, turning to Sylvia, altering her tone, 'about something she told me . . . something she told me on one of the last occasions I visited her.'

It had been shortly before that final, rapid decline, said Cecily. Cora had sat in her usual chair, overdressed, tiny and hunched. She had asked Cecily about her journey, whether she had had a good crossing. And Cecily had smiled and nodded. What else could she do? Cora had asked her the very same question on her previous visit. She was confused, thought she was back in Rome, and there seemed little point in attempting to dislodge her from her dream. She told Cecily that she was glad not to be in England, 'so cold at this time of year', and then she leaned forward in her chair and said, 'I shan't ever go back there, you know. Not now.'

'Well, you can be wherever you wish to be,' Cecily replied.

'He wants to visit Cyprus in the spring . . .' she said, absently.

'That would be nice.'

'We might go to Egypt, see the Nile, the pyramids.'

'How lovely.'

'But I'll never go back there. I can't ever go back there.'

'No.'

'You understand, don't you?'

Cecily nodded.

'And he shan't go back either,' she continued. 'He prefers it here, you see. Oh yes, he always did . . . he never wanted to leave me, but he had to. It wasn't because of Freddie. He didn't know . . . had no idea,' she added, lifting her hand to the locket round her neck.

None of it had made any sense to Cecily. And she was herself distracted, keeping an eye upon the time, glancing to the clock on the mantelpiece. And the muddled ramblings of a deluded old lady had not been compelling enough to unravel. Not then. The same names came up again and again: Freddie and George, or Georgie, and Jack and

Fanny. All jumbled in with 'he' and 'she' and 'him' and 'her', and 'they'. How could it make sense? A lifetime spewed out without any chronology; the names of people long since gone, and – bar one – never known to Cecily. It was sad, pathetic, and the events of the preceding decade had washed away any romantic ideas Cecily might have had about the elderly woman sitting in front of her. Reality had arrived in 1914, futility in 1917.

'Did you see him?' Cora had asked, moving in her chair, tilting her head to peer at Cecily.

Her spine had curved with age, pushing her head forward so that it hung down and appeared too large for her small frame. Mrs Davey said she barely touched food, and though she had long given up smoking, Mrs Davey told Cecily that she still enjoyed the occasional glass of wine.

'See whom, dear?'

'Well, Jack, of course. They're outside . . . they'll be back at any minute. I said to them not to go far, said you were coming . . .'

And thus it went on, this movement back and forth in time, and names, and words, and words and words. Then silence. From time to time the flicker of amusement crossed her face, and she almost laughed; and then she would frown, appear perplexed or bewildered, move about in her chair, scanning the room with her eyes, searching for . . . sense? Order?

She said, 'He was a shoemaker.'

'Who, dear?' Cecily asked. 'Who was a shoemaker?'

'He was . . . Uncle John . . .'

'Uncle John?'

'Do you remember him?'

Cecily shook her head. 'No, I never knew him. Was it a long time ago?'

'Best forgotten,' she said, then added, 'You mustn't tell her, don't tell Fanny we've spoken of him.'

'Of course I shan't tell her . . . but what happened to him?'

She didn't answer. She disappeared back to that place Cecily couldn't reach. But the pain – on her face, in her eyes – was easy enough to see.

'What happened to Uncle John, Cora?'

She winced, closed her eyes and shook her head. 'Mustn't tell.'

'Mustn't tell what?'

She opened her eyes, and without looking at Cecily, staring down into her lap, she whispered, 'I killed him.'

For a moment Cecily said nothing. She was unsure what to say. 'I'm quite sure you did not kill anyone,' she said at last, in an unusually condescending tone.

Cora looked up at her. 'Oh, but I did. I hit him over the head with it!'

'With what? What did you hit him over the head with?'

'It had to be done . . . had to be done. He was a brute, a monster . . . and I didn't understand.

We went to Jersey,' she went on, her eyes half closed, lowering her head. 'Yes, Jersey . . . to the Lebruns . . .' She raised her head again. 'Do you recall them, Philip and Mary?'

'No. I never knew them.'

'We couldn't go back, you see. No, not ever, she said. But Mr Staunton was a good man, such a *good* man.'

'Mr Staunton? Jack's grandfather?'

None of it made any sense.

'Did Mr Staunton know any of this . . . about Uncle John?'

But she didn't answer, didn't seem to hear. 'Fanny warned me. But I never thought they'd find me.' She glanced up at Cecily. 'It was my brother, you know, my eldest brother, Samuel . . . he ended up there, in Jersey . . . working for the Lebruns. I suppose Mary thought she was bringing us back together. But he wanted money, nothing more. He said he'd write to the newspapers, tell them.' She shook her head. 'My aunt had only just married again . . . become a contessa. I suppose he thought I was rich . . .'

'You mean to say you were blackmailed . . . by your *brother*?'

'He said he'd tell *him* . . . tell him where we were, how to find us. But how could he tell him if he was dead? And I *had* killed him . . . Fanny told me. Yes, it wasn't bigamy, she said, because he was gone . . . it was only bigamy if I had not killed him, you see.'

No, Cecily did not see. Could not see. It was all coming too quickly. Bigamy, blackmail, murder, it was bizarre, too preposterous to contemplate, almost impossible to comprehend.

'She was his housekeeper, you know,' Cora was saying, 'and he was such a good man . . . Mr Staunton.'

'Mr Staunton?'

'Yes, Mr Staunton . . .' She lifted her head and looked at Cecily. 'Have you had your hair done, dear?' she asked.

When Cecily stood up to say goodbye, moved over to her and took her hand, she said, 'But you don't have to go upstairs yet. Fanny will be with the little ones, will have put them to bed by now.'

In the hallway, Mrs Davey appeared.

'She's very confused,' Cecily said.

Mrs Davey nodded. 'They're all here with her. She can't escape them, or the past. But she's happy enough . . . happy to be amongst them.'

'I'm not so sure,' Cecily replied, putting on her gloves. 'She has some uninvited guests, I think.'

'Do you think any of it is true?' Cecily asked Sylvia now.

Sylvia took a moment, then she smiled and said, 'Well, of course it's not true! Oh, there may have been an Uncle John, once, somewhere in her family, and he may have been something of a brute, but I'm afraid everything else is complete nonsense. She was clearly deluded, as you say – very confused.'

'But where on earth did it all come from?'

'From her imagination . . . she was always one for a story. You should know that. Don't you remember all her tales about Rome and Paris?'

'Yes, of course I do, but they *were* true, weren't they?'

'Hmm. Not all of them, no. Cora liked to add her own twist, embellish, add a little detail here and there. She adored drama, and the truth of the matter is, she could not recall her childhood even twelve years ago. But it's sad, makes me very sad, that she was so lost at the end . . . so estranged from reality.'

'Yes, yes. You're right. Of course, you're right.' Cecily glanced to her wristwatch. 'Gracious, I should be going soon.' She reached for the paper bag on the table: 'I've brought you the letter, and my manuscript,' she said. And Sylvia, thinking she had misheard her, almost laughed. '*Your* manuscript?'

'Yes, I mentioned it to you on the telephone, remember?'

And just as the sun slowly rises, the horrendous reality of the situation began to glimmer and break in Sylvia's mind, the word 'manuscript' echoing once more down a crackling telephone line. She said nothing, and Cecily handed her an envelope with the words 'Miss S. Dorland' written on the front in Cora's hand, and underlined twice. Cecily said, 'I've had this letter for so long, seems rather strange to be finally handing it over to you.'

Sylvia tried to smile. 'I shall look at it later,' she said, putting it to one side, watching Cecily as she pulled out a small pile of paper held together by a red elastic band. 'And here is the manuscript,' she said, rather triumphantly, Sylvia thought. And she pushed the bundle across the table towards Sylvia. The capitalised title on the frontispiece read, *A Desperate Heart*.

'It's a novel then?' said Sylvia.

'Yes, as I said on the telephone, it's loosely based on Cora's life and, I hasten to add, not quite finished. But I'd value your opinion . . . She had such a remarkable life, inspiring, I think.'

'Yes, it was certainly that,' Sylvia conceded.

'I'd appreciate your opinion . . . thought you might take a look, point out any obvious mistakes . . . and I wondered if you might be prepared to elucidate on a few other matters . . . and not necessarily for the book.'

'Oh?'

'The truth is, I'm still rather confused about Cora's marriage to Edward. Why she kept it a secret for so long, and why she married a man so very much older than she was. He was an old man and she still quite young, not that much older than me when she married him. I know it can't have been a . . . a proper marriage, a physical relationship, nor even for the company, the companionship of a husband, because they never lived together. I presumed it was for some sort of security, but then . . .' she paused.

'Then?'

'Then, more recently, I've been pondering her relationship with George. You see, I'm aware that she knew him long before she married Edward, and though she was always rather guarded about their friendship, later, when she was . . . confused, she spoke of him so much. It was always George this, George that. She very rarely mentioned Edward, or Jack, or Antonin.' She paused again, scrutinising Sylvia. 'I realise now that they were closer than I had at first thought, that she may . . . well, may perhaps have been in love with George – and not his father?'

She said this as a question, but Sylvia offered no reply. And she quickly went on. 'Of course, I may be wrong, but even so, it must have been queer to George for his friend, one of his contemporaries, suddenly at that late stage to become his stepmother.'

Sylvia smiled. 'Oh, I don't suppose George ever viewed Cora as a mother, even a stepmother. But you are correct, they were close, very close friends, and for many years.'

'You were there, at the wedding? You knew them both, George *and* Edward?'

Sylvia nodded. 'Yes, I was there. I knew them both.'

'And you never detected anything . . . between Cora and George?'

CHAPTER 23

In the taxicab, en route to the Café Royal, Cecily wondered if she had misinterpreted Sylvia's reaction to her novel, which had been odd to say the least. She had forgotten about Sylvia's obsessive nature, that all-consuming love she had for Cora – anything and everything to do with Cora. She had appeared surprised when Cecily mentioned and then produced the manuscript, despite the fact that they had spoken about it on the telephone, for hadn't Sylvia said then, *Oh how lovely, I'm so pleased?*

But Sylvia seemed to think she had some divine right over Cora's life, as though she owned the copyright to it, all of it. As though only she knew the truth. And oh, how she guarded it! When she said, 'I'll try and take a look at it, but I am actually rather busy,' Cecily could have laughed, and almost had. For what was there for Sylvia to be busy with, there at the Windsor? What was there for her to do?

She lit a cigarette. The traffic on Oxford Street had ground to a halt and she stared at the murky shapes waiting in queues to be transported home.

But she saw none of them. The photograph, reminiscences, and the memory of that summer had stirred her, taken her back. Back to a time when everything shone, back to a time when even the prospect of war had not been enough to dampen hopes and dreams . . .

She had been home for a day when Rosetta mentioned his name, told her that Jack Staunton was in Bramley, at Temple Hill. 'Don't suppose her ladyship's too happy about him going off up in them aeroplanes neither.'

'Aeroplanes?'

'Well, yes, he's learning to fly. Been having lessons over at Farnborough. You ask your mother if you don't believe me.'

So she had asked her mother. 'Is it true that Jack Staunton's back and that he's learning to fly?'

'Yes, it's true. Though for the life of me I can't understand why he's got himself caught up in that nonsense.'

'I can,' Cecily said, watching her mother, bent over the sewing machine. 'Do you know how long he's home for?'

Her mother didn't look up. 'He's been to call a few times, enquired after you, asked where you were,' she said, fiddling with the fabric under the needle as she spoke.

Cecily sat down in the chair opposite her mother. 'But how long is he here for?'

Madeline glanced over her spectacles at her daughter. 'I'm not sure, he didn't say. But I told him you'd been in Paris for almost a year. He couldn't believe it. Yes, I said, she's never going to settle in Bramley, not now. But I told him that due to the situation you'd come home and were living in London. Very wise, he said, very wise. And Walter, too, is keen to see you. You know he adores you, would marry you in a heartbeat, and yet you keep him hanging on . . .' she looked away, shook her head. 'It's cruel, I think. Really, I do.'

Cecily rose from her chair, walked to the window. Daylight was fading, the tops of the trees golden in the twilight. 'I can't marry Walter. I've told you before, I don't love him in that way.'

'In *that way*?' her mother repeated and then laughed. 'My dearest girl, do you really think all of life is about being in love? It's about making the best of what we have, and being gracious – and thankful – in our acceptance of that.'

Cecily closed her eyes, didn't answer for a moment, and knew full well that she should not answer. She knew that she should leave it at that. But she couldn't. She turned to her mother. 'No. You're wrong. It's not about acceptance, Mother. It's about creating the life you wish for . . . dream of. Creating a better world, a better place in which to live. Otherwise, what is our life about? What is our legacy?'

'My legacy is you,' Madeline replied quickly. 'You and Ethne.'

Cecily sighed. 'The world is changing, Mother,

and even if there is a war, it will continue to change, for better or worse. We can't stand still, we can't stop progress.'

'Progress? Your generation are too preoccupied with progress. Is it not enough to have a life and someone to love?'

Cecily didn't answer. Yes, she thought, of course it is. It's the most important thing, surely, to have someone to love, to be loved.

'I'm surprised he hasn't called today,' her mother went on. 'Jack Staunton, I mean. I told him you'd be home Saturday. In fact, I was surprised he wasn't at church this morning. Of course, she never goes . . .'

Jack Staunton. Each mention of the name caused a flutter.

'Oh well,' Cecily said, 'we probably have nothing in common now. He was always . . . rather arrogant, I think.'

'Jack? No, he's not arrogant, dear, quite the opposite. And, considering everything . . .' Madeline paused, looked across the room to the empty hearth, 'considering everything, it's really very encouraging.'

She had wondered what her mother meant by 'encouraging', but chose not to ask. 'Poor Walter,' her mother began again, 'seems to work all the hours God sends.'

'I can imagine,' said Cecily, turning away, staring out through the open window in the direction of Temple Hill. 'I wrote to him, you know.

When Mr Gamben died, I wrote separate letters to each of them . . . How is Annie?'

'As happy as the day is long.'

Cecily smiled. 'All she ever wanted was to get married and have a family.'

'Well, it's enough for some of us. And Luke's a good husband to her. He loves her and he loves that baby.'

'I'm happy for her.'

She was looking forward to seeing Annie again, but they had lost the place with each other during the course of the past two years. And Walter, dear Walter, he had almost proposed to her the night before she left for Paris – would have done so had she not stopped him. And was it not in fact Jack Staunton's words she had borrowed to deter Walter, when she told him that she had no wish to be tied down, no desire to be married for at least another five years?

Jack. Almost three years had passed since she had stood and kissed him at the top of that hill. Almost three years since she had felt her heart split in two and thought she'd never, ever recover. Almost three years . . .

After he left she had wondered if he would write, had longed for him to, just to see her name in his hand. And she had waited. But nothing came, not even a postcard. Then, early the following year, having managed to persuade her mother to allow her some of the money her father had left to her, she had gone travelling with Aunt Kitty and cousin Erica. They had been away for six months, had visited Paris, the Riviera, Rome, Naples, Florence, Geneva, the Rhineland, and almost every place with a church or cathedral in between. By the time she returned home, Jack had been and gone. He had stayed at Temple Hill for only a few weeks that summer, due to his own somewhat hectic itinerary. Then another Christmas came and went without any sign of him. He was ski-ing, Cora had said. And that Easter, 'away with friends . . . on the Riviera.' Their paths, it seemed, were destined not to cross, and Cecily – by then determined that they should not cross – enrolled on a secretarial course in London (with French as an extra). By winter she had returned to Paris, sharing what she described to her mother as a shoebox off the Champs-Elysées with a girl from her course.

'Almost three years,' she said out loud in the taxi.

'Almost three years,' she murmured, standing by the window in her mother's workroom.

'Mm? What's that, dear?'

'Oh nothing. I think I'll take some air, have a walk in the garden.'

As she moved towards the doorway, she said, 'Oh, and how is Cora?'

'I'm not entirely sure. No one ever sees her but Mrs Fox seems to think she's gone a little doolally.'

Cecily stopped. 'Doolally?'

'Mm. Communing with the dead, she said.'

'And how does she know?'

'Edith Davey – the housekeeper up at Temple Hill, is very friendly with the cook at the rectory. They speak.'

'You mean they *gossip*,' Cecily said and moved on.

Outside, the air was soft, fragrant with the scent of honeysuckle and jasmine. It felt good to be back there, home, out upon that hillside once more. And yet so much of the place reminded her of him. But how could that be? How could the place she had lived for so long be infused with the presence of someone who had only been there, in her life, for a matter of weeks? How could he do that to a place and to her?

It made her angry and perplexed her. I have done it, she thought, sitting down upon the warm stone of the steps to the lily pond; I have hung on, dragging a romantic notion forward, from here to Europe and back again, and then to Paris and London. I have done it to myself. So, he called and enquired after me, she mused. It means nothing . . . nothing. He has nothing better to do with his time here . . . is most likely awful now . . . like those graduates in London who say, 'Bramley? Is that a new college?' and then laugh. Well, if he comes, if he were to appear now, I shall be indifferent, she thought. Yes, I *am* indifferent . . .

She had been sitting on the steps for no more than five minutes when she heard the voice. 'Hello stranger, your mother said you were out here.'

'Reckon we'd be better cutting down Piccadilly,' the cab driver said, interrupting.

'I'm in no rush,' Cecily replied.

She was only thirty minutes late, only nine years behind, and she wasn't ready to step back into *now*. Not yet. She wanted to remember, needed to savour those weeks, those few weeks, not quite amounting to months, that they had had together before the war, before he said, 'I'll be back soon.'

They had picked up where they left off. Resuming what was unconcluded with a new sense of urgency and without any questions. Resuming a courtship begun three years before. Those who did not know might have used the word 'whirlwind'. Because within weeks Jack had asked her to marry him, at the top of the hill – the place they had first kissed. And within a heartbeat she had said yes.

But he was like that, she thought now. He knew what he wanted and went after it, as though aware of the limitation on time. As though he knew.

They married four days after the declaration of war, at St Luke's in Bramley, and afterwards Cora hosted a small reception in the garden at Temple Hill. The week after their return from honeymoon – five days in Brighton – Jack signed up. Like most others he enlisted for a 'temporary commission for the period of the war'. He was assigned to the Rifle Brigade. But of course it was not where he wanted to be. Jack wanted to be in the air. And he was one of a few who had already taken a turn up in the sky.

Jack got his wish early the following year. After attending a military school in Birmingham and gaining his flying certificate, he was attached to the Royal Flying Corps' Number One Squadron, and almost immediately deployed to the war zone, piloting biplanes over the fields of France and Flanders on reconnaissance missions. He was happy to be doing his duty and thrilled to be flying.

Cecily lived in fear and dread. She never knew for sure when her husband was flying, or where he was, would only find out about his movements after the event, in the form of a letter, a telegram or, occasionally, a phone call. Shortly after their marriage she had had a telephone installed at their cottage. 'For emergencies only,' she had said, only to regret it later. Because the very last thing she wished for was any emergency call. She wanted to hear from him, Jack; wanted to hear his voice and know only that he was safe, alive.

Whenever he managed to secure leave, he came home to Cecily at their rented cottage on the north-west fringe of Bramley – exhausted. He was understandably sombre, less ebullient. But by then everything and everyone was changing. Young, fit and able-bodied men had disappeared from the village, and it was left to the women to do the jobs the men had previously done. Cora's servants had been halved in number, and then halved again, as her kitchen and parlour maids joined the war effort, and left for farm or factory work. Her precious garden had been dug up, turned over to produce vegetables and accommodate livestock. She was left with Mrs Davey, and a daily, and her gardener, Mr Cordery, who was too old to enlist.

Cecily followed events in the newspaper; she read of the losses to the British Fleet and to the army, and then, with even greater horror, of the losses to the Royal Flying Corps. She became used to the distant sound of air raids and bombs dropped by German zeppelins along the coast. And Cora told her it was different to any of the wars she had known before. It was a modern war, she said, voracious in its appetite for young souls, relentless in its cruelty.

On Jack's last leave, Cecily savoured each second of each minute, barely sleeping so that she could watch him while he slept, take all of him in. And that was all he did, sleep, for three whole days. But on his final day they had gone back to Brighton, with Cora.

The place had been crowded with army personnel and couples unashamedly walking hand in hand; young women in their Sunday best clinging on to their sweethearts; parents walking proudly alongside their uniformed sons – all of them enjoying those precious hours before the inevitable 'Adieu' and that grim journey back across the Channel. Under the strange and intense winter sun that day, the young men in uniform appeared to Cecily almost iridescent. They were there and alive, but not really there; destined for glory, destined for death, they were already going, already gone, already ghosts.

And there were the others, too, the walking wounded and injured, in mud-caked tattered uniforms, staggering on crutches, sitting along the promenade in bath chairs; some missing limbs, others disfigured or badly burned. Jack had made a point of stopping to speak to them, shaking hands, slapping backs, making jokes. They all did that, Cecily noticed. As though they had been at some macabre, nightmare party and could laugh about it now, momentarily, before re-entering that doorway, and the cacophony of the theatre.

Cora had seen injured soldiers many times before, she said, after the Crimea, as first deserters and then disorientated soldiers slowly made their way home to England; and on the streets of Rome, after Garibaldi marched on the city. She told Cecily that she thought her sensibilities had long ago been anaesthetised to life's tragedies and war's casualties, but even she struggled with the sights that day.

They had sat hand in hand opposite Cora on the train journey back to Linford. And from time to time Jack lifted her hand to his lips and held it there, eyes closed, as Cora chattered on. But there had been signs, even then, of Cora's confusion and muddled memory; early signs, which went unnoticed.

'Did we have luncheon today?' she had asked.

And they both laughed, thought she was ragging them. Jack said, 'Yes, and you said it was daylight robbery. Three shillings, remember?'

She shook her head.

'Whitstable oysters, consommé, turbot Marguery, fillet of beef and peach cardinal. A feast!' Jack said.

She smiled. 'Ah yes, of course.'

Later, alone in the bedroom of their cottage, they had lain on the bed staring at each other. He said, 'Don't cry, please. I'll be back soon, a few weeks . . .'

'Promise me, promise me hand on heart you'll come back . . . promise me you shan't let yourself get killed?'

He held his hand to his heart. 'I promise.'

'And you'll never ever forget that promise, will you?'

'Never.'

Against the odds, Jack had survived almost two years in the Royal Flying Corps, and had been promoted from Flying Officer to Lieutenant. But he had been in Number One Squadron, deployed on reconnaissance duties and not fighting. When he telephoned Cecily two days after returning to duty to tell her that he was to be promoted to Captain and that the squadron was to become a dedicated fighter squadron, she said nothing. She closed her eyes and knew: knew immediately that aerial combat would be infinitely more dangerous than reconnaissance. But he seemed oblivious to any peril, and spoke only of his new aeroplane, a

Nieuport 17, and its powerful engine and large wings.

The telegram to say Jack was 'missing' arrived the day after Cecily found out – had it confirmed – that she was expecting the first of their 'unruly horde'. She had already posted a letter to her husband, saying:

My darling man, I have news! Are you sitting down? I imagine that you are. I imagine you are lying on your horrid uncomfortable bunk as you read this. But even so, brace yourself, darling . . . you are to be a father! Yes, that's right, YOU ARE TO BE A FATHER! This means that you really do have to stay safe and come back to me . . .

Cecily did not cry, she did not shout. She sat down. And she stayed very still and very silent for some time, holding on to that telegram, pondering that word: missing. Missing was not dead, she reasoned; missing was inconclusive. And Jack had promised. It took her a while to realise that the strange whimpering sound, the sound of an injured animal, was coming from within her and not from outside.

Hours later, she walked out from her cottage towards the village, towards Temple Hill and Cora. It was early autumn, the sky was clear and cloudless, the hedgerows still green, and purple with blackberries. But she saw none of the day. She walked in a daze along the gritted road, past the whitewashed cottages and tile-hung shops of the village, across the stepping stones of the ford, and up the rabbit-hole tunnel towards the house. *Not dead, not dead . . . missing, not dead . . .* From time to time she placed her hand upon her stomach and thought of the life within her. And in her head she heard his voice: I promise . . . never.

She kept her gaze steady as she passed her former home, determined not to look at the gate, lest something of him – and her – was still there, an impression caught in the ether and only visible once lost. But at the very top of the track, as she emerged from the shadows, the sound of a motor-cycle's acceleration on the other side of the valley made her stop and look up. She followed its sound along the winding lane towards the village, turned and stared back down the track, willing him to appear, anticipating the sight of him coming up the hillside towards her, to explain. She thought she could hear the machine, spluttering, stumbling through the ford and out the other side. But no one and nothing appeared at the bottom of the track, and as the sound of the engine slowly faded she too moved on.

Cora was in her usual place, usual chair, leaning forward and peering through her old lorgnette at the newspaper laid out on the card table in front of her.

'Aha!' she said, glancing up as Cecily entered the room. But her smile quickly fell as she took in

Cecily's expression. And before Cecily could speak, she whispered the name as a question. 'Jack?'

Cecily nodded. 'Missing.'

Cora closed her eyes.

If there was a specific time, a moment Cecily could identify as the start of Cora's mental collapse, when she had finally given in, given up, surrendered her mind, her sanity, that was it. The prospect of his loss – more loss – was simply too much.

As though shutting out reality, trying to deny that moment, Cora kept her eyes closed. But even through sealed eyelids tears escaped. And Cecily, unsure and impotent, powerless to alter facts and details, unable to offer hope, simply stood and watched. Then, with her eyes still closed and seemingly unable to speak, Cora nodded. As though it were news she had been waiting for. When she finally opened her eyes, she said, 'We shan't give up hope. We must wait for him. He'll find his way back to us. He'll find his way home.'

The newspapers were quick to include Jack's name in the Roll of Honour. Captain J. G. Staunton, RFC was listed under 'Missing', above the column titled 'Previously Reported Missing, Now Reported Killed', and another, 'Previously Reported Missing, Now Reported Prisoners of War'. And the *London Gazette* kindly included him in their 'List of Dead'.

Jack had been missing for seven months by the time the letter arrived from the War Office. It enclosed a copy of the Geneva Red Cross 'List of Dead', and read: 'Staunton J.G., RFC, seen to fall in an air fight near Bixschoote . . . In view of the lapse of time, this report will be accepted for official purposes as evidence of death.' Ten days later, Cecily gave birth to their son.

As the taxicab turned on to Piccadilly, Cecily glanced at her wristwatch and thought of her boy. He was staying for a few days with her mother and Rosetta, whom he adored, and who idolised him. Rosetta had looked after him as a baby so that Cecily could continue to teach at the school. And her new charge had given her a new lease of life. Each day and in all weathers a bonneted Rosetta had pushed the perambulator proudly through the village, disappearing into the lanes, singing songs to little Jack. One of his first words had been 'Etta', which Rosetta had now officially adopted as her name.

Even then, during those very first days and months of her son's life, Cecily had spoken to him about his father, telling him how brave and fearless he was. And as her son grew bigger, she would hold him on her hip, pointing to the man in the framed wedding photograph on the mantel-shelf and repeating the word 'Daddy', until one day he finally said it as well: 'Dada!' And Cecily wept.

She had taken her son to visit his great-grand-mother, but by that time Cora had been distracted at best, and entirely absent at worst. There were glimmers, the odd moment when she seemed to know, appeared to realise that the baby in front of her was in fact Jack's son, her great-grandson. But there had also been occasions when she had stared at the baby in Cecily's arms, frowning, and asked Cecily to whom the child belonged. Once, possibly prompted by confusion over the name Jack, and after Cecily had once again tried to explain that Little Jack was Jack's son, she had asked her, 'Is it *my* baby?'

It was sad and bizarre and comical. And Cecily had had to remind herself how Cora might think such a thing. Lost in time, she had grasped the name, the name of a former husband with whom she had had her babies.

'No, dear, he's not your baby. He's my baby,' she replied, looking at the old lady through tear-filled eyes.

How Walter had laughed when she told him of that. He said, 'How can a woman of eighty odd think she has a baby?'

'Because she doesn't and can't let herself see the here and now. Inside her mind she's still young, forever young. She's gone back in time.'

Walter Gamben had been returned from the killing fields of France invalided, minus a leg, in the spring of 1918. Cecily had visited him at the military hospital at Winchester. Months later, after he had been discharged and returned home to Bramley, he had asked her to marry him. It was Armistice Day, the whole village half-deaf and dizzy from the sound of the church bells, everyone riding on a wave of euphoria, drunk on the idea of peace and the future. How many marriage proposals must there have been that day, Cecily later thought.

She had told Walter that she could not marry him, that she was still in love with her husband, still in love with Jack. She had tried to explain to him that some small part of her refused to believe that Jack was not coming back. For he had promised her and she could not give up on that promise. Not yet. Walter said he understood, and that he'd wait. 'Even if I have to wait ten years,' he said, smiling at her with such optimism, such hope. Then he said, 'You know, I sometimes feel guilty . . . guilty that my happiness has been brought about by another's misfortune. For had Jack been here you wouldn't be with me now.' Cecily told him he was wrong, told him she would still have been there for him; 'the what ifs could go on and on – what if I'd never met Jack, what if there had never been a war – but we're all part of each other's lives, each other's story, and always will be.'

But it was the unwritten story, the one about herself and Jack, that she most often returned to, and dreamed of: the *what if he is alive, what if he comes back to me.* She had already spent what seemed like a lifetime imagining that story. A story bound up in missing faces and places, and journeys yet to be taken. It was the fantasy of youth and idle optimism, pulled forward in time and springing back like elastic. Nothing could change the past; it had happened, it had gone, but what if . . . what if . . . what if . . .

But the war had ended and Jack had not returned. He had not come back to her. He had not been able to keep his promise. And as life took on a new normality, hope faded and loneliness set in. Each evening, alone in her bed, Cecily returned to her musings, to Jack, and their unspent future . . .

They would have been happy together, surely, blissfully happy and in love. They would have gone on to have more children, that 'unruly horde' they had spoken of. And they would have lived in Bramley, possibly at Temple Hill. After all, it was the perfect house for a large family. There would have been a swing in the garden, a slide, bicycles lying about the place; and noise, oh, so much noise. She would glance up from the manuscript in front of her, look out through the window and see them, see him – her husband, the father of her children. And he would sense her gaze, turn to her and smile.

How it could have been, how it should have been, if only . . .

It had been impossible for Cecily to let go of that dream, and of him, Jack. It sustained her, kept her warm, offered her sanctuary and became her escape. It was the luxury in her life, that imagining, that what if. And she realised she could write it any way she wished, change and alter it at whim; introduce new situations, new characters, test Jack's love for her and test her own for him. And thus, night after night, she rewrote history. There was no declaration of war and Jack never fell from the sky. No one aged or died, and time simply moved back and forth, like waves upon a shore. Days were repeated, rerun with amendments and with added colour and detail. And she returned again and again to that moment when the world had spun on its axis and everything around them – and beyond them – had seemed possible and within reach.

Cora had once said to her, 'We all have a plan . . . a plan of how our lives will be, but it is never what happens because we're all mortal, all fallible. And because human beings make mistakes – follow others' mistakes. We are easily led from our path. But we can find our way back, eventually, if we are able to remember what it is we first wished for.'

On Armistice Day, after she had returned home from the celebrations, after Walter's proposal, Cecily sat up until dawn reading through her old journals. Thinking of her son, his future, she deliberated on destroying the blue cloth-covered books. So much had been promised, so much had been hoped, and she had no wish for him to one day read and feel that loss. Then she picked up her pen and wrote:

It is that morning of once before now, that morning I first saw you . . . and I feel the heat. I see lambent ferns and waist-high nettles . . . a demoiselle butterfly skimming the pond. I see dragonflies, minnows and jam jars, yellow gorse and purple heather, and poppies, scarlet and black. I see fox-coloured tiles and tall chimneys, and lines of silver on blue. And you say, we have our whole lives ahead of us. Our whole lives, you say, looking back at me.

Now it is early evening. The sun has slipped beneath the trees. I move through the last remnants of slanting sun upon grass, golden, parched and dry, and I hear you whispering: when this whole rotten business is over . . . when this whole rotten business is over, you say. And my heart burns but I am still. I can wait. I can wait.

The sun slips further, I hear the first owl, and I feel the edge of summer.

The baby in my arms laughs as I swing him through that fading twilight, round and round, and round again. And when I stop and look up I see you standing by the hedge once more in your cricket whites, smiling back at me, at us.

Yes, it was a stunning thought, my darling. You were my stunning thought, burning and poignant and blurring my mind.

Cecily glanced up at the lights of Piccadilly. That dark time had gone. It was over. The only thing that mattered now was the man waiting for her in the bar of the Café Royal. And their future together.

'Anywhere here is fine,' she said to the cab driver, pulling her wallet from her bag.

CHAPTER 24

The letter lay unopened on the shelf of the mantelpiece. Sylvia sat with Cecily's manuscript scattered about her.

She had looked through it, read a number of chapters. But it was appalling – and quite insensitive – she thought, for Cecily to have brought it to her. Then again, the girl had always been presumptuous. Had overstepped the mark years ago. And Cora was naive and silly to have trusted her so. As for the manuscript, it was, as far as Sylvia could make out, simply the work of a rather vivid imagination, and not an accurate account of Cora's life at all. *Loosely based*, Cecily had said. Well, it was certainly founded on delusions, presumably Cora's. What on earth had she told Cecily? And what could she, Sylvia, say to Cecily about it?

It was curious to Sylvia that Cecily had been unable to remember the people at the farm. When Sylvia said, 'And what about that nice young family at Meadow Farm?' Cecily had stared back at her blankly. 'The Abels, I think they were called,' Sylvia had added. No, Cecily shook her head.

'They can't have been there for very long,' she said. 'It's been with the Stephenson family since before the war.'

Of course Sylvia was testing Cecily to see what she knew. When Cecily went on to talk of Cora's confused ramblings, and the mention of 'someone called Uncle John', it was obvious to Sylvia that she had never been told the name, the full name. Thus, she had never made any connection with the people at the farm. Uncle John was simply Uncle John: a monster, deprived of identity, and now confined to fiction. Sylvia had made sure of that. And she had done so out of loyalty and love, nothing more.

In truth, Cora had never *consciously* told Sylvia the full name either; certainly not then, not that summer. But Sylvia had a long memory, there had been little to cloud it. And even during Cora's fever, at the height of her delirium, when she repeated the name out loud, Sylvia already knew it. She knew John Abel and the Uncle John mentioned in Rome all those years ago to be one and the same.

When Sylvia visited the farm, she had done so in order to establish whether one John Abel was related to the other John Abel. It seemed almost too much to hope that this would be the case, that a young farmer would be able to furnish her with those missing pieces of a story which had fascinated her for the best part of fifty years. And yet, there were too many coincidences for there not be a link, for she had heard the rector inform Cora that the family came from Suffolk.

Sylvia had duly told the young man that she heard he hailed from Suffolk, and then lied, telling him that her parents, too, came from that county, the Woodbridge area, and that they had spoken of a John Abel, one who had married a woman by the name of Frances . . . a Frances who had gone to live overseas? The young farmer clearly knew something of the story, for he had nodded and, glancing at his wife – smiling knowingly, Sylvia thought – he said yes, that would be his Great-Uncle John. Then he turned to Sylvia. 'You're not from the Mother's Union, are you?'

Sylvia shook her head.

'Parish council?'

'No. I'm simply staying in the village for a while and I . . . I heard the rector mention—'

'Ah! That old busybody, I might have known.'

'John!'

'We came here to get away from nosy parkers,' he said, staring at Sylvia.

'John!' his wife said again.

'I do beg your pardon,' said Sylvia, turning away, about to head back to the village.

Then he began, 'I never knew him, but I know enough about him . . .'

He had been a shoemaker, he said, like his father before him. 'It was the family trade, see, then.' And yes, she was correct, his namesake had married a woman named Frances, or Fanny, as she was known, the daughter of a local tin man. They had moved away from Woodbridge to the East End of London. But things had gone wrong there, for his great-uncle's wife had 'up-ed and off-ed', left her husband and disappeared without trace. 'It were the great mystery in the family, that.'

'And your uncle – great-uncle – whatever happened to him?'

The young farmer looked at his wife and then back at Sylvia. 'He's long since been gone.'

Sylvia smiled, nodded. 'Of course, I realise he must have passed away by now but do you know *where* he passed away? Did he . . . live for long after his wife departed?'

'Lived till he were nearly ninety. Never married again, couldn't, you see.'

'Yes, I see,' Sylvia said, thinking aloud. 'But something must have made her – your great-uncle's wife – flee like that, in the depths of the night, and taking the poor child with her?'

'Who said anything about night? Or any *poor child*?' he asked, narrowing his gaze.

'Oh, forgive me. I'm a writer. I somehow imagined that it was at night . . . and I thought I heard tell that there was a child involved.'

The three of them – Sylvia, the young John Abel and his wife – stood under the shade of a stone archway leading to the farmyard, where a pile of manure lay steaming in the sunshine. John Abel leaned on his rake as he explained to Sylvia that it was his grandmother who had first told him the story of how her brother's wife had vanished.

'She knew her, of course, knew Fanny Abel. Didn't like her.' He shook his head. 'Said she had had highfalutin' ideas. Woodbridge not good enough for her . . . London not good enough for her! No pleasing some folk, eh?'

'No, indeed.'

'And you're right, as it happens, there were a child, a girl, but not theirs, some relation of hers, of Fanny Abel's. My grandmother reckoned she and the girl must have went overseas, changed their names, because he looked for them for years, did Uncle John, placed advertisements in the newspapers, done all of that.'

'And he never discovered what became of them?' Sylvia asked.

'Didn't your mother say she ended up a duchess or something?' the woman broke in, addressing her husband.

'That's right!' He laughed; then, scratching his head, he said, 'No, no, it weren't Fanny Abel, 'twas the girl, the girl what ended up a duchess.'

Now Sylvia laughed too. 'A duchess! Gracious me. But however did your mother hear that?'

'Woodbridge is a small place, missus . . .'

'Miss.'

'Aye, Woodbridge is a small place, and she knew the family, see, some of the family at any rate. One of them had went off to work at . . .' he looked towards his wife.

His wife stared back at him blankly for a moment, then she said, 'Wasn't it Jersey?'

'Jersey, that's it. He went off to be gardener to some folk at Jersey, but they must've had connections in Woodbridge, I reckon – imagine it's how he got the job. Anyhow, they knew, must've known, because they were the ones it came from, the ones what told him. Imagine, eh? Imagine finding out that your own sister was aristocracy!'

'Ah, so he was the girl's brother, this gardener in Jersey?'

He scratched his head again, looked back at his wife. 'I think that were it, weren't it? You remember better than me.'

'Yes, that's it,' his wife replied.

'Aye, well, they'll all long since be dead so we'll never know now, but I fancy the notion that I'm related to the nobility,' he said, smiling and winking at Sylvia.

'Fascinating. And your great-uncle, he died eventually at . . . at Woodbridge?'

'He was locked up,' the woman replied quickly.

'Locked up?'

'Mm. Put away. Best thing for him,' she said, glancing from her husband to Sylvia. 'He was a . . . a—'

'Nothing were proven,' the farmer interrupted, suddenly raising his voice. 'It weren't proven and shouldn't be repeated. Some silly young girl's word against his.' He turned to Sylvia. 'Best let sleeping dogs lie, eh?' he said. Then he raised his cap to Sylvia, 'Good day to you, missus.'

Walking back from the farm that day, Sylvia knew what she had to do. But, trying to look forward and not back, she struggled to contain her emotions, struggled with the knowledge that she had been the one to lie. The confirmation that Uncle John had not only existed but that he had lived to the age of ninety meant she owed Cora an entirely different story, one that absolved her and gave her back the life she could and should have had.

But could she? Sylvia thought now; could Cora ever have had that life, the life she so wanted – with him, George? Sylvia reordered her thoughts. She did not want to think of her own intervention. She *had* made amends. She had given Cora that life, given it to her in a book begun as a memoir now rewritten as a work of fiction. Yes, she had given her back her life, something Cecily could never do. That was why she came to me, Sylvia thought, to sanction Cora's memories, to fill in the gaps. *You were there*, Cecily had said. Yes, she had been there.

When Cora married Edward Lawson at the town hall of the eighth arrondissement in Paris, three days after her fortieth birthday, she became step-mother to her son's father, wife to his grandfather. But only Sylvia and Cora's aunt knew this. Edward remained almost as oblivious as his son. And he, like others, was intoxicated by her – that aura of experience, that enigmatic smile. For Cora had lived, she had seen life, and felt it, too. And now she seemed to guard its secret. If one could only keep hold of her, pin her down. In the meantime, one could watch. Watch *her*. The way she spoke – to a waiter, a dignitary or a dear old friend – was something to behold. The way she tilted her head and blinked as she listened to those same people as they spoke to her; the way she drifted effortlessly from one language to another. And the places she knew and the people she quoted, and her knowledge, and empathy, that ability to relate to each and every person, no matter how extra-ordinary, no matter how mundane, as though she was completely captivated, immersed in their experience.

And all the while George saw this. She belonged to him, and yet he had never owned her. He loved her, but he had thought he needed something more. Something he would see and know, something he would recognise when it presented itself to him. It had been her; it had been her but not her. How could it be her? He had walked away. How could it be her if he had walked away? And his father, pandering and fawning like a lovestruck adolescent – it was despicable, sickening. It had made him feel physically sick. Cora was almost young enough to be his granddaughter!

And that day, that fateful day in Paris, when Cora married Edward, how bittersweet it had been. Even at the time, the marriage had had the scent of scandal about it. In ignorance, people's main concern had been the fact that Edward, a long-time widower, respected member of the English establishment and father of England's greatest painter, had elected to wed a woman almost three decades his junior, *and* one residing on the continent, *and* one with a dubious past. For no one was quite sure of her credentials or where she hailed from. But it mattered not to Edward. He was in love, bewitched, mesmerised. No one in attendance at the nuptials could have been in any doubt about that.

Cora's son and her aunt were both present at her marriage, and a notable mix of artists, architects, English, French and Italian friends – including the Hilliers and George – attended a second ceremony at the British Embassy and a reception there afterwards. It was unbearably hot: the temperature in Paris that summer's day hit one hundred degrees Fahrenheit. And though each of the long windows of the embassy rooms remained wide open, the air was stifling, oppressive.

Circumnavigating the room, holding on to the arm of her new husband, Cora looked radiant and much too youthful, people commented, to be the mother of a young man. Edward smiled broadly, barely lifting his eyes from his new bride. And in his speech he thanked his son, George, for bringing himself and Cora together.

That was when Sylvia noticed George's expression, one she would later describe as 'bewildered detachment'. He shuffled, looked down at the floor and kept pulling out his pocket watch, as though he needed to check the time of his next appointment. Oh, how Sylvia had felt for him! Whatever he had done to Cora it seemed cruel beyond words that she was standing there in front of him as his father's bride – his stepmother.

Was Edward Lawson aware? Sylvia had wondered. Did he know what had taken place – what was, perhaps, still taking place – between his son and his new wife? But surely it was obvious. It was to Sylvia. For she had studied them for years, followed the strange and fragile dynamic of this denied, ongoing and furtive love affair.

When George shook his father's hand, he simply said, 'Congratulations, sir,' and then added, 'I wish you both a long and happy life together.'

'I only hope that one day, and in the not too distant future, you can find yourself a Cora,' Edward replied, red-faced, delirious with the occasion. 'But I don't suppose there is another Cora in the universe,' he added, gazing at his wife.

No, there was not another Cora in the universe. How could there be? Who, other than Cora, would have had the vision, imagination and skill to invent such a character? For Cora *had* invented herself, and then reinvented herself again and again, honing and perfecting her creation, each one of her selves better than the one before. But she had had no choice. Robbed of identity early on in life, she had had to become someone else.

And that day, all George could do was stand back and watch, like everyone else. Watch a woman who seemed only to improve with age.

Sylvia was not sure if she was the only one to notice the one person Cora did *not* kiss on that her wedding day. They came face to face, stood and smiled at each other, but nothing more. And later, as everyone was leaving, bidding each other a weary adieu, and kissing once again, Sylvia saw them standing together in a corner. Cora had her hand upon George's arm, and it seemed to Sylvia as though George was refusing to look at her. Then, at last, he raised his eyes to her and smiled: a sad, affected smile. As Cora turned and walked away, towards Edward, George watched her intently, but she never looked back at him. Not once. Though Sylvia had willed her to.

Later, Sylvia travelled back to the hotel with George, who seemed exhausted, monosyllabic. The hotel lobby had been busy and – 'Much too hot to retire' – George suggested they take a nightcab together in the lounge. He ordered iced tea for them both and they sat in silence for some time, watching others come and go: the rigmaroles of travellers.

'It was an elegant reception,' Sylvia said at last.

'Mm, yes,' he replied, absently, gazing across the room.

'I'm sure she'll be happy . . . sure they'll both be very happy.'

He said nothing.

'She looked very fine,' Sylvia persevered. 'Everyone looked very fine.'

He moved forward in his chair, placed his glass down upon the table in front of him, and with his eyes fixed on it, he said, 'Why did you tell me those things, Sylvia? Why did you make up that story about Cora, all those years ago, and then tell me?'

'I'm not sure what you mean. Which particular story are you referring to?' she asked. 'There have been quite a few, you know.'

He lifted his head to look at her. 'The one where Cora was wanted for murder. The one you told me in such extraordinary detail in the Piazza del Popolo that day. *That* story.'

Sylvia glanced at the letter. She was unsure about opening it, reading it. Unsure what it would say. It could say so much, she thought. Until opened, it could say so much . . .

And it was typical of Cora to have the final word. Even from beyond the grave she *would* have the final word. But there was a sense of unspent luxury to be derived from looking at the envelope, anticipating its contents, her words. It was bulky, clearly contained more than one sheet of paper, and the knowledge that it had been written some years ago was intriguing. It came from one who had not only gone, departed this life, but from another time also. It had been sealed by Cora, passed on to Cecily and then kept, stored in an unknown place through seasons and years, until now, when it had finally arrived at its destination, its intended recipient. There was something impossibly romantic about all of this to Sylvia. And, in a peculiar way, it seemed a shame to break the seal, open up the pages, read the words.

Sylvia would wait; find the right moment. It deserved that. *She* deserved that.

CHAPTER 25

The plane came down near Bixschoote, in Flanders. Others had seen him fall. That he had survived the crash was almost unimaginable, but not impossible. He was an accomplished pilot, without doubt one of the best. And he had already had a few 'star turns', earned his badge as a flying ace, shooting down more than a dozen enemy aeroplanes.

Those working in the fields stopped. They raised their heads to the blood-orange sky, to that halting, whirring sound. And as they watched its steady, smoking descent, they began to walk and then run across the flat earth. They saw it bounce and burst into flames, saw a figure emerge from the burning wreckage, stagger, and then fall. They took off tunics and shirts and jackets and smothered the flames. And then they carried the burned body back to the farmhouse of Monsieur and Madame Ricard.

For a number of weeks – no one would ever know how many – the rescued pilot lay unconscious in a cellar in Flanders. When he finally opened his melted eyelids, he was unable to see, unable to hear, unable to speak. Badly burned, with broken legs, broken ribs, a broken shoulder and fractured wrists, he drifted in and out of consciousness for more weeks, oblivious to his surroundings, unaware of what had happened. When he did, eventually, gain consciousness, complete consciousness, he was unable to tell anyone his name, unable to remember. His memory had gone. But he had spoken, had uttered a few words the evening he was rescued, before he passed out.

Monsieur and Madame Ricard's daughter, Susanne, told him that when he was rescued, as the plane burned, he had told her that his name was Jacques, and later, in his delirium, he had spoken of a Cee-cee, or something sounding like that. But all clues to his identity – his uniform, any papers or documents he had had on him – had perished.

Jacques' recovery was slow. It was months before he was able to climb from his bed and stand on his feet, months before he was strong enough to learn to walk again. But as his physical wounds slowly healed, his mind began to throw things back to him, offering him snatches of nameless people and places, glimpses of moments: a church steeple, a village green; an elderly woman with a shock of white hair and piercingly brilliant blue eyes; and a girl, a young woman, whose lips he so wants to kiss.

As time went on these things came back to him

more, in dreams and, encouraged by him, in conscious moments, too. The elderly woman, the one with the white hair, speaks to him in French, and another woman – one he suspects is his mother, suspects has gone, died – sometimes appears at the foot of his bed. But the girl, the girl with the lips he longs to kiss, comes back to him more than anyone else. She smiles at him from shadows, in sunlight and moonlight, next to painted gates and sun-bleached canvas, sitting on a garden bench and lying back upon a bed. And she says his name: she says *Jacques*. He knows that this is the Cee, the Cee-cee. And in his dreams she stands very close to him, staring at him, smiling. She says, 'Promise me . . . promise me.' She says, 'Never ever forget.'

But how many months have passed? He has no idea. No idea. He belongs nowhere, has nowhere to go. And though they continue to hide him, he catches time: colours changing, fallen leaves, snow, and then the thawing, a gradual warmth. He hears them speak of ploughing, planting, and then harvesting. When Susanne returns from one of her meetings, she talks of a final push, and tells him, 'It will be over soon, the war.' A final push, he thinks. But he can't remember any war. Can't remember where he came from, or who he is. And he sees only the scarred face of a stranger looking back at him from the glass.

Susanne has nursed him, bathed his wounds and changed his dressings. She is the one who has fed him, brought him up from the cellar to look at the sky, the sunset. She is the one who helped him take those first steps through the pain. And she speaks to him in English. She says, 'The body chooses how and when it heals itself. It chooses its time, like the mind. When the time is right, your memories will return.'

But as summer slips to autumn, nothing comes: no parents, no siblings, no family. And Cee-cee continues to stare back at him, elusive, impossible for him to take hold of: 'Never ever forget.'

Lying in his bed, staring up at the cobwebbed beam, he hears the tail end of a conversation, one he has heard before, one that makes no sense. A woman says, 'She is afraid of being discovered, being found.' Another asks, 'Why?' The woman says something he can't quite hear, and then, 'My husband adored her.' But who are these people? And whom do they speak of? Later, when Susanne finds him sitting on the floor, weeping and surrounded by broken glass, she wraps her arms about his neck and holds him to her. She strokes his head, whispers in his ear, and she says his name: Jacques.

She has a familiar softness, a scent similar to something before. And there's a craving in him, a longing to languish in that softness, to taste and know that scent. But something stops him and he pulls away.

'I'll be dead to them all by now,' he says. 'Forgotten . . . mourned and forgotten.'

She shakes her head. 'I think not, Jacques. I think there's someone waiting. Don't you?'

He wanted to say yes, because he hoped that there was, and part of him – that irrational, instinctive, illogical part of him – knew that there was. Yes, Cee-cee was waiting. Somewhere. She was waiting. And in his dreams he wanted to take hold of her, tell her that he was alive and coming back to her, if only he could remember. He wanted to reach out and touch her and know that she was real, and maybe then he would remember who he was, had been.

He was sitting on the bench outside the farmhouse when he heard the noise. He could see Monsieur Ricard nearing, coming up the cypress-lined lane on his bicycle, ringing his bell and calling out, 'Vive la France! Vive la France!'

Unsteadily, he rose to his feet.

'The war is over. *Finis!*' Monsieur Ricard shouted, dropping his bicycle to the ground. '*Finis!*' he said again, crossing his hands in front of himself. Then he grabbed Jacques by the shoulders, kissed him on both cheeks and rushed in to the house. '*C'est finis! C'est finis!*'

At the celebrations in the local village square, Jacques joined in with the others, drinking and singing and cheering 'Vive la France!' and falling into the fountain wrapped in a flag not his own. And later, as dawn broke, standing by the gate to the farmyard, Susanne wrapped her arms around his neck again and said, 'So, Jacques, do you want to kiss me?'

It was a clumsy, drunken kiss, and only made his head spin more. But the sensation of another's lips upon his own, of arms wrapped around him and a world spinning was too familiar. And as he pulled away, trying to steady himself, his mind, he saw two figures standing at the top of a purple-coloured hill under a vast blue sky, kissing.

'Cee-cee,' he murmured, 'Cee-cee . . .'

Susanne stepped back, listening, watching.

'Cee-cee-ly . . . Cee-cee-ly,' he said, and he fell against the gate and dropped down to his knees. His head bent, he stared at the ground and didn't speak. Then he raised his face, closed his eyes to the light and exhaled one word: 'Cecily.'

'Cecily? And who is Cecily?' Susanne asked, crouching down next to him.

'She's my girl,' he said, opening his eyes, looking into hers. 'She's my girl,' he repeated, shrugging his shoulders and trying to smile. He glanced away, tilting his head to one side, frowning, searching. 'No . . . no, she's my wife, I think.' He straightened himself, nodded his head. 'Yes . . . she is, she's my wife. I'm married. I'm married to Cecily . . . my Cecily.'

And he placed his head in his hands and began to weep.

CHAPTER 26

He was there, sitting up at the bar reading a newspaper, and she smiled as she moved towards him. Even now, four years after his return, four years after he had returned from the dead, Cecily's heart leapt at the sight of him, his presence made all the more precious by his long absence.

But he had kept his promise, as she knew he would: he had come back to her.

Cecily had refused to relinquish hope. Inspired and reassured by stories in the newspapers, tales of missing soldiers and prisoners of war returning home months after the cessation of fighting, she had clung on, waiting, expectant. And though she had never quite been able to envision how he would return, when he would return, or how she would react or how he would be, she knew in her heart that he was not dead. And if he were not dead, he would, eventually, find his way back to her.

When it happened, there was no forewarning, no trumpet call, nothing to herald his arrival.

It was early evening, a weekday – perhaps a

Tuesday or Wednesday, she could never quite remember. The sky was overcast, the air damp and threatening rain. She had gone out to the garden to take in the washing hanging from the line he had put up for her, years before. She was already late to collect her son, had spent the previous hour reading and marking Class Three's homework. As she gathered up sheets that had hung out since dawn, a figure appeared on the periphery of her vision. She did not turn, not immediately. She heard her name, a familiar male voice. But it had happened before, and would happen again. The sound of Jack's voice, her name, carried in the wind, echoing back to her, inflected in sighs and sounds. But the blur at the edge of her vision did not move and began to take on a shape. And as she turned her head, turned to face him, she saw at first only a bearded stranger, a black eyepatch and a stick; a dishevelled man in shabby clothes. And when he stepped forward and began to move towards her, she stepped back, pulling the collected bedlinen in front of her as though it were a shield.

Later, she would replay this scene over and over, see it in slow motion: see herself, arms filled with linen, turn slowly, so slowly, and him, at the end of the pathway, standing watching her, perfectly still; see herself step back as he begins to move towards her, see her arms fall, white linen float down to the grass; and as the landscape moves, the sky comes down and the earth rolls out like an unfurling carpet, bringing him back to her.

'I was beginning to think you were taking your revenge,' he said, easing himself up on to his feet.

'Revenge?' she repeated, wrapping her arms round his waist.

'Keeping me waiting so long,' he whispered. 'I missed you.'

'And I missed you. But thirty minutes is *not* two years, Jack Staunton.'

He smiled, shook his head. 'It wasn't two years . . . was it?'

'Almost.'

She placed her bag on the marble counter, watched him as he turned to the barman to order her a drink. Even now, she found it difficult not to stare. Older, injured, war damaged, he was perfect to her. The burns, flesh still charred when he had appeared to her that day, had healed as best they ever would. There were scars: scars from new skin and scars on old skin. The skin grafted to his face, his eyelids, cheeks and nose, as well as to his neck and hands, masked some of the damage to his young, once fit and able body. And the somewhat patchy beard he would not part with.

But the lack of early, proper medical attention to Jack's injuries, including his two shattered legs, meant they had not healed the way they should have, could have. One leg remained badly twisted, at the knee and at the ankle, and made walking difficult without the aid of a stick.

Watching him, she said his name, and he turned to her. 'What's that?'

'Oh nothing. Nothing at all.'

'So, tell me,' he began, sitting down and swivelling his chair round to face her. 'How was Cynthia? Did she like it, your story?'

'Her name is Sylvia, Jack, not Cynthia.'

'Of course, Syl-via.'

'Think . . . saliva?' she suggested. 'Though it's not her name.'

He smiled. 'How was dear Saliva?'

She shook her head: 'You really have no recollection of her at all, do you?'

'No, should I?'

'Perhaps. She was, I think, your grandmother's oldest friend. And that summer – the one when we first met, before the war – she was there, quiet, unmarried, rather touchy, slightly troublesome, and quite obsessed with Cora.'

'I'm sorry,' he said, 'but you are painting a pretty dismal image. Do I really need to remember Sylvia?'

She lifted her hand to his face. 'No, my dear, you don't. The only person you need to remember is right here. Anyway,' she went on, 'in answer to your question, I've left it with her, which was the plan.'

Sylvia had read some of her manuscript there and then: some of the first chapter. As Cecily sat drinking the tea a woman called Wendy had brought in to them, she had watched Sylvia's mouth twitch, watched her raise a hand to her spectacles, pushing them back up her nose, watched her turning pages. She had listened to her breathing, the occasional sigh. Eventually, Sylvia had looked up at her, smiled and said, 'hmm, yes . . . interesting.' And that was all.

Cecily had wanted more, had said again, 'I'd value your opinion . . . I'll leave it with you if I may.'

'How was she with you?' Jack asked.

Cecily shook her head. 'She's no different. No different at all to how I remember her,' she said, lighting a cigarette. And as her husband took a glass from the barman and placed it on the polished marble in front of her, she smiled at him.

'What is it?' he asked, taking hold of her hand. 'Tell me.'

'Oh, I was just thinking about everything, on the way here in the taxicab. I was remembering all those days and nights . . . all those days without you . . . and thinking about Cora, remembering all of it.'

He nodded. 'I knew it would be tough. But I did offer to come with you . . .'

She shook her head. 'No, it was best, I think, that I went on my own. Anyhow, you don't remember her.'

'And perhaps with good reason.' He pushed his folded newspaper across the marble. 'Take a look,' he said.

A headline read, 'Lawson's Lost "Aphrodite" Found.' Beneath it, a small back and white image of the painting, and Cora's young face staring out at her.

She said, 'You did the right thing.'

'You mean *you* did the right thing. She left it to you. Left everything to you.'

'She thought you were dead. We have done the right thing,' she added, placing her hand over his.

'It always strikes me, the irony – me having lost my memory, coming back to my only blood relation, who had no memory of me, could not remember me.'

'But she did! She did remember you. She spoke about you all the time, it's just that she didn't recognise you, didn't recognise the *you* that returned, and she had gone anyway, left us by then . . .'

He glanced down at her hand over his. 'It makes me sad to think she never knew, never realised that I'd survived and come back.'

'I've told you before, you need to try and take comfort from the fact that in her mind you were there, with her. Everyone she ever loved was with her.'

Cora had failed to recognise the battered, bearded man with eyepatch and stick as any relation. And certainly not as her grandson, not as the unblemished, handsome young man who had gone off to fight, to fly aeroplanes. He had been killed and, in an attempt to accept that, or perhaps in order to protect herself from that, she had simply slid further into a world inhabited by ghosts. She did not hear the war veteran in front of her claiming

431

to be Jack or, if she did, chose not to. Too much time had elapsed, and those in front of her were not those she remembered.

On one occasion she had even spoken to Jack about Jack, telling him he must meet her grandson. 'He likes cricket,' she said, vaguely. 'He's a leg-spin bowler, you know.'

Cecily and Jack gave up trying to explain. They visited her, sat with her, listened to her nonsensical conversation and jumbled words and names. Sometimes she recognised Cecily, and once she asked her, 'Who is he, that man? Is he *your* husband?' As though he might perhaps be *hers*. 'Yes, he's mine,' Cecily replied, smiling at Jack, winking. 'He's mine and I love him.' Cora's face had erupted into a smile, a wonderful breathtaking smile Cecily would always remember. 'And does he love you?' she asked.

Cecily turned to Jack. 'Well?'

'With all my heart,' he said, looking from Cecily to his grandmother.

And for a moment, just a moment, Cecily thought she saw something in Cora's eyes, a fleeting recognition, as she stared back at him and said, 'Yes, of course you do.'

'What time do we need to be there?' Jack asked.

'Seven, I think. Mr Davidson, the curator, wants to meet us, meet you. He wants to introduce you to the biographer.'

'Whose biographer?'

'Lawson's, of course. Don't tell me you've

forgotten, I told you this morning, remember? The retrospective is to coincide with the publication of the book, *The Life, Letters and Work of George Lawson.*'

'But why do they want to meet us? If it's to talk about the painting, I know nothing about it. Do you?'

Cecily shook her head. 'No, nothing really, other than it's by him, and of her.'

'Oh God, they're probably going to ask all sorts of questions, like when and where it was executed and so on and so forth.' He shook his head. 'You know I can't handle too many questions.'

She tightened her grip on his hand. 'Don't worry. I'll answer any questions they might have as best I can.'

He glanced to his watch. 'I suppose we should get a move on.'

She didn't reply. And when he turned to her, he asked, 'What are you smiling at now?'

She shook her head. 'Oh, nothing really,' she said. 'I was just thinking about how Sylvia will react to my novel. I just hope she's not shocked.'

'Why on earth would she be shocked?'

'Because . . . because it bears little comparison, I think, to the true story.'

'She's a novelist, it's fiction. And you said you gave them all a happy ending. Can't do better than that.'

Yes, she had given her heroine a happy ending, an ending no biography or memoirs could ever do. Whether it was the right ending, the one Cora would have wished for, she would never know but she suspected that perhaps it was. Because though Cora had never confessed to any great love affair with the painter, George Lawson, she had spoken of him in such a way that it had been plain to see she had once loved him. When she told Cecily of her marriage to his father, Edward, she had simply said that he was a good man, a good husband, but that it had been a mistake for her to marry again. And by the time she told Cecily about that marriage, Jack had gone, and Cora was already muddled about who was who and where she was. Quite often it had been difficult for Cecily to know whom she was speaking about, and she continually made mistakes with names and places and dates. But there had been clues: in the painting, and in the names themselves. She had, after all, named her son after George, and mentioned that he was godfather. Could he, Cecily wondered, have been the father of her son?

It had been a thrilling thought for a while, that Jack could be Lord Lawson's grandson, that her own son could be his great-grandson. But as Cora sank further into her dementia it became impossible to ascertain the truth, and impossible to pose those questions. Cecily had waited, hoped that Cora might say more, say something, and though she had, none of it made any sense.

Now, it no longer mattered whose son Jack's father had been. Jack had no memory of him, none at all, and very few of his mother. 'But do I need to remember?' he had asked her, whenever she tried to coax memories. 'Can't we just live for now, look forward?' The only thing that mattered to Jack was here and now and the future. And so that's what mattered to Cecily now, too.

'When are you going back,' Jack was asking, 'to pick it up?'

'I said I'd call in on Friday before we go down to collect the children.'

'It'll be interesting,' he said, smiling, lifting his glass, 'for you to hear what she makes of it all.'

'She won't like it,' Cecily said. 'I know that. But I'm going to ask her again about George Lawson and Cora.'

'You really want your story to be true, don't you?'

'No, not necessarily, but I would like to know the truth.'

'Did you tell her about the Uncle John character, the blackmail?'

She sighed. 'Yes, and she said the same as you. Said it was all nonsense.'

'I never said it was nonsense,' he replied, tenderness in his voice. 'I simply said that it didn't seem feasible. She may well have received some unpleasant letters, though you never found any, did you?'

'No. No, there were very few letters at all.'

They sat in silence for a moment, then she said, 'You know, you once told me – years ago, I think it was on your last leave – that you'd found out something about Cora.'

He laughed. 'You're not expecting me to remember what it was now, are you?'

'No, I suppose not,' she said, sighing. 'You said you couldn't tell me until you had spoken to her about it . . . whatever it was.'

'Well, whatever it was, we'll never know.'

CHAPTER 27

Sylvia had already moved the envelope about the room: from the mantelshelf to the window sill and back again. Now it lay on the table in front of her. She enjoyed looking at it. It made her happy to see it sitting there, waiting to be opened. She would find the right time. Until then, she could wallow in its potential, imagine its contents . . .

My own dearest Sylvia, Forgive me, forgive me, forgive me . . .

My dear Sylvia, Can you find it in your heart to forgive me?

Dearest Sylvia, Soon, I shall be gone, and I cannot bear that thought without first making amends with you . . . my only true friend . . .

Dear Sylvia, Mr Cordery is planting out the herbaceous border and I was wondering if there are any violet plants to be had in London at this time of year . . .

Sylvia, I am at a loss to know WHAT to say to you, even now. The fact that you took it upon yourself to speak to X and visit Y is beyond me, but . . .

Sylvia placed the envelope on the table in front

of her. She poured herself a sherry. Then she sat down. She tried to ignore the cream paper in front of her. She looked about the room, sipping the warm liquid in her glass. It was at moments like these she often wished that she had taken up smoking, or another hobby: something one could pick up and put down, something to distract oneself with. But now the envelope was shouting out at her, begging to be read. And that was what she had been waiting for: beseechment.

She picked it up, read her name out loud. Then, slowly, running her index finger under the flap, she severed the seal and lifted the paper to her face. It smelled of violets, the scent of Cora. And she sat with it, unsealed, in her hands for some time. It was the first step. She glanced at the clock: five to seven. She would wait five more minutes.

It was a difficult five minutes. Time seemed to slow down, minutes stretched out, self-consciously, as though knowing they were being watched. Finally, the clock chimed the hour and she pulled out the sheets. One, two, three, four, five, six, seven, eight: eight pages from Cora! Her heart soared.

The letter was dated 15 September 1917. Sylvia lingered for a while on that date, making calculations: seven years after they had last seen each other . . . six years ago . . . and wasn't that the time when Jack went missing? She read the first three words a few times over, out loud and slowly, knowing she could loiter there in safety: 'My dear

Sylvia . . . my *dear* Sylvia . . . *my dear* Sylvia . . .'
It was a good start, a nice opening. She cast her
eyes down over the page. Certain words sprang
out: Cecily's name, Jack's name, the word blackmail and a few capitalised words, which appeared
to her rather angry. She took a deep breath and
began.

My dear Sylvia,
How very queer it feels to be penning a
letter to you once more, and in the knowledge
that by the time you read these words I shall
be no more . . . for I am to ask Cecily to pass
this on to you in the event of my death, which
I fear cannot be too far away.
Much has happened since we last saw each
other & none of us I am certain could ever
have imagined or begun to comprehend the
obscene horror upon us now. I am unable to
make any sense of the carnage & see only the
<u>WASTE</u>. Like everyone else, I have prayed
& pleaded with God, I begged him to keep
Jack safe, to end this fighting, but my darling
boy is 'missing', & though I try to keep Hope
and Faith, to live within that state, God's
voracious appetite for young souls offers me
no hope at all. I do not see my grandson
returning & experience tells me I will not be
spared.
It is this sense of waste that has caused me
to reflect upon my own life, & I see now

only the brevity of our time here, that it lasts but a moment, & I begin to understand that the most important thing of all is to be <u>TRUE</u> to oneself . . . something I have struggled with, due perhaps to the absence of anyone to remind me & other things which I shall come on to. I realise also that before I am able to forgive myself I must forgive others . . . and so, dear Sylvia, I want you to know that <u>I forgive you</u>. Though I cannot condone your underhand tactics, & consider blackmail wholly immoral & beneath you or any decent human being, I am quite sure by now you bitterly regret such an undertaking. However, I know you were desperate, & I see also that I was much to blame. Furthermore, I know that you were not alone, & that the coincidence of another at the same time as yourself was unforeseen & not in your plan.

The withholding of information can be peculiarly frustrating, not least for the withholder . . . What you failed to grasp was that I had to protect dear Jack. He had a future ahead of him. Indeed, he WAS the future, the very best of me, and all I had left of George. It was this, & this alone, which caused me to question the merit & potential ramifications of allowing the truth to be told. No one else mattered a jot. They have all gone, and though George & Edward's reputations would be held up to scrutiny, their judgements perhaps questioned, I think the truth would only add to intrigue & the myth of George in particular.

I am including some pages from your notebook, the ones I tore out – confiscated, though I rather think they read like a novel &, if you were to do anything with them, I would prefer that you took out the extraneous detail & imagined dialogue . . .

As regards 'The Beginning', that part of my story you were so very desperate to hear about & for so long, and which I rather think you know a little about by now, I leave it for you to decide whether or not to include it in any book. Is it relevant? Of any interest? I am still unsure. Also, I must admit that my memory is not what it was, & thus some things continue to elude me. However, & most peculiarly, certain details of my early life, which have remained something of a blur for so long, have recently come back to me, & I am able to confirm a few Facts. So, to the beginning . . .

Heart pounding, Sylvia turned the page.

I was born & baptised Coral Lillian Stopher in the year eighteen thirty-three. My parents' names were <u>Coral & Samuel</u>. Both originated from Woodbridge in Suffolk, which is where

I was born & where my father was employed as an under-gardener & outdoor servant at a place called <u>Standen Hall</u>. I lived at this place – with my parents, sister & two brothers – in rooms above the stables. The Lillian in my name came from my maternal grandmother, a woman I cannot recall and possibly never knew, and my parents used this name for me, its abbreviated version – Lily. Thus, I was once Lily Stopher.

When I was perhaps six or seven years of age we left Standen Hall, for reasons I know not, but I suspect that my father lost his job there for he had nothing to go to and we nowhere to live. It is my belief now that we were homeless for some time, for I have memories of walking many miles & of sleeping out in fields, under stars.

It was around this time that my mother disappeared, though I do not recall her actual departure or any 'Goodbye', she was simply there and then not there, & I always assumed she would be coming back, that she had not abandoned us, perhaps because I had been told by someone at some stage that she had simply 'gone for a while'. Not long after this my father too must have 'gone', for I have very few memories of him without her, my mother. As I say, my memory is not what it was & there are gaps and this time is one of them.

My siblings were eventually placed into the care of various scattered family members, & I into the care of my maternal aunt, who had married a shoemaker, a man by the name of john abel. Aunt Fanny and Uncle John at that time resided somewhere in the vicinity of Bethnal Green the Whitechapel area, in East London, and I recall little of it apart from the brutality of the man, my uncle. He fitted into that world & my aunt did not. But I do remember our rooms, how cramped and gloomy and very small they were, & how vast and sinister-looking the lunatic asylum on the old Roman road. That building haunted me before I understood why. I had no idea then that it was in fact the very place my mother had 'gone for a while'.

My memory of our departure – the night we fled, & the events preceding it – is now muddled & vague . . . due perhaps to the fact that it is a memory for so many years unpractised, not exercised, but instead <u>exorcised</u>. I can have been no more than twelve years of age, certainly of an age when I should be able to recall more, but though I have tried I am unable to summon detail, or perhaps I have no wish to.

Here, there was a line crossed through, and crossed through so many times it was impossible to make out the words.

What I do know is that my aunt and I took off into the night knowing we had committed a crime, knowing the law would not protect us, knowing people were hanged for murder and tried for desertion, knowing my aunt could not afford to go through Parliament and obtain a divorce. We travelled first to Jersey, later to Paris, & thence onwards to Rome, where my aunt had secured a position as housekeeper for a Mr Staunton. It was the start of a new life, she told me, and a place where no one would ever find us. She was true in this, for in the doing I never again saw any member of my family.

It was many years later that I learned the truth of what happened to my mother, that when she left us she had in fact walked to London, whereupon she was found in a desperate & hysterical state on the streets, and later committed to the Bethnal Green Lunatic Asylum. She had been incarcerated there for over twelve years by the time the cholera epidemic swept through its doors and rescued her. As to my father, he passed away the year I was twenty-one, at the workhouse at Colchester, the very same place he had been headed when he left my siblings & myself in a derelict barn by a roadside. One imagines he had gone there looking for work and, unable to secure any employment, could not face returning to four hungry, motherless children.

My mother's fate has been an immovable stain on my mind, for I long ago realised poverty & insanity to be irrevocably linked – that one simply preceded the other, and my mother's madness to be the direct result of a bleak existence. My aunt once told me that three of her eight brothers had been committed to the Country Lunatic Asylum, the same three who had tried to move on in life, the same three who had had Removal Orders placed on them, returning them back to where they had started, back to the parish of their birth. I understood early on how madness could rescue a person & obliterate pain, that money afforded comfort & comfort afforded reason.

My life overseas enabled me to crawl out of that mire & become someone. Had my father not lost his job we would not have become homeless, & perhaps my mother would never have taken it upon herself to walk away one day down the old London Road. We would have remained together, & I would have had a family, my own family. But I would never have met George, never have become who I am – or once was. These are the things I ponder upon now, how my life should have been or could have been. And it is a queer conundrum. One offers me an identity, a family, and perhaps a sense of belonging . . . the other, opportunity. But

445

which, I wonder, would I have chosen, then, had I been able?

So that was the beginning, Sylvia. That part of my story you so wished me to tell you. I was born poor, horrendously poor, nothing more or less. Unlike you, I was not a banker's daughter, I was a servant's daughter . . . and, even worse, an unemployed under-servant's daughter. Poverty made my mother go mad, ruptured my family, & drove my aunt to desperate measures.

When I told you in Rome all those years ago that I had killed a man, I was not lying, for it was how it seemed to me at that time. I yearned to tell the truth, to confide in someone, you, and for you to understand that possibility & be able to make a choice, to be my friend or not, & to see me as more than that which I had come from. And you did . . . and yet you used my confession & my trust in you to betray me, electing to repeat it, without context or furnishing of background from me. However, it is a long time ago, & we are older and wiser, and the world has changed.

Please do not be sad about this last chapter – ironically, the start of my story – or about our 'upset' or by my passing. My life has been rich and full, & friendships do not last forever. In many ways you have achieved much more in your life than I. You leave a legacy in your words, your books, & I leave nothing other than my memories, which I am doubtful anyone will be interested in now, but perhaps.

Here the pen changed. And the hand, too, appeared altered.

I have spent a great deal of time cogitating & pondering this letter, and if I am to be honest, completely honest — and that is my intention — there is another matter to set straight, and this may come as something of a shock to you.

As regards my 'Comte de Chevalier de Saint Léger', he never existed.

Sylvia looked up. 'Never existed? But of course he did! I met him, I met him in Rome . . .'

There was no wedding at Le Havre or anywhere else, & there was no fine chateau in the Loire. There is and never was any Comte de Chevalier de Saint Léger. There was however an Antonin de Chevalier, my rather gallant French army officer & lover of three years. When I met Antonin, after Freddie passed away, I longed to escape from Rome, longed for change. I had been living on hope for so long, the hope that G would return there & to me, and, like any insubstantial diet, my near empty life had left me famished & weak. When I took little G off to France – to stay, or so I told everyone, with Antonin's family – it was not with the intention of staying away for two years, & of course I had had to tell my aunt that I was engaged to be married, otherwise she would never have allowed me to go. When I wrote to her, and to you too, about the place 'Chazelles', it was not altogether a lie, the house was indeed called Chazelles, but perhaps more dilapidated farmhouse than castle, & buried in obscurity in rural Nièvre.

It was in fact my aunt who decided that I was residing in a castle & that Antonin's family must have a title lurking somewhere, all good French families did, and she embraced this notion long before I. That is not to say it was forced upon me, but rather that I chose not to enlighten her on the truth of my circumstances. I chose not to disillusion her. She had been through so much & had such hopes and dreams for me. I think I realised then that I could return to Rome as someone else, someone quite different, & so caught up with my new & improved self & the possibilities ahead that it was impossible for me to relinquish the idea of that new identity. Everyone who mattered in Rome had a title – genuine, defunct or bogus – so why should not I also?

After Antonin was killed I had no choice

but to return to Rome – as his widow. My aunt believed I had married Antonin at Le Havre, and we had indeed been living as man & wife, I was long used to referring to myself as such & had been 'Madame de Chevalier' for over a year. I am not altogether sure now where the 'Saint Léger' came from, or why I added it to the name. I rather think I must have felt the name needed something more, and that it had a nice ring to it. The only time I can recall any problem was when I married Edward – with all the various paperwork, or lack of. But of course he saw to all of that.

One thing I wish to make clear is that there was no plan or premeditation on my part. It was an evolutionary process, a small detail, which began as a misunderstanding & developed into something more. In the end, of course, the name secured not George but his father, a man who would have done anything to stop G & me from marrying when we were young. I suppose one could say then that my revenge – if indeed it was revenge – was not simply on George but on his father, too. And yet, like my first marriage, that union was an arrangement that suited both parties. Edward offered me much needed security – a home (my first & only home) & an income. In return, I gave him the Countess de Chevalier de Saint Léger Lawson. Je pense, quid pro quo.

But enough. It is late & I am weary . . . and yet it is impossible for me to end this without mentioning George. I think you & you alone know that my life has been shaped and defined by him, his presence, that he was and remains my only one true love. That love began over seventy years ago in Rome, is with me now & shall go with me after death. If I am to be remembered for anything, I hope it will be for my love of him, & as the mother of his sons.

And so, I leave it with you, dear Sylvia, to decide how & what to record, if anything at all. I have always felt alone in this world, an exile even before I became one. But we are, I think, all in transit . . . hopefully, to something better.

The letter was signed: *Yours, Cora Lawson.*

Sylvia stared at the signature. Then, as though emerging from the depths, she gulped and swallowed, and began to weep.

By the time Sylvia first met her, Cora had already dropped the last letter of her given name and assumed the name Staunton, the name that would become hers through marriage. At that time, the focus of attention had been on Cora's aunt, the new Mrs James Staunton. There were rumours then that Mr Staunton had advertised for a new wife. And there was gossip and intrigue then about who she was or had been, and where she hailed from. Everyone knew there was a secret, but no one guessed that the secret was murder – attempted or otherwise, or desertion, or bigamy. No one had had the imagination for that: no one apart from Sylvia.

It had at first been all the little things, the tiny incidental details, which allowed Sylvia to build a picture. And then the mistakes: the mention of an 'Uncle John', and Cora's knowledge of things she should not have had knowledge about; and sometimes the fear, as well. Long before Aunt Fanny's tutelage paid off, before the reinvention was complete, Cora had been a mass of contradictions, both in character and in what she said. And Sylvia, the budding novelist, had not only been captivated and inspired, she had taken note. Cora was older than her years and Cora still cried for her mother; Cora was streetwise and savvy, and Cora was afraid of strangers; Cora was reticent and studied, and Cora was verbose and impetuous; Cora was from Suffolk, and Cora was from London; Cora had been an only child, and Cora had siblings – all dead. And so it went on.

It was easy enough to see that Cora lied, but what Sylvia wanted to know was *why* she lied; what inspired the lies and contradictions. When she had asked Cora, 'Did you run away?' Cora had not appeared shocked. They had been sitting on the bench by the fountain in the Piazza d'Ara Coeli, and Cora had simply stared at her and said

451

once more, 'I am not allowed to tell anyone . . . but I'll tell you one day, I promise.' And then she lifted Sylvia's hand and kissed it. No one had kissed Sylvia's hand before, no one had ever promised her anything. No one was like Cora.

Then, George Lawson arrived in Rome. Cora fell in love and had no time for sitting by fountains with Sylvia. Cora changed. And stories were practised and put in order. Sylvia heard them, each one slightly more polished than the last, until there was a final, definitive version. And it was impressive; Sylvia could not have done better herself. But George Lawson was not the man for Cora. Sylvia knew this. He was self-centred and ambitious, determined to prove himself. He would not stay in Rome; he would not marry Cora. He was using her.

When Sylvia penned her note to George, telling him she had information she thought he ought to know, her only thought had been Cora: protecting her from an inevitable heartbreak. And when she met him that day and he said, 'If this is another rumour about Cora or her aunt, I rather think I've heard them all,' Sylvia knew he had not heard what she was about to tell him. No one had. Not even Cora.

She explained that this was *not* idle gossip but had come from Cora herself, and though she had been sworn to secrecy, she felt duty bound to tell him. Yes, he wanted to know what it was Cora had told her. And so Sylvia told him the truth. Or what she thought might be the truth.

She had no idea then that her actions – motivated by nothing other than love, the desire to protect the person she loved – would carve the future path of Cora's life; or that as a result of those actions Cora would spend all of her days estranged from love, would make it her mission to prove something and become someone, or that that someone would be George Lawson's stepmother. Sylvia never imagined that.

And yet it was she, Sylvia, who had comforted Cora after George broke off with her and left Rome. It was she who had held Cora in her arms and smiled down at her when she said, 'You're the best friend anyone could ever have, Sylvia.'

CHAPTER 28

The doorman saw them into the taxicab. It wasn't far to walk, but it was easier for them, easier for Jack. Piccadilly was busy and progress was slow. Through the window Cecily watched the drifting crowds, those milling about the statue of Eros, amidst pigeons and fruit barrows, under the rain-laden sky; she could hear the echo of music drifting out from an arcade, and newspaper boys shouting about curses and Pharaohs, and 'Lord Carnarvon struck dead!' And there was perhaps some queer synchronicity at work that day, she thought, when the taxicab finally pulled up opposite the Academy, outside the *Egyptian* Hall.

They were on time. West End church bells were chiming seven o'clock as they walked through the entrance of the Academy. Mr Davidson was waiting. He stepped forward to introduce himself. 'Please, do come this way,' he said. He led them through the vast lobby, past vaguely familiar sculptures – Cecily knew she had seen before – then down a corridor and into a panelled room. There, another man stepped forward to shake their hands. 'Stephen Fowler, a pleasure to meet you both.'

Mr Davidson asked them to take a seat. They sat side by side upon a long leather chesterfield sofa. He laid out some paperwork on the table in front of them – which Cecily was expecting, which their solicitor had already looked over – for her to sign. After signing her name – Cecily Staunton – a few times over, Mr Davidson offered them a glass of sherry. Still on his feet, he made a toast: 'To "Aphrodite"!' And the three raised their glasses and repeated it. Then he sat down in the armchair opposite Mr Fowler, and said, 'As you know, Mr Fowler has spent these last few years researching Lord Lawson's life and work, and he has a few questions he'd very much like to ask you.'

Cecily reached over and took hold of Jack's hand. She said, 'I'm happy to answer anything I can. Unfortunately, my husband's memory is not what it was.'

The men nodded at Jack.

Mr Fowler began. 'The painting, "Aphrodite", was, I believe, executed at Lucca some sixty years ago. Would that be correct?'

Cecily heard Jack sigh. 'I'm really not sure when, exactly, it was executed,' she answered, 'Cor— my husband's grandmother had it hanging in her hallway for a number of years, certainly since nineteen eleven, but I'm afraid I have no idea where it was before that, or any dates.'

Mr Fowler smiled and waved a hand, as though

it was of little importance. 'She was, we believe, his regular sitter during his time at Rome. And we are, I think it is safe to say,' he paused and turned to the other gentleman, 'almost certain that she was his "Madonna". The faces are identical, the treatment the same. Wouldn't you agree, Mr Davidson?'

'Oh, without doubt.'

Mr Fowler cleared his throat and went on. 'For my own part, there's . . . a niggling. Yes, a niggling. Call it a dilemma, if you will.' He paused, lowered his head and glanced over his spectacles at Jack. 'Your grandmama gave birth to a child some nine months after she had returned from her stay at Lucca with Lord Lawson and Mrs Hillier. That child – your father, sir,' he said, nodding to Jack, 'was given the name George, and George Lawson was duly conferred godfather.' He said this last word rather more loudly, and then paused, again, as though giving Cecily and Jack time to absorb these facts, an unfolding theory. 'Lord Lawson wrote often of this child – your father, his godson – George, or Georgie, as he seemed to prefer to call him. And sums of money – considerable amounts and over many years – were sent to banks in Paris and Rome . . .'

It was obvious to Cecily where the conversation was headed, what was being implied, and so she continued to hold on to Jack's hand, gripping it tighter from time to time.

Mr Fowler sighed heavily. 'Unfortunately, almost all of Lord Lawson's personal correspondence was destroyed by his family after his death. He was secretive by nature, and his surviving journals and personal papers are . . . hard to decipher – written in code, perhaps. But there's one name, a name that appears time and again in his early journals, and then again in later ones. It's a name I have been unable to identify or locate. And so, what I would like to ask you is,' he paused, looked from Cecily to Jack and back to her, 'what was the countess's given name?'

'Cora, her name was Cora,' Cecily replied.

He looked away, shook his head.

'That's not the name?'

He closed his eyes and sighed. Then he looked at her. 'No. And it's a shame,' he said and laughed. 'I thought I had discovered the missing piece,' he said, wringing his hands. 'Yes, the missing piece,' he said again.

Mr Davidson turned to him. 'Hmm, not even remotely alike,' he said.

'There were . . . no other names? Middle names?' Mr Fowler asked, looking from one to other once again.

Cecily turned to Jack, shaking her head. 'Not that I'm aware of,' she said. And Jack shrugged his shoulders. She looked back at Mr Fowler: 'But what is the name you're looking for? Perhaps it will mean something if I hear it.'

'Lily. The name is Lily.'

Cecily managed not to say anything, or nod. But she did smile.

CHAPTER 29

Cecily said she could not stay long. 'Jack's waiting at the hotel, and we have to get back to collect the children from my mother's.'

'Ah yes, of course,' said Sylvia. 'How are they? I forgot to ask you last time.'

Cecily opened her bag, pulled out her wallet and took something from it. 'Here,' she said, extending her hand.

Sylvia stared at the photograph: a dark-haired boy in a sailor suit, holding another child, his sister, on his lap. 'Aha, so that's little Jack.'

'Actually we call him Jay. It was too confusing with two Jacks in the house . . . He'll be five in a few weeks' time. And that's my baby, that's Lily,' she said, moving over to Sylvia to look at the photograph with her. 'She's grown a lot since then – they both have. She'll be three in October.'

'Lily? And what made you choose that name?'

'It's what my father called me when I was young, before he passed away. He always called me Lily.'

'I see,' said Sylvia, staring at the photograph.

Unlike the little boy, whose hair was straight,

and parted at the side, the baby in the picture had a mop of dark unruly curls. And whilst the boy looked back at the camera with a serious face, the baby looked elsewhere, laughing.

'So when was this taken?' Sylvia asked.

'Oh, only a few months ago, at Christmas,' Cecily replied, smiling at the image. 'But children grow so quickly.'

'Jack must be very proud.'

'He is . . . adores them both.'

Sylvia handed back the photograph and Cecily returned to her chair.

'It would've been nice to have seen Jack,' said Sylvia.

'I know, I'm sorry, but he's not always comfortable with strangers.'

'*Strangers?*'

'He doesn't remember people, Sylvia. He has very few memories of anyone really, from before the war.'

'I see. And the children, little Jack – I mean, Jay – how was it for him when his papa returned?'

'Daddy,' Cecily corrected her. 'It's been four years, Sylvia. Jay was little more than a baby when his daddy came back.' She shrugged, 'Jack's simply Daddy, like any other . . .'

Sylvia nodded. 'And Jack copes? Copes with the children?'

Cecily laughed. 'Oh yes, he copes very well. In fact, he rather prefers their company to anyone else's. They don't see his disability, his injuries, they see the man, their father. Jack as he is now is the only Jack they've known.'

'And you? It must be quite . . . quite hard for you, dear.'

She shook her head and laughed again. 'No, it's not hard for me, not hard for me at all. I feel immensely lucky – extraordinarily lucky. My husband came back, with four limbs and a face, scarred perhaps but recognisable – to me. God spared Jack, spared me. I have my husband, the father of my children. I have *everything*.'

They moved on. Cecily told Sylvia that she and Jack had attended the private view of the exhibition of George's work, adding, 'We've loaned them the painting, the one from the hallway at Temple Hill.'

Sylvia tried to remember.

'The one of Cora? Painted by George in Italy?'

No, she could not recall it. But it did not surprise her to hear that Cora had had such a painting, she said. 'I've no doubt she had quite a few by him.'

'No, that was the only one.'

'And so it's on loan to the Academy?'

'Yes, indefinitely. It's one of the few pieces we're not inclined to sell. Jack says it's our pension,' she added, smiling.

'And I imagine it'll provide a very generous pension, too.'

'We have everything we need,' Cecily went on, 'and anyhow, it would cost a fortune to insure and look quite out of place in our cottage.'

They sat in silence for a moment or two. Sylvia

deliberated on what to say about the manuscript, lying on the table in front of them. But she was still distracted by Cora's letter, acutely conscious of its presence beneath her, under the cushion. It would be interesting to see if Cecily mentioned it, asked her about it, she thought.

'About your novel,' Sylvia began, 'it's a reasonable enough story though I'm not sure one could say it is Cora's story.'

'It's fiction, Sylvia,' Cecily said, a little defensively, Sylvia thought. 'I should perhaps have explained that . . . it's inspired by her life rather than based *on* her life.'

'But you said *loosely based*; you did use those words, Cecily.'

Cecily smiled, nodded. 'Yes, I did, and perhaps that was misleading,' she said. 'But I must ask you, did you like the ending?'

Sylvia glanced across the room, up to the cornicing. She could see a cobweb or two. She would have to speak to Mrs Halliday about it later, get her to send someone up. Then Cecily spoke again. 'Is the ending feasible?'

She turned to Cecily. 'Nothing is ever *entirely* unfeasible in fiction,' she said.

'And in Cora's life?'

'I'm afraid I can't say. You would have to ask Cora that question, I think.'

'But she's not here, and you are. Do you think it's possible that Cora and George could have married, had circumstances been different?'

Sylvia laughed. 'Had circumstances been different, my dear, anything might have been possible. And as I said before—'

'No, you didn't say before,' Cecily cut in, exasperated, irritated. 'Oh, and there's something else: why did Cora think George was buried in Rome when his grave is here in London?'

'Because she needed to . . . and because I gave it to her.'

'You *gave* it to her?'

Sylvia nodded. 'I wrote it that way, in *A Roman Affair*.'

For seven days after George's death, his body lay in the Octagon Room at the Academy. Crowds of mourners queued to pay their respects, to file past the coffin festooned with flowers and wreaths, and draped in patriotic colours, like a war hero who had died for his country. The newspapers proclaimed his death a 'tragedy'; the nation was bereft.

Weeks earlier, George had been diagnosed with angina. His doctors had informed him that he needed to cut down on his workload, needed to take a rest. He had written to Cora in Rome, telling her that he planned to take a sabbatical, and that he would like to spend it in Italy, with her. And she had quickly replied, full of plans: they could take a house outside Rome, somewhere quiet, she suggested; and they could perhaps travel north, if he felt up to it, to Bagni di Lucca, where the waters and hot springs would surely do him a power of good. Yes, she would look into it, she told him.

When Cora learned of her son's accident, she immediately despatched a telegram to George informing him of the situation, telling him that she was about to set off for England. Two days later she sent another – to inform him of Georgie's death. Stunned by disbelief, by the sudden and abrupt end to her son's life, she failed to notice George's silence, his absence at their son's funeral. She had no idea that hours after George received her second telegram he had had a stroke; no idea, as she stood in a snow-covered churchyard with one George that the other had just taken his last breath.

Cora insisted on going to the Academy. She told Sylvia she could not return to Rome before paying her final respects. And so, stiffly upholstered in mourning, she held on to Sylvia's arm as they climbed the steps of the entrance to the Academy. She seemed able, Sylvia thought then, to divorce her shattered spirit from that swell of public hysteria. For no one in that murmuring line of sombre-faced strangers would ever have guessed. No one shuffling across that marble floor could know that she had just buried her son; or that the man whose coffin they queued to see was in fact the father and the man she had loved for almost half a century.

And yet, it seemed to Sylvia that, in death,

George Lawson, late President of the Academy, England's greatest painter, unmarried, with no apparent heir, and owned by everyone, belonged only to one: the woman gripping her arm.

When a man, some sort of official in uniform, asked, 'Did you know him?' Sylvia quickly replied, 'Yes, we both knew him . . . long before he became famous.'

'Thought so. Saw you'd both dressed proper. Not everyone has the decency to do that these days,' he said, and moved on.

When it came to their turn, Sylvia stepped to one side and Cora walked forward alone. She placed her hand upon the coffin, closed her eyes for a moment, and Sylvia saw her mouth a few words. Then she turned to Sylvia and nodded. They walked back through rooms softly humming with desultory conversation, following the snaking line out into the lobby and past Clifford's 'Tinted Venus' without a second glance.

'Yes,' Sylvia said again, 'it was my gift to her, dedicated to her . . .' She paused and smiled. 'But I'm afraid you'll have to wait for my new book for your answers,' she added in a new bold voice.

'You've written a book about her, about Cora?'

'Well, they've all been about her, one way or another, I suppose. But this one is different. It's the story of her life,' Sylvia said, 'the *true* story.'

'Oh, and according to whom?'

'Well, according to me, of course. As you know, I was there for a great deal of it, and, as Cora's confidante, was for most of her life privy to her innermost thoughts and secrets. That is why she wished me to record her memories, but alas it was not to be.'

'How wonderful,' said Cecily, rising to her feet. 'Well, I shall look forward to reading it. What's it to be called? Have you a title yet?'

'*The Memory of Lost Senses.*'

'*The Memory of Lost Senses,*' Cecily repeated. 'Mm, I like it.'

She pulled on her coat and picked up her manuscript.

Sylvia watched her and said, 'I thought you had something to tell me, something about Cora?'

'Did I? Oh no, I simply wondered about the letter – her letter to you, that was all. Was it . . . was it as you imagined . . . what you expected?' she asked, fastening buttons.

'It was indeed, and it will help me with the final part of my book,' Sylvia said, moving forward in her chair.

'Please, don't get up, I can see myself out.'

There was no kiss.

Wendy was quick to respond to the bell, and even quicker to return with the bucket of coal. 'Having a clearout, are we?' she said to Sylvia, crouching down by the hearth, eyeing the paper and envelopes, the tattered shoeboxes piled up on the table.

'Sorting through . . .'

'Don't forget, it's Mrs Evesleigh's birthday. There's tea and cake in the lounge at four.'

'Ah yes, of course,' Sylvia replied, watching the flickering.

'Do you want me to take any of this?' Wendy asked, nodding her head towards the table. 'I can dispose of it, you know. You don't want to be having a bonfire in your room, now do you?'

Sylvia feigned a little laugh. 'Thank you, Wendy, but I shan't be having any bonfire, at least, not today. Just burning a few old letters, that's all.'

There was plenty of time, Sylvia thought, hours until Mrs Evesleigh puffed out her cheeks to extinguish a few tiny pink candles. In the meantime, Sylvia could have her own burning ceremony. And it gave her something to do: a task for the afternoon. I am the only one who knows, she thought, placing the first envelope upon the fire, watching the cream-coloured paper slowly ignite and burn . . . *the only one who will ever know.*

Cecily stared out of the train carriage window to row upon row of soot-blackened houses, back-to-back gardens, washing lines and fences and paths, huddled and dismal under the lowering smog. She caught glimpses of crossings and platforms and faces, and high streets foreign to her; shops she would never enter, trams and buses she would never take. She forgot for a while that she was about to see her children; forgot Jack, sitting opposite her.

She had known about Lily for years, known since that stormy summer's afternoon when they sat waiting for a deluge that never came; when she told Cora that her father had called her Lily, not Cecily, and Cora had said, 'Mine too.' But what could be gained by revealing the name? What could be gained now? Everything was in place and where it ought to be; and she had left it so.

Jack had said, 'A coincidence, eh? The name being Lily.'

'Hmm, it's a common enough name, I suppose.'

They had been in another taxicab, heading back to their hotel, exhausted from standing about the crowded picture galleries of the Academy surveying George Lawson's life's work; and, at the same time, elated from seeing their painting hanging there. But Cecily's private joy had been the 'Madonna', Lawson's most famous work, the one which had catapulted him to success and, for years, had been enjoyed only by royal eyes. The painting was vast. It took up an entire wall of one room – easily the most crowded room. And there, right at the centre of the enormous canvas, a vaguely familiar face: eyes downcast, almost closed, and lips slightly parted as though in mid-sigh. And for Cecily it spoke of the pain of love, and of a life of loss.

'Do you think they were actually implying that my father was Lawson's lovechild? That he and Cora had had an affair?' Jack had asked, staring out at the wet lamplit street.

'It did sound like that, didn't it?'

'Scurrilous . . . Perhaps I should sue them,' he had added, turning to her, smiling.

She could not tell him. She had promised Cora. And that promise – like Jack's to her – had been kept.

But that morning, when she had called on Sylvia to collect her manuscript, and had teasingly said, 'Oh, I have something to tell you, something about Cora,' she had thought of telling Sylvia; or rather, of leading Sylvia to a place where she might tell *her* more. But it was clear to her that Sylvia was not going to divulge anything, whatever she knew. And she had been in an odd mood, odder than ever. There had been little point in asking about Cora's letter, though she had, simply for politeness' sake.

'She just seems so . . . so bitter,' Cecily said now, continuing to stare out of the carriage window, musing aloud.

She was rankled by Sylvia's attitude, and wondered why she had been so unkind, for she had said nothing at all constructive, offered Cecily no words of encouragement or praise. *A reasonable enough effort . . .*

Then Jack said, 'Perhaps it was unrequited love.'

Cecily turned to him. 'The only person she's ever loved is Cora.'

'That's what I meant. There's your answer,' he said, raising his eyebrows, smiling at her.

When they arrived back at Bramley, Jay was waiting at the bottom of the track, perched on the wall of the bridge where the ford had once been. He looked smaller than she remembered – even from a few days ago. And as she stepped down from Mr Cotton's motorcar, he was there, helping his father climb down at the other side, wrapping his arms around him as though he'd been gone for years and not days. He barely drew breath as he walked back with them, regaling them with what had happened in their absence: Lily had refused to eat Rosetta's dumplings, had thrown one across the kitchen floor; she had behaved atrociously at bathtime, 'screaming the whole place down, *and*,' he added, with emphasis and pausing for dramatic effect, before what Cecily knew to be the *pièce de résistance* – 'she took a wee in the garden, on Granny's lettuces.'

'Jack!' said Cecily, in an attempt to silence her husband's laughter.

Then, as though remembering something called manners, Jay looked at his mother and asked, 'Have you had a nice time, Mummy? What have you been doing?'

'Well, I went to call on an old lady, a friend of your great-grandmother's.'

'Golly,' he said, 'she must be *ancient*!'

'Yes, she is quite old. She's a writer, a novelist, like me.'

'What does she write about?' he asked, moving on up the track, clutching his father's hand.

'Mm, romantic things . . . men and women falling in love, that sort of thing,' she replied.

'Ugh!'

'But she's been writing a book about your great-grandma, a book about her life.'

'Why doesn't she write a book about Daddy?' he asked, releasing his father's hand, rummaging in his pocket and pulling out a piece of folded paper. 'That'd be far more interesting than a book about some old lady, specially a *dead* old lady.'

Cecily smiled. 'Jay, she wasn't just some old lady; she was Daddy's grandmother, your great-grand-mother. And she wasn't always dead, or old. She was once a little girl and lived in a castle, and she lived in a castle in France as well. Imagine that?'

But they had reached the gate and her son had turned away from her, stretching out his hand to present his father with the paper aeroplane he had made for him earlier that afternoon. And Cecily, home again and feeling complete, paused for a moment to savour it, savour it *all*: the familiar scent of pine and woodsmoke, the soft twilight air; that sense of wholesomeness she knew money could not buy. Then, feeling the pull, she turned her eyes to the ever-narrowing track, beyond the silhouetted limbs of arching branches to the circle of light at the top. And she watched her, Cora – Lily – turn and walk away, vanishing into the dusk, into her world, another place in time.

One day Cecily would tell her children of their great-grandmother, that she had been Lord Lawson's stepmother, been his Madonna and his Aphrodite, too. And that she had been quite a character.

But for now it was enough to be home, with Jack, with her children. And as she watched her husband walk up the pathway holding on to their son's hand, and saw Rosetta appear in the doorway, their daughter on her hip, she knew everything that mattered was there in front of her.

She heard the latch on the gate drop, clickety-click, her feet upon the path, and a door quietly close.

It is evening and the sun is still high, shining in through the wisteria tumbling across the small open window. The room is hot, the black paint on the window frame bubbling and peeling in soft curls. She sits barefoot on her aunt's lap and it feels good to be held, secured. She can hear her sister in the field outside, her cousins and little Johnny, too. 'Your mother has had to go away for a while, just for a while,' her aunt says, answering her questions, stroking her hair. 'She needs a little rest.'

'And Father?' she asks, swinging her legs up, glancing to her toes, her feet.

'Well now, your father is . . .' but she doesn't finish the sentence. She says, 'And you're to come and stay with me and Uncle John in London. Now isn't that nice?'

Samuel has already gone — to relations in Framlingham, someone said.

'And Jemima and Johnny, are they coming as well?' she asks.

'No, dear, they are to stay here with your Uncle Daniel,' her aunt says.

She nods. She knows she must be brave, must not cry. Then she turns to her aunt, looks up at her and says, 'But when will she be back? Do you know? Did she say?'

'Oh, soon,' her aunt replies, kissing her forehead. 'Very soon.'

'And will she know where I am, will she know where to find me?'

'Well, of course she will, Lily. She knows you're with me . . . knows you're safe with me.'